"You already closing up shop?! Don't worry! I never had any plans on shoppin' at your damn store in the first place! *Hya-hya-hya-hya-hya-hya-hya!*"

"Ha-ha-ha-ha-ha!"

MESTELEXIL THE BOX OF DESPERATE KNOWLEDGE

Golem/homunculus. Kiyazuna's greatest masterpiece. Regenerates no matter how many times he has been killed. He can conquer his cause of death each time he revives.

Anyone who knew how terrifying Kiyazuna the Axle was would leave the area before they could get involved with her or watch from a safe distance and make sure not to interact with her. Being feared and avoided by her fellow minian races was, if anything, an absolute joy to Kiyazuna the Axle, who was filled with spite and malice from birth.

KIYAZUNA THE AXLE

Self-proclaimed demon king and Craft Arts genius. Led by her brutal and savage nature, she made Mestelexil. Participates in the Sixways Exhibition.

SHALK THE SOUND SLICER

A skeleton without any memories of his previous life. Possesses godlike speed that outpaces even sound and the ability to transform his body and render any distance meaningless.

A damn monster.
Mele the Horizon's Roar.
What a bastard.

"Perfect. All right, Shalk. I'll tear you apart and take the whole world with ya."

MELE THE HORIZON'S ROAR

A gigant beloved as a village's guardian deity.
The powerful arrows he fires can transform
geography itself from across the edge of the horizon.

The air screamed like a lightning strike.

The terrifyingly massive and boiling-hot earthen arrow passed through Shalk's position.

The speed as it pierced the atmosphere was so great, the soil burned from the high temperature of the adiabatic compression. The arrow passing through the surface was enough to melt even the bedrock, which had been frozen over by a dragon's breath.

What was made clear in this attack, the point he truly needed to fear, wasn't the instantaneous and fatal destructive force.

YUNO THE DISTANT TALON

A young girl who's a survivor of the ruined Nagan City. Accidentally learned a certain secret and has since left Haade the Flashpoint's command.

"M-Miss Yuno."

"You should've killed me immediately, then! I mean, I…"

LINARIS THE OBSIDIAN

Vampire successor of the spy guild Obsidian Eyes. Capable of using the vampiric powers of subjugation through airborne infection rather than blood infection.

The body Yuno pinned down was very slender. If she went any farther, she just might have snapped her neck.

Eyes wet with tears were looking up at her.

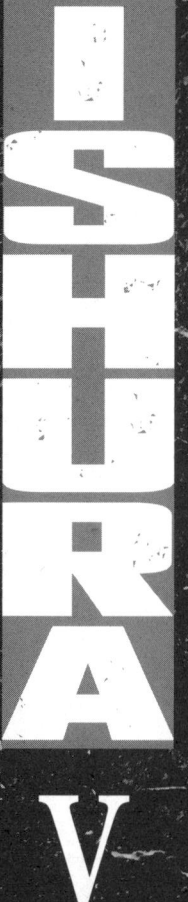

ISHURA

V

Grotesque Seeds Lay Dormant

Keiso

ILLUSTRATION BY

Kureta

YEN
ON
New York

Keiso

ILLUSTRATION BY

Kureta

Translation by David Musto

This book is a work of fiction. Names, characters, places, and incidents are the product of the author's imagination or are used fictitiously. Any resemblance to actual events, locales, or persons, living or dead, is coincidental.

ISHURA Vol. 5 SENZAIIGYOSHU
©Keiso 2021
First published in Japan in 2021 by KADOKAWA CORPORATION, Tokyo.
English translation rights arranged with KADOKAWA CORPORATION, Tokyo, through TUTTLE-MORI AGENCY, INC., Tokyo.

English translation © 2023 by Yen Press, LLC

Yen On
150 West 30th Street, 19th Floor
New York, NY 10001

Visit us at yenpress.com
facebook.com/yenpress
twitter.com/yenpress
yenpress.tumblr.com
instagram.com/yenpress

First Yen On Edition: November 2023
Edited by Yen On Editorial: Payton Campbell
Designed by Yen Press Design: Andy Swist

Yen On is an imprint of Yen Press, LLC.
The Yen On name and logo are trademarks of Yen Press, LLC.

The publisher is not responsible for websites (or their content) that are not owned by the publisher.

Library of Congress Cataloging-in-Publication Data
Names: Keiso (Manga author), author. | Kureta, illustrator. | Musto, David, translator.
Title: Ishura / Keiso ; illustration by Kureta ; translation by David Musto.
Other titles: Ishura. English
Description: First Yen On edition. | New York : Yen On, 2022.
Identifiers: LCCN 2021062849 | ISBN 9781975337865
    (v. 1 ; trade paperback) | ISBN 9781975337889
    (v. 2 ; trade paperback) | ISBN 9781975337902
    (v. 3 ; trade paperback) | ISBN 9781975337926
    (v. 4 ; trade paperback) | ISBN 9781975363079
    (v. 5 ; trade paperback)
Subjects: LCGFT: Fantasy fiction. | Light novels.
Classification: LCC PL872.5.E57 I7413 2022 | DDC 895.63/6—dc23/
    eng/20220121
LC record available at https://lccn.loc.gov/2021062849

ISBNs: 978-1-9753-6307-9 (trade paperback)
       978-1-9753-6308-6 (ebook)

10 9 8 7 6 5 4 3 2 1

LSC-C

Printed in the United States of America

The identity of the one who defeated the True Demon King—the ultimate threat who gripped the world in terror—is shrouded in mystery.
Little is known about this hero.
The terror of the True Demon King abruptly came to an end.

Nevertheless, the champions born from the era of the Demon King still remain in this world.

Now, with the enemy of all life brought low,
these champions, wielding enough power to transform the world,
have begun to do as they please,
their untamed wills threatening a new era of war and strife.

To Aureatia, now the sole kingdom unifying the minian races,
the existence of these champions has become a threat.
No longer champions, they are now demons bringing ruin to all—
the shura.

To ensure peace in the new era,
it is necessary to eliminate any threat to the world's future,
and designate the True Hero to guide and protect the hopes of
the people.

Thus, the Twenty-Nine Officials, the governing administrators of Aureatia, have gathered these shura and their miraculous abilities from across the land, regardless of race, and organized an imperial competition to crown the True Hero once and for all.

POWER RELATIONSHIPS

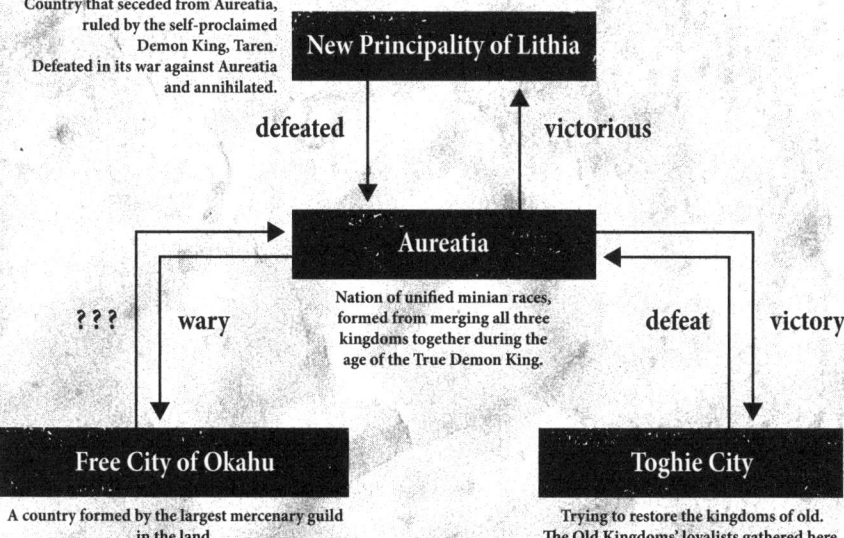

New Principality of Lithia
Country that seceded from Aureatia, ruled by the self-proclaimed Demon King, Taren. Defeated in its war against Aureatia and annihilated.

defeated

victorious

Aureatia
Nation of unified minian races, formed from merging all three kingdoms together during the age of the True Demon King.

??? wary

defeat victory

Free City of Okahu
A country formed by the largest mercenary guild in the land.
A group of elite soldiers that deploys a military force on par with any nation-state.
Completely independent of any outside authority.

Toghie City
Trying to restore the kingdoms of old.
The Old Kingdoms' loyalists gathered here.
And taking advantage of the Particle Storm's attack,
declared war on Aureatia and were defeated.

ROSCLAY THE ABSOLUTE

Knight Minia

Sponsor
ELEA THE RED TAG

KIA THE WORLD WORD

Elven Word Arts Master

Sponsor
HARDY THE BULLET FLASHPOINT

SOUJIROU THE WILLOW-SWORD

Blade Minia

Sponsor
YUCA THE HALATION GAOL

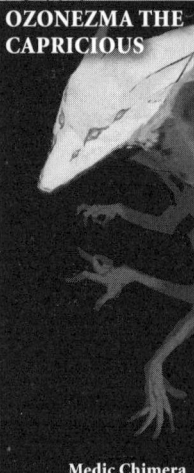

OZONEZMA THE CAPRICIOUS

Medic Chimera

UHAK THE SILENT

Oracle Ogre

Sponsor
NOFELT THE SOMBER WIND

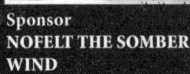

ZIGITA ZOGI THE THOUSANDTH

Tactician Goblin

Sponsor
DANT THE HEATH FURROW

SHALK THE SOUND SLICER

Spearhead Skeleton

Sponsor
HYAKKA THE HEAT HAZE

MELE THE HORIZON'S ROAR

Archer Gigant

Sponsor
CAYON THE THUNDERING

LUCNOCA THE WINTER

Silencer Dragon

ALUS THE STAR RUNNER

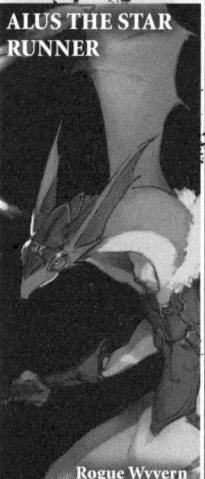

Rogue Wyvern

TOROA THE AWFUL

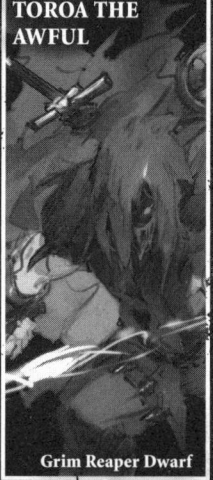

Grim Reaper Dwarf

PSIANOP THE INEXHAUSTIBLE STAGNATION

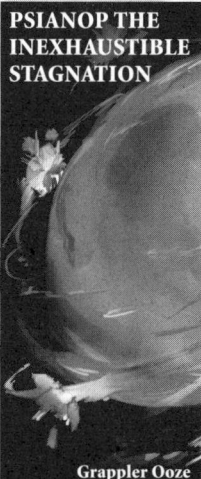

Grappler Ooze

SIXWAYS EXHIBITION

ZELJIRGA THE ABYSS WEB

Clown Zmeu

MESTELEXIL THE BOX OF DESPERATE KNOWLEDGE

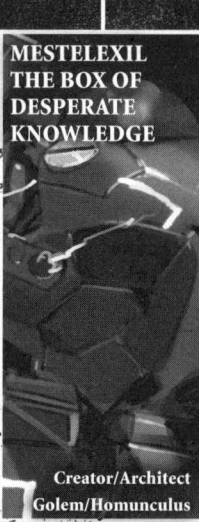

Creator/Architect Golem/Homunculus

TU THE MAGIC

Juggernaut

KUZE THE PASSING DISASTER

Paladin Minia

GLOSSARY

❖ Word Arts

① Laws of the world that permit and establish phenomena and living creatures that physically shouldn't be able to exist, such as the construction of a gigant's body.
② Phenomenon that conveys the intentions of a speaker's words to the listener, regardless of the speaker's race or language.
③ Or the generic term for arts that utilize this phenomenon to distort natural phenomena via "requests" to a certain target.

Something much like what would be called magic. Force, Thermal, Craft, and Life Arts compose the four core groups, but there are some who can use arts outside of these four groups. While necessary to be familiarized with the target in order to utilize these arts, powerful Word Arts users are able to offset this requirement.

❖ Force Arts

Arts that inflict directed power and speed, what is known as momentum, on a target.

❖ Craft Arts

Arts that change a target's shape.

❖ Thermal Arts

Arts that inflict undirected energy, such as heat, electrical current, and light, on a target.

❖ Life Arts

Arts that change a target's nature.

❖ Visitors

Those who possess abilities that deviate greatly from all common knowledge, and thus were transported to this world from another one known as the Beyond. Visitors are unable to use Word Arts.

❖ Enchanted Sword • Magic Items

Swords and tools that possess potent abilities. Similar to visitors, due to their mighty power, there are some objects that were transported here from another world.

❖ Aureatia Twenty-Nine Officials

The highest functionaries who govern Aureatia. Ministers are civil servants, while Generals are military officers.
There is no hierarchy-based seniority or rank among the Twenty-Nine Officials.

❖ Self-Proclaimed Demon King

A generic term for "demonic monarch" not related to the One True King among the three kingdoms. There are some cases where even those who do not proclaim themselves as a monarch, but who wield great power to threaten Aureatia, are acknowledged as self-proclaimed demon kings by Aureatia and targeted for subjugation.

❖ Sixways Exhibition

A tournament to determine the True Hero. The person who wins each one-on-one match and advances all the way through to the end will be named the True Hero. Backing from a member of the Twenty-Nine Officials is required to enter the competition.

CONTENTS

SEVENTH VERSE: SIXWAYS EXHIBITION III

AUREATIA TWENTY-NINE OFFICIALS

Fifth Official
VACANT SEAT
Previously the seat of Iriolde the Atypical Tome. It is now vacant following his banishment.

Tenth General
QWELL THE WAX FLOWER
A woman with long bangs that hide her eyes. Sponsor for Psianop the Inexhaustible Stagnation. Timid and always trembling in fright. For some unknown reason, even compared to the rest of the Twenty-Nine Officials, she possesses superlative physical strength.

First Minister
GRASSE THE FOUNDATION MAP
A man nearing old age.
Tasked with being the chairperson who presides over Twenty-Nine Officials' meetings.
Not belonging to any of the factions in the Sixways Exhibition and maintaining neutrality.

Sixth General
HARGHENT THE STILL
A man who yearns for authority despite being ridiculed for being incompetent.
Sponsoring Lucnoca the Winter.
Has a deep connection with Alus the Star Runner.
Not part of any faction.

Eleventh Minister
NOPHTOK THE CREPUSCULE BELL
An elderly man who gives a gentle, kindly impression.
Sponsor for Kuze the Passing Disaster.
Holds jurisdiction over the Order.

Second General
ROSCLAY THE ABSOLUTE
A man who garners absolute trust as a champion.
Participates in the Sixways Exhibition, supporting himself. The leader of the largest faction within the Twenty-Nine Officials.

Seventh Minister
FLINSUDA THE PORTENT
Corpulent woman adorned in gold and silver accessories.
Leads the medical division.
A pragmatist who only believes in the power of money.
Sponsoring Tu the Magic.

Twelfth General
SABFOM THE WHITE WEAVE
A man who covers his face with an iron mask.
Previously crossed swords with self-proclaimed demon king Morio and is currently recuperating.

Third Minister
JELKY THE SWIFT INK
A bespectacled man with the air of a shrewd bureaucrat.
Planned the Sixways Exhibition.
Belongs to Rosclay's faction.

Eighth Minister
SHEANEK THE WORD INTERMEDIARY
A man who can decipher and give accounts in a variety of different scripts.
Acts in practice as First Minister Grasse the Foundation Map's Secretary.
Maintains neutrality just like Grasse.

Thirteenth Minister
ENU THE DISTANT MIRROR
An aristocratic man with slicked-back hair.
Sponsor for Zeljirga the Abyss Web.
Infected by Linaris the Obsidian and now under her control.

Fourth Minister
KAETE THE ROUND TABLE
A man with an extremely fierce temperament.
Sponsoring Mestelexil the Box of Desperate Knowledge.
Possesses preeminent military power and authority and is resisting Rosclay's faction.

Ninth General
YANIEGIZ THE CHISEL
A sinewy man with a snaggletooth.
Belongs to Rosclay's Faction.

Fourteenth General
YUCA THE HALATION GAOL
A simple and honest man, round and plump. Doesn't have a shred of ambition. Head of Aureatia's Public Safety branch. Sponsoring Ozonezma the Capricious.

Fifteenth General

HAIZESTA THE GATHERING SPOT

A man in the prime of his life with a cynical smile.
Prominent for his misbehavior.

Sixteenth General

NOFELT THE SOMBER WIND

An abnormally tall man.
Sponsor for Uhak the Silent.
Originated from the same Order almshouse as Kuze.

Seventeenth Minister

ELEA THE RED TAG

A young, beautiful woman who rose up from her prostitute ancestry. Supervises Aureatia's intelligence apparatus.
Sponsoring Jivlart the Ash Border. Keeping Kia the World Word a secret to use as her trump card.

Eighteenth Minister

QUEWAI THE MOON FRAGMENT

A gloomy young man.

Nineteenth Minister

HYAKKA THE HEAT HAZE

A small-statured man who supervises the agricultural division. Straining himself to become worthy of his position in the Twenty-Nine Officials.
Sponsoring Shalk the Sound Slicer.

Twentieth Minister

HIDOW THE CLAMP

A haughty son of a noble family and at the same time a popular, quick-witted man.
Sponsor for Alus the Star Runner.
Sponsoring Alus to ensure he doesn't win.

Twenty-First General

TUTURI THE BLUE VIOLET FOAM

A woman with grizzled hair tied up behind her head.

Twenty-Second General

MIZIAL THE IRON-PIERCING PLUMESHADE

A boy who became a member of the Twenty-Nine Officials at just sixteen years old.
Possesses a self-assured temperament.
Sponsoring Toroa the Awful.

Twenty-Third Official

VACANT SEAT

Previously the seat of Taren the Punished.
However, it is currently vacant following her secession and defection.

Twenty-Fourth General

DANT THE HEATH FURROW

An exceedingly serious man.
Commands the northern front army, containing Old Kingdoms' loyalists' forces. Part of the Queen's faction—and harbors ill feelings toward Rosclay's faction.
Sponsoring Zigita Zogi the Thousandth.

Twenty-Fifth General

CAYON THE THUNDERING

A one-armed man with a feminine speaking manner.
Sponsor for Mele the Horizon's Roar.

Twenty-Sixth Minister

MEEKA THE WHISPERED

A stern woman who gives a rigid and rectangular impression.
Acting as the adjudicator of the Sixways Exhibition.

Twenty-Seventh General

HAADE THE FLASHPOINT

A man who sincerely loves war. Sponsor for Soujirou the Willow-Sword. Prominent figure accompanied by the largest military faction.
Regarded as the largest rival to Rosclay's faction.

Twenty-Eighth Minister

ANTEL THE ALIGNMENT

A tan-skinned man wearing dark-tinted glasses.

Twenty-Ninth Official

VACANT SEAT

ISHURA

Keiso

ILLUSTRATION BY **Kureta**

Seventh Verse:
SIXWAYS EXHIBITION III

Two small months before the Sixways Exhibition was set to begin.

Hidden within a dense forest on the outskirts of Aureatia was an old mansion standing on the banks of a clear freshwater stream. A lone carriage was parked outside the front gate.

An elderly gentleman, dressed from head to toe in black, alighted from the carriage and knocked three times on the mansion door.

An old leprechaun woman came out to meet him and respectfully bowed to the guest.

"My, my, if it isn't Master Miluzi. Thank you for making the long trip out here."

The elderly man raised his cap up to his breast and returned the bow with a friendly smile.

He was Miluzi the Coffin Edict—a Craft Arts caster who had once fought against Kiyazuna the Axle, and creator of the mighty and unrivaled golems Reshipt and Nemerhelga.

"Not at all, Miss Frey. I should be the one thanking you. Were it not for your support, my past deeds would have made it impossible for me to enter Aureatia."

"For us, it was no problem at all. My lady is waiting for you, so please come in."

Every nook and cranny of the manor's interior was illuminated, enough to make one forget it was the dead of the night. However, there were thick, black curtains covering the windows, ensuring that none of the light escaped into the darkness.

Before long, Miluzi and Frey arrived at the hall for receiving guests. Waiting there to greet Miluzi was the young and beautiful owner of the manor.

"Do come in, Master Miluzi. My name is Linaris. I shall be the one to host you today in my father's stead."

Linaris tilted her head slightly and flashed a charming smile.

Though she was draped in a lovely dress that also seemed to glow, the bare skin of her shoulders and back seemed to shine even more radiantly.

She was the only daughter of Rehart the Obsidian and the final leader of Obsidian Eyes.

"How very courteous of you—thank you. I never would have dreamed that Master Rehart of all people would have such a beautiful daughter... Should I be calling you Obsidian now, young lady?"

"No."

A strained smile came across her face; she looked at the chair in the back of the hall.

The figure was slumped deep in his chair and remained perfectly still. He likely wasn't even breathing.

"There is only one Obsidian. That name belongs to my father."

"Indeed, you may have the right of it."

Miluzi was one of those people who knew very well the deeds of Rehart the Obsidian before his death. The heartless leader of Obsidian Eyes, always skulking in the dark underbelly of the world, Rehart was far more ruthless to his allies than he was to his enemies.

While he did possess powers of vampirism, allowing him to control the minds and actions of those he had given his blood, many seemed to bend to his will purely out of fear. Was the same true of Linaris as well?

Miluzi sat down at the large dining table, opposite the young lady.

Wild-duck meat dressed with black honey. A salad of root vegetables and cheese. A translucent, amber-colored beef-bone broth.

"Master Miluzi, let us make a toast. To our friendship."

"Yes, and to our meeting today."

The two gently clinked their glasses together.

Savoring the fragrance of the high-quality red wine, they took a sip.

"...Obsidian Eyes. Ahhh, they're all such distant memories now. Yet at the time, I felt like I wouldn't be able to forget any of it even if I tried. Until I heard your messenger say that name...it felt as if I had been in a long sleep, with my memories of that bygone era as my only comfort."

Miluzi the Coffin Edict was a self-proclaimed demon king. In the past he'd led his own country, and prior to the age of the True Demon King, he had fought a fierce war over resources with Kuta Silver City before its transformation into the Land of the End.

During that war, Obsidian Eyes had been an enemy, delivering a terrible blow to his nation.

"Back then, I was still but a young girl myself. Nevertheless, I've heard that the technological wonders you produced were like those sung about in the poems of legend."

"It is truly an honor to hear that. Miss Linaris, do you...or rather—does Obsidian Eyes not hold a grudge against me?"

"Not at all. Is there anything more wonderful than two people who once crossed blades getting the opportunity to meet again and reconciling in friendship? We knew of each other's strength even more than we know our allies'. Why, nothing would make me happier than if we could join forces together right now."

"...In that case, to celebrate our reunion, shall I regale you with stories from back then?"

"Oh yes, by all means."

Underneath the chandelier, the elderly demon king softly told the tale.

"Much like you were once a child...in the beginning, I, too, was nothing but a mere home tutor, employed by a noble family on the frontier. While I am sure it comes as no surprise at all, I was teaching Craft Arts, you see. However, I wasn't a very skilled teacher."

"*Tee-hee...* You are quite the comedian, Master Miluzi. I find that very hard to believe."

"I, myself, am embarrassed to admit it, but I was still young. Whenever I would teach, I would think—why can't I get them to understand such basic fundamentals? These frustrations would claw at me constantly. In order to provide better instruction, I had those nobles teach me their noble script. In their estate, they had old academic records that their ancestors had left behind. The contents of the records were completely unknown to anyone."

It was not uncommon for records elucidating the natural sciences, through experiments, observation, or calculations, to be kept in a noble family's home. And in many cases, an aristocratic family's unique writing script had been constructed specifically to leave them behind. The nobles of antiquity once secured their control by bestowing—and monopolizing—the power of knowledge.

"They had these records at hand for so long, and yet no one read them?" asked Linaris.

"That's right. It seemed that none among their generation had opened the books even once. Even though they'd hired a home tutor, mind you. Quite the peculiar story, isn't it? However, these records were extremely detailed...and day after day, I learned. I would revise some of the older sections that turned out to be incorrect, and when they detailed an experiment, I would try to replicate it on my own."

There were large disparities in these records, depending on their pedigree, and some of them were complete nonsense. In this way, Miluzi was fortunate that these were the books that served as his first teacher.

"...It was then that a realization struck me. I was, in truth, not cut out to be a teacher. I was much more suited to teach myself Craft Arts on my own. Although I had been hired as a home tutor, I felt I was in the aristocrat's mansion not to teach, but to learn."

"I have heard it said that all teachers learn for themselves through their instruction. It must have been the same for you, Master Miluzi."

"I was just being selfish... Still, thanks to this, I was called the best Craft Arts user in the city—and soon, the best in the nation. It was around that time that I met a man named Barnard the Essence as well. He was a visitor...and troubled that he couldn't reproduce the machinery from the Beyond, where he grew up. You must have heard talk of that as well, Miss Linaris. What they refer to as the 'steam engine.'"

"...Yes, I have ridden in a locomotive once before. It's a wonderful invention."

"In order to mass-produce cylinders that didn't leak any steam, I used Craft Arts to set up processing machinery that possessed even greater precision. My invention was well-received, and many people congregated to us. I gathered comrades together with Barnard, increased our workforce, and aimed to increase production even further using golems..."

"......"

Linaris stopped talking and simply stared at the elderly man's face.

She had likely heard what came next.

"...Before long, we became a country. I thought to incite a manufacturing revolution in this world, independent of any of the kingdoms, using this new machinery. However, such excessive power couldn't remain unconcerned with the wars and politics among nations. To the One True King...I was a threat."

Miluzi was a demonic monarch. Someone with too much power, who didn't align himself with the One True King.

Self-proclaimed demon kings didn't all necessarily become one on purpose.

"The factory I had painstakingly designed…and the town I'd built for its employees were burned to the ground. My friend Barnard was poisoned, and when I made golems to bolster my own defenses, the enemy struck me down with even greater might. It felt like I was always tormented by a lack of resources and manpower."

"…Master Miluzi."

"Yes, I understand, young lady. I also know that even though you and your organization were behind it, you were simply acting on orders from said country, nothing more. However, after my nation fell, I lived on in order to find a new purpose for my existence. If I had died before coming up with an answer, it would have felt like I had failed Barnard."

It was also fair to say that Miluzi lived so he could settle things with the many enemies who'd stymied him in the past.

This included Kiyazuna the Axle, who'd been trampling over the world with Craft Arts that surpassed Miluzi's; as well as his mortal enemy in Obsidian Eyes, who had menaced his country.

Finally…the surviving family of the One True King, who scorned him as a demon king—the Queen of Aureatia.

Across from him, Linaris cast her long eyelashes down as she spoke.

"…Master Miluzi. Please, I implore you not to speak any further."

"Miss Linaris. I truly thank you from the bottom of my heart for inviting me here. You told me that you bear no grudge toward me, yes?"

Miluzi took the cane he had left propped up.

"I, however, do bear a grudge. It's time for you all to die."

A shock wave shattered the window.

A figure resembling a bird's skeleton violently flew into the hall while aiming the sights on its right arm at Linaris.

"Reshipt Modified."

It was a golem.

"Reshipt io halese. Nearug samart. Wbunt—" (From Reshipt to Halesept's eyes. Fissured pupils. Pillar of—)

"Get your hands..."

Long before the Thermal Arts incantation could resolve, a colossal figure attacked with razor-sharp claws.

The golem was knocked out of the air and crashed into the floorboards.

The intruder was a massive lycan. Obsidian Eyes. Harutoru the Light Grip.

"...off my lady. Lowly scum."

There were deep gouges in the wall and ceiling from the entrance to the wall—which had been used as a foothold to create more marks, up to the ceiling. The traces of his movement meant that Harutoru, in the span of single second, had gotten above Reshipt's head during its high-speed flight, all without making a sound.

"My daughter, and Obsidian's daughter. Who will surpass the other?"

Suddenly, there came an explosion of compressed air.

The golem cut off the part of its own arm that Harutoru had pinned down and flew outside the lycan's range.

Miluzi still had his sights fixed on the young woman.

"I think there is still more for me to show you... Now then, Reshipt Modified."

"Kweey, kweey, kweey."

A bizarre cry echoed from the golem's head, which resembled an empty bird's skull.

Then six blades extended up from what served as its rib cage.

"My lady. Please stay there and don't move."

"...I understand."

Harutoru stood in front of Linaris on top of the dining table. He seemed to understand that the blades were a type of projectile weapon. This presented the possibility that with his almost armor-like body hair, he could withstand the six-projectile burst.

"Kweey, kweey."

Reshipt Modified aimed its sights on Linaris, and then—

—the moment before the blades fired, a chakram flying in from the golem's flank stopped the initial movement. It was a weapon shaped like a spiral hook.

Without paying any heed to the interference, Reshipt Modified's attack fired off in rapid succession. Then it halted.

Fired. Stopped. Stopped. Stopped. Stopped.

In the span of a single breath, the six blades, which were supposed to be fired off in a volley, were all jammed the moment before launch. With each attack, a chakram had tangled itself in Reshipt's blades.

"How dare you try something so foolish…against our lady…?"

At some point, the lights in the hallways had been extinguished. A curious and mysterious voice was heard from within the darkness.

"Be ashamed of your idiocy. I am Wieze the Variation. Seventh-formation rear guard."

Three more circles emerged from the darkness. Reshipt Modified knocked them out of the air with its landing gear. The spiral hooks entangled in the golem's joints and, through their rotational speed, severed its legs. Knocked off its center of gravity, its body faltered in midair.

"Reshipt Modified! Turn around fast—"

It was then that an explosive sound tore through the air.

A lightning-fast flash streaked from top to bottom, and Reshipt Modified was bisected lengthwise.

"Oh my, what do we have here?"

The tiny old woman floated down between each half of Reshipt Modified and landed. She was the matron of the house, Frey the Waking.

With a cordial smile adorning her face, she spun her cleaving cane behind her waist.

"It seems my whole arm has gone numb. That is quite a hard daughter you have there."

"……"

Still seated at the dining table, Miluzi closed his eyes.

Obsidian Eyes—the damnable adversary that had slaughtered his citizens and burned his country to ash. He recalled that the members from that day long ago had been the same sort of horrible demons he was faced with now.

"It seems I've been defeated once again."

"…How unfortunate, Master Miluzi."

Linaris also remained seated, quietly staring across the table from him.

The battle between them had been decided without either of them moving a single centimeter.

Miluzi might have been able to brandish the gun concealed within his cane, but it was likely that this, too, would have been entirely meaningless from the start. Linaris quietly spoke to Miluzi.

"In these moments, I always… I always hope that if I haven't truly been forsaken, then perhaps someday, regardless of any benefits, reason, or sense of justice…a friend may appear who will accept us all."

"I feel for you. However…I'm sure such a thing will never happen. Not for you, nor for myself."

In the distant past, Miluzi had been a mere home tutor. Not any sort of demon king.

However, he became an enemy. Not to anyone in particular, but to a great number of people—a *vague and nebulous* enemy. As he spired further, meeting the animosity he faced with the animosity of his own, Miluzi the Coffin Edict had, at some point, become the enemy he was thought to be.

Now he had become someone who was capable of wearing the face of a mild-mannered gentleman as he tried to kill another.

"Will you kill me?"

"No."

"Then will you make me an ally?"

"No."

"...What, then?"

"Master Miluzi. Regarding the reason I invited you here today..."

He wasn't going to be killed or become their ally. When one was dealing with Obsidian Eyes, such treatment could only mean one thing.

Miluzi was unable to move. It was almost as if the power of Linaris's eyes on him had frozen him in place.

Meeting face-to-face spelled immediate defeat—could anyone in the world even imagine such a vampire?

"...I would like to ask you about Master Mestelexil."

As long as something held secrets, Obsidian Eyes would peer into it all...

...with those golden irises, beautiful enough to make one forget everything else.

The residential district in the center of Aureatia had been readjusted into a regulated grid through a massive-scale city-planning project. This plan had continued from the time of the Central Kingdom.

This uptown, high-class residential area was relatively close to the palace, and many of the Twenty-Nine Officials of Aureatia set up their manors here. However, the residence of Dant the Heath Furrow was a humble one.

The apartment building where he lived was distinctly faded compared with the surrounding homes; his own apartment was equipped with the bare minimum required for a dwelling. It was only big enough to fit a room for his aging mother and his study.

While he understood the opinion that, as one of the Twenty-Nine Officials, he should be living somewhere that reflected his station, Dant had been staying here since long before he made a name for himself as a general.

This wasn't because Dant lacked ambition. He merely had a faint aversion to something beyond his station ballooning further and further. It may have been a result of the education his mother had given him.

However, at this point, Dant the Heath Furrow needed to deal with something that had swelled to a size far too large for his hands to grasp.

One small month before the beginning of the Sixways Exhibition.

When Dant visited the room, Hiroto the Paradox was having a late lunch.

"Have you gotten used to life in Aureatia, Hiroto?"

"If I had just a bit more freedom to come and go as I pleased, then there'd be nothing to want for."

His appearance placed his age at thirteen or fourteen years old. He had gray, almost white hair. Hiroto was an extremely light eater, and that sole aspect of his was even more childish than his looks would suggest.

The apartment building's third floor, which had once been totally vacant, was presently in Dant's possession. It had become necessary to place the Gray-Haired Child in the same building as himself and keep him under observation.

"After all, this is a great chance to see and learn about Aureatia's culture with my own eyes. Did you know? Simple pictures and symbols are used to some extent as a replacement for written words even in this world, but when you look at the regional differences in them, you can see, for example, what sort of progress and development that city was able to accompl—"

"That's not necessary." Dant spat out crossly, sitting down in a chair.

It was fair to describe Hiroto the Paradox as the type of person he personally found the most unpleasant of all. Shrewdly maneuvering and conspiring, Hiroto believed that words spoke far louder than actions.

"I only want one thing from you. Crush the designs of the reformation faction and the other ragtag rabble and protect the Queen."

The Sixways Exhibition. An idiotic national undertaking meant to decide on who the Hero was through true duel matches between sixteen candidates. Behind the scenes, there were the plans of Aureatia's Third Minister Jel and Second General Rosclay to establish a symbol of authority and power to replace Queen Sephite. As part of the Queen's faction, it was something Dant absolutely could not afford to overlook.

"If you're saying that this cultural understanding, or what have you, is needed to plan out a battle strategy, then Zigita Zogi can handle it, right? You're not going to be the one coming up with the strategy yourself anyway."

"True."

Hiroto calmly nodded.

"When it comes to this battle, neither my skills nor my intellect will prove useful in the slightest. If anything, being under surveillance like this is the more reassuring option. The reformation faction won't cast any half-baked suspicions at us this way, either."

"……"

Even Hiroto the Paradox was not a true ally to the Queen's faction.

Though Dant had joined forces with him for the time being to oppose the reformation faction and their majority position, Hiroto had the Free City of Okafu at his back. Okafu was a nation of elite mercenaries led by the visitor and self-proclaimed demon king Morio the Sentinel. In fact, attracting them to the Sixways Exhibition stage may have been equivalent to selling out Dant's own country to protect it.

If by any chance this man looks to harm Aureatia...I'll kill him on the spot before the reformation faction can do it themselves. Then I'll take responsibility... I'll pay with my life. A hero candidate sponsor should have at least that much resolve.

"Regarding Ozonezma..." Hiroto suddenly began, as if the thought had just come to him. "Are there any signs that some of the other camps are looking into him at all?"

Hiroto the Paradox had dispatched two of his men to participate in the Sixways Exhibition: Zigita Zogi the Thousandth and Ozonezma the Capricious. On top of that, Ozonezma was a candidate *he had made Fourteenth General Yuca sponsor* to ensure he wouldn't be traced back to Hiroto.

"...As far as I was able to see, Rosclay and Haade only took a cursory look into his background. Ozonezma's sponsor, Yuca, isn't very skilled at subterfuge to begin with, after all. He's always getting pulled into counterinsurgency work all over and doesn't have the spare time to enact some large-scale operation... They likely don't have any reason to be wary of his camp's movements."

"Fair enough. To put it another way, it's nigh certain that

someone will eventually try to use some roundabout means to attack him."

"I'm thinking the same thing... How do you plan to deal with it?"

"That won't be necessary," said Zigita Zogi.

A goblin poked his head out from the neighboring room. He was the hero candidate Zigita Zogi the Thousandth.

"Master Ozonezma is bait. It will take a fair amount of preparation and a considerable number of men to investigate a hero candidate in Gimeena City, as it's removed from Aureatia. Be it General Rosclay or General Haade, if they attempt to meddle with Ozonezma, we should be able to detect it from here in Aureatia. The investigation will become a burden, but they won't be able to leave him alone, either. The plan is for this, as a result, to chip away at their reserve forces that are keeping us in check."

"Is it really going to go that smoothly? Doesn't seem like there'll be any noticeable effect."

"I am saying that there are things to glean from how each camp deals with this situation. Not allowing Master Ozonezma to enter Aureatia is his own personal wish, yes, but it won't prove disadvantageous to us, either."

"...So then which camp are you going to look into?"

"The ones we're investigating are..."

Zigita Zogi unreservedly rolled out the map of Aureatia in his hands onto the floor.

He slapped a finger on a spot in this city.

"Last night, there was a violent incident involving gunfire at the Blue Beetle tavern. Two of the people who happened to be present were Shalk the Sound Slicer and Tu the Magic. They are both hero candidates. This means there are some who immediately stepped forward after the sixteen candidates were announced to perform a forceful bit of reconnaissance."

"Last night—really? That's far too fast."

"You're thinking the same thing, then, Dant?"

There was someone who'd immediately moved to investigate their enemies as soon as the hero candidates' names were announced. That itself wasn't anything abnormal. In fact, there were likely still competitors whose combat abilities remained a total mystery, even to Rosclay the Absolute, who was working on the side of the tournament organizers.

Additionally, for any of the different camps, investigating the other competitors would only happen after the public announcement of the hero candidates. If they didn't, the timing of their attack would then make it clear to everyone whose information they had their hands on.

Still, to go into action on the very first day... That's practically admitting that they had information on who they were ambushing from before the public announcement, isn't it? Once the names were publicized, it wouldn't be completely impossible to get a hold on where throughout Aureatia's vast borders they were located and find a chance to ambush them, but...

At the very least, there had to be some purpose behind these movements. To those most engaged in intrigue and schemes, this purpose was an enigma that couldn't be overlooked—much like how Ozonezma's existence appeared to the other camps.

"On the very day the hero candidates were announced, the hunt for particular individuals began: someone who was able to attack individuals with the skills and expertise to appear in the Sixways Exhibition, then draw out the slightest amount of that person's power; Someone who could be tasked with a mission and faithfully carry it out; Someone who gathered power and influence, formed a plan, and immediately put it into action; Finally, someone who could be used and tossed aside without issue should the situation call for it. Assuming the Aureatia military wasn't a part of it, the pool of individuals who could be obtained through ordinary personal connections would be rather limited."

"But if the Twenty-Nine Officials openly used Aureatia's regular soldiers to look into their opponents, that would instead reveal their own moves to everyone else. Right?"

"That is why I agree it was far too fast. The attackers at the Blue Beetle were mostly like not Aureatia soldiers."

"…Not necessarily. Even so, there's another way. Outside mercenaries could— Wait."

Dant realized: This Sixways Exhibition had begun long before the start of the first match.

…Zigita Zogi. Hiroto's adviser whom he had raised from a young age. A goblin, a race existing in this very world. Dant had recognized Hiroto the Paradox as a true monster, but Zigita Zogi was a similarly terrifying being.

"Okafu! So that's why!"

"Well, that was my intention, yes. Winning over the Free City of Okafu to our side first was, in addition to securing a fighting force we could freely utilize for ourselves, to make it so other powers *couldn't freely utilize the Free City's mercenaries for themselves.* To attract mercenaries in a large quantity, and of better quality than Okafu's—that would be a considerably difficult task. However, the other party in the Blue Beetle attack did just that."

"Milord Dant, do you have any ideas as to who may possess a powerful private army?" asked Hiroto as he silently chewed on the scraps of meat still left on his plate.

"Assuming, then, that this excludes any regular Aureatia soldiers... Among the Twenty-Nine Officials, it would be Haade the Flashpoint, since he presides over the military...or Kaete the Round Table, presiding over Aureatia's industry. He's Mestelexil's sponsor. You need a fair amount of power and authority to secretly have your own private army, after all. That, and those two could mobilize any force well, whether it was their own army or not."

"What about the *Fifth Minister*, then?"

"......"

Dant silently glared at Hiroto the Paradox.

This man was serious about approaching the fight with a complete understanding of Aureatia's political situation. Not only that, but his understanding was also far deeper than the Aureatia side had anticipated.

"There is no Fifth Minister within the Twenty-Nine Officials. That said..."

Just like it had been with Twenty-Third General Taren, among the seats of the Twenty-Nine Officials, there existed a few seats that remained empty without any designated replacement—the fifth seat was one example.

"...the former Fifth Minister, Iriolde the Atypical Tome. Though not a military officer, he could likely gather any number of bureaucrats with superb tactical minds. Not only that, *but he would also do it, too...* You think there's someone being backed with his support mixed in among the sponsors?"

Zigita Zogi answered Dant's question in Hiroto's stead.

"No. That is not what we're saying... The point is that if there is already a suitable person to suspect, then it was worth it for the other camps to attempt this rushed attack."

"You mean that as long as there's a suspect, they'd be able to disguise themselves as part of their forces?"

"In that sense, this is a slightly unfavorable situation, isn't it? There is a whole small month before the start of the games. Our first trial will likely be to survive until they begin."

"...A small month," Hiroto murmured. He looked to be done eating and was wiping the corners of his mouth. "The reason there's a small month delay between the hero candidate announcement and the first match is because of Rosclay, yes?"

"Ostensibly, it's to give time to acclimate Word Arts to this region. If there are any who fight primarily with Word Arts among the hero candidates, their presumed focal point would be a well-worn vessel, along with the water, wind, and earth on the battlefield. If they're simply coming to an understanding with natural objects of those three elements, then one small month should give them enough time to acclimate. That's the justification," said Dant.

"I see. On the battlefield, you always have to anticipate the use of Word Arts, after all."

Those who utilized Word Arts needed to familiarize themselves with the targets they were applying them to. Even though it may have physically been the exact same water or wind, if they were in a different region, the characteristics of those elements would change slightly, making it possible that they'd be unable to produce the desired effect.

Nevertheless, for those with exceptional aptitude for Word Arts, having an entire small month would make it possible to create for themselves a focal point that was complex enough to go beyond these three elements. Conversely, there were also those whose aptitude for Word Arts wouldn't even let them communicate with a single drop of water if it was on unfamiliar soil, even after spending a whole small month attempting to do so.

Thus, this reasoning, with its vast individual variability, was nothing more than an excuse for the public.

"In truth, it takes time to gather information on the hero candidates. Rosclay has the authority to use the data from their small-month-long investigation to then decide the tournament bracket. Rosclay, out of all the sixteen candidates, will start from the most advantageous position to advance through to the end."

"That said, as we confirmed moments ago, he can't openly use

Aureatia troops to do so. The information gatherer would then need to have a power that possesses soldiers outside the Aureatia framework. In which case, looking at it from our opponent's perspective, there is another suitable suspect, just like the former Fifth Minister, isn't there?"

Zigita Zogi's hypothesis hinged on the presumption that their enemies were properly trained soldiers.

The power, then, that clearly met all these conditions beyond the Aureatia army themselves would be…

"The Free City of Okafu. There's a possibility that our opponent here is trying to force suspicion on us."

"……!"

Someone who was able to attack individuals with the skills and expertise to appear in the Sixways Exhibition, then draw out the slightest amount of that person's power; Someone who could be tasked with a mission and faithfully carry it out; Someone who gathered power and influence, formed a plan, and immediately put it into action; Finally, someone who could be used and tossed aside without issue should the situation call for it.

Zigita Zogi was absolutely right. Given that Hiroto's camp had monopolized the Okafu mercenaries for themselves, from the perspective of the other camps, they would be the first people to suspect.

"…In which case, that discredits your assumptions here. Now there's a meaning to plan this attack for Rosclay, too. You all are going to be the first ones the reformation faction will try to knock out of the Sixways Exhibition before it even begins. They're shining suspicions on the Okafu army and trying to create an excuse to disqualify them," said Dant.

"That's fair. Or perhaps..." Hiroto followed up Dant's words. "...there is the possibility that this is the attempt of an undisclosed third party to sow bad blood between the reformation faction and the Okafu army."

"In which case, it could be Haade, Kaete, Iriolde... Wait. This is getting us nowhere. If we start thinking about who's pulling the strings behind the ones pulling the strings, we'll go around in circles forever. How do you plan to verify this, exactly?" asked Dant.

"......"

Rosclay the Absolute's reformation faction, which was spearheading the Sixways Exhibition.

Those within Aureatia who opposed the reformation faction, like Haade the Flashpoint and Kaete the Round Table.

Iriolde the Atypical Tome, possessing tremendous influence and power from outside the Twenty-Nine Officials.

Finally, Hiroto the Paradox, backed by the Free City of Okafu.

The ambush incident at the Blue Beetle itself was a trivial little skirmish. However, any one of them could be a possible suspect behind it.

Zigita Zogi murmured, "...Master Dant. It's possible that our enemy may be on the outside of this never-ending circle."

"What do you mean?"

"I imagined, as a camp's motive behind enacting this sort of scheme, what would be the most troublesome possibility for us. In other words, supposing someone somewhere isn't trying to pit one camp against the other for their own benefit but whose goal is purely *to make camps fight among themselves—*"

It was then that a crackling mechanical static echoed in the room.

"Pardon."

It was the communication radzio installed in the neighboring room. Zigita Zogi swiftly stood up and went to pick up the receiver.

Left behind, Dant could only sigh.

"…Hiroto the Paradox. Do you think we can win?"

There were machinations whirling about this battle that even an experienced military officer like Dant the Heath Furrow couldn't fully deal with. The Queen's faction, which placed the royal lineage above all else, had become a minority at this point. This was because the Sixways Exhibition was happening solely so the reformation party, seeking a Hero to replace the Queen, could come to power.

For Dant, his current situation—borrowing powers from outside the kingdom like the Free City of Okafu and the Gray-Haired Child to resist the current tide—was the same as conceding his own defeat. Supposing he did indeed come out victorious in this fight, it was possible that instead of the reformation faction, it would just be the Gray-Haired Child usurping Aureatia's rule instead.

"I don't have much strength to speak of, personally," Hiroto replied. "But I have made the wishes of all who have ever voted for me come true. Without any exceptions."

"…Hmph. You must be lying."

"Is it so difficult to believe the words of a politician?"

Hiroto laughed as well. Perhaps this was the man's attempt at a joke.

Zigita Zogi may have been a freak, equipped with intelligence more outstanding than any minia, but he was still ultimately a goblin. Monstrous races devoured the minian races. In which case, was Hiroto an ally to the monstrous races?

If he insisted he could make everything come true, was it even possible for him to make conflicting forces like the minian races and monstrous races *both come out victorious*?

Finished with his call in the other room, Zigita Zogi poked back in.

"This is quite troubling. Master Hiroto, we have learned the identity of the ones behind the attack at the Blue Beetle."

"...What happened?"

"They were soldiers from the Free City of Okafu."

"So it really was some of theirs, after all. I don't necessarily believe so myself, but... Did Morio the Sentinel betray us?"

"No. Even if he was going to, he wouldn't yet. Suspecting him would likely be just what our enemy wants."

Zigita Zogi's meticulousness, laying out his information network across all Aureatia, was what saved them. Before anyone else, they, the concerned parties themselves, had been able to sense this disquiet.

The ones who were starting to investigate the hero candidates weren't some unknown soldiers from a third party. It was their own collaborator making inroads into Aureatia. A soldier from the Free City of Okafu. A breakaway? A masquerade? A spy who had slipped into their ranks long before? Somebody was pulling the strings from the shadows. In a worst-case scenario, their camp could very well be destroyed from within.

Then once the origins of the assailants who'd attacked other hero candidates became known, it would be their turn to suffer a fatal blow.

"For the time being, I will try to cover up this latest incident as much as possible. Even assuming we do eventually disclose the information we hold, this is still quite an ill-boding tide. Also, supposing that this Okafu soldier defected and broke away from his city—Master Dant, there is something I would like to ask you," posed Zigita Zogi.

"…What's that?"

"What do you say to the possibility that perhaps a vampire is involved in this case? A former agent of Obsidian Eyes, Zeljirga the Abyss Web, is among the hero candidates, I believe."

Infiltrate an organization and create traitors at will.

That was the most terrifying power of the once-active Obsidian Eyes… However.

"That…can't be possible."

"Your basis for that?"

"Obsidian Eyes, led by Rehart the Obsidian, has already been wiped out. Thirteenth Minister Enu undertook an operation to subdue them and is monitoring Zeljirga as her sponsor."

"You're sure that he isn't being manipulated himself, then, yes?"

"It's obvious, isn't it? He was in charge of a vampire-subjugation operation. *He assuredly injected himself with the antiserum beforehand.* Given that they've already finished inspecting him for any hints of infection following his operation, we can be certain he hasn't been turned into a corpse."

"That's certainly right. Supposing that even then, Obsidian Eyes is continuing their operations…"

Zigita Zogi once again sat down beside the map.

"…it would mean that the Thirteenth Minister was betraying the minian races of his own volition."

In this world, races that brought harm to the minian races were defined as monstrous races.

Having both the minian races and the monstrous races coming out victorious was inconceivable.

For the past several days, Kuuro the Cautious had been sleeping at the clinic in central Aureatia.

He was not a patient himself. He had bent the staff's arms to loan him an empty hospital room and continued to guard the defeated hero candidate—Toroa the Awful.

As long as he was Toroa's bodyguard, he couldn't let the admitted patient out of his sight. While Toroa continued to live here, Kuuro had no intentions of stepping outside the clinic, either. Eating the rations he had brought in with him, he quietly spent his time during the day ensuring he didn't get in the way of the other patients. He could ascertain how Toroa was doing without going to see him directly, but he still visited his hospital room around two times a day to chat.

On the other hand, his partner was apparently paying visits to Toroa's room with far greater frequency.

"Hey, Kuuro, listen. They said Toroa's wounds look a lot better today than they did yesterday. Incredible, huh? The doctor was really surprised, too."

The creature who fluttered around Kuuro's head like a

songbird was a tiny girl, small enough to fit in two hands. She was a homunculus with two bird wings instead of arms. Her name was Cuneigh the Wanderer.

"The Life Arts aren't supposed to be having that strong of an effect yet, but they say he's already beginning to heal."

"That's great news. The more I hear about him, the more outrageous he gets."

He was the man who'd leaped into the middle of the Particle Storm—a calamity capable of laying waste to entire cities. He had been gifted with vitality worthy of his monster moniker.

"...My bodyguard job lasts only until he gets discharged, too. Has this whole arrangement been a big headache for you, Cuneigh?"

Gently catching Cuneigh as she fluttered into his palm, he then placed her inside his inner coat pocket. Cuneigh gleefully squinted her eyes as she smiled.

"Nuh-uh, not at all! Actually, I enjoy getting to talk with Toroa. Also, if I go up on the roof? I can see the street performers in the plaza! Since it's so far, I can't really catch the music or their voices, but the children admitted in here all really look forward to it, too!"

A street performer. Must be Zeljirga. Her sleight of hand's always been real impressive. Even though I can see everything, she still might fool me.

In the past, Kuuro was once an assassin belonging to Obsidian Eyes. He had been feared for his Clairvoyance, a composite sensory ability that surpassed physical vision and was capable of perceiving any and all phenomena with ultra-precision.

The hero candidate Zeljirga the Abyss Web was his colleague

at the time. She was a woman of the zmeu race, with a lizard's head and skin. Almost obnoxiously cheerful, the exact opposite of Kuuro, she was an assassin who lived to make others laugh with her clownish antics.

...Judging by the intentions behind that "street performance," it's very unlikely that she's acting out of a personal desire for Toroa's enchanted swords. Her close proximity to this clinic is either because the conditions simply lined up for her, or conversely, she's monitoring me to ensure I don't make any strange moves.

Currently, there were no signs that Obsidian Eyes had their sights on Toroa's enchanted swords and were planning to attack. Supposing that she did make a move—even if it was with a military force indirectly manipulated, regardless of any vampiric power—Kuuro would be able to expose everything about the attack, including the secret intents that lay behind it.

Possessing supreme sensory abilities and knowing everything there was to know about the spy guild's techniques, Kuuro the Cautious's very existence was their natural enemy, preventing Obsidian Eyes' activity. While they weren't in a definitively hostile relationship, to Obsidian Eyes, Kuuro was sure to be someone they wished to eliminate first and foremost.

"In any case, hearing that Toroa's recovering quickly is fantastic news."

"Yup! Sure is!"

Toroa in perfect form was truly an unrivaled monster. Once his wounds were healed, he wouldn't need Kuuro to guard him anymore.

Kuuro would return the favor he owed Toroa from their fight against the Particle Storm then depart Aureatia immediately. Cuneigh might be reluctant to leave, but for both Obsidian Eyes and for Kuuro himself, that seemed like the best possible conclusion.

The problem is the few days until Toroa's wounds heal... The question is if all the powers in play will keep nice and quiet until then.

That wasn't going to happen.

Kuuro's Clairvoyance perceived the scene through the dividing hospital-room wall.

There were five men standing in front of the door to Toroa's room. Footsteps. Posture. The type and weight of the weapons they were concealing. Not there to visit Toroa as he lay injured nor messengers sent by his sponsor—they were undisputedly Aureatia soldiers.

...They're hiding short swords inside their coats. Never smelled this scent before... Some explosive I'm unfamiliar with? Then there's the strangely shaped weapon on their belt. Similar to a small handgun. Sitting on their dominant hand's side. I gotta be careful of that.

Finishing his thoughts on the scene in a single second, Kuuro stood up. He put on his flat cap.

"Cuneigh, wait here. Don't leave this room."

"Hmm? Okay."

"I'll be right back."

He quickly exited out into the hallway.

Once he climbed the stairs, it was only a few paces to reach Toroa's room.

The five Aureatia soldiers were prying open the door to the room and getting ready to rush inside when Kuuro arrived.

"...Hey, you five over there."

The soldiers laid their eyes on Kuuro. One of the men spoke up with an annoyed tone.

"What's this, some kid?"

"Piss off. I'm a leprechaun. You got some business with the patient in there?"

"We're with the Aureatia army. We're here on an official directive from the council. If you don't have business here yourself, then beat it."

"You have a seal from the council? You should have a warrant from whoever sent you guys here, right?"

"Of course we do. On the orders of Aureatia's Fourth Minister, Kaete the Round Table, we are here to seize Toroa the Awful's enchanted swords."

The soldier produced the seal.

Kuuro was, if anything, impressed by the behavior.

They've got guts, I'll give them that... Coming to take them like this without trying to be coy about the one who put them up to it.

Still, he also understood that the men had come to steal the enchanted swords and wouldn't take no for an answer.

"...Sorry to say, but Toroa there commissioned me to guard him. If you all plan on stealing those swords by force, then I'll have to get forceful myself."

"Pfft. Get a load of this guy."

The man who appeared to be the commanding officer of the group smirked.

"Let's go out front. I want the whole avenue to get a good look at the fate of this bastard who dares defy Minister Kaete."

Kuuro was perceiving the vicinity around the clinic at all times. They weren't using this opportunity to bring Kuuro outside and attack Toroa with a separate force.

Seriously...these are a rare breed to see nowadays.

Kuuro followed their orders and went outside the clinic.

These Aureatia soldiers likely thought that Toroa, with his injuries, would be an easily dispatched opponent. Given that, Cuuro believed it was necessary to ascertain what was the source behind their swelled confidence.

"All right. Around here should be fine," said the soldiers.

"...Tell me something. Are these sorts of...*pretend duels* a popular pastime in the Aureatia army?"

"Not at all. This isn't a duel."

At that moment, there was a dry gunshot, and Kuuro's small body collapsed to the ground.

"It's an execution."

Sniper fire from a distance.

Not only that, but from an abnormally long distance...that went beyond all this world's existing knowledge of weaponry.

The commanding officer stooped down beside Kuuro's collapsed body and smiled like a wolf.

"Kuuro the Cautious. Surely, you didn't assume that we knew nothing about you, hmm?"

The blatant attack on Toroa had been bait from the very beginning to lure his bodyguard, Kuuro, out onto the main road with its unobstructed sight lines. If they were expecting to go up against someone with deviant sensory abilities, they simply needed to attack him from outside the range of his perception.

"Break in again. If Toroa the Awful looks like he's going to bolt by himself, you can let him go. Prioritize securing the enchanted swords above all else."

"...I get it. An interesting weapon you've got there."

"......"

Kuuro spoke, still collapsed facedown on the ground.

"A lot of areas to adjust on the gunstock. So it can adhere close to the body and match up with the shooter's physique and quirks, huh...? The barrel looks like it's covered, but it's actually constructed to be free-floating and only contact the mechanical action. This mechanism's gotta be to increase its accuracy. Producing a gun this accurate goes beyond any Craft Arts or machining techniques... This has to require an outlandish degree of engineering precision—"

"I-impossible."

Kuuro the Careful appeared to have been shot through and collapsed on the ground. He only *appeared* that way.

There was no blood splattered on the street. Given how inconceivable the situation was, the Aureatia soldiers hadn't been able to immediately pick up on this abnormality, either.

"H-he—he *dodged* it...?!"

"Impossible! That shot came from over nine hundred meters away!"

Kuuro the Cautious hadn't collapsed.

"You seem to know a lot about me, right? You didn't assume that *a mere nine hundred meters* behind me was beyond my sight, did you?"

Faster than the sniper rifle could launch its bullet, he had perceived not just the muzzle it came from but also everything down to the rifle's internal construction, then dodged the bullet by falling to the ground.

The soldier behind him went to retrieve a gun from his breast pocket. It was a firearm called an automatic pistol, whose stopping power and burst speed far exceeded the latest model of small firearms; however...

"*Hnaugh!*"

"Tell the doctor you've got a torn flexor tendon."

...Kuuro stood back up like nothing had happened. Not only that, but he had also finished making his attack far faster than the soldier could pull the trigger on his gun.

Tucked inside his coat sleeve was a collapsible crossbow.

The soldier still had his gun trained on Kuuro but was unable to fire. The second joint of his finger had been pierced through by an extra-fine arrow and was no longer capable of moving.

"You really think I don't know that's a bomb?" Kuuro said without looking at another soldier who was trying to make his move.

He was conscious of it all, even the initial movements of an attack occurring from a total blind spot.

"......!"

"...Good judgment. You're not going to be able to throw that thing my way. I could pierce through your wrist right before you release it and make you blow yourself up, for one... Even if it's some weapon I've never seen before, I can pin down its intended use just from the initial movements the person wielding it makes."

He slightly cocked his head.

Another gunshot rang out.

Not a single hair on his head scattered into the air. Kuuro dodged the second nine-hundred-meter sniper shot without the slightest hint of difficulty.

"Y-you monster...!"

"The man you guys are trying to attack is much more of monster than me."

Kuuro brushed sand off his fallen hat and placed it back on his head.

His opponents were regular Aureatia soldiers. Although they were the ones who'd started this fight, there was no need to stir up the situation any further. He was all too accustomed to having his life threatened already.

"...Be good and get lost before I end up stealing all the information you have," said Kuuro.

After he had settled things, Kuuro once again headed toward Toroa the Awful's room.

"Got into a little trouble, did you, Kuuro?"

It went without saying, but Toroa had also been fully cognizant of what had occurred outside his hospital room. Bending his enormous upper body, he apologized to the leprechaun.

"Sorry. Ended up causing you trouble," said Toroa.

"It wasn't a big deal. I just figured it'd go smoother if I handled things."

At the very least, he had resolved things without any deaths.

The weapons Toroa wielded were not anything like Kuuro's arrows with their low degree of lethality. He had a treasure trove of enchanted swords, boasting the potential to deal instant death. If Toroa himself had dealt with the Aureatia soldiers, at the very least, it wouldn't have ended with nothing more than a torn tendon.

"That said, though…I think you need to be cautious of Kaete the Round Table. I've never seen a gun constructed like that before in my entire life. Its precision was on an entirely different level, even compared with the Gray-Haired Child's latest models."

"A weapon no one's ever seen before, huh…? Kaete the Round Table is Mestelexil's sponsor, right?"

"Yeah."

Cuuro and Toroa, along with Mestelexil. There was a slightly bizarre connection between the three of them.

The trio had fought to the death as the supernatural disaster of the Particle Storm swept over them. The reason Kuuro was guarding Toroa now was to repay him for saving his life at the time.

In addition, just as Toroa had saved his life, Mestelexil and Kiyazuna had saved Kuuro's life as well. Be that as it may have been, though, it certainly hadn't been their intention.

After thinking a moment, Toroa began to speak.

"…Back then, I witnessed the way Mestelexil fought. Guns that spit out bullets like rain. Bombs that tracked me and flew at ultra-high speeds. Weapons that caused only acute pain, totally invisible. All the weapons he produced looked more calamitous than any enchanted sword... That stuff was truly on an entirely different level."

"A weapon that creates weapons, then. That means that Kaete the Round Table is mass-producing those weapons and making his soldiers use them, huh?"

"That might be it. This doesn't just apply to enchanted swords, but see... A weapon's greatest strength *is the ability for anyone and everyone to wield it.* There's no logical reason why the weapons Mestelexil makes would only be able to be used by the golem himself."

"If that's the case, their groups come up with some truly crazy ideas in their heads. I was able to settle things peacefully this time, but no guarantee that next time'll go the same way."

"...It's okay. When that time comes, I'll handle it myself."

Mestelexil was a nigh-invincible weapon just on his own.

However, if Kaete the Round Table, leader of Aureatia's third-biggest faction, was to make use of Mestelexil, the golem's true value would far outstrip his fighting power.

While Mestelexil the Box of Desperate Knowledge was the ultimate immortal construct, at the same time, he was a factory that tirelessly produced weapons from another world.

These assailants didn't attack us without thinking. They must have come here believing they had a chance of beating Toroa.

Kuuro thought back over the words and actions of the soldiers under Kaete's command.

That confidence he'd felt from the soldiers had come from having a mighty weapon backing them up after all. Just as throughout history, a single enchanted sword had influenced the tides of war, the visible strength that came from having a superior weapon bestowed morale on the entire force.

What a pain. Damn near everyone's crawling around with their individual motives. Rosclay the Absolute. Haade the Flashpoint. The Gray-Haired Child and the Free City of Okafu. The Old Kingdoms' loyalists. Obsidian Eyes...

Among them all, Kaete the Round Table wasn't the type of opponent to lay out multiple layers of schemes against his enemies. The ones Kuuro needed to be cautious of were still the Gray-Haired Child and Obsidian Eyes.

However, Kaete's group alone was the only one able to utilize technology that even Kuuro's Clairvoyance was barely able to comprehend, and they could do so in large groups as well. The more time they were given to produce these technologies, the worse it would get.

On top of that, if by any chance there was a weapon...beyond what he saw in that fateful battle, that even Kuuro's senses couldn't perceive...

There might be a chance...that Kaete the Round Table is the most dangerous power out of them all.

In central Aureatia, children could often be seen playing in the city streets. This was thanks to the safety of the neighborhood, as well as the many different parks that'd been established in the area.

In this part of the city, with the start of the Sixways Exhibition close on the horizon, there were all sorts of different performances being held day and night, delighting the eyes and ears of every child present.

Mixed in with this scene were the figures of a strikingly bizarre parent and child.

"M-M-Mama! Th-there are dolls...moving...like they're alive! Is that even possible? They aren't actually alive, though!"

"A puppet show, huh...? I loathe the damn things. There's always gotta be someone behind them controlling them and stuff, so what's even fun about it? Adding a puppet into the mix is just adding one extra step to the whole process, right?"

The old woman, small but possessing a brutal aura, was named Kiyazuna the Axle. Her child, meanwhile, was a colossal construct encased in navy-blue metal armor—one of the hero candidates, Mestelexil the Box of Desperate Knowledge.

"Geez... All right, then, wanna go see that puppet show, huh?"

"I—I want one, that Mama, can enjoy watching, too!"

"*Hee-hee-hee*, ya don't say! You really are a good kid, aren't ya?"

The self-proclaimed demon king who'd previously rampaged across the world as one of the kingdom's greatest enemies had been freely strutting through the streets of Aureatia ever since Kaete the Round Table had invited her into the city. There were many citizens who complained about the danger of letting a serious criminal like Kiyazuna free to do as she pleased, but there wasn't anyone who was able to lodge a complaint straight to the old woman's face.

"Hey, hey, shoe store there, you already closing up shop?! Don't worry! I never had any plans on shoppin' at your damn store in the first place! *Hya-hya-hya-hya-hya-hya-hya-!*"

"*Ha-ha-ha-ha-ha-ha-ha-ha-ha-ha-ha-ha-ha!*"

Anyone who knew how terrifying Kiyazuna the Axle was would leave the area before they could get involved with her or watch from a safe distance and make sure not to interact with her. Being feared and avoided by her fellow minian races was, if anything, an absolute joy to Kiyazuna the Axle, who was filled from birth with spite and malice.

"Y'know, I don't care if people're cowering in fear like this, but how're you supposed to enjoy yourself, Mestelexil? You haven't been out in a while, so you must wanna have a look around, don't ya?"

"Y-yeah! Making, weapons all the time, gets boring!"

"Oh yeah, I bet it does. That bastard Kaete, how dare he work my precious child to the bone like that!"

Mestelexil's creations were weapons from the Beyond. Kaete the Round Table apparently wanted to distribute them en masse to his personal army as fast as possible, but as far as Kiyazuna was concerned, just rushing through production like this wasn't going to bring about the drastic effect he wished for; at most, it would just make Mestelexil even busier.

That was because his functions extended only to the production stage of the weapon-manufacturing process.

Mestelexil himself possessed latent structural knowledge of these weapons and, therefore, could wield them as if they were an extension of his body. However, in order for anyone else besides the golem to collectively utilize these weapons, time to explain the specifications of said weapon and to then give the proper instruction on how to use them was absolutely vital.

At the moment, only firearms that didn't need a high level of understanding could be used. The defensive heavy machine guns were admittedly serviceable from a tactical standpoint, but highly advanced weapons, like fighter aircraft and strategic arms, would still be hard to utilize on a systematic level for the time being. The Chariot Golems, which Kiyazuna produced herself, could already serve as a substitute for various types of combat vehicles.

Geez, that dumbass Kaete isn't any different from those guys who prize enchanted swords over everything, is he?

Entering the Sixways Exhibition was fine. Conspiring to bring about an industrial revolution was fine, too. He could produce weapons and use them however he wanted—she didn't care.

However, that was all under the pretext that *Mestelexil wanted to do the same.*

Kiyazuna had brought Mestelexil here to Aureatia to give him as much freedom and amusement as this world, completely devastated by the era of the True Demon King, could possibly offer. She also brought him to avenge the death of her son, the Nagan Dungeon Golem, by butchering his killer, Soujirou the Willow-Sword, during the Sixways Exhibition with the citizenry in full attendance.

Kaete's ambitions, the hero talk, and all other such nonsense were, at best, just matters that happened to coincide with her own goals.

"*Ha-ha-ha!* Th-there's, something going on, over there!"

"Hmph, a performing magician, huh? That's Zeljirga, one of the hero candidates, too. Wanna take a look?"

"Yeah!"

The street-performer zmeu they saw from a distance was Zeljirga the Abyss Web. There were major differences between the color of each zmeu's skin and the shape of their faces, making it easy for even people of other races to individually identify them. Zeljirga was suitably described as a minian-shaped lizard.

When the two approached her, several groups of parents and children fled in fear.

"Well, lookie here! Seems like business is booming for ya now, ain't it?"

"B-business, booming! *Ha-ha-ha-ha-ha-ha!*"

Zeljirga acknowledged Kiyazuna's presence, giving an exaggerated bow.

"*Ah-hya-hyah!* Well, a nice hello to you, my new customers! I can see you have your child with you here as well. Just a teeeeensy bit bigger than me, isn't he?"

"...*Hee-hee*, Zeljirga the Abyss Web. You sure you should be fooling around all day? Your big match is just around the corner, ain't it?"

Direct contact between hero candidates before matches was generally forbidden. However, given that they were all living together in Aureatia, it had also been decided that the arrangements wouldn't punish candidates for chance encounters. They were ensuring that they were able to lay down arbitrary punishments at will, to some extent, in response to trifling moments of unlawful activity.

"I mean, if you stand out that much, you know..." said Kiyazuna.

"*Ha, ha-ha-ha!* Mama! If we defeat, a hero candidate, Kaete will be happy, right?! Sh-should I kill Z-Zeljirga, too?!"

"Hey, now. She might just end up getting beaten to death in some unfortunate accident instead, right?"

And it almost went without saying, but Kiyazuna the Axle was, of course, not bound by any of these regulations.

"Oh, come now!" Zeljirga said. "I'll have you know the children love a little accident or two! To be perfectly honest, I think I've gotten more customers to laugh with my failures than I have with my performance! And what would be this child's name, then?"

"I—I am, Mestelexil!"

"And a fine name it is! Now then, Mestelexil, do you like balloons? What about puppet play?"

"I like both! *Ha-ha-ha-ha!* Do you like, puppets, Zeljirga?"

"Oh, but of course. I have plenty of puppet friends, in fact!"

Zeljirga lightly knelt down. Though her right hand had been empty until that moment, in it appeared a large puppet big enough to fit in two hands.

It was a cloth puppet covered in a wavy fabric, with a bird's head. Most of its body was hollow and likely able to fold up to a size much smaller than its appearance suggested.

"This here's Morf!"

"*Ha-ha-ha!* Wow, amazing!"

"Watch carefully now. He's going to say hello. 'Mestelexil! Hi!'"

Morf's head flopped down to the side.

Zeljirga questioningly tilted her head in the same direction as the doll.

"Hmm, now this wasn't supposed to happen here... 'Nice to meet you, Mestelexil!'"

The doll made adorable movements in time with Zeljirga's voice.

"H, e, l...lo—"

However, on the final syllable, Morf lost all its strength and went limp.

"Uhhh, now just give me a moment, if you will! It looks like Morf here's having a bit of an off day! Let's see... Did I put my tools in my bag? I do apologize, but I can finish this up in no time, I promise..."

Despite the audience in front of her, Zeljirga turned around and began fishing through her bag...while behind her, Morf abruptly sat up and briskly began trotting along.

"*Ah-ha-ha-ha-ha-ha-ha-ha!* I-it is, moving! Wooow!"

"What'd you say?"

Right as Zeljirga turned back around, Morf flopped down to the ground.

"Honestly, no more joking with me, okay? Now then, where were they...?"

Once she took her sights off him, Morf begin to start walking again as if alive...and kicked Zeljirga's back. She left out an exaggerated scream before toppling over.

"*Bwaaaugh?!*"

The laughter of the children watching, including Mestelexil, echoed.

"...Did someone kick me just now?"

She picked up Morf, which had immediately collapsed behind her, and cocked her head in confusion.

After making a believable show of turning screws and making slight adjustments, Zeljirga took another bow to her audience.

"Okay then, allow me to introduce him! This is my partner, Morf! Say hello again...or actually, why don't we hold off on that for now? I honestly have a bad feeling about that."

Zeljirga released the tool she held in her other hand.

Except it wasn't any type of tool, but a simple bottle opener.

"At any rate, he should be all patched up now! Now then, everyone, I invite you to watch my friend—and you are my friend, right?—Morf's song and dance!"

A music box began to spin, and the puppet danced in time with the music. Zeljirga manipulated the puppet to pace about the ground before spinning into the air and splitting into two the instant everyone's gaze went off it. All while, the zmeu made it pass through objects that should have obstructed the strings attached to it.

"Wooowee! I-isn't that, amazing, Mama?!"

"Huh, impressive technique there."

Even Kiyazuna the Axle, despising puppet theater as she did, still let her honest admiration slip out. The same was true of the moment Zeljirga first produced the puppet, but there couldn't have been many people in the world capable of sleight-of-hand tricks that were dexterous enough to fool the sensors from the Beyond that comprised Mestelexil's sensory system.

"*Ah-hya-hya!* Thank you very much, all of you! Yes, well, there were some parts in there that were a bit disgraceful on my part, but I do hope you'll overlook all that as simply part of the entertainment… If you'd indulge me, I'd be even happier if you'd overlook it tomorrow, too!"

"Z-Zeljirga! How did you do it?! I—I don't, understand at all!"

"A thanks to you, too, Mestelexil! It seems you were blessed with a truly excellent upbringing by your mother here! It was a terrific honor to have the chance to perform my art for a fellow hero candidate!"

"*Bah.* You think some empty flattery's gonna make Mestelexil and me here go easy on ya, huh?"

Kiyazuna flashed a cocky smile. She agreed, for one of the minian races, Zeljirga's skills were impressive. Nevertheless, compared with the truly powerful like Toroa the Awful, Mele the Horizon's Roar, Lucnoca the Winter—or above all, Mestelexil—she understood from her observations here that the zmeu was little more than an illusionist playing tricks on children.

"If I were you, I'd probably turn tail and run right about now."

"I do indeed have a tail, I suppose! I am a zmeu, after all! What did you think, Mestelexil? Don't you want to see something *even more entertaining* on the Sixways Exhibition stage?"

"I—I do! Zeljirga, can I come, and see your tricks, again?"

"*Ah-hya-hya!* Absolutely, you're always welcome! Children are my absolute best friends, hero candidates or not! Be sure to come back again with your mother there!"

"Yeah! Zeljirga is a, friend! That was, fun!"

"I am absolutely delighted to hear that! Here, would you like a piece of candy for the road?"

"Sheesh... What sorta golem eats candy? Time for us to get goin', Mestelexil."

"Okay! *Ah-ha-ha-ha-ha!*"

Kiyazuna scratched her head, her malice seemingly drained away, and turned on her heels—

"*Ha-ha!*"

It was then that one of Mestelexil's arms moved with lightning-fast speed. A needle was repelled off the golem's armor, falling to the ground with a light *clink*. Kiyazuna had no idea what sort of mechanism had sent the needle flying in the first place.

"......"

Some sort of liquid shimmered on the needle's point. If Kiyazuna's skin had been grazed even slightly, she wouldn't have escaped the fatal side effects.

"...That's a shame, ain't it, Zeljirga?"

Still with her back turned, the self-proclaimed demon king sneered savagely, the corners of her mouth smirking up to her ears.

"*Ah-hya-hya...* What do you mean, I wonder?"

"If we end up matched together, we'll make sure to be nice and thorough when we kill ya, okay? Don't need to get so impatient now."

"How very kind of you! Please do be gentle."

Even when dealing with a tiny needle, imperceptibly fired, with every point of origin unclear...he could snatch any dangerous object flying toward himself or Kiyazuna out of midair, following up after it to defend against it. Mestelexil the Box of Desperate Knowledge was a golem who possessed the most formidable body in history, even without weapons.

Dexterity that could completely deceive someone standing right in front of her. A golden opportunity where her target's state of mind had relaxed. Even then, with both of these conditions coming together perfectly, assassinating Kiyazuna the Axle with a surprise attack had been virtually impossible.

"Y-you can't, beat, me!" Mestelexil shouted as he whirled his circular head section, with its single eye, to and fro. "B-because I am, I am, the strongest of all! *Ha-ha-ha-ha-ha-ha-ha-ha-ha!*"

Why were Kiyazuna and Mestelexil openly joining in on the Sixways Exhibition, exposing themselves to the world at large without being daunted by the hostility they stood to face? The reason was quite simple.

The pair understood that they were without equal.

CHAPTER 5 ◀◻▶ Kuta Silver City

The terror of the True Demon King, originating from the ruins of the True Northern Kingdom, swept across the world and was an omen that every city would meet its end in madness. That had been just as true for Kuta Silver City.

Three years earlier. Following the True Northern Kingdom, the suzerain of the United Western Kingdom fell to ruin, bringing extreme turmoil to the political landscape of Kuta Silver City, the largest metropolis on Western Kingdom soil. The middle-class citizens craved long-awaited peace, while in contrast, the armed conflict between Kuta Silver City and other powers, including the Central Kingdom, ceaselessly repeated itself... Thus, it wasn't rare for some person's mangled corpse to pop up somewhere.

This corpse had been stuffed into multiple hemp bags and dumped into the river, so in order to identify the bodies, Obsidian Eyes needed to retrieve the remains from the bags and attempt to piece them together. The damage to the whole body was horrible, and it was clear that most of the injuries has been inflicted while the victim was still alive.

A residential basement on the outskirts of the city. By this point, Obsidian Eyes needed to hide themselves from the city's army.

"...Is this Rehem? Where'd everything from the nose to the chin go? This iron... It's been melted down and coiled around the bones—what kind of torture did they put her through?"

The one charged with autopsying the body was a lycan and the ninth-formation vanguard in Obsidian Eyes, Harutoru the Light Grip. He was an assassin who utilized his superb muscular strength as a weapon, but he also had a physician's understanding of Life Arts.

"I-I'm sorry, sh-she was the only one I found... Hyne got his face burned, and it's unsure if he'll regain consciousness..." Fourth-formation vanguard, Hyakrai the Tower replied, struggling to force the words out. After retrieving the hemp bags filled with the corpse and carrying them to this basement, he seemed to lack the mental willpower to even stand up from his chair.

"I think Teeks is dead, too. His corpse has yet to turn up, though..."

There was one another among them.

"Rehem! J-just look...at what a handy partner you've become now! After all, see, look! Now I'll be able to easily carry you around with me from here on out! What do you say, Rehem?! Will you lend me your face? *Ah-hya-hya-hya-hya!*"

"......"

"......"

She returned Rehem's head back to its original position, perfectly straight-faced.

"...Ah, well...you see...I was just trying to find a bright side to all this."

A zmeu woman. Her name was Zeljirga the Abyss Web, fifth-formation vanguard. Rehem the Fog Hand and Zeljirga had been partners for many years of life-and-death danger.

"Don't clown around in a situation like this," said Harutoru. "We already know the one who got the three of them. Shinji the Piece Column, the right army staff officer for the city army."

"...Piece Column. B-but our contract with Kuta Silver City shouldn't be over yet. How could they betray us without any prior counsel like this?"

"They must've planned on using a surprise attack to get rid of us from the very start! Those three were the ones in charge of dealing with Shinji the Piece Column! From the very start, they planned on using us...on using Obsidian Eyes and throwing us away once they were done!"

"...A scorched-earth slaughter. Even during the previous campaign against Miluzi the Coffin Edict, i-it was nothing but dirty work for us... To ensure that the Central Kingdom and Kuta had an excuse to give to their governments...th-they were scheming to make us take the blame for carrying it all out. *Heh-heh-heh...* V-very rational. With the characteristic depravity of a visitor."

Shinji the Piece Column was a visitor staff officer employed by the Kuta government. Feeling cornered by the rampant terror of the True Demon King, Kuta Silver City needed to suppress any sort of resistance, even if it meant using a visitor of uncertain origins to do so—and regardless of whatever sort of methods that visitor, bereft of this world's common sense and morals, may have tried to use.

"Oh, look, you two! If I do this to this part of Rehem right here, I can just pull this out here, and...she's making a super-funny face, don't you think?!"

"......"

"......"

Zeljirga timidly took both of her hands off Rehem's corpse.

The other two continued their conversation, still harshly seething with murderous rage.

"We will get our revenge, no matter what. I'm going to teach them a lesson, Hyakrai. No matter what command may say...these hands are going to take Shinji's head!"

"Th-this is clearly a challenge. That's why they let us find the bodies! They're trying to use our retaliation a-as an excuse to hunt us down!"

"Um, guys...?" queried Zeljirga.

"Hyakrai! We may be sinners, strayed from the correct path. But even then, we became Obsidian Eyes precisely because we didn't want to be thrown out like genuine trash! I'll talk with our leader!"

"W-wait a second, Harutoru!"

"......"

Left behind by herself, Zeljirga fiddled with her partner's hand. It was on the only arm still connected to her torso.

She held its hand, shook it, and let go. The wrist limply drooped down.

Rehem the Fog Hand wouldn't ever cook again, nor would she say another straight-faced joke. Zeljirga would no longer need to pull out all the stops to try and get her to burst into laughter, either.

To the public, Rehem was nothing more than a convenient sacrificial pawn, easily disposed of and whose identity would never come to light. Those who operated in secrecy and lived in darkness were never going to be trusted.

"...Everyone is so frightening, aren't they, Rehem? It'd be much better if they'd just laughed instead."

Zeljirga let slip a whisper that fell on the deaf underground walls.

For the rest of that day, she did exactly as her own words dictated.

She tried to mellow out her comrades as they grew restless with bloodlust and plunged toward their ruin.

She cheerfully sparked up a conversation with her compatriots as they had their meal.

When she made her report to Rehart the Obsidian, as always, she mixed in an all-too-obvious tall tale as well.

The young lady Linaris considerately reached out to Zeljirga, but the zmeu used sleight of hand to surprise her with a flower, just as usual.

...The sun rose. Zeljirga shut herself away in her room and didn't come out until late the following evening.

"...Ah-hya-hya."

Facing the dark window, she forced out a hollow laugh.

"Ah-hya-hya-hya... Everyone is just so angry. It really is exhausting, isn't it, Rehem?"

Harutoru and the others' claims were rejected. In order to avoid full-scale conflict with Shinji the Piece Column, their alliance was unilaterally discontinued. Obsidian Eyes would most likely be departing from Kuta Silver City soon.

Staying locked up in her room while everyone else was working could have earned Zeljirga some sort of punishment. However, at the moment, she couldn't show any concern toward it.

Zeljirga the Abyss Web was from the True Northern Kingdom, which was annihilated shortly after the True Demon King appeared.

While the zmeu, with their reptilian outward appearances, were defined as one of the minian races, they had markedly different origins from the others. Therefore, when the orphan Zeljirga was bought as a slave, her intended use was not for labor, but as foodstuff to satisfy a noble's sick curiosity.

The reason Zeljirga had survived until division among the slavers led to them killing one another was because she had a bit more needlecraft knowledge than the other zmeu. Her work meant her turn to be eaten had been postponed later than the other slaves.

She didn't gain her freedom. Next, she was bought by a bandit group and given the dirty task of disposing of people's bodies.

Zeljirga was highly praised for her unmatched dissection skills, but the right to refuse the bloodstained work was never there for her. There was some instances where she disposed of the children whom she had been bought with. That bandit group was also wiped out in a few years' time.

It happened again and again.

Throughout Zeljirga's life, death would rapidly close in on her, then be replaced by fresh terror right before it could seal her fate. The exceptional dexterity in her fingertips was always *postponing* Zeljirga's demise—like a tightly tangled string, it kept her tethered to the abyss and would never let her go.

Zeljirga's smile never once faded.

It wasn't that she was emotionally broken. Or though that may have been the case, Zeljirga didn't see it that way herself. Ever since she had lost her homeland, she had been placed in environments that would steal these emotions and her smile...which made her believe all the more that she *needed to keep practicing them both*, or else she'd lose her way to return to a decent world, like the days long ago spent with family and friends.

She believed that for those who had nothing, a smile was the most valuable thing of all.

"Ah-hya... Hya-hya-hya..."

Rehem the Fog Hand had been her only partner.

These were the times she had to be sure to laugh, faced with such an enormous loss.

"Hya-hya, honestly, what am I going to do? The laughs won't stop..."

"...Miss Zeljirga."

She heard a faint voice through the door.

"Miss Zeljirga. Are you crying?"

"My lady."

It was Linaris's voice. She was the beautiful young daughter of Obsidian Eyes, turning fourteen that year.

Currently, this manor was filled with anger and hatred. Zeljirga needed to be there to make her laugh at a time like this, and yet she was making the young lady worry about her instead.

"Please, my lady, don't let yourself worry about me! These past two days, I haven't given any water to the house plants, you see… *Ah-hya-hya-hya!* I need to have a full two days of water—for the plants, of course! I think we'll get a great harvest from our green potted friends—just you wait!"

"……"

"…Umm, what's wrong? I'll admit that joke may have lacked some of my usual luster, but…"

"Um, Miss Zeljirga, please allow me to apologize for that. I hope you're able to cheer up."

"Oh, please! I am the absolute definition of cheer! What do you say, my lady? If you'd like to see some rope tricks, I can show you quite a cheerful sight indeed!"

In complete contrast to her words, Zeljirga was leaning up against the door, holding her knees to her chest.

It seemed as though there wasn't a single way to soothe this sadness and indignation.

"Miss Zeljirga? We might have to leave Kuta."

"…Yes, I understand. I assumed that would be the case."

"Is there anything you still wanted to do? Anywhere you wanted to go?"

"*Ah-hya-hya*...and what exactly would you be implying by that?"

"...I myself never even imagined...that we would be leaving here so soon."

Zeljirga could tell that Linaris was sitting in the hallway, leaning her back up against the door.

Linaris was a frail young girl, much more so than the average vampire. The pheromones that allowed her to command thralls should have manifested when she entered puberty, but she couldn't wield that power, either.

Always being protected inside the manor's walls, Linaris would have only walked the dazzling nighttime streets of Kuta Silver City a handful of times.

"...The steam train."

Zeljirga unexpectedly vocalized her wish.

She was sure that destruction was on its way for this city as well. Fear and despair were sneaking near, and eventually, it would all end. Even the bright and beautifully developed city landscape was already just a surface-level facade.

Nevertheless, the nighttime scenery had been truly beautiful.

"My lady, did you know? A steam train like those that run in the Central Kingdom passed through this city just four days ago. It went through the noble quarter, traveling over the connector bridge from the commercial district...crossing the canal into the industrial district."

"…Is that so?"

"I heard that it moved with such force and made a huuuuuge noise along the way! It's a truly wonderful invention, and a very rare sight indeed! I would have loved the opportunity to ride in one even once…is what Rehem told me! Did I trick you into thinking I was talking about myself? *Ah-hya-hya!*"

"Miss Zeljirga."

Linaris spoke with a gentle tone from the other side of the door.

"Let us go board it together. Right now."

"*Ah-hya-hya*, oh, please, my lady! Surely you jest."

"I suddenly have the desire to see this steam train for myself. Don't you think it would be much more reassuring to have someone accompany me?"

"…Even if that someone is a clown with only rope tricks to her name?"

"I was told that you would perform them for me if I so desired."

"Even if I'm a good-for-nothing who wasn't able to protect her partner?"

"You'll be good for something, I'm sure of it. After all, there isn't anyone else who will play with me."

Zeljirga scrubbed her face roughly.

A clown couldn't show their grief-stricken face to anyone else.

She believed that for those who had nothing, a smile was the most valuable thing of all.

◆

The lamplights lit up the night like a starry sky.

Even when Linaris was wrapped up in a modest overcoat the color of dead leaves, her countenance, like a moon lowered from the heavens, did not fail to capture the attention of everyone they passed on the street.

Conversely, Zeljirga had carefully hidden her face with her scarf. She also carried a large duffel bag in one hand. While Linaris rarely traveled outside the manor, there was a chance that Zeljirga's appearance was already known to the man in control of the city army, Shinji the Piece Column.

She was fully aware that what she was doing right now was an act of foolishness unbecoming of Obsidian Eyes.

...I won't do anything uncalled for. I'll board the steam train with my lady and then return to the manor. As long as nothing happens until we're back, that'll be it.

Night stalls lined each side of the street on the way to the station, and the row of lamps suspended outside the shops lit up the streets in a myriad of colors. Like a cluster of hazy balls of light, the focal points of the scenery were blurred.

"Oh, Miss Zeljirga, look here!"

The young porcelain noblewoman shone vividly in the Kuta night, all the many things she was seeing for the first time sparkling in her eyes.

"Look at all these candies and their strange colors...! How do you think they turn them that color? It's unbelievable... I never imagined candy could look so pretty on display like this!"

"Hmmm! My lady, it pains me to say this, but I do not have any acquaintances who specialize in candy, so nothing comes to mind at all! *Ah-hya-hya!*"

After she replied, Zeljirga paid the owner of the street stall in silver coins.

"In that case, how about we purchase these candies for ourselves?! Please, my lady, pick out any number of colors you'd like."

"What? No... *Tee-hee!* I shouldn't!"

"As long as you keep it a secret, no one will be the wiser! If you fear the candies will spill your secrets, then pop them in your mouth—that will work to keep them quiet!"

Linaris picked out a white-and-green colored candy. Zeljirga's was pink.

There was likely no difference in flavor between any of the colors. They were just pleasing to the eyes.

Candy was a wondrous thing because it could effortlessly bring smiles to people's faces.

"...Oh, this is simply too much. I can't even take two steps without stopping... Miss Zeljirga, what's that over there?"

"Please, my lady, feel free to pause as much as you like. That's a street performance using light-up balls. As you can see, they've lit a fire inside a spherical cage. They use celestine powder to kindle the fire, and that's what gives the flame its magenta hue."

"Thank you! Everywhere I turn, there's something I've never seen before...and I let my good spirits get the best of me. Still... *Hee-hee.* Their tricks may be quite pretty, but your sleight of hand is far more brilliant, Miss Zeljirga."

"Oh, please, my lady, you flatter me... *Ah-hya-hya!* Though perhaps you're right!"

The two enjoyed the nighttime sights on their way to the station.

They ate sweets baked with flour and sugar.

The two laughed together at the illustrated fortunes they received, because they were so terribly far off the mark.

They looked out at the ships traveling up and down the canal, which were coming to dock in the harbor one by one.

The pair ended up at the lamplit station, where the final train of the night was getting ready to depart; it would bring the laborers of the industrial district who worked the latest hours of all back home. There were very few passengers purposely boarding here from the commercial district for the outbound train.

Linaris stood on the sparsely populated platform, waiting for the train.

Zeljirga narrowed her eyes and looked at her beautiful figure.

"Hey, Miss Zeljirga?"

Velvety black hair, and reflectively ivory skin. Her long skirt swayed in the wind and loosely billowed.

"*Ah-hya-hya!* What is it, my lady?"

"Were you able to smile for me?"

That's right. Zeljirga had realized for herself.

Just as Zeljirga herself wished to always be her usual self... Linaris, too, wished the same of Zeljirga. Linaris simply wanted her to smile, not for someone else's sake nor by forcing herself.

Clutching her bag tight to her chest, Zeljirga answered:

"Of course. I'm smiling right now."

"I'd like to see you smile more. Even more."

"……"

From before she awakened to her terrifying superpower as a mutant vampire, Linaris already possessed a similar power. The gift to penetrate a person's heart and perceive their deepest emotions.

The steam whistle shook the air, signaling the train's imminent departure.

"Time to board, my lady."

"...So it is."

Going inside the night train, the pair sat down side by side.

From the railroad track, which had been built in an elevated position, they could look down over Kuta Silver City as the lights began to go out. The vast cityscape spread out before them like a starry night sky. They drank in the sight of the thriving city they would be departing soon.

The sheer tranquility made the scenes of brutality seem a world away.

"...Thank you, my lady."

"I just insisted you join me on my self-indulgent little outing, nothing more."

"Even then... Ahhh, it was fun."

The nights inhabited by those who dwelled in darkness were scenes of carnage, filled with blood and conspiracy.

Even if it was for only one night. Zeljirga had never even imagined that she would be able to spend such a peaceful, beautiful night free from fear.

"Perhaps... In my lady's case, she could—"

There was no need to finish the thought. Linaris adored Rehart the Obsidian more than anyone else. Zeljirga knew that she would never leave the Obsidian Eyes of her own accord.

But because she lacked the conventional strength of a vampire and had yet to develop the ability of vampiric subjugation, there was a chance that unlike Zeljirga, she could live outside this world of darkness.

Zeljirga wanted her to enjoy a life of happiness and genuine smiles, not the ephemeral ones bestowed by a clown's camaraderie.

"Miss Zeljirga, the train's leaving."

"So it is."

"...Ohhh. So we're going over to the town, then."

"Indeed. We're crossing over a very long bridge, high above the city. It's almost like we're flying, isn't it?"

The steam train swayed, and the sounds of the wheels rang out. Light streamed below them.

Zeljirga closed her eyes... She always wanted to have a smile on her face. She wanted to make Linaris laugh.

"Why, that reminds me, my lady! This is a rare opportunity, after all! Why don't we go have ourselves a peek into the head car? You won't be able to see a steam engine like this very often—I guarantee it! After all, perhaps there isn't any steam engine, and they just have a whole bunch of leprechauns pedaling for dear life!"

"Yes, absolutely! Come, Miss Zeljirga, let's us—"

"Ah, yes, well... I beg your pardon! I am experiencing a slight physiological phenomenon. You might say I have a disposition toward carriage sickness, and this is, well... I hesitate to describe it aloud, truth be told..."

"...Right here, on the train?"

"Yes! I'm afraid it will be *quite* an unsightly thing to witness, indeed! If you could, perhaps, take your leave for a short while! *Ah-hya-hya-hya!*"

"……"

Linaris anxiously took Zeljirga's hand and looked quietly into her eyes.

Zeljirga didn't say anything more and gave a troubled smile.

A sharp young girl. Any and all clumsy lies were seen through completely when placed before these golden pupils.

"In that case, I'll be off."

"Yes, yes. Please take your time and enjoy!"

Linaris quietly disappeared, heading toward the head car.

There were no other passengers left in the car besides Zeljirga. She spoke up without turning around.

"Well, now."

Just then, there was a new group, stepping in from the train car behind her own.

The several dozen men in ordinary clothes were Shinji the Piece Column's personal soldiers.

"...You didn't think I hadn't noticed, did you? The eyes of the land's greatest spies? The fifth-formation vanguard of Obsidian Eyes... Me, Zeljirga the Abyss Web?"

All of them unsheathed their weapons—a mix of short swords

and small crossbows, all small items in order to disguise themselves as passengers when boarding the train.

"Announcing yourself, eh, Zeljirga? Quite the resolve you have. Those other Obsidian Eyes bastards could learn a thing or two from you," the head of the group replied.

He wore an insidious smile, the edges of his lips twisted upward.

"We're gonna give you a great opportunity to prove to us if that resolve of yours is the real deal or not. You should be happy. You'll get to live a bit longer."

"Were you the ones who tortured Rehem?"

"We're asking the questions. Who's that other girl with you? Whoever she is, with a body that tiny, I'm worried she'll kick off after just two or three bouts of fun."

A few of the soldiers let out a stifled chuckle.

"So it is you all, then."

She was aware her ice-cold tone sounded as if it were coming from someone else.

Zeljirga had understood the answer for a long time—the reason why she hadn't ever once been able to experience such a peaceful night like this before. She had long become a creature of darkness.

Between the commercial district and now, she hadn't dropped her guard for a single second.

She faced her lady with a smile.

"I know everything. Rehem didn't cough up any information, did she? In order for that prick Piece Column to get to the base of operations, the only option he had was to wait until one of us appeared out in the open. Irredeemable fool. Not a single one of us will say a peep, you know. We're Obsidian Eyes, after all."

"That's your answer, then. In that case, we'll start by cutting off your left—"

"I'll say it one more time."

A sound of vibrations through the air.

Two of the soldier's heads were severed at once, something reflective wrapping around them and suspending the heads in midair.

Zeljirga wasn't even looking toward the soldiers. She didn't wield any obvious weapon in her hands.

The reflection of the nighttime lights dimly made the wire, like a spider's web, stand out.

"Hopeless fool. Let me tell you the name of the one who bestowed Hyne the Swaying Indigolite with his chain techniques. Let me teach your folly in challenging a master of thread to battle in an enclosed space like this. And finally—"

The soldiers fired their arrows.

The horizontal sweep of Zeljirga's arm was faster.

The crossbows, seconds before firing, had their aim manipulated, as if they were living creatures, and shot the soldiers next to them.

There was one who moved to attack her with his short sword. Zeljirga bent her thumb slightly.

The thread suspended in various places snapped, and in a flash, it instantly strangled all the soldiers in its path.

"*Ugh, hrnk!*"

"Gaugh!"

"Gwahak!"

"—more than anything, I'll teach you the price of trampling over my lady's moment of respite with those filthy boots of yours."

Before any of them could blink three times, all the soldiers had been neutralized. As soon as the enemies had stepped into the train car, now transformed into a spider's web, they had already lost the fight.

"Ngh...hrk... I-impossible...!"

Zeljirga turned her eyes to her enemy. It was an icy glare she would never direct toward Linaris.

"Be sure to learn from this pain. All of you. Each and every one of you deserve to die a thousand deaths."

The warp threads, extracted from tarantula webs, boasted a tenacity that even an ogre's abominable strength couldn't cut, while the weft possessed a crossedge sharp enough to slice through a wyvern, bones and all.

Zeljirga's monstrous ability to dynamically control their trajectory and speed exhibited a high level of technique that even a tarantula couldn't replicate.

"First, I'll weave threads around the cavity in your thyroid cartilage."

She wrapped the end of the thread digging into the soldiers on a metal umbrella hanger. She was pulling out a new thread.

From the very start, this wasn't a fight. To Zeljirga, this was an execution.

"If I constrict you at an angle, the thread will wrap around the cartilage covering your windpipe, ensuring your suffocation is as agonizing as possible."

She described in gruesome detail what was happening to the soldiers as she paced alongside them.

This sadistic practice served no other purpose than to sow fear in the soldiers as they breathed their last.

"Even when the tongue is pulled backward from within and moves down your throat, blocking the windpipe completely, blood will still pass through the carotid artery. That will ensure your brains will maintain consciousness while you savor the anguish of your final moments."

The soldiers were still alive; however, with their entire bodies bound and unable to move, they weren't even allowed to scream. One, then another—she strangled them all. And all the while, the look on her face was complete indifference.

"U-unh."

"Help—"

As they flailed their arms like dying insects, their eyes bulged in their sockets, almost ready to burst from their skulls. The soldiers convulsed in haunting unison as they died one after the other.

The sounds and movements were not minian at all, but rather resembled some sort of creepy, unsettling creature.

"..."

Zeljirga didn't smile. She simply watched.

She had decided whom she would leave for last. She had already identified the commander of this unit.

His equipment and position within their formation. The slight look he sent to the soldiers who'd been attacked. To Zeljirga—or to anyone else within Obsidian Eyes—that information alone was more than enough.

She loosened the bindings on the commanding officer, the sole assailant left alive, just enough for him to barely get his words out.

"You're the one in charge, aren't you?"

"…Wh-what're…you going to do with me? Will you have your revenge by…t-torturing me?"

"No. You're going to deliver a message for me."

Zeljirga had carried a large bag with her when she went into town with Linaris.

She opened it up and passed her eyes over its contents.

The commander was terrified.

"*E-eek*… Huh?!"

"'We'll have our revenge, no matter what.'"

It was Rehem's head.

"Now I'll be able to easily carry you around with me from here on out."

"…Remember? We're Obsidian Eyes. 'We'll have our revenge, no matter what.' Shinji the Piece Column likely believes that his wretched methods are the best tactics of all. So we'll take a page out of his book. We'll drag you into a hellish nightmare that will make what you just witnessed like paradise in comparison. Pass that message along."

"*U-ungh… Aaaugh!*"

The steam train was approaching the canal. Inside the car,

filled with what were now silent marionettes dangling from deadly strings, Zeljirga opened up the door of the moving train car.

"You all *didn't board* this train. Your presence is totally unnecessary in my lady's memories of tonight."

She pulled a thread. The carcasses spilled out into the night. There was no one to witness the horrible scene over the starlit canal.

The commanding officer trembled at the ruthless barbarity, far surpassing anything he could imagine, and with any dignity he had now gone and surrendered.

"O-okay, I—I get it…Zeljirga. I'll tell him. I'll tell right army staff officer Shinji…to wash our hands of anything to do with Obsidian Eye—"

"You misunderstand me."

In the next moment, the commanding officer was thrown out into the darkness.

With his screams of terror drowned out by the din of the steam train, his four limbs were all severed in midair. Left with only his head and torso, he sank into the waters of the canal, still conscious.

"You're passing that message on to *Rehem*."

Witnessing his final moments, she closed the door. The only thing left behind inside the train car was a small splatter of blood.

Completely ignorant of the massacre that had occurred in the rear passenger car, the steam train chugged along.

◆

"Miss Zeljirga! They let me see inside the head train car! The train conductor was so friendly!"

"Oh! Is that right? How wonderful! Machines are exciting, aren't they? *Ah-hya-hya-hya!* Pagireshe and Rook love those sorts of things as well!"

Listening to Linaris regale her upon returning, Zeljirga just smiled as always.

It wasn't a lie. She wasn't pretending to smile.

Now, with Rehem dead, Zeljirga was sure this would be her final night. Zeljirga felt true heartfelt gratitude to the young girl for giving her this pleasant memory.

"Ahhh... I'm relieved. I'm very glad I was able to make you smile, my lady."

"...Miss Zeljirga."

She had been able to protect Linaris. However, Rehart the Obsidian was a cruel man. Simply exposing his one and only daughter to meaningless danger was enough of a reason for him to dispose of Zeljirga.

"Well...I know it's a bit too late to say so, but this wasn't exactly a good idea, now was it?! Given how dangerous things are right now... Bringing the commander's young daughter outside, and for what? Just to have a bit of nighttime fun in town?! Laughter that could invite danger... Why, as a clown, I should avoid that most of all! *Ah-hya-hya—*"

"Hey, Miss Zeljirga."

Interrupting her laughter, the girl's small, delicate hand took Zeljirga's.

Her golden, jewellike eyes were right in front of the zmeu's.

"Let me tell you something nice."

"Something nice, you say? Well, if there is anything in this world better than your beauty, my lady, that would be quite the discovery! And what might that nice thing be?"

Putting a finger up to her lips, Linaris smiled.

"If we keep this a secret, no one will ever know."

Linaris had always known the danger behind what she was doing.

Even if she had, though, just how much had this night done to save Zeljirga's heart?

No matter how much time passed...the beautiful smile she saw in that steam train would never lose its luster.

"What happened tonight...will be our secret. I was in the manor the entire time, and you were as well, Miss Zeljirga. Nothing happened at all. Right?"

"*Ah-hya...hya-hya-hya*, my apologies, my lady, I've laughed so hard, some tears seemed to have slipped out..."

"...It's okay. I can't see your face if I do this."

Linaris hugged Zeljirga close. Zeljirga could hear a frail, ephemeral heartbeat.

The nights inhabited by those who dwelled in darkness were scenes of carnage, filled with blood and conspiracy. Even then—

"My lady... Ahhh, it's no use. I'm truly ashamed. No matter how much I try to laugh it off, this is how I am. Long ago...I knew nothing of war and fighting. But I just— I just don't have any other path to walk..."

"I know. I, myself...wish to protect that path for you. Forever and ever..."

"...My lady, no, please..."

"Listen, Miss Zeljirga. Please keep smiling for me."

The light of the steam train cut through the night.

Four small months after that night, Shinji the Piece Column suddenly disappeared, his whereabouts unknown.

From that point on, whatever happened to the military strategist was an utter mystery.

After the True Demon King's death, in the middle of Sakaoe Great Bridge Town, where the then-Demon-King lurked, people discovered a brutally murdered body, weather-beaten and bound by thread, but the identity of the body was unknown.

◆

Aureatia, with the Sixways Exhibition on the horizon. In a plaza facing the main avenue, there was a zmeu clown who put on street performances every day.

She was said to have betrayed Obsidian Eyes, once a threat to miniankind, and a key player who'd helped destroy it.

A spy guild draped in mystery—ruthless, wicked, mighty— an organization that people living a normal life would never be involved with. Much as Shinji the Piece Column had done, the butchery of allies that each country engaged in during the madness of the True Demon King's era was attributed to the Obsidian Eyes.

For slaying this terrifying group, Zeljirga was said to have the qualifications of a champion.

"Now, now, gather round and take a look! These water bubbles are parading along in a perfectly straight line!"

Zeljirga presented her tricks in the plaza as if she was a true street performer.

She used threads to move a puppet. Surrounding them with water droplets, she then knit beautiful geometric patterns. Cheers rose from the children watching.

Even now, she still remembered the circus performance she saw so very long ago together with her family and how she had worn a truly heartfelt smile.

"Wonderful! It's like it's alive!"

"Zeljirga, what're you gonna do next?"

"My, my, my, there is plenty of time—no need to get anxious! Next, how about I show you a car that flies through air? Or how does a duel between two puppets sound?! *Ah-hya-hya-hya!* Zeljirga the Abyss Web won't hold back when delivering one of her spectacular performances!"

Surely none of the children, eyes sparkling in awe of her performance, would have imagined the possibility that an enigmatic creature like those in Obsidian Eyes was next to them at this very moment.

Or the fact that those who were constantly exposed to the terror of death, no matter how much they tried to put on a smile, had lost the ability to live out their life in public society.

There wasn't a single person who thought about trying to save an outcast who'd fallen into that position.

Just as it was with Zeljirga, beasts that had tasted the blood of their own were entirely different species altogether.

After all, one day, she was bound to devour her own kind once more.

...The havoc of war will once again be brought to this world.

Right now, Zeljirga was able to make people laugh. Even if her technical mastery had come from staining her hands with blood and repeatedly butchering others.

Perhaps there may have been a chance for her to go on living without killing a single person.

However, the zmeu woman had now become an entirely different creature from the girl living in her homeland long ago. Although she would always remember the smiling face she wore that day, it was too late for her to ever go back to that again.

The only world we can find our way in...is a chaotic war where none of us will ever be cast aside.

The only thing awaiting Obsidian Eyes was annihilation.

In which case, hope for Zeljirga consisted of one thing only.

My lady.

The clown smiled, manipulating vividly colored fireworks with her strings.

The children let out cheers, and copper coins were thrown her way, dancing through the air.

No matter how much time passed, it would never lose its luster.

Please smile. I promise... For you, I will be victorious!

The Aureatia Industrial Ministry courtyard was a wide-open space surrounded by high walls, which made it a pleasant place to relax as well. This allowed one to enjoy the sunlight and greenery while still inside.

However, the head of the industrial ministry—Aureatia's Fourth Minister, Kaete the Round Table—had never felt any need for such a relaxation area. He didn't make any attempt to have a moment of unguarded rest in public and loathed such a waste of time.

Despite his handsome features, he was a man with a cruel gleam in his eyes, as if he was always irritated. Known as being part of a fierce military faction while serving as the civilian officer in charge of Aureatia's industry, he was the bureaucrat who was the closest to being an all-around genius among the Twenty-Nine Officials, save for Rosclay.

His knowledge relating to his main duty of industry was without question, but he had also cultivated his swordsmanship, archery, gun skills, Word Arts, and more to a high level. Due to the military successes he had as a commanding officer during the age of the True Demon King, he also possessed the exceptional authority to command a part of the military, even as a civil official.

It left no room for doubt from anyone who knew the man that he was born with the natural gifts of a champion; however, there was almost no one who adored Kaete the Round Table as a person. This was due to a disposition that went beyond just fierce and into the realm of ferocious.

"Fourth Minister! P-please listen! I have something to tell you!"

"......"

Walking through the courtyard corridor, Kaete continued to ignore the voice that had been calling to him from behind. If he ignored the call three times, Kaete thought that they would grasp that he was reacting with tolerance to their irredeemably rude accosting, but it seemed these men lacked such powers of comprehension.

Stopping in his tracks, he turned around. One was elderly, while two were young. They looked to be secretaries for a government official.

The first word out of Kaete's mouth was—

"Decapitation."

"What...?"

"You wanted to petition me for something, didn't you? Are you aware, then, of the damages you've incurred by making me pointlessly waste my time when you haven't even finished the proper paperwork yet? If you insist you're prepared for the suitable punishment, then I'm saying you can pay the prize up front. Decapitation."

He watched the three secretaries' reaction.

Faced with his extremely irrational declaration, their bodies were trembling, but their fists were balled.

Looking at their comical courageousness, Kaete simply snorted.

"I'll notify you of the date for your punishment later. I'll be sure to listen to whatever inconsequential nonsense you have to say then, when you have a chance to defend yourself."

From the very start, he had no intentions whatsoever of giving his ear to anything a rude petitioner had to say. Such people were often fools who could only come up with illogical reasoning, even with the proper paperwork.

"…W-wait… Please wait, Fourth Minister!"

"Beat it."

Right now, he had something more important to take care of, and he needed to devote all his strength there—in short, the Six-ways Exhibition.

However, a woman casually appeared from the shadow of the pillar in front of him.

"C'mon, now. Knock it off, Kaete. Don't go bullying them too much, y'hear?"

A middle-aged woman with her graying hair tied up behind her head—Aureatia's Twenty-First General, Tuturi the Blue Violet Foam. In contrast to Kaete, she was an eccentric woman who served as a military officer almost without any personal military power of her own.

"I get it. So then these three are…"

Kaete immediately understood the meaning behind the situation.

"…under your orders, then. Quit bothering me with this drivel."

"Aww, but don't you feel sorry for them? These three said they're from Nagan. Y'know what happened to Nagan and how it ended up, right? They're unhappy that there hasn't been any apology or excuse from Kiyazuna the Axle, basically. At least hear them out."

"…Oh?"

A faint smile came to his lips, and Kaete turned around to face the three men again.

"I more or less guessed what this was about, but…it looks like my conclusion was hasty."

It was only his mouth that smiled. His eyes flickered with far worse cruelty and scorn.

"I never expected your petition would be several times more worthless and stupid than I could even imagine."

"W-worth… It's not worthless at all! N-Nagan was our home! There are some who lost friends and family! What're we… What're we supposed to do with our indignation?! Why was Kiyazuna the Axle not punished but *welcomed* into Aureatia?!"

One of the three, struggling not to cower in fear, retorted. It was fair to say he was a rare breed for summoning up the courage to speak to Kaete the Round Table face-to-face like this.

Though to Kaete, he truly and deeply didn't care whatsoever.

"Beyond irrelevant. Your whole family deserves to be exterminated for such idiocy— Ah, right, you must not have such a family anymore. Hmph."

"M-milord Kaete. I…I, too—"

"Silence. I'm only talking to this man who stepped forward first. Thus, I'm only answering his question. Shut your mouth and die."

Kaete put his hand on his sword hilt. It wasn't a threat—he thought he'd be fine to cut the man's head off right here and now. There were too many foolish citizens. Death was the only way to make amends for stupidity.

The young one who first stepped forward seemed to have used up all his courage, and even when given the chance to speak further, he was unable to continue his comments.

"…First of all, you've mistaken the person you should be seeking reparations from."

Irritated, Kaete informed them of the logic that anyone should have been able to understand.

"The Nagan citizens are the ones who should be making amends for the incident with the Dungeon Golem. You people."

"Wh-what…? How could you—?"

"What? Do you have some objection to that? Did you think Kiyazuna the Axle— Did you think she built Nagan for rabble like yourselves to live there? That was her enormous, personal property that she manufactured in a land far away from any other people. If all of you had received an official commission from the kingdom to investigate or destroy it, that would be one thing, but what argument can you give for arbitrarily labeling Nagan a labyrinth and scheming to illegally steal its technology, all before you brazenly began establishing schools and your own homes? Go ahead, tell me."

"B-but…Nagan Labyrinth City w-was from the time we were born—"

"*Ha*, see, you get it. You all were nothing more than a group of bandits from birth. Wait, no… Since you weren't even aware of that fact, I'd say it makes you even worse than bandits," Kaete said, bringing his face close to the young one. "But rejoice. Kiyazuna the Axle's demon king designation has already been lifted, and the things I just touched on have all been taken care of. And *without punishing any of* you Nagan citizens, mind you. If you've got a problem with the results, you can go ahead and hold a retrial. For your people's crimes, that is."

"*Nhg…nngh… Sniff, hnggh…*"

"Disgraceful. Not even worth decapitation. Get lost."

Leaving the Nagan citizens frozen in place, Kaete finally made for his office.

Picking up her steps and following after him, Tuturi poked her head out from behind.

"What do I always tell you? You gotta stop threatening people with 'decapitation this, crucifixion that.' I'm not saying it's bad or anything, but when you throw in all the extreme stuff, it'll start sounding less real, y'know?"

"I'm always serious… You're bad enough yourself, Tuturi. The only thing you're good at is idly prowling around to interfere with other officials' duties. Get to work."

"Well, I mean, I still technically got a job to do, all right? I can't do anything until then, is the thing. C'mon, Kaete, enter-taaaain me!"

"……"

Tuturi the Blue Violet Foam wasn't incompetent like Harghent the Still or Nophtok the Crepuscle Bell. Kaete didn't hesitate to label the people meant to be governed as the ignorant populace, but he also didn't ignore the movements of excellently capable talent, either.

"…You weren't part of Rosclay's group, were you? Who gave you that assignment? What are you preparing? What are you planning?"

"Heh-heh-heh-heh!"

The Sixways Exhibition—amid this political strife set to influence the world's future path, it seemed very unlikely that a woman of Tuturi's caliber wouldn't be supporting any of the powers at play. She could have incited the Nagan natives to obtain some careless comment or promise from him, then use that as a foothold to bring about Kaete's downfall.

Though, in Tuturi's case, he couldn't rule out the possibility that it was done simply to annoy him, either.

"If you don't plan on answering me, then get lost," Kaete said.

"...Well, if you insist like that, I guess I'll go pass the time somewhere else. Later."

Tuturi aimlessly wandered off. Watching her depart, Kaete clicked his tongue.

...There were some who claimed that with the menace of the Old Kingdoms' loyalists and the Free City of Okafu gone, Aureatia's long-maintained state of war was over. These were the thoughts of people who couldn't see the true nature of things.

If Rosclay or Jelky didn't send her, then the person in Aureatia capable of getting her to make a move naturally starts to narrow down. Haade, in control of the military. Or possibly...former Fifth Minister Iriolde is pulling the strings from retirement. In any case, it doesn't change what I have to do.

The world's only kingdom, Aureatia. Beneath the peaceful veneer, their war had already long begun.

◆

Kaete opened the door to his office and was taken aback.

"...What is all this?"

The books that had been neatly lined up on the bookshelf were scattered all over the floor. In this world, without the popular dissemination of written language, scholarly texts that used noble script were an extremely rare resource.

On top of this, wholly unfamiliar lab equipment had blanketed one of the walls, with clear marks left behind that indicated some sort of acidic and toxic chemicals had been used. His luxury rug had holes burned into it in a spray pattern.

The windows were left wide-open, and strange conducting wire had been pulled in from outside in large quantities.

A fire had been lit, too. The flame, meant either to heat medicine vials or process metals, was brazenly roaring in Kaete the Round Table's office.

"Well, ain't you late?"

Topping it all off, the one who'd created the horrible sight was openly sitting in the middle of the room.

"Looks like chemically processing deep celestial charsteel's still impossible after all. I already imagined as much, but... Hey, Kaete. This record's a sham. No way they did what they said they did with that era's technological level."

Kiyazuna the Axle. A self-proclaimed demon king of unmatched atrocity who showed no allegiance to the kingdom whatsoever, instead wholly devoted to researching construct creation, even creating Nagan Labyrinth City along the way.

She was also the creator of one of the hero candidates, Mestelexil.

"......You."

Kaete immediately closed the door behind him.

"Grams! All I said was I'd show you those records! I don't ever remember agreeing to these sorts of experiments!"

"Well, if I don't do it while I'm researchin', I'll plum forget all about it! Knock it off with the 'Grams' crap, too."

Kiyazuna's eyes had already turned off Kaete and was observing some sort of crystalline structure under a microscope.

"What am I supposed to do if someone mistakenly thinks we're related? You ain't my grandson, for one, and you ain't one of my children, neither."

"When you...act so conspicuously like this, I'm the one who has to deal with it. While you're at it, stop going out for walks with Mestelexil, too."

For the time being, he picked up the scattered books and returned them to their places on the bookshelf.

Inside the horribly messy room, his efforts seemed all too futile.

"Some Nagan natives came to lodge their complaints with me today. There are a whole slew of people just among the Twenty-Nine Officials who have motives to come after you. You've never once imagined the amount of hard work I've gone through because of you, have you?!"

"*Feh!* That's why I'm helping you out, ain't it? Financing the funds, controlling public opinion, all that sorta...all that small stuff that I owe you's gonna get paid off with this next big *boom*. Smash every other faction in the Sixways Exhibition and take over Aureatia! Murder everyone who goes against you, and you'll be able to live a nice peaceful life. Ain't a bad deal, huh? Right?"

"Grams, you seem to think I've got unlimited authority and power here, but...my faction doesn't hold a candle to the scale of Haade's or Rosclay's. Give several factions a justification to crush us, and we'll lose just in numbers. I don't know how many times

I have to explain this, but we absolutely need to increase weapon production fast, before a full-blown conflict breaks out. There isn't any time to let Mestelexil play around."

"Hmph... Mestelexil ain't your tool. This snotty-nosed dolt's older, and now he thinks he can start blabbering like a damn politician. All that because you grew up dawdling around here in Aureatia while you went ten years without ever coming to see me, that it?"

"Let me be clear here, but the whole reason I even went to the kingdom?! It was because no number of lives would've been enough for a flesh and blood minia to tag along with you, Grams!"

Fourth Minister Kaete, leading the third-biggest faction in Aureatia after Second General Rosclay and Twenty-Seventh General Haade.

However, there were very few people who knew the teacher Kaete had learned from was, in fact, the self-proclaimed demon king Kiyazuna.

Given a seat among the Twenty-Nine Officials because of his prominent abilities, he had been supporting Kiyazuna's activities from the shadows, long before he ever sponsored Mestelexil, and saw to it that the hands of the kingdom's suppression campaigns never reached her.

It wasn't merely once or twice that Kiyazuna's unbridled behavior had resulted in Kaete's guts going cold. It was practically a miracle that he'd been able to get Kiyazuna into Aureatia while keeping the relationship between the two a secret. If Kaete hadn't used the Particle Storm incident to his advantage, it would have been difficult to provide his former teacher with the distinguishing accomplishments he would have needed.

"Geez... So, in short, we just gotta win, right? Mestelexil's here to do just that!"

Kiyazuna lay down on the floor as she was sulking. She was a teacher unbecoming of her age.

This Mestelexil that Grams made is invincible. There's no doubt about that.

He didn't actually say it out loud to avoid souring his teacher's mood, but Kaete didn't look toward the future of the Sixways Exhibition with the slightest hint of optimism.

But...even if Mestelexil doesn't lose at all, it's very unlikely that we'll win through to the end of the tournament.

Sponsoring a hero candidate itself wasn't meaningless. Much like the Free City of Okafu...given that a faction possessing a hero candidate had a *provisional hero* with them, as long as the candidate wasn't eliminated, it also served to guarantee said faction's survival.

However, by forcing through the unreasonable annulment of Kiyazuna the Axle's demon king designation, the connection between Kaete and Kiyazuna had, in part, become public knowledge. If Mestelexil advanced through the tournament and rose up to become an obstruction toward Rosclay's faction, that would be when they'd use any and all political power at their disposal to make Mestelexil lose and take down his whole camp with it.

Thus, the true battle I'm supposed to look ahead to is that inevitable clash. Assuming...we don't secure the fighting strength needed to surpass Rosclay's overwhelming numbers, then we won't really be victorious *in the Sixways Exhibition.*

In some respects, Kaete the Round Table stood in a far more dangerous position than anyone else in this battle.

He had very few allies. Kaete. Kiyazuna. Finally...

"Ain't anywhere to step in here. Whew, boy, one helluva mess..."

Appearing in the room was an older man wearing a cynical smile.

Aureatia's Fifteenth General Haizesta the Gathering Spot. This man had been able to break into the room without the use of any lockpicking skills.

"...Don't pry open the lock. My camp has no need of knaves lacking etiquette."

"*Nyeh-heh-heh.* Getting sacked just for coming and going a bit? Gimma a break."

In his hands was a machine equipped with a display and joysticks. It was an item that was totally inconceivable with this world's level of technology.

"Hey now...I went and looked into our opponent Zeljirga, okay? No signs that she's in touch with anyone else... Maybe that earlier announcement about betraying Obsidian Eyes was the real deal after all."

The machine was a controller for a weapon called a reconnaissance drone.

It was small and quiet. Above all, it was technology *unknown to* the people of this world. Even if Zeljirga was a spy with Obsidian

Eyes, it would have likely been impossible for her to escape from the wholly unimaginable method of surveillance before she contacted Obsidian Eyes.

"And what the hell are we supposed to do with that trivial amount of info, you slimy brat?"

Before Kaete could open his mouth, Kiyazuna berated Haizesta.

"If you got time to spare on kiddie chores, hurry up and slip some laxatives in Zeljirga's or Enu's food instead. Hell, you were 'posed to be the one in charge of stealing those enchanted swords of Toroa's, ain't ya?"

"*Nyeh-heh-heh.* Ohhh, a plan without any thought to the consequences—I like that... You're turning more and more into my kind of woman every day."

"You're the absolute worst."

Kiyazuna's wrinkled face distorted even further with disgust.

"...Save your worthless bickering for somewhere I don't have to look at it. First of all, Toroa the Awful's already lost. No reason to focus so much attention on him," said Kaete.

"Hah? We leave him alone, and some other group'll snatch him for themselves. What, you gotta problem with my strategy, huh?"

"Grams, you just wanted toys for Mestelexil... At least, right now, there shouldn't be anyone on Aureatia's side trying to make a move on him. They know full well the danger of going toe to toe with Toroa the Awful. Don't sic my men on him just 'cause you feel like it."

—That said, Kaete couldn't say that robbing Toroa the Awful's enchanted swords had been a complete mistake. Given the aim of

Rosclay's faction was to eliminate all latent threats to Aureatia, there was the possibility that the swords could serve as advantageous bargaining chips if they secured them for themselves. Either way, before Kaete's camp and Rosclay's camp plunged into full-blown war, he had needed to give his soldiers a chance to use the weapons of the Beyond in a real combat situation.

"Getting back to the topic, we need to come up with a plan for the sixth match," said Kaete.

"Hmph, it's simple, ain't it? We'll win by killing that Zeljirga woman dead," responded Kiyazuna.

"Seriously, enough with the myopic thinking. Much more than Zeljirga, it's her sponsor, Enu, who's the problem. His unit's starting to survey the castle garden theater. Might be planning to set some sort of trap."

"That so, eh...? What the hell happened to the agreement about not going in there unless there's a match? Just how are they checking the damn place, then?"

"They're examining the surrounding area, just not inside. Enu is using his power as head of city planning. He appears to be doing it under the pretext of improving the traffic conditions that come with the Sixways Exhibition, but he's measuring the distance between the surrounding buildings and recording their bearings in detail. Pulling this stunt now, right before the start of the sixth match, is basically confessing that he has some sort of scheme up his sleeve."

"*Hmph.* Sniper fire on the arena, is that it?" Kiyazuna spat, seemingly disgusted.

"...Obviously, that possibility was brought up before the tournament had even begun. Whether from some tower or elevated ground, there aren't any sniper spots with sight lines that reach inside the garden theater."

The Sixways Exhibition matches, as long as there weren't any hindrances or any demands to the contrary between both combatants, had all been ruled to take place inside the castle garden theater. That was in part for audience seating capacity and to guarantee a fair competition. As such, preventing foul play was paramount, as outside interference was difficult given the arena inside was surrounded on every side by high walls.

The castle garden theater was protected by soldiers who belonged to the garden theater itself and weren't with any of the factional hero candidate powers, and generally, sponsors were only allowed to have their subordinates on the premises during a match.

"Inside or outside, as long as our enemy's making their move, we can't sit by and let it happen, now can we? For our match, too... *Nyeh-heh-heh.* The problematic castle garden theater, eh. You already agreed on the arena a while back, too, right?"

"Shut up, Haizesta," grumbled Kaete. "If Enu is planning on setting up some sort of trap, then really, it's about whether there's anything that'd be possible from outside the castle garden theater or not..."

Zeljirga may have been a former spy for Obsidian Eyes, but it was wholly unbelievable to think she had the abilities to face the unparalleled Mestelexil head-on and triumph. Putting it another way, then, this meant that Zeljirga was sure to carry out some sort of scheme ahead of time in order to win the sixth match.

"Just gotta smash it all up," Kiyazuna said unconcernedly. "Who cares if we know what they're up to or not? Those assholes set something up in the castle garden, so we just gotta smash the entire damn place and take their trap with it, right?"

"Grams! I told you those types of…" Kaete started to protest, but he stopped midsentence. "…No, actually, you're right. We can just make them change the location right now."

"Excuse me? *Now?*" Haizesta asked back with a dubious look. There were only three days left until the sixth match.

"Our end prerequisite for victory is weapon production through Mestelexil, and to use the Sixways Exhibition to buy time for it. There's no need to spare effort on a man like Enu. If it can be handled just on my end, then it can be done far more efficiently than with soldiers or drones," said Kaete.

Enu the Distant Mirror was the most eccentric one of the Twenty-Nine Officials. There were very few who understood what his objective was in the Sixways Exhibition or even if he was truly trying to win in the first place.

It was this reason that Rosclay's camp had avoided a match against Zeljirga. Rosclay saw the grouping of Obsidian Eyes and Enu the Distant Mirror as a threat—two uncertainties combined together.

In which case, in a battle between Kaete and Enu, two elements of concern for Rosclay's camp, some degree of aggression was likely to be overlooked. For the opportunists waiting for their chance, there was no better development than two forces they needed to deal with both crushing each other.

"*Heh-heh*, looks to me like you thought up something," said Haizesta.

"I can just redesignate the terms and the battlefield on my end. I'm not going to let Enu get his way," Kaete replied.

"Oh boy, now we got two violent bastards in here... *Nyeh-heh-heheh*... All righty, I should just look into the moves Enu's making, then, right?"

"Sure, knock yourself out. Do anything too debaucherous, and I'll have Grams turn you into a construct before you can get your head lobbed off. You wouldn't want that, now would you?"

"*Nyeh-heh-heheh*... Getting turned into a construct by a fiiine woman like her? Wouldn't bother me one bit."

"Ugh, everything outta that mouth of yours is disgusting. Like hell I'd even waste time making constructs outta flesh," Kiyazuna chimed in.

When Kiyazuna let out a yawn, a heavy metal *clang* echoed from out in the hallway.

The laboratory equipment lining the walls shook and knocked into one another.

"K-Kaete!"

Ducking through the broken door and appearing in the room was a colossal golem covered in navy-blue armor. Kaete the Round Table's biggest and most powerful trump card—Mestelexil the Box of Desperate Knowledge.

"I finished, today's amount! I can p-p-play now, right?!"

Mestelexil carried with both hands a large number of automatic rifles—they were a model of weapon from the Beyond known as the AK-47.

Witnessing how Mestelexil's massive frame ravaged his office interior even further, Kaete now wore a wearied look.

"…That's too little. Way too little. You're slacking off, aren't you?"

"N-no, I am not! *Ha-ha-ha-ha-ha!*"

"Wait just a damn minute, you complaining about how my boy does his job?! Well?! Are you?!"

"*Nyeh-heh-heh…* Nice and lively, ain't it?"

"Dammit, each and every one of you, I swear…"

Pressing his palm to his face, Kaete sighed.

Why did he have to deal with this when he already had a depressing task ahead of him as it was?

"I got to clean things up in here…"

They were, indeed, the third camp in Aureatia's political power struggle.

Wicked and powerful—as well as the most discordant.

Kaete the Round Table. Kiyazuna the Axle. Haizesta the Gathering Spot. Mestelexil the Box of Desperate Knowledge.

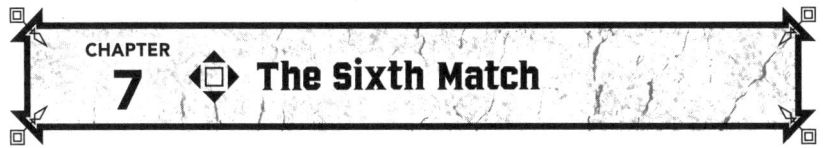

In the Sixways Exhibition, the desperate fights to the death didn't only unfold between the hero candidates standing on the battlefield. Negotiating the terms and conditions, and beginning with a battlefield and match date that would guide said candidates to victory, was a serious matter handled by the candidates' sponsors, holding sway over their political careers.

The Coordinating Room—meeting premises used to host such negotiations—had been newly constructed to coincide with the opening of the Sixways Exhibition. The Coordinating Room was protected by strict security, and sponsors were able to hold one-on-one negotiations with guaranteed safety. Inside the facility, there were several other rooms in addition to the main meeting room, including a nap room, all constructed with the estimation that a single period of negotiations could potentially take up more than a day's time.

The day before the Sixth Match. Brilliant balloons were coloring the sky, and the sound of fireworks had continued unabated since noon.

"Now then, Kaete. I don't really think there's any reason to alter the match conditions at this point in the game. The citizens are looking forward to tomorrow's fight. In which case, it's our duty to make sure their expectations are met without incident."

"...Expectations? Hmph. What should I care about the expectations of the ignorant rabble?"

The two people facing each other in the Coordinating Room were the sponsors involved in Sixth Match. Aureatia's Fourth Minister and Mestelexil the Box of Desperate Knowledge's sponsor, Kaete the Round Table. Aureatia's Thirteenth Minister and Zeljirga the Abyss Web's sponsor, Enu the Distant Mirror.

Kaete folded his legs with a pompous flair, while conversely, Enu looked just as expressionless as usual.

"They're no different from a pack of soulless wild beasts. They fear, flee, and, in the depths of their hearts, crave a new tragedy. That foolish nonsense is nothing but a way to vent a fear that's taken on a new shape."

To Kaete the Round Table, it appeared like not one person understood the true nature behind it all—or, perhaps, tried not to see it. Even after the True Demon King was dead, many fools longed for their own destruction.

The New Principality of Lithia was burned to ash. Both Aureatia and Lithia themselves should have been able to adopt some other means to solving the situation.

Gruesome massacres were occurring out on the frontier, like what had happened at Alimo Row. People who persisted in their oppression of the Order appeared from among the citizenry, and the Old Kingdoms' loyalists' lust for war led them to take advantage of the Particle Storm.

In the fourth match, in full view of the public, the man who was supposed to be a symbol of hope—Rosclay the Absolute—was reduced to a pitiful state. It was the Aureatia public itself that had hoped for such a sight.

This world continued to go mad.

"By exposing the states of these hero candidates killing each other to the public, we're substituting where they're focusing their urge for slaughter. Ultimately, the goal of this Sixways Exhibition is to add more fuel onto the flames of violence."

"As a method of public control, that may indeed be quite an intriguing discussion. You're striking right to the essence, in a certain sense."

Enu merely nodded slightly. Kaete couldn't read any emotion from his wide, owlish eyes.

"…And what's the topic of our negotiations, exactly?" asked Enu.

"The venue for the sixth match *has been* changed."

"…What?"

"I'll say it again, in case you didn't hear me. The sixth match is going to take place not in the castle garden theater, but in the old town plaza, like for the first match."

Kaete told him, as if it was a completely settled matter.

Even after receiving Kaete's entirely too one-sided notice, Enu showed no signs of agitation. He remained dispassionate and cold as he replied:

"We reached a consensus regarding the arena in talks two big months ago. Talks between you and myself. This has already been accepted by the council, and even should either one of us have a desire to change it, it should be impossible to overrule that. Or perhaps this is some new attempt at a joke, Kaete?"

"The real joke is that bold-faced performance of yours. Did you really think you could finish your little survey of the castle garden theater without me finding out?"

"Hmm? Find out or not, that is nothing but an urban survey-ing plan that I previously submitted to the assembly, progressing as scheduled. It's part of my official duties within the Twenty-Nine Officials, so if anything, it would be a bigger problem if you *didn't* know about it."

"A piss-poor front, I'd say."

Enu's urban surveying plan had been thrust through hastily, using a transport stoppage that occurred in Gimeena City as an excuse. His claim was that he needed to perform surveys and stud-ies as part of an effort to streamline the traffic in the vicinity of the castle garden theater, seeing as it was going to be the biggest nucleus of traffic as the Sixways Exhibition continued.

"Fair enough—it was approved, wasn't it? Then why don't I cut down some of the time and effort that 'work' of yours will take? The castle garden theater... Right this moment, your men are sur-veying it. Am I right?"

There was an intense tremor.

While the sound was small and far in the distance, even the walls of the Coordinating Room swayed with a deep and low quake.

"……"

"Now, I'll ask you again. What were your men doing?"

There were no windows in the Coordinating Room. However, at that moment, there was a thin black cloud trailing up to the sky in the direction of the castle garden theater.

Inferring from the scale of the explosion, the conclusion would probably be that at least a full storeroom of firepower must have been ignited. It was an amount of explosives that absolutely couldn't be smuggled in by one or two intruders, and Kaete's camp wouldn't be brought up as part of the criminal investigation—

Composition C-4.

—so long as they based their thought on this world's level of technology.

It was a highly effective plastic explosive from the Beyond, able to be detonated remotely.

"…Kaete. Do you know what you've done?"

"You're wrong there. What *you've* done. Assuming that right now, there was some sort of accident in the area around the castle garden theater…and the busy team performing the survey work was not only unable to find anything out of the ordinary, but moreover, unable to provide a single piece of evidence to who the culprit was, then I'm sure you realize who'll be the first one suspected."

One day was left before the beginning of the sixth match.

Enu's survey was suspicious, but there wasn't any time to grasp what sort of foul play he was devising.

However, if there was someone whose position appeared

dubious in the eyes of many, the solution was simply to then make the suspected foul play a reality.

"The investigation into the explosion will take three days, at least. Renovating the castle garden theater's security based on the investigation, two days. Let's test that duty you spoke about to the test. Go ahead—try holding the match without incident."

"......"

Changing the date the day before the match. Common sense dictated such a reckless act would be impossible.

However, Kaete the Round Table was a despot. He had been capable of going through with a rather reckless plan of his own, knowing full well that there was the chance that innocent civilians would get caught in the explosion. If anything, some number of victims made it all the better for him.

The masses were nothing more than beasts being led by fear in the form of the Sixways Exhibition. In which case, if a different fear was thrust straight out in front of them, they were sure to want a venue change for the match themselves.

"Now then. As of just a moment ago, we need to adjust the conditions of the match. We're going to delay the sixth match and change the venue to the old town plaza. If you have an alternative solution, go ahead and give it, Enu the Distant Mirror."

"...It appears I don't have any choice. Naturally, I will have them investigate this bombing. I'm sure it won't take them long to prove who ordered it."

"Hmph. Suppose I'll hope for the same."

Kaete the Round Table was a despot, but because the ignorant masses were as they were, he was thoroughly aware of what sort of actions they'd take.

Even if they tried to obey the previously agreed-upon rules and made the match take place in the garden theater, with the fear of another explosion, they wouldn't be able to overcome the citizens' protest. Holding a match in the castle garden theater now was an unrealizable and reckless move. No matter what Enu the Distant Mirror may have been scheming to do to the venue, this one move had changed everything.

Then as long as he fought through direct combat, where all intrigue held no meaning...Mestelexil the Box of Desperate Knowledge was an unrivaled hero candidate, in the truest meaning of the word.

If there was one point of concern left for Kaete, though...

"Enu. Let me ask you something," Kaete said, stopping right before he was to leave the room. "You went and put down Obsidian Eyes, right? Did you really get inoculated with the antiserum?"

"Of course. You and I should've both gotten the serum around the same time."

"..."

He was right. There wasn't any room for doubt there. Even if Zeljirga was secretly maintaining her connection to Obsidian Eyes, it would have been inconceivable for her sponsor, Enu, to be manipulated, too.

"...Enu. Why then...are you taking on the Sixways Exhibition?"

"There needs to be another method aside from fear to control the people," Enu replied matter-of-factly in a flat tone.

"If that's your thinking, well, I strongly feel that way, too. While we may become enemies, on that point alone, I sympathize with you."

Kaete didn't turn around to look back at Enu, but there was a terribly eerie sound to his words.

Just where did this man's goals lie...?

"I couldn't care less. You'll be knocked out of the tournament in this fight anyway," said Kaete.

◆

Finished with his meeting in the Coordinating Room, Kaete met up with Haizesta on his way out.

Though they were both among the Twenty-Nine Officials, the sight of Kaete wearing a picture-perfect bureaucrat outfit while walking alongside Haizesta and his dingy unshaven face must have made for a terribly abnormal combination.

"The explosion was a success."

Haizesta the Gathering Spot's role had been to remotely detonate the high explosive, which had been placed inside a food storehouse near the castle garden theater, while observing the flow of the crowds from a high vantage point.

"For injuries, there are only three or so people with light wounds. Just enough to leave behind some wounded, but not enough to kill... *Nyeh-heh-heheh.* One of 'em was a woman aged like a fine wine, too... Maybe I'll send her some flowers while she's in the hospital. *Nheheh...*"

"No nonsense. I'll cut your head off."

"It's a joke. I know plenty well that it'd be real bad to leave any evidence behind for this little op... Still, you sure we shouldn't have used those drones? And here I finally got used to controlling the buggers..."

"The superiority of those reconnaissance drones lies in the display that transmits images instantly. We need to generate power and charge them every time they're activated, and someone always has to be there controlling it. If we're looking for a machine we can utilize at will, then the golems Kiyazuna the Axle makes are far superior."

"Well now. That's really something."

Tricking the eyes of Enu's soldiers who were in the area while they were conducting their survey, then setting up the explosion mechanism had been extremely simple. Using one of Kiyazuna's mini flying golems, they slipped through the surveillance network from midair, cutting off the high explosive and dropping it below.

In the future, this sort of bombing tactic could make it possible to bring down an enemy army without a single personnel loss.

"Anyway, just relax, okay? I didn't give any room for Enu to come up with some excuse, trust me. It exploded in a way that ensured the citizens witnessed it all, not just that guy's subordinates, too. *Nyeh-heh-heheh*. Gonna take up a whole bunch of his time and energy just to clear his name..."

"Hopefully."

Kaete didn't want to defeat and degrade Enu, but he didn't want to stop it from happening, either.

To prepare for the day when he'd be going up against Rosclay's camp, he simply wanted to dispose of any unpleasant obstacles he could, even if only temporarily.

"What about your job, then, huh?" queried Haizesta.

"I got Enu's word. I had anticipated the chance he'd come after me, as the sponsor, myself, but... Hmph. Looks like a letdown in that regard."

Kaete took out the tiny machine he had hidden in his clothes. It wasn't a weapon from the Beyond. It was a small golem that Kiyazuna had created with specialized sensory abilities. If anyone besides Kaete and Enu had broken into the facility, it would have detected them with its sonar mechanism, and it would've prepared to make the next move as necessary.

"Was there even a reason to be scared anyway? Like there's any assassins out there who could sneak into the Coordinating Room," said Haizesta.

"Stupid oaf. The fact that Aureatia soldiers have strictly tightened up the security and blocked anyone uninvolved from getting in...means that for someone with the skills to fool Aureatia soldiers, *they could set up an attack completely unopposed.* Assuming Enu is indeed allied with Obsidian Eyes, that place would give him his best chance. Even something so basic's too much for you to understand?"

The Coordinating Room was supposed to be a safe zone, built for negotiations. As long as the Sixways Exhibition was involved, however, there wasn't a true safe zone anywhere. That was the major premise behind this battle.

"…But even then, these enemies of ours never attacked… Well then. I mean, at that point, maybe it'd be fine to say Zeljirga's clean… If anyone's scheming anything, it's on Enu's end."

"Except there's no way of knowing what's in that guy's head. The man's always been eerie."

For starters, Kaete thought, why had Enu, who was supposed to be the head of the urban planning section, volunteered his name to subjugate the remnants of Obsidian Eyes? Around the time Aureatia was established and they began reorganizing the districts, he had worked together with the medical division as part of his metropolitan epidemic prevention plan. That connection, somewhere along the line, led him to being in charge of stamping out vampires.

Enu, too, possessed a highly trained field-operation squad, despite being a civilian official himself. Almost as if he had been aiming to stamp out Obsidian Eyes long before the start of the Sixways Exhibition—

"…Ha."

Kaete laughed at himself derisively.

What, because he's a creepy man? What about it?

In the end, Haizesta's opinion on the subject was the more correct one. There wasn't any need to read deeper into things and be afraid.

Even if they had held their match in the castle garden theater as scheduled, Mestelexil should have naturally claimed victory. There were no means that Enu could have at his disposal to surpass Mestelexil's immortality.

At the very least, Kiyazuna and Haizesta had been asserting as much the whole time. Kaete may have been meaninglessly fighting against an invisible enemy and just exhausting himself in the process.

But there's still a remote chance. Always.

Rosclay had avoided going up against Zeljirga. If, by any chance, Aureatia's strongest man also had a hunch that *there was something peculiar about her*, it was indeed the insignificant opponent in the very first round whom he had to be the most proactive against. Kaete couldn't help feeling like that was what his instincts were whispering to him.

...If, by any chance, there's someone unknown to me making their moves...

◆

Night. In a room inside the lakeside manor, a returned spy was giving his report.

"The match venue has been changed."

Obsidian Eyes seventh-formation rear guard Wieze the Variation had a body that had been deformed from birth. He could only walk by crawling around on all fours, but his abilities of surveillance, lurking in gaps and high places, was exceptional.

"The sixth match will be delayed by two days, and it will be held in the old town plaza. The official announcement will likely come tomorrow morning."

"...I see."

Meanwhile, in the case of the young well-to-do woman receiving the report, everything about her outward appearance was put together perfectly. Vivacious and pale skin, together with a slender yet smoothly curvaceous body. She was the girl commanding Obsidian Eyes, named Linaris.

"We should think about how to act from here. Will you assist me while I get my thoughts in order?"

"Of course."

Considering Kaete the Round Table's temperament, she had predicted that there'd be some sort of interference in Enu's survey plans. It wasn't difficult to imagine that the smooth approval of the survey plan had happened with the intent of the leading faction to fan opposition like this to begin with.

Nevertheless, the enemy's moves were far more forceful and destructive than she had expected. Never would she have imagined they would kick up an explosion themselves and make it impossible to use the castle garden theater as a whole.

"Will Aureatia be able to identify the criminal behind the explosive?"

"No. I stole the investigation data, but it seems impossible for simple gunpowder or oil to have caused it. Similarly, the method used to set up the explosive is unknown. Given it was such a large-scale explosion, I can only assume they used an extremely high-powered explosive that we have no knowledge of."

"As long as the substance can't be explained with our current sciences, then they can't investigate the crime under the premise that such a thing exists. I see what they were doing."

"At the very least, I don't believe we will be able to grab any evidence on Kaete the Round Table before the start of the match. Changing the match venue is one thing, but…we didn't anticipate we'd be unable to use the garden theater like this."

While they needed to work out some sort of strategy, there weren't many moves Linaris could make. The soldiers of Obsidian Eyes were powerful, but their group comprised barely ten people in total, and it would be premature to systematically mobilize the corpses they had lurking in various organizations.

Linaris placed a slender finger on her lips.

"…Could we show that the castle garden is safe? Control one of Master Kaete's soldiers and make them surrender themselves as the criminal behind the explosion. So long as the perpetrator's arrested and the goal behind the attack is brought to light, I'm sure it'll make the people's confusion subside faster."

"I see. Just as our enemy created their own example of foul play, we can create our own criminal to be responsible for it. Indeed, I couldn't think of a better way to get our revenge."

"*Tee-hee.* Not that revenge was my intention, mind you."

Linaris smiled stiltedly.

"At the very least, it will be necessary to fight Master Mestel-exil in a match before the eyes of the public. My concern is that if another camp besides Master Kaete's…such as Master Rosclay's or Master Zigita Zogi's camp were to bring Master Kaete's faction down before the sixth match starts, we will end up losing our big chance."

"...A two-day postponement. Hopefully, there won't be any problematic developments until then."

"First, we'll get in touch with Miss Zeljirga and prepare to interfere with the other factions. More than anyone else, it will be Miss Zeljirga who will be the one putting her body on the line."

Zeljirga the Abyss Web was sent out to do her street performances day and night, and it seemed as if she had absolutely no connection to the organization whatsoever. Even using drones, a technology they were totally ignorant of, proved unable to catch any suspicious movements on Zeljirga's part.

Nevertheless, as long as she was among the land's greatest spy guild, Obsidian Eyes, there was always a method to communicate with Linaris and the others.

The combination of the tricks she put on display. The order of colors to the balloons she brought out. The subtle differences in the shapes of her confetti. Zeljirga was constantly sending signals using her street performance—openly, in front of the public's eyes. The techniques that could freely control the perceptions of others, making things visible but never revealing their truths, was Zeljirga the Abyss Web's true power as a clown.

While maintaining her link to Obsidian Eyes, she moved out in the open as a hero candidate. It was something only she could do.

"Do you think Zeljirga...can win against this Mestelexil?"

"She doesn't necessarily need to win. Just as long as she can survive."

Linaris smiled.

The reason she made Zeljirga enter the Sixways Exhibition was definitely not to have her advance through the tournament. If Obsidian Eyes was only concerned with victory, the best method would be to assassinate the sponsors one by one and induce victories by default.

"Thank you very much, Master Wieze. You may return to your mission.

"Understood. If you'll excuse me, my lady."

Wieze departed the parlor.

"……"

This latest incident was an unexpected turn of events, but still tolerable. Obsidian Eyes would speedily carry out the young woman's will without any changes. The sixth match was going to be held.

In just a few days...Miss Zeljirga will have to fight. Against Master Mestelexil, with her life on the line.

Every time she became cognizant of this reality, she felt fear coldly shiver down her back.

The fear that Zeljirga might die.

The fact that it was Linaris and Linaris alone who was leading this operation.

She had been forced to come to a decision. Gamble with Zeljirga's life and take on the Sixways Exhibition? Or do nothing while they all eventually died off as ghosts of the times?

...It's okay. I can do things like Father. When he levelheadedly treated everyone and everything like pawns...he always understood what the best possible options were... Always.

She pressed her hand up to her mouth. No one was watching. Wieze had left, and Linaris was alone in the large parlor.

An age of chaotic war that Father sought to realize...without anyone being sacrificed or anyone's identities behind exposed. I... A daughter like me, at the very least, *has to achieve that much.*

Linaris had a brilliant talent for intrigue, but because of it, she knew how precarious it was.

Just as she had been unable to anticipate the castle garden theater explosion, Linaris knew there were bound to be unforeseeable circumstances. She was risking Zeljirga's life, someone she loved like family, while based on this uncertain footing.

Everyone has done this. *My father. And the leader before him... I must be able to do it, too.*

◆

The sixth match underwent major changes out of necessity, right before it began.

The match between Mestelexil the Box of Desperate Knowledge and Zeljirga the Abyss Web would occur not in the castle garden theater, where there had been a bombing, but in the old town plaza, where the first match took place.

Compensating the stores that served as brokers for the spectator seats had required an enormous sum, but Aureatia's Third Minister Jel the Swift Ink had issued orders and directions to various places with incredible finesse—proving to all that even these circumstances were nothing more than one of the many possibilities that had been predicted ahead of time.

Mestelexil's sponsor, Kaete the Round Table, glared at the venue from his sponsor-exclusive seat. Kiyazuna the Axle was there as well in the seat beside him.

"…Can't say the conditions are great."

Richly colored balloons floated in the blue sky, with a flurry of confetti waving in the air. A scene of festive citizenry.

"I had estimated with the sudden venue change that there'd be a bit of a smaller audience… With this, Mestelexil won't be able to put his true value on display. Any gas or rocket bombs'll get the rabble caught in the attack."

As long as one was a hero candidate, a major premise to the title was that one needed to constantly demonstrate that they were an ally to the minian races.

Kaete was personally unconcerned if ten or a thousand of Aureatia's citizens got caught up in the blast, but he wanted to avoid having Mestelexil get recognized as a self-proclaimed demon king and become targeted by the rest of the hero candidates as a threat to be culled.

"You stupid or what? Wasn't any need for that sorta stuff to begin with. Against an opponent like Zeljirga, a little poke to the head, and it'll be over. Her brains are gonna splatter everywhere! *Hee-hee-hee-hee!*"

"I don't want to give Zeljirga any more time to set something up. It would be ideal to snuff her out with the opening punch right as the match begins."

"Hell, that's easy enough."

Kiyazuna bit down on the sweet rice cake she'd purchased from one of the stalls. She was enjoying her life in Aureatia a little *too* much.

"Soujirou the Willow-Sword apparently used just a single sword to hold out against Ozonezma's Gatling gun–like throwing-knife barrage. There's the incident with Kuuro the Careful as well. Shooting her dead right from the start isn't a guarantee, Grams."

"Bah, enough! I'm sayin' it'll be easy-peasy! You think I haven't anticipated that much?"

Mestelexil stood in the ring. Both of his shoulders were fitted with thin mailbox-shaped equipment, two lined together on each side.

"The LRAD 2000X. It's a directional acoustic weapon that selectively suppresses targets in front of it. Sound doesn't need any line of sight; there ain't no way to preemptively fight against it, and you can't block it with a shield, neither. The thing'll blow out your ears if you get hit by it, sure, but the ones Mestelexil's got have a lot more functionality than that. They'll knock ya unconscious in an instant. Let 'em rip right as the match starts, and that's it. The end."

"...Seriously? They really can do everything, can't they? Over in the Beyond."

Kiyazuna the Axle seemed sloppy in every possible way, but at the same time, she was careful.

Spending a majority of her many years in the maelstrom of

battle, the self-proclaimed demon king had inevitably grown into an unrivaled master of war.

"Time to see. Gonna be a hoot if that Zeljirga got scared and ran away."

Right as Kiyazuna muttered this, a zmeu appeared on the opposite side of the arena. Zeljirga the Abyss Web.

She carried the fifty-centimeter-long bird puppet she had used for her street performance, Morf.

"My, my, my, look at this! I am glad to see all our guests are enjoying themselves! Don't worry, though, I promise to bring even bigger smiles to your faces! Please, I would love if everyone here watched my ultimate performance!"

The cheers she received were largely made up of children's voices.

"Zeljirgaaa!"

"Zeljirga's here!"

"Hello, hello! Morf here is downright ecstatic to see you, too!"

Waving at the crowd, she took out a balloon for all to see and folded it around and around. Was it her pride as a clown that stirred her not to neglect her craft, even right before a true duel of life-and-death?

"…How's it look to you, Grams?"

"Hah?"

"I've never heard of someone using a puppet to fight."

"Well, it's gotta be a weapon. No way it's empty inside, that's for sure. Whatever it is, Mestelexil's X-ray sensor will see anything there clear as day. No damn point in trying to disguise it."

The Sixways Exhibition was a one-on-one true duel. Just as it was for Toroa the Awful with his enchanted swords and Mestelexil's acoustic weapons, as long as the combatant could wield their weapon unassisted, there wasn't anything banned from being brought or used in the duel. Be it a firearm or a puppet.

"Z-Zeljirga!" Mestelexil shouted. He practically dashed over to Zeljirga as she entered the stadium. "W-will you, show me, your magic tricks again?"

"Yes! You'll get to see the best of my craft! With that in mind, I do hope you'll go easy on me, Mestelexil...or maybe you'll be nice and lose for me, hmm?"

"*Ha-ha-ha-ha-ha-ha!* I am going, to win, for Mama! I'm not, holding back!"

"Isn't that wonderful? Having someone to dedicate your victory to."

Zeljirga squinted as she smiled.

Match six. Mestelexil the Box of Desperate Knowledge versus Zeljirga the Abyss Web.

"Silence, both of you."

A large-framed woman stepped forward between the two, who were standing opposite each other.

Aureatia's Twenty-Sixth Minister, Meeka the Whispered. A woman with a stern look of iron.

"Candidates are not to put on any sort of show unrelated to the match at hand. Understand, Zeljirga?"

"...*Ahem!* Oh, this was, well... Er, my apologies."

"And to the other candidate, are you ready?"

"*Ha-ha-ha-ha-ha-ha-ha!* I—I am ready!"

"This match will be like all the others. I shall lay out the accords of the true duel. One side is knocked down and doesn't get up. One side willingly admits their defeat with their own words. These two outcomes shall decide the match! In regard to any matters outside these conditions, I, Meeka the Whispered, on my honor, will judge with impartiality. Do you both consent to these rules?!"

"*Ah-hya-hya-hya-hyah!* But of course! I, Zeljirga, shall fight fair and square!"

"I—I, I am! *Ha-ha-ha-ha-ha!* The strongest!"

"Mestelexil, I shall consider that your consent! At the sound of the band's gun, begin!"

Meeka turned her back to the arena and retreated to her judge's chair at the top of the stone steps.

Everything would start with the shot from the band—but right before that moment that all the onlookers would concentrate on...

"*Ha-ha—*"

...Mestelexil made an unexpected move. He whirled around and fired into the air.

He appeared to move faster than the ringing of the match's starting signal.

"What in the—?"

Kaete looked at what Mestelexil had just fired at—a balloon. The balloon, descended down to an abnormally low altitude, was right around Kaete's head.

The gunshot from the band rang. The match had begun. Zeljirga sprang into action.

Crap. Mestelexil...

The shot through the balloon ignited and then exploded.

...will respond to any danger to Grams before anything else!

White smoke poured from inside the balloon over the audience seats. Combined with the smoke screen from the fireworks Zeljirga had scattered at the start of the match, the audiences' sights were completely blocked out.

"Whoa!"

"What's going on?!"

"Was that an explosion?!"

Kaete's sense of danger had been correct after all. Zeljirga had gotten the first move.

"...Dammit! Grams! You all right?!"

Mestelexil's attack prior to the start of the fight fortunately hadn't been seen as breaking the rules.

He had been manipulated into using what was supposed to be an instantaneously lethal opening move to instead shoot down the balloon.

"Nothing but cheap tricks! Mestelexil! Forget about it and shoot 'er dead!"

"Ha-ha-ha-ha-ha-ha-ha-ha-ha!"

Gunshots, like a metallic scream, reverberated. The smoke screen, which blocked visible light, was also meaningless when up against Mestelexil's array of sensors. The bullet holes from his

Gatling gun bore through the uninhabited ruins of the old town, and they began to partially collapse in.

However, Zeljirga's form wasn't inside the smoke—in her place, the puppet she controlled came flying out alone.

It rushed with speed wholly inconceivable from any ordinary marionette. Mestelexil blocked it with an arm.

Even after being blocked, the puppet wasn't repelled, continuing to rotate and spit out sparks with a high-pitched noise. It had speed and power that far exceeded any bullet.

"...Morf!"

◆

Fooling the eyes of the audience with the balloon uproar and the smoke screen, Zeljirga hid herself in one of the abandoned ruins adjoining the plaza. Everything as of that moment had gone exactly as planned.

The residents in the vicinity of the old town plaza had been evicted in order to use the place as an arena for the Sixways Exhibition. Just as Psianop and Toroa had done in the first match, it was possible to dash inside said evicted buildings during the match—however, this was simply an exception to the rule that exploited a hole in the definition of the arena.

Using a mirror trick, she kept her eyes on Mestelexil.

...*Let's start with the opening move.*

From her faraway position, Zeljirga was controlling the golem puppet, which was continuing to fly with abnormal power output, using the threads on her fingertips. The Morf puppet recited Word Arts.

"—*Saknamop lastarmokg.* (—Bore closing twilight)

"Amteneaor sharbardhor nes tort sind get zept merticst—" (Fill the vessel with corundom thorns, separate root, stem, and leaf from the horizontal plane knot, worldly affairs are gold—)

Coming up at the end of the incantation, Mestelexil reconstructed his right arm into a shotgun. The puppet radiated a bright heat ray, melting through part of the golem's right arm and chest as it passed by Mestelexil. Mestelexil's breast plating melted under the high heat, and for a moment, he lost sight of the speedily flying puppet. A heat-induced sensory error.

The puppet's true identity was Reshipt Modified-II. A golem meant for suicide attacks, wholly specialized at its charging drill offensive and nothing else.

Obsidian Eyes had hidden this golem inside the balloon that had caused the earlier explosion. The doll that Zeljirga had initially brought in with her, similarly, was the necessary opening move to launch a surprise attack through its substitution.

Miluzi the Coffin Edict's trump card. Compared with Mestelexil, its capabilities are almost laughably inferior.

Nevertheless, just as it had been with Reshipt and Nemerhelga...there was one sole part of its functionality that could stand shoulder to shoulder with Mestelexil's abilities. Reshipt Modified-II was a model even further specialized in one particular function.

Zeljirga needed to constantly keep directing and controlling

Reshipt Modified-II's high-speed movements through her tarantula threads. Reshipt Modified-II wasn't equipped with any directional capabilities of its own.

"*Hrnk, phew...* This...is seriously...hard...work!"

She wrapped the end of the threads—which were violently struggling under the tremendously high speeds—around the nails on the floor, dispersing her strength and using her fingers, and sometimes her feet and teeth, to handle the complicated and simultaneous controls. Every time she tried to pull a thread, her fingers would bear the load of its tremendous velocity, and blood seeped from Zeljirga's fingertips. The bones in them would creak, and she bent them until they were just about to break.

Reshipt Modified-II went halfway around the arena, at high enough speeds to look like little more than a glint of light, and went behind Mestelexil.

Conversely, Mestelexil stood in the middle of the arena and didn't move.

"O-oh, it's you, Morf! What is it?"

However, he generated a countless number of gun barrels all over his body.

...Uh-oh.

She immediately let go of the threads around her fingers. Mestelexil's precision deflection shooting landed three hits on Reshipt Modified-II as it flew at high speed. The only reason it wasn't hit any further was because Zeljirga had released some portion of the threads, erratically altering its flight path.

With its trajectory thrown off by the shots, Reshipt Modified-II crashed down into the rubble and stopped.

I can't believe it was able to immediately respond to such speeds...and shoot it down, too!

Reshipt Modified-II's main body was protected in the front by sloped armor, so the crash didn't cause a fatal malfunction. However, there was a slight distortion in its machinery. She could tell that through her threads.

"Hey, Mestelexil! That scrap heap's just buying time! Find Zeljirga and kill her!"

Kiyazuna issued her orders with a loud shout.

Zeljirga didn't let the chance slip by and pulled on the threads connecting to Reshipt Modified-II.

"G-g-got it! Mama—"

Charge again.

The golem furiously flew out from the mountain of debris. Its propulsion was still working.

It wasn't aiming for Mestelexil. Without any directional control, Reshipt Modified-II pierced through to the second floor of the ruined residence. Raining down a shower of debris, it interfered with Mestelexil's next move.

Only five left. No, six... I didn't expect to have so many tarantula-silk control lines severed just to suppress his opening moves. I can probably only set up for one more attack. Dear me, honestly...

She heard a soft *thud.*

A pain in her upper left arm.

"......!"

It'd been pierced with an arrow.

When had he gotten in so close? She hadn't sensed him at all.

Behind Zeljirga...a large number of machines, resembling bird skeletons, silently hovered in the air.

"Golems...!"

Autonomously driven, airborne, and tasked with searching for the enemy, even when Mestelexil wasn't moving. Mestelexil was producing this swarm of golems right at the same time he was countering back against Reshipt.

The information had been obtained from the battle with the Particle Storm, and she would've known about this aspect of his unlimited capabilities.

A golem who could make golems.

"Ah-hyah-hyah-hayh... What does knowing about something like this even do for me?"

The golem swarm fired their arrows all at once. Zeljirga's threads had caught up a majority of the golems right before they fired, mixing them into the debris to avoid the attack and live through the lethal storm.

She was skewered. Her left knee. Waist. Stomach. The tip of her left foot.

A fatal wound and a wound to both arms, which she used for her clown craft, were the only things she needed to avoid.

The attack wasn't going to end here. The fact that the scouting golems had found where she was hiding meant...

Here it comes!

Using her uninjured right leg, she immediately jumped out of a window. An explosion.

Zeljirga tumbled out into the arena, as if swept away by the shock wave and air blast, which felt strong enough to shatter her bones.

The ruins that she had been hiding in moments prior had lost over half of its total cubic volume.

"SMAW rocket launcher."

As Mestelexil muttered, he folded up the cannon barrel that had spread out from his waist, which had been opened up by his reconstruction.

Her wounds were deep. She had to handle the next attacks.

How? Where?

Mestelexil's singular eye aimed at Zeljirga. On his back was some box-shaped equipment.

"*Ah...hyah*, well now...it's good to see you aga—"

An invisible yet colossal something slammed Zeljirga's body.

It was as if the very air itself had crushed her. It had surpassed the range of what her senses could tolerate, making her unable to perceive it as sound, either.

—A directional acoustic weapon.

"LRAD 2000X."

Zeljirga lost consciousness.

◆

"Hmph. We won, then."

Sitting next to Kaete, Kiyazuna instead seemed displeased as she spoke.

At times like this, she felt absolute indignation at the fact that her son had been injured, however slightly—something her pupil Kaete could understand.

Since he, too, felt the same sort of anger.

"...The incident with the balloon was clearly an intentional accident. I was thorough in ensuring there were no traps in the arena, but...the sky was a blind spot even to me. I should have expected it."

While he had correctly sensed some danger, he hadn't been able to properly guard against it.

Mestelexil had won as if it was a matter of course, but Kaete himself truly felt like he had lost.

"Bah, who cares? It wasn't much of a problem anyway."

"Mestelexil has a semiautomatic counterattack logic incorporated into his construction. That's why they didn't fill it with explosives, but a smoke screen heavier than air. It's just a golem puppet, but I can't believe that some connection of Enu's was able to make something so well-built."

"Nah. That thing's one of Miluzi's golems."

"...It's what?"

Surprisingly, Kiyazuna was gazing down at the battlefield, still propping up her cheek on one hand. Or rather, she was staying on guard.

Miluzi the Coffin Edict. The person who developed this world's steam engines. A self-proclaimed demon king recognized in the later days of the True Demon King's age, and whose whereabouts were unknown. In particular, he was said to rival even Kiyazuna the Axle when it came to the level of completion he had in his golems.

"The individual quirks of the creator show up in how a golem's made. That puppet there was definitely made by Miluzi, but... Miluzi'd *make something like that*? Strange."

"Huh? I have absolutely no idea what that's supposed to mean...!"

"The design philosophy behind it ain't his style. It's almost as if some other person was forcing him to—"

Kiyazuna's words stopped there.

There was a strange phenomenon in the area. Zeljirga was standing up.

"Hey. Grams."

"Nah-uh, no way...it's impossible. Physically impossible."

There existed examples of warriors who had lost consciousness without falling down and still continued to stand. However, after getting directly hit by an acoustic weapon and fainting, *getting back up from the ground* should have been impossible.

"Proceed," the adjudicator Meeka tersely declared.

◆

Ahhh, this is funny, so funny. The ground's wobbling back and... *No, that's not it.*

Aware of the fact that she had stood up on her own feet, Zeljirga strove to maintain her consciousness.

If she didn't stand up, there was a chance she may never wake up.

She had fallen into a dreamless darkness up until just a moment ago.

I'm the one who's wobbling, and I...I'm fighting.

She moved her fingers. One, two, three. Using the movements that had become customary from her training with threads, she regained the sense that she was herself.

"Huh? We're still, fighting? Okay, then i-if I...defeat her, one more time, I win!"

The adjudicator Meeka appeared to be explaining to Mestel-exil why the match was restarting.

She was grateful. Right now, a few brief seconds were more valuable to her than tens of years.

Pathetic, Zeljirga the Abyss Web. Mestelexil being an invincible and immortal golem, all of it... You knew all that a long time ago.

Her standing up just now wasn't due to Zeljirga's own strength, either—there was someone who was moving her body and had made her stand up in her stead.

The two had made a promise to do just so in case of an emergency.

Zeljirga was one of Linaris's corpses.

Thank you very much. My lady.

Zeljirga had volunteered to be a hero candidate in the Sixways Exhibition. That was easily done. Most who willingly undertook these sort of missions would find themselves on the borderline between life and death. For her...for someone from the old Obsidian Eyes, this was simply a part of everyday life.

It must have been a heartbreaking feeling for Linaris. That was all the more reason for Zeljirga to laugh.

"...*Hya, ah-hya...*"

"Zeljirga. M-Meeka...told me something g-good!"

Mestelexil's singular eye rolled around his head with excitement.

"She said, it's okay, for you to surrender! If you do...I won't, have to kill you, will I?! *Ha-ha-ha-ha-ha-ha!* Since, you are, my friend!"

"Ahhh, yes...that's right... Silly me. I forgot."

Having watched so many children delight at her craft, Zeljirga understood. Mestelexil was an invincible weapon. Nevertheless, at the same time, he was a young child.

Except in this world, there were children who could kill even those they once saw as friends.

Zeljirga was just such a creature. Mestelexil was likely the same.

Creatures of battle, who definitely couldn't live in a world of peace.

The minute nicks gouged into Mestelexil's armor had long been repaired.

The smoke screen was gone, and there was nowhere to hide. Zeljirga was covered in wounds from head to toe, and she was facing Mestelexil head-on. The gap in their strength was so vast that she knew the moment Mestelexil shifted his gun barrel the slightest millimeter, that alone would blast her from this world into the next.

We don't need to win.

Obsidian Eyes' duty was not combat. It was fair for her to say that the moment she got into a battle with Mestelexil the Box of Desperate Knowledge, that alone meant defeat.

"Zeljirga the Abyss Web, do you wish to surrender?"

But there's also no need to lose, *then, is there?*

Zeljirga shook her head in reply to Meeka the Whispered's question.

"*Ah-hyah-hyah...* Before I end up losing here, there's only one thing I want to do. Since you're a friend of mine, Mestelexil..."

Gasping for breath in her current state, Zeljirga produced her final weapon.

"...this is for you."

"Candy—"

It was just a piece of candy.

At that moment, Mestelexil turned around in the direction of Kiyazuna. In that instant that he took his focus off Zeljirga, she released the final two threads she had kept gripped tight in her hand.

"Again... Attack again!"

From the sidelines as the pair faced off, Reshipt Modified-II, all its moorings released, flew ferociously into the air. It rammed itself straight into Mestelexil's chest like a warhead and begin digging into him.

"*Resipkt io halese. Win halt elk, nertak mamert—*" (From Reshipt to Halesept's eyes. Gear in the soil, flower petals as golden film—)

Rotate. Bore. Incant.

"Wh-what?"

"—*Saknamop lastarmokg.*" (—Bore closing twilight.)

Reshipt Modified-II fired a heat ray from completely point-blank range. Heat arts radiated from its built-in magical tool at its maximum energized state. Together with a temperature hot enough to melt its own body down, Reshipt Modified-II penetrated even further and tried to pierce all the way—to Mestelexil's life core, the homunculus.

"*Ha-ha-ha-ha-ha!* That, tickles!"

Then it was smashed into smithereens.

Mestelexil hadn't even needed to rebuild his weaponry. With his individual power output, which surpassed any and all other golems, he had simply crushed Reshipt Modified-II, which had been digging into his plating, with his fist.

Neither defenses that could withstand gunfire nor the offensive power to pierce through armor were a match for Mestelexil's capabilities.

However.

"My lady..."

Zeljirga the Abyss Web couldn't have possibly overlooked that ever-so-brief moment when the golem was destroyed.

A fine thread, impossible to catch without straining the eyes long and hard, was stretching into the crack in Mestelexil's head section.

Reshipt Modified-II was the guide for Zeljirga's thread.

"...I, Zeljirga the Abyss Web, to live up to your faith in me, have successfully pulled off my performance."

Like a spider's web after the rain, there was a trick to make water droplets blanket a thread.

It may have been nothing but an inconsequential bit of street magic, useless in battle.

A single meager drop of the blood-borne pathogen afflicted the homunculus life core.

"......"

"Mestelexil. This gambit..."

The perfectly ordinary piece of candy fell to the ground.

That day she first met Mestelexil, Zeljirga had shown him a piece of candy right before shooting at Kiyazuna. The reason he had suddenly turned back to Kiyazuna was because that threat had been instilled in him subconsciously.

"...wouldn't have been possible if you weren't my friend."

The strongest weapon in the land lost power right on the spot, collapsed, and didn't get up.

◆

"What...What happened?"

Despite watching the whole battle right from the sidelines, Kaete the Round Table couldn't comprehend the conclusion.

Mestelexil was an immortal construct. If the golem died, the homunculus would regenerate the golem, and if the homunculus died, the golem would regenerate the homunculus. On top of it, annihilating both at the same time was impossible.

In the unlikely scenario where defeating Mestelexil was

possible, it still shouldn't have looked anything like what had played out before them.

"Hey! Mestelexil! Get up—what's wrong with you?! You're gonna lose!"

Kiyazuna stood up, her vigor suggesting she might barge into the arena at any moment. Kaete had to stop her from rampaging out of control, but he had an even more terrifying premonition.

A surprise attack from above... Was something that mundane really the truth behind this terrible foreboding? An attack using a balloon would have been utterly impossible to pull off in the castle garden theater, the original venue. Why did one of Miluzi's golems show up here out of the blue? The balloon isn't the only problem... My attempt to change the arena... Mestelexil's participation in the Sixways Exhibition in the first place... If there was someone...pulling the strings to make all that happen...

"Mestelexil! C'mon!"

"...! Grams, get back!"

Kaete immediately pulled Kiyazuna's hand. Suddenly getting up, Mestelexil rushed toward Kaete and Kiyazuna's spectator seats. Leveling and demolishing the seats, the golem continued on unfazed through the old town.

Meeka the Whispered shouted:

"Fourth Minister Kaete! Apprehend Mestelexil this instant! Sponsors must have control over their hero candidates! I rule that he has fled from the match!"

"How dare you order me...!"

Kaete had to instantly quell his rage.

Kiyazuna was already running off without a word. His only option was to follow after her.

No one outside Kaete's camp could have understood just how abnormal the situation was, whether he tried to explain it or not. There shouldn't have been anyone out there in the world who had more control over Mestelexil than Kiyazuna the Axle.

"This ain't his own will," Kiyazuna muttered as they ran. "He can become independent someday and turn against me, I don't care, but this is something else entirely!"

"Then is there some sort of technology that could steal control from you...?! He may be a golem, but he's still just a machine!"

"No. Unauthorized hacking, credential spoofing—all that only works for machines from the Beyond. Golems are Word Arts creatures. Controlling authority? That couldn't—"

Right as they approached an old town back alley, Kiyazuna suddenly stopped.

He was the only example in the land of a construct being controlled under two different wills. Therefore, if he did have a vulnerability that couldn't exist in other golems...

"...It could. Of course. The shared curse...! Mestel and Exil's lives are both equally valuable, but Exil has more authority, since it holds the knowledge from the Beyond! If they had to make judgments with the same authority, it'd disrupt the order of command! You understand this reasoning here, Kaete?!"

"Roughly, sure! But are you saying they killed the homunculus side, then?!"

"That stupid puppet was aiming for Mestelexil's head section right from the damn start! If you're talking about a living, breathing creature, than there's one thing that'll force 'emselves into an ultimate position of authority!"

"...Vampires...! So Zeljirga really is linked up with Obsidian Eyes?!"

It was a difficult conclusion to accept. Kaete had painstakingly confirmed for himself that it *wasn't* possible.

Did Enu the Distant Mirror know what was going on? Exactly how far had the roots of this conspiracy spread?

"What other explanation is there?! Those bastards... I'll flatten 'em all! This is war!"

"I told you, just calm down! You might not know this, Grams, but there's more to turning someone into a corpse than just wounding them! You need to administer a considerable amount of the parent unit's bodily fluids to do it! Isn't it unnatural that the wounds from this fight would've been enough to infect him?! So just one drop or some fine particles wouldn— *Gaugh!*"

Kaete was suddenly grabbed by the nape of his neck an'd dragged down to the ground.

He could tell that something had flown right over him, a hairbreadth above his nose. A chakram.

"We gotta do this fast! They're already here to finish the job!"

Kiyazuna was staring up at the roof of a building at the end of the street. There, set on all fours, was a bizarre-looking minia. Kaete jolted up like a spring and immediately drew his sword.

"Grams!"

A lycan, emerging like a shadow, stopped Kaete's sword with his large claws.

Up until that second, he hadn't noticed him drawing near—the footsteps had been inconceivably silent despite his massive frame.

"*Grrrrr.*"

When the lycan gave a low growl, Kaete's sword was twisted under the enemy's grip, which was beginning to shove Kaete along with it. Kaete immediately took his hand off his sword and prioritized covering his ears more than defending himself.

The lycan swung his claws up into the air, and the sniper from afar readied two new chakrams.

"Good job coverin' those ears, Kaete!"

There was an explosion of bright light. The violently loud roar shook all the lycan's five senses, and thanks to the light, nearly as bright as the sun itself, the faraway sniper lost sight of their target, too.

The hexagonal and cylindrical weapon Kiyazuna the Axle threw was an M84 stun grenade.

"Great, now we gotta scram!"

"I can't hear a single thing you're saying!"

As the concussive sound and bright light subsided, the two figures disappeared.

◆

The old town plaza began to fill with nervous and confused whispers.

Mestelexil the Box of Desperate Knowledge had suddenly lost control after losing the match, then disappeared somewhere. A sight yet to be seen in any of the other five matches.

However, amid all the hubbub, there was a single young girl heaving a relieved sigh.

Her face was covered in a black veil, concealing her eye-catching beauty.

...Thank goodness. I'm so glad. Truly...truly so happy.

There was someone who had been manipulating Zeljirga's physical body while she was unconscious, as well as Mestelexil's, who'd been newly brought under her command. The vampire parent unit, Linaris, had needed to be there in attendance.

Without making a single conspicuous movement, Linaris had simply used her thoughts to command her corpses from her seat in the audience.

I was able to spare Zeljirga's life. It all went...exactly according to my calculations.

From the very start, Obsidian Eyes had intended on making the arena change from the garden theater to the old town plaza.

By using all the obstacles available in the ruined buildings and audience seating, they were able to limit the weapons Mestelexil could utilize and cause a distraction from above with their balloon trap. Furthermore, with the last-minute venue change, they hadn't given any time to the other factions besides Kaete's camp to set up some large scheme for the match, either.

Kaete the Round Table was an arrogant man filled with self-confidence. Even though they were the very citizens he was supposed to govern, he didn't hesitate to refer to those he deemed lacking in ability as *ignorant rabble*. However, on the other hand, he was extremely sharp-witted when it came to the movements of those he acknowledged as superbly capable—he had a psychological tendency to be deeply suspicious of everything and everyone.

Zeljirga's thread attacks, no matter what sort of strategy she tried to employ, would be incapable of defeating Mestelexil. In which case, Kaete the Round Table would believe *there was some sort of scheme* beyond them.

In order to lend support to those suspicions, Enu started his surveying operation. Kaete would then suspect his enemy was setting up some sort of trap in the castle garden theater. Since Zeljirga alone had no means of victory, Kaete would assume a scheme involving the arena would be the only way to defeat Mestelexil and then investigate into the truth behind said scheme.

However, there wasn't anything to find in the castle garden theater. Enu had simply been surveying the area, and nothing more.

They'd been setting up *something*, but *there wasn't actually anything at all*.

There was only one method left for Kaete to escape from his misgivings:

Fundamentally changing the location of the duel itself.

Then a request to change venues was put forth, just as Linaris had anticipated, and the match occurred under terms that gave Obsidian Eyes a one-sided advantage.

Obsidian Eyes' intelligence gathering had begun long before

the beginning of the Sixways Exhibition. The battle with the Particle Storm, which had called all the shura to one location, was something that Linaris had plotted herself, mobilizing Atrazek the Particle Storm to do so.

The plan was to observe the monsters that had been drawn together and ascertain which would be the most useful pawn among them.

The answer was Mestelexil the Box of Desperate Knowledge.

With this, we don't even need to fight *in this Sixways Exhibition anymore.*

Linaris the Obsidian's supernatural ability of forced control through airborne infection was without equal, but it wasn't totally invincible.

Most of the important figures like those in Twenty-Nine Officials and the Queen had been inoculated with the antiserum. It was also powerless against constructs that didn't have any blood. While it was a power that could limitlessly manipulate soldiers and the public, what about when it was against the sort of eminently powerful people nominated as hero candidates? Fragile Linaris herself had to infect them directly, or she needed to stand up against them with someone mightier.

The Sixways Exhibition imposed the restraints of a royal tournament on these powerful individuals, and it was an event that made it possible to fight under fixed match conditions.

With this, we've gained it for ourselves...the military strength to bring down the mightiest players directly.

Mestelexil was now a part of Obsidian Eyes.

A golem, a homunculus, and a corpse.

A factory producing weapons from the Beyond, and an immortal soldier who could not be destroyed.

"And with everything staying secret."

The young woman sneaked a finger up to her lips as she disappeared into the middle of the crowd.

◆

A half day had passed since the conclusion of the sixth match. Evening had come.

Kaete and Kiyazuna still remained unable to make it out of the old town.

"…Bad news. They got this exit under watch, too."

Pulling back the reconnaissance golem, Kiyazuna clicked her tongue in frustration.

The covert lycan soldier, and the sniper on all fours. These were the two they needed to be wary of the most. They were both unbelievably skilled, and it would be difficult to break through using just the improvised golems Kiyazuna had created.

"This has to be Obsidian Eyes after all; there's no other explanation. How long have they had their sights on Mestelexil? What's their goal…? Systematically hijacking the entire Sixways Exhibition?!" asked Kaete.

"Geez, you didn't prepare for this and make some sorta underground shortcut or anything?"

"Even if I had, that'd be the very first place that'd get pinned down in this situation! Our information's been leaked here!"

"Fine then, you tellin' me to stay here in this boring hellhole until I turn into a dried fish?!"

"...That's all we can do."

Although not the main two they were faced with, a presence that appeared to be hostile was patrolling the alleys and sewers. All the paths they could use as their escape route had been seized and rendered unusable.

Conversely, the two of them, lying in hiding, were still alive. These movements meant...

"The way they're acting, it seems less like they're trying to find us and more like they're trying to stop us from escaping, don't they...? If they're cutting off our contact with anyone outside and waiting until we grow impatient and show ourselves, then why? For example, they might be wary of the possibility that we're waiting in ambush with weapons from the Beyond instead. As long as they don't have a full understanding of the capabilities of the Beyond, they might be taking strict care not to move unless it's in response to the movement on our side."

"Hmph... Basically, they're a buncha scaredy bastards, eh? Then what're we supposed to do?"

"If we don't ever return home, either my soldiers or Yuca's public safety force will eventually come looking for me. If we can meet up with those squads and escape, the enemy won't be able to readily ambush us."

The match had been ruled in favor of Zeljirga. However, Kaete hadn't given up on victory yet.

Even if he was knocked out of the Sixways Exhibition, if he could take back Mestelexil, then there were plenty of routes to victory. He'd wage war against Rosclay and Haade, then overthrow everything, along with the results of the Sixways Exhibition. Regardless of Mestelexil's victory or defeat, nothing about his plan had changed.

"At any rate, keep making golems, Grams. Doesn't matter how makeshift they are—we need to gather as much fighting power as we can for our next encounter, or it'll be impossible to fight our way through."

"*Feh*, Aureatia's damn soil's the problem...! If I could just get back to my lab, I could get all kindsa rare materials ready."

"...! Wait."

Kaete stopped moving, hearing a voice echo in the streets outside.

The voice was searching for Kaete's location; that was without question... However—

"Former Fourth Minister Kaete the Round Table is hiding out in the vicinity of this street! His crimes include grievous rule-breaking actions in the Sixways Exhibition and the recent bombing at the castle garden theater! The individual who committed the bombing on Kaete's orders has already appeared before the assembly—"

"Tha—"

It was an Aureatia soldier calling out with a shout. It was an announcement of his status as a wanted criminal.

"That can't be…! Impossible! Curses, what is this…?!"

"*Hee-hee-hee-hee-hee!* This happened because you're always up to no good."

"Still, this is some sort of mistake! What're they talking about?!"

Former Fourth Minister.

If he ended up losing the faction he was meant to lead, why, even if he regained control of Mestelexil, it wouldn't mean a damn thing.

"Guess I gotta use this after all."

Kiyazuna produced an instrument of some kind.

It was equipped with a display, and when it connected to a simple battery, two faint points of light appeared on it.

"Dammit, dammit… Grams…what is that, then?"

"If we're dealing with a vampire, we only got two options, right? Kill the parent dead, or kill Exil dead and make him regenerate from scratch."

"…So if he's forced to regenerate, it'll mean returning to the state he was in before the infection, then?"

"More accurately, it'll erase the overriding authority on Mestel. Normally, if Exil was hit by some poison or illness, Mestel's made to immediately cure 'im with Life Arts on the spot—the reason he's not is 'cause the orders from an overruling authority are inhibiting that function."

"You can't remotely order him to self-destruct? Any construct needs some sorta function like that."

"Huh? The hell I need some way to blow up my own children. Dumbass."

"That's not… Forget it. Let's stick to the topic. The only method's to kill him on the inside, then… How're we going to destroy Mestelexil's armor and kill Exil? That's a tall order, no matter who you task with the job."

"Even more than that, stupid. The amniotic fluid preserving Exil's been affected by the vampire pathogen, too. Just kill Exil, and he'll get infected right after he's done regenerating, then that'll be that. Gotta be an attack that sends all the amniotic fluid flying, too, or it's still impossible."

Mestelexil's mechanical perfection was now baring its fangs at them.

The peerlessly elite Obsidian Eyes had them surrounded, and all Aureatia was now their enemy.

"…Impossible or not, I at least know where Mestelexil is. In case my boy ever got lost, see… We'll be able to track him down."

"Track him… So that display's a tracking signal…!"

"Obviously, using GNSS is still too much for this world—gotta blast a bunch of man-made satellites out past the stars first. With a LORAN system, it'll only show coordinates, so its accuracy ain't reliable at all. Just shows a broad estimate of his distance and direction."

"Hold up, we're talking about tracking Mestelexil, so where does *beyond the stars* come in to play? Are you sure that thing'll work?"

"*Heh*, when have I ever been wrong, eh? We doing this or not?!"

For some reason, Kiyazuna seemed livelier than she had been moments earlier.

—For the entirety of Kiyazuna the Axle's lifetime, she'd had nothing but enemies around her.

A born villain. Kaete was surely the same.

"...We are."

Villains never gave up, even when all the conclusions had been made.

"Right. I'm not letting this end here. We're getting Mestelexil back. Whether it's this Sixways Exhibition...or this factional war for powers, I'll overturn the results of it all...! Kaete the Round Table...isn't just going to lie down and die!"

Match six. Winner, Zeljirga the Abyss Web.

Peering into the past. The third match of the Sixways Exhibition was over, and Yuno the Distant Talon had no place to go.

More accurately put, she'd ended up voluntarily throwing away her place to go. She had secured a life for herself here in Aureatia as Twenty-Seventh General Haade's secretary, yet once again, she had given in to her violent emotions and chosen the path of destruction.

...I betrayed his trust. Betrayed General Haade... It wasn't like I hated him or that I wanted to cause trouble for him, either, yet...

Leaving her post due to nothing but her own personal feelings, she'd saved a young girl she happened to come across named Linore and accidentally learned Haade's camp's most important secret. If he found out that Yuno had deciphered what was written in the letter, there was no question he'd have her killed.

Thus, she had nowhere to return. Together with Linore, she wandered the forest on the outskirts of Aureatia.

"...Wh-where—?"

Her quivering voice called to Linore in front of her. Following after the girl had been her only option.

"Where are we going? That road we passed by could've gotten us out of Aureatia."

On both sides of the road, the thick forest was obstructing the way. Yuno checked behind her over and over. If they were being followed, they were extremely unlikely to get away.

"...You do not need to worry at all. There's no risk of being followed."

Linore had learned the same potentially life-threatening secret herself, yet unlike Yuno, she had remained perfectly calm. Not just calm, but her expression made it seem like she was continuing to think something over.

She had a face that almost unconsciously left Yuno spellbound, as beautiful as a nighttime dream.

"But if we really were being tailed, it'd be impossible for us to know..."

In the middle of her sentence, the sound of horse hooves approached, and Yuno caught her breath. She might have actually let out a bit of a scream. Linore quietly lingered where they were and waited for the carriage to reach them.

The carriage came to a halt beside her.

"My lady. I have come to receive you."

"—Thank you."

The driver bowed to Linore. She appeared to be an elf woman, but both her eyes were covered with a bandage. Though, if she had truly been covering her eyes, how was it possible for her to drive the carriage?

"Huh? Um...what?" asked Yuno.

"And who might she be?"

"She is...Miss Yuno the Distant Talon. She's...um..." Linore stuttered.

For some reason at that moment, Linore furrowed her willowy eyebrows, looking a bit at a loss.

"...my...friend."

"I see. Do you plan on inviting her into the manor?"

The driver leaned her upper body down from the driver's seat and met Yuno's gaze.

Yuno felt a mysterious chill run down her back.

She experienced a sensation similar to the moment right before Soujirou the Willow-Sword went into action.

"Well..."

"Hold up, I don't understand anything going on here... There's a manor up ahead of here? And 'my lady'...?"

"Please listen, Miss Yuno. If, perhaps, you do not have a home to return to, that is. I thought, um, I could give you shelter...in my manor for a time..."

"......"

"......"

Linore smiled bashfully and tilted her head to the side.

"...How would that sound?"

"Ummm, o...kay... Sure...?"

Yuno nodded, shifting her eyes between the driver and Linore.

In any case, right now, she didn't have anywhere else to go.

◆

She threw her back onto the large, soft bed.

Holding her palm up before her eyes, Yuno sighed as she thought over the terribly hectic day she'd had.

Too many unbelievable things had happened, both in Yuno's own heart and beyond it.

I will get revenge.

Inside her mind, she whispered the first thing she needed to do—Linore the Shadow Laden. Haade's plan. Soujirou the Willow-Sword's third match, which she hadn't been able to see through to the end. Finally, Yuno's own future.

Even if, at this very minute, she had a number of fears and apprehensions, she absolutely couldn't change what she needed to prioritize the most.

She would get revenge against the powerful and strong, who trampled over everything and everyone without any bit of self-reflection.

Among all the strong and powerful, she still prioritized one above all and would kill Kiyazuna the Axle.

Revenge. Revenge. Revenge. Revenge.

She had to feel the animosity. Up until now, Yuno hadn't been able to maintain such hatred in her heart.

The strength capable of killing Kiyazuna the Axle may have been eternally unattainable for a girl like Yuno. Nevertheless, if she were to ultimately lose the truth in her heart, then what else was she supposed to use as anchorage?

Yuno rolled over on her stomach and buried her face in the white pillow.

...So peace of mind. Satisfaction. Happiness. I can't let myself

start to feel that way. As long as I don't forget this hatred, I can still continue to be my true self...

A reserved knock came from the door.

Still feeling dismal, Yuno roused her body and answered: "Come in."

"Pardon me."

It was Linore. She wore a pure-white nightgown. She seemed to have already finished her bath, as her evenly cut, shoulder-length black hair was still damp.

"Am I bothering you?" asked Linore.

"I-it's fine."

Yuno immediately averted her eyes. Linore had an allure that made it impossible for her not to, even though they were both girls. Her golden pupils and nearly translucent ivory skin were part of it, but...

I didn't realize...

...the thin nightgown clearly displayed all the contours of her body.

...how big...how big her chest was...

"Miss Yuno. Please allow me to apologize again for today's events. I am also terribly sorry for making you feel nervous...when I invited you into my manor."

"Whatever... It's no big deal. We've both got our secrets to hide, right?"

"No, I need to apologize. You gave your name to me; however, I have been hiding my own. My true name is Linaris."

"...Linaris."

She had infiltrated the Sixways Exhibition arena, stolen important documents, and done it all under a fake name.

It was evident that she wasn't someone with honest or respectable goals in mind. Even despite that, was Linore—rather, was Linaris—trying to show some measure of good faith toward Yuno, who had accidently run into her and become her accomplice?

"What is your group's objective, then? You're against Aureatia... right? General Haade has a lot of factions opposing him, so you might just be someone within Aureatia anyway, but..." Yuno trailed off.

"Allow me to explain that to you as well. We are Obsidian Eyes."

"......!"

Yuno subconsciously looked at Linaris's face. The look in her eyes was serious, and she didn't seem to be lying.

Obsidian Eyes. The spy guild *said to* have been constantly maneuvering in the shadows of the Demon King War.

For the average person like Yuno, such rumors were the only things that reached her ears. It was also possible that these rumors themselves were groundless hearsay in order to deceive the movements of each country's own spy forces. On relatively rare occasions, there were mercenaries who said they were formerly a part of Obsidian Eyes, but she heard a majority were just dubiously claiming themselves as such.

"So then have you been hired by someone, like the Free City of Okafu...or the Old Kingdoms' loyalists, to try taking Aureatia down? Even if that's true, getting a young girl like yourself involved in the infiltration...," said Yuno.

"…I ask you to forgive me…for I cannot say anything beyond that. If you happened to learn more, then it could very well put your life in danger."

Yuno averted her eyes down to the floor.

"Well then, why… Why are you fighting in Obsidian Eyes, Linaris? Just earlier today, you might've been killed on the spot if things had gone a bit different."

"That's because…"

Stories had long been told, for example, about bandits or assassin organizations making kidnapped children do work for them.

Linaris was a well-raised young girl and close in age to Yuno, too. There had to be some sort of personal circumstance involved, at the very least. Maybe she was similar to Yuno, fighting to claim revenge against the life she had led.

"I wonder…why?" Pressing her hand up to her chest, Linaris murmured, as if the words were catching in her throat.

"I need to… I feel that I have to…or else, my own life can never begin… Perhaps, that is why I am trying to carry this through. Miss Yuno…why, then, did you do something like that?"

"…Your life can't begin…"

That was it. Her reply seemed to put words to Yuno's own heart, too.

Yuno leaned her body forward and spoke.

"Listen, Linaris. I want to get revenge."

"…You mentioned so at the garden theater as well. Do you wish to get revenge on Master Soujirou the Willow-Sword?"

"Not just him…I think. I'm a survivor of the now-annihilated

Nagan City, and…that terrible day, Soujirou cut down the Dungeon Golem. That's why I'm…I'm still alive right now."

Dying would be a waste. That was what Soujirou had told her.

That life got fun after you lost everything.

"I didn't want my life to get crushed underfoot as if it had never mattered to begin with. I didn't want to feel expendable. That's why the thing I want revenge on isn't just Soujirou—or the one who made that Dungeon Golem, Kiyazuna the Axle, but something more, something bigger than that."

Sitting upright in the bed, Yuno hugged her pillow and sighed.

Yuno was weak. Not only in terms of strength or wits, but even her mental state was chaotic and unreliable, making it seem like she wouldn't be able to achieve a single thing she wished for. Even so—

"I want to beat the strong."

Her own way of phrasing it made her sound just like Soujirou. That's how it seemed to her.

"You have been through quite a bit of hardship, haven't you?"

Linaris placed her hand over Yuno's.

"…*Tee-hee*. We are a bit alike, don't you think?"

"I—I…"

The soft, delicate fingertips touched the back of Yuno's hand.

Simply looking at her beautiful face up close threatened to drive her mad.

"…I wouldn't know either way. I mean, I don't even know what you've been through, either."

"Would you like to know?"

"Doesn't matter to me… It's not like I want to ask enough to impose about that sorta stuff anyway…"

Yuno already had her hands full with her own problems to begin with. She didn't want to get involved in anything more complicated than she already had, even if it involved Linaris.

"Miss Yuno…have you grown to hate me?"

"…If you're talking about the thing with General Haade, I'm just as much to blame."

"Th-then in that case…"

Linaris awkwardly ran her hand through the hair on one side of her face.

"…would we…be able to become friends?"

"…Yeah."

Friends. Back when she lived ignorantly in Nagan, Yuno had friends as well.

Now…even after she had begun living in Aureatia, she didn't have a single friend her age.

"We might be able to do that."

"Oh, thank you so much."

Linaris smiled with a look of relief.

In this moment, Linaris…this pretty girl, as far removed from Yuno as the angels depicted in stories seemed just like any girl her age.

It's the same.

Just like Lucelles had once been.

Why—why does this girl?!

Yuno pulled Linaris's wrist. An angry urge that even she couldn't comprehend possessed her.

"*Hngh!*"

Linaris suddenly fell off-balance, the act bringing her flopping down on top of the bed with it.

Grabbing both of her wrists, Yuno placed one knee on top of her stomach.

"Wh-what...?"

"Why're you relieved?"

"M-Miss Yuno."

I need to always keep myself thinking solely about my revenge.

"I...! I'm Haade the Flashpoint's secretary, you know. My job might just be to sneak into your ranks like this and look for information. What, you hadn't imagined that?"

"*Koff*, th-that's not—"

The body Yuno pinned down was very slender.

It was difficult to claim Yuno had any physical strength to speak of, yet it was enough to hold Linaris down, and if she went any farther, she just might have snapped her neck.

"That goal of yours... *If you truly have to see it realized*, then you should've killed me immediately for knowing your secret! I would've done just that. I definitely...wouldn't be relieved or let down my guard, that's for sure...! I mean, I..."

"*Unh...*"

Eyes wet with tears were looking up at Yuno.

".......!"

If this girl really was part of Obsidian Eyes, then there was no reason why she couldn't dispatch a single young girl like Yuno. Some type of concealed weapon could surely do it, but there was also poison or drugs, like Linaris had used to make that one security guard faint. There was no way she didn't possess any means of resistance.

If this girl, Linaris, really was fighting with the same resolve Yuno had, then she should've been able to, at any moment.

"I...I was...just happy..."

"......"

"...that we...could become friends..."

"......! Sorry."

Yuno let go of her hands. Yet another fit of madness.

It wasn't that she wanted to hurt Linaris. Far from it, she might have even wanted to become friends with her herself.

Was it possible that, with her own hands, Yuno would only continue to sabotage and destroy any and all peace and tranquility she found?

"I'm sorry. I never... I never wanted to do anything like this. After looking at a letter like that, there's no way I could ever go back to General Haade again...so even I get that's why you trusted me and were honest with me, and yet...I—I...keep doing things, things even I don't understand."

The area around Linaris's neck was disheveled, and her porcelain collarbones peeked through.

All Yuno felt was a terrible sense of guilt.

"...*Koff.* Please don't let it bother you... I understand. It makes sense you might be shaken up and confused. For tonight...please give yourself a nice long rest, and then...please carefully think over yourself and your situation."

Yuno tried to come up with something to say, but she couldn't.

Linaris turned back around once and smiled weakly as she walked away.

"Good night."

◆

A young minia man had been standing right next to the door to Yuno's bedroom.

The man didn't have any distinguishing features, but he held a drawn long sword in his hands. His name was Hyakrai the Tower, of Obsidian Eyes.

"M-my lady. Are you all right?"

"Yes."

Exiting the bedroom, Linaris sheepishly dropped her eyes.

"You caught quite an embarrassing moment of mine."

"Y-Yuno the Distant Talon...should be disposed of. How awful... She's mad. At that moment, i-if she had stretched her hand out to your neck, my lady...I—I would have c-cut off her head, whether you ordered me to or not. Y-you should've put a stop to such violence...yourself, my lady."

"......Perhaps, that is indeed...what I should've done. I apologize for making you worry, Master Hyakrai."

Yuno wasn't aware of it herself, but she, too, was already one of Linaris's corpses.

A mutant strain, capable of airborne infection, and the only example of such in all the vampires' history. Anyone who got close to Linaris the Obsidian, even once, would become a corpse, regardless of whether Linaris wanted them to or not. With a single order from Linaris, the parent unit, she could prevent a corpse from any and all movement or stop their natural respiration and cause them to die. That was what it entailed to be under the control of a vampire.

...Not yet.

Linaris touched the base of her neck.

...We may still be able to remain friends. Not yet—just for a little while.

Like Shirok the Sextant and Miluzi the Coffin Edict. Or like the possibility that once existed with Kuuro the Clairvoyant.

"M-my lady...is too kind. Those types of scum always turn traitor... E-even if right now, she doesn't intend to do so, her true feelings will change at moment's whim. Because her mind is weak. I...I know those types well."

"You might be right. Still...until that time comes, and she truly turns on me..."

They were all Obsidian Eyes. Dwellers in darkness who would mercilessly run through anyone in order to save their comrades in arms.

That was exactly why discarding and abandoning comrades was something to be feared. Linaris believed so.

"...Miss Yuno is my friend."

Or was it nothing more than a selfish wish, contrary to her father's ambitions?

Separate from the apartment building he rented from Dant, Hiroto the Paradox had a specialized office in Aureatia's upper-class residential area. He had secured this reception room, equipped with ultra-luxurious sofas and other furniture—high enough quality to avoid any bad impressions—along with an endless supply of tea and snacks, first thing after he joined the Sixways Exhibition.

The Gray-Haired Child. Hiroto the Paradox's strength was that he only battled in a domain where he excelled. As long as he had a negotiating room, where conversations couldn't be heard and which he could use at will, it would serve as a far more effective resource for Hiroto than any military force or information.

Though he was under Dant the Heath Furrow's surveillance at all times, Hiroto invited many people to this room, from bureaucrats to shop owners, and continued to expand his circle of acquaintances in various forms.

Now an opportunity to use this reception room in the middle of a Sixways Exhibition match had come.

Right as the match between Soujirou the Willow-Sword and Ozonezma the Capricious was occurring, Soujirou's sponsor—

Aureatia's Twenty-Seventh General, Haade the Flashpoint—requested a meeting with Dant.

"I know what you're aiming for in the first round."

They were the first words from Haade's mouth.

"Your hidden motive here is that if Ozonezma wins the match, you're going to immediately integrate my camp into yours... and under your guidance, you'll try to bring all the anti-Rosclay groups together."

Haade the Flashpoint was nearly the oldest member of the Twenty-Nine Officials, but he was still a titan who held a tremendous influence on the entire military. After Rosclay's faction, known as the reformation faction and which was scheming to abolish the monarchy, he was the leader of the second-biggest faction—the military faction.

Facing him on Hiroto's side of room were Hiroto the Paradox, who had a connection to the Free City of Okafu, and Twenty-Fourth General Dant, part of the smallest of all the factions, the Queen's faction. Finally, there was the goblin tactician, Zigita Zogi the Thousandth.

"Ozonezma's been part of your camp from the start. Am I wrong?" asked Haade.

"Indeed, Ozonezma the Capricious is part of our forces."

"...What the hell, Zigita Zogi?"

Zigita Zogi was the one to answer the question. He continued on, paying no heed to Dant's reprimanding.

"Come now, Master Dant. There's nothing to keep hidden at this point. Given that we did everything we could to repel such a massive amount of interference, it's only obvious he'd have an inkling toward who was providing Master Ozonezma his support. Besides, we need him to come to us with this conversation, and not to Master Ozonezma himself, too."

"So behind this cooperation between Ozonezma and Zigita Zogi is you, then?"

Haade then shifted his sights to Hiroto.

"The Gray-Haired Child… Heard quite a lot of rumors about you. Not all of them are good, either."

"Nevertheless, it is an honor that you would remember my name, my good sir Haade. I'm Hiroto the Paradox. I am also responsible for acting as a negotiation intermediary for times like this, under the Twenty-Fourth General. Let's talk."

Hiroto extended his right arm, and Haade accepted his handshake.

As he had the external appearance of a thirteen-year-old boy, Hiroto's hand was far smaller than Haade's.

"You're a visitor after all, eh? Your hands are young. Even with leprechauns and elves, a hand's age doesn't lie."

"You're absolutely right. Shall I talk a bit about the Beyond, then? For example, in Aureatia now, you have steam-engine trains running, but—"

"Very kind of you, but I don't have time. I'll get straight to the point. A little while back, there were some number of Okafu's mercs who turned up dead—by the looks of it, there's someone out there slipping spies into different organizations. I want the Free City of Okafu, as a collaborator in the Sixways Exhibition, to take action and uncover these guys. Long and short is, I want Okafu to supply information."

"Of course, we would be thrilled to cooperate with the good General Haade himself. Am I safe to assume you will share the information from Aureatia's own investigation?"

"Sorry, but I can't do that. Long as we don't know who we're actually dealing with, best thing's to cut down any routes for information to slip out. So I'll offer up a bargaining chip instead. Sorry, this isn't from Aureatia, exactly, but…"

Haade kept up his stern visage as he spoke.

"…I'm fine with putting up a united front against Rosclay. If Soujirou loses this match, it'll get harder to defeat the guy politically either way. I want to join with your forces."

Hiroto observed Haade, never dropping his flawless smile from his lips.

They could absorb the second-biggest faction, Haade's camp, into their own. Given a confrontation with Rosclay's camp was inevitable, to Hiroto's camp, the deal was more than they could ever ask for.

The promise of lies and the truth both being revealed by logic was reason enough to go through with it. He needed to ascertain what the man wanted and what he was afraid of.

It's the opposite.

Without moving a muscle on his face, he traced his enemy's thoughts in the second before he answered with words of his own.

Haade's camp, or Kaete's camp. Or possible even Iriolde's. There is definitely a camp enacting a large-scale covert operation in this

Sixways Exhibition. Yet here is a request for a one-sided informa-
tion exchange in regard to that investigation. He's trying to confirm
Okafu's level of involvement by how I answer here. It doesn't seem
like he'll seriously follow through on his request. Then what is he
really asking for here? Haade first tried to verify our goal from the
third match. If Soujirou loses, he wants to join forces—if this con-
dition to the deal is the true request and he's just wrapping it up as
a bargaining chip, what does that mean? The first possibility that
comes to mind is that he has a plan that is guaranteed to absorb our
camp into his own. As for another possibility...Haade is trying to
win the first round by any means possible. In other words, he doesn't
necessarily need to have Soujirou as his candidate if he's able to get
the results he wants...

His brain went through his massive number of thoughts one
by one—he still didn't have enough information.

He would need to hear Haade give them additional answers
himself.

"These mysterious covert operatives. We have been referring to
this force as 'the invisible army.' Since there are some who appear
to be part of this invisible army within Okafu, we have just begun
conducting our own internal investigation. From the beginning,
we intended on sharing information regarding this subject if there
was anyone else who wished to get rid of this mutual enemy. Given
the need to prevent any leaks of information from Aureatia's investigation, it would be best not to join forces instead. As you just said
yourself, we have confirmed that spies have infiltrated Okafu as
well," said Hiroto.

Hiroto tried the most straightforward method of agitation. He only rejected the request that appeared to be the man's true objection.

"That's welcome news. But we still have to win the Sixways Exhibition, too. The worst outcome is while we're all busy dealing with this invisible army or whatever, Rosclay ends up winning the whole thing. If Ozonezma does get through the third match, he'll meet Rosclay in the second round. How're you planning on fighting him if that happens? Believe me, that guy's advancing through."

"...*Ha-ha-ha*. Fair enough. If we challenge him as an opponent in the second round, it will be the same as having Aureatia itself as an enemy. If you're taking that carefully into account with your proposal, that is very appreciated."

"Master Haade. Actually...in addition to your cooperation in the Sixways Exhibition, there's something we'd like to ask for, as collateral for the information from our investigation."

Zigita Zogi interrupted the conversation from the sidelines. He had purposely cut Hiroto off to ensure they weren't pressed for a clear answer about joining their forces. Hiroto understood that.

Haade puffed cigar smoke.

"I'll hear it out. What is it, then?"

"To get straight to the point, do you have any guesses at the true identity of this invisible arm?"

"Former Fifth Minister Iriolde the Atypical Tome," Haade immediately replied. He was one of the possible suspects whom Hiroto's group had previously considered. "He's a damn monster who's sat fat on top of this country's aristocrat class since the Central Kingdom era. Back then, there were people with his personal support in every damn government agency, and he knew everything that went on in the Central Kingdom, down to how many rats lived in the sewer. Might still be true now.

"But would such an influential player really stay retired from public life without trying to force himself into the Sixways Exhibition?"

"Just the opposite. Jel and Rosclay thoroughly crushed Iriolde to make sure he didn't get involved with it. Suspicion of corruption, unfair hiring practices—whatever it was, no lack of examples with the old bastard, see. Guess you could say he had it coming, but basically, it means Iriolde has his reasons to pick a fight with the Aureatia assembly."

"…I see. However, I have a differing opinion on the identity of this invisible army. I believe there is a chance our enemy is a unit of corpses being commanded by multiple vampires."

"…Vampires?"

"Indeed, the former Fifth Minister's influence is extremely powerful, and he might have many potential allies in many of the different factions. However, that still only concerns Aureatia. The invisible army has also infiltrated our forces in Okafu as well. Mercenaries without any involvement with Aureatia or the old Central Kingdom. There are several examples, in other organizations beyond our own, of people disappearing after exhibiting suspicious behavior. When comparing those names, none of them had any relation to the other— No. *The correlating factor that they were all unrelated was far too obvious to ignore.* In other words... we can look at this enemy of ours as possessing a means to freely flip a random target into a spy."

"With vampires, the most recent example would be Obsidian Eyes. So for instance, you think Zeljirga the Abyss Web is able to set up this massive conspiracy? While performing in the street?"

"No."

"If so, it would mean that there is a powerful parent unit among the remnants that Enu the Distant Mirror failed to slay."

"That's one possibility. However, given what we know of vampire biology, creating this number of corpses in such a short time clearly doesn't add up. Therefore, as of right now, our realistic explanation is the existence of multiple parent units."

"That's an intriguing idea. So this thing you want as collateral for our collaboration—it's got something to do with that?"

"That's right. In order to investigate further into this enemy of ours, I would like to receive the vampire antiserum."

"...Hmm, I see."

Before the era of the True Demon King, their continent had a history of waging wars against vampires. It was in that era when a vampire antiserum formula was discovered. It was technology that hadn't cropped up on the goblins' new continent, where Zigita Zogi and the others had been born.

"I'd love to share some with you, but it'll be tough, to be honest. I don't really know much myself, but the ingredients needed to manufacture it are unique, and apparently, there's a limit to how much you can make at once. I think there's some number left over from the Central Kingdom era, but over half of the Twenty-Nine Officials still haven't even been inoculated yet. If we're going to push them aside and hand some over to you all instead, with my level of authority, the best I could do is one vial, maybe."

"…One vial," Hiroto answered in Zigita Zogi's stead. "That's plenty. If Zigita Zogi can be inoculated, then even in the worst possible situation, we will still be able to keep our organization functioning. One vial of antiserum. That will be the conditions for our deal."

Hiroto knew the rarity of vampire antiserum. A mere one vial—while terribly unreliable terms for the deal—was, in actuality, very difficult to obtain. He couldn't let this chance slip by.

"Then we're good on how to deal with the invisible army, right? Getting back on topic, what're you going to do about the Sixways Exhibition?"

"How are we going to fight in the second round—is that it?"

Hiroto pondered. Was he really supposed to answer right here that he would join forces with Haade? The general wasn't a simple enough man to let Hiroto keep his position ambiguous.

If the proposal was simply that he wanted power to oppose Rosclay, then Hiroto was definitely supposed to accept it. However, if that wasn't the case—he needed to confirm if he had some other hidden intentions as well.

"Incidentally, General Haade, there is something that's been on my mind."

"What?"

Hiroto didn't necessarily have a complete read on Haade.

However, he could ask questions that would lead him to the heart of the matter.

"How exactly did you intend on fighting in the semifinals?"

There was a brief silence.

Hiroto could feel in his skin that the atmosphere in the room had changed.

Haade opened one eye wide, then slowly took a puff of his cigar...before pushing it into the ashtray and extinguishing it.

"...I could I ask you lot the same question, couldn't I?"

"Tee-hee. You might be right there, but—"

Right at that moment, the reception room door opened. An older female staff officer entered the room and whispered something in Haades' ear. He frowned, standing up and donning the coat he had hung on the wall.

"There's been a slightly problematic incident. Someone's tried to steal a missive of mine at the castle garden. A castle garden soldier apparently cut him down, but the culprit resisted and cut the soldier's arm, too. Feels bad since I'm the one who dropped in, but I want to go back and question the soldier myself. I'll be sure to make it up to you."

"Tried to steal...? So spies were mixed in with your men, too, huh?"

"Yeah, Dant. Looks like they can slip in anywhere they want. *Invisible army*'s the perfect name for 'em. You better pay close attention yourself while the Sixways Exhibition is going on."

Haade, accompanied by his staff officer, departed the reception room.

Zigita Zogi slowly stuffed his cheeks with baked treats while he gazed out of the window at the carriage galloping off. He commented as if to himself. "That staff officer just now was readied ahead of time."

"True. Just a little bit more, and I felt like we could've gotten some important information out of him... The general's a shrewd man."

"What do you mean? You're saying he fabricated some incident to force the conversation to end?" Dant asked.

Dant cast doubt on their conversation for the first time.

Ostensibly, this was a meeting between Dant and Haade, but for their string of back-and-forths, Dant had stood silent with his arms crossed. He likely felt that when it came to Hiroto the Paradox's specialty, negotiation, it was best to not speak up unnecessarily.

"The incident itself is not a lie, I would say. Otherwise, he'd run into trouble when it was investigated later. However, even if there hadn't been such an incident, he must have prepared some sort of urgent topic ahead of time. So then that staff officer's entrance would've been a setup they had planned in advance just in case. He could've tapped a small radzio hidden in a pocket to signal her," said Zigita Zogi.

"...How do you know that? You didn't see him actually do that, right?" asked Dant.

"It's plain enough."

Hiroto answered the question this time.

"Right before he left, Haade pressed his cigar into the ashtray to put it out, correct? Unlike cigarettes, you don't normally snuff out cigar flames like that. You lean it against the ashtray and wait for it to go out naturally... Since even if a cigar's flame goes out, you can light it again and still smoke it. Haade knows this, of course—which means then that the moment before the staff officer came to him, he already didn't have any intention of smoking his cigar any further. That would signal that he knew he was taking his leave shortly."

"...I get it. You might be right there. Guess I should've known more about how you smoke a cigar, then. So that'd mean that the question about the semifinals was an inconvenient topic for Haade?"

"I can't say with one-hundred-percent certainty, but..."

It was because Haade felt it was a sign. That was how Hiroto perceived the reaction.

In regard to the question itself, Haade likely could've come up with any number of stopgap answers. However, he was scared of treading the waters that lay beyond it.

"Though there isn't anyone who can hope to best Master Hiroto during face-to-face negotiations. He likely understood that for himself. He hammered home the linchpin, the possibility of a collaborative relationship, and left... Although our side obtained more information, the conversation ended with him achieving his bare minimum goal, too. He's acting very carefully on one hand, but on the other, he's resolute. If Haade the Flashpoint intends to win against Rosclay in the second round—it seems he has some sort of big trick up his sleeve when the time comes," said Zigita Zogi.

"...A big one, huh," Dant bitterly murmured. "Big ambitions. Big goals. A mighty hero. That's all it is with him, and everyone else, too..."

◆

After this meeting, Ozonezma the Capricious lost. The all-powerful and horrible trump card that had been hidden even to Hiroto's camp was Ozonezma's own cursed past itself. As someone who knew the True Hero, he would eradicate all those who fraudulently claimed this achievement—realizing the very goal he had been risking his life for was a mistake, he chose to withdraw himself.

Dant visited Hiroto's room on the third floor of the apartment complex in order to give him the full account.

"Ozonezma lost."

"...So I heard."

"I want to ask you something. Did you think he was going to win?"

"With a relatively high probability, at that. To be honest, I'm having a hard time believing it myself."

Hiroto wore an almost bitter smile.

"So even the Gray-Haired Child can have poor judgment, huh?"

"Yes. Unfortunately."

For Dant, it was a complicated fact.

It certainly wasn't that Hiroto the Paradox had the strength to always calculate what was going to come and prepare for it. If anything, that was the tactician Zigita Zogi's area of expertise. Just having Hiroto the Paradox with him didn't mean he was always going to win.

But seeing him look upset by the reality of Ozonezma's defeat, Dant felt like he finally was able to spot a glimpse of humanity contained within the man before him.

"...I've wanted to ask this for a while."

Dant sat himself down in a chair.

Currently, Zigita Zogi wasn't with them. He was out conducting his own investigation ahead of the morrow's fifth match.

"What is your personal goal here?"

"Exactly as I've told you before. The resurgence of the goblins on this continent. A peaceful coexistence with the minian races."

"That doesn't answer my question. That's *Zigita Zogi*'s goal, isn't it?"

The main fighting power of their force—from the mercenaries of the Free City of Okafu, to even Ozonezma, who had been given a hero candidate slot—acted according to Zigita Zogi's strategies. In truth, the Gray-Haired Child, considered the biggest mastermind in modern history, didn't lead his camp at all and seemed devoted to simply assisting Zigita Zogi's plan instead.

"Would you be satisfied if I said it was out of pure self-interest? If I'm able to gain a seat of power during a critical era of reform, then I'll be able to create vested interest for myself, even long term."

"That's not it. If you were that materialistic, then we wouldn't be going through trouble like this. Even I can understand that."

"You've got me… I had decided to avoid speaking about this in front of my constituents, but…"

"……"

Hiroto vacantly stared out of the window and ran his eyes over the starlike gas lamps.

For a few moments, there was nothing but silence.

Then he gave a terrifying answer.

"…I don't have any."

Hiroto the Paradox let out a chuckle and then a sigh.

"…Excuse me?"

"It's the truth. I don't have any goal myself. A course for Zigita Zogi to reestablish the goblin race. A opportunity for Ozonezma to subjugate hero candidates. Securing a participation spot with your cooperation, General Dant, was simply to fulfill my commitments to help them with each of their different goals, and I myself don't intend to work on a goal that goes beyond my wishes as their supporter."

"…………"

"That's why I've been careful not to say it. *It sounds like a lie, doesn't it?* Constituents are funny in that they claim to want an upright politician, clean of any materialistic motivations, but inwardly, they firmly believe that such an individual can't possibly exist. That's why I am not trusted enough to speak truthfully about a goal like this."

"That's absurd…"

Dant tried to suppress the vertigo. It was inconceivable. Could there really be someone capable of behavior that essentially amounted to taking over the land's last great nation without goal or thought to any reward?

Still, Dant knew. Hiroto wasn't lying.

"So basically…that's all there is to it? Their battle in the Sixways Exhibition here is simply compensation to their supporter… and that itself is the result you're looking for?"

"…That's right. General Dant, what do you think a politician is?"

Hiroto picked up a piece on the strategic map, which was still spread out on the floor.

"Let us say that right here is an individual named *A*. He has a goal he wishes to achieve, but it would be difficult to accomplish with his strength alone… Conversely, there is someone he has absolutely no contact with right here, *B*. B has a separate goal of his own, but just like A, it will be impossible with his power alone."

"Hold on. What do you mean by 'A' and 'B'?"

"…Ah, right, well… Think of them as a type of symbol from the Beyond for now. Anyway, the two of them presently don't have any knowledge of the other's existence. If things stay that way, it'll mean neither of them will achieve their goal—that's where *C* appears."

In between the two pieces Hiroto lined up together, he placed a small additional piece.

"C can't do anything. He doesn't possess power that could help A or B, and he probably doesn't even have accurate knowledge regarding their goal at all. He's the weakest of all."

"You're saying that supposing A and C or B and C pooled

their power together, they'd still only be able to display the same amount of power as if they were alone?"

"That's right. However, C possesses a power that these other two don't. The weakest one among the three gathered is good friends with both A and B. Through C's intermediation, A and B form a brilliant cooperative relationship, and they can achieve both their goals. Perhaps, there might be a bit of compensation for C. The end result is that all three characters are able to become happy together."

"......"

"This C is a politician."

The sound of a carriage cantering down the faraway road faintly reached the pair. All was calm.

In the small apartment-complex room, where no other eyes could reach them, Hiroto was giving a speech to a lone listener.

"There are those who assert that a politician needs to have charisma that attracts others, proper knowledge and strategy, conversation skills to prevent any slip of the tongue, and a grand vision of the future. This understanding is mistaken. It's best to pass things off to those capable of such feats. I believe that the only power a politician requires is the ability to become friends with anyone. Connecting through personal relationships those seeking power for their goals and those who can lend power for their goals—for that, a politician's will isn't required and won't have any problems, whatever the goal may be. Since it is the politician's supporters who should decide that."

"Basically, this is what you're getting at... Hiroto the Paradox.

One, you alone were born a politician. And two, as a politician, you're not doing anything out of the ordinary."

"If the people desire an honest and upright politician with no self-interests, then that is the politician they will get."

Hiroto the Paradox's outward appearance was young. However, there was no mistake that he had lived longer than Dant.

A visitor's age was their age when they were driven from the world of the Beyond.

Had he recognized the structure of society through this viewpoint of his all while in his early teens?

"That is nothing more than extreme populism. If you keep chaotically realizing your supporters' wishes, then society will eternally stagnate. If you're not lying right now, then I think what you're describing is a truly nightmarish politician," said Dant.

"Perhaps. However, I'm able to choose for myself who to receive support from as well."

"……"

The Queen's faction, which Dant belonged to, was the weakest in all Aureatia, and it generally would've been the very first group stamped out during the Sixways Exhibition.

And yet…regardless of the actual circumstances at play, Dant was still able to keep fighting. He was borrowing the power of goblins, mercenaries, and this mysterious visitor politician.

Was that really all because Hiroto had chosen for himself whom to make his ally?

"…Hiroto the Paradox. I heard you created a goblin nation-state."

"That's right."

"Why did you decide to ally yourself with goblins?"

Hiroto was, without any doubt, a minia. When he came from the Beyond, minian civilization was surely the first one he came into contact with. Allying with one of the minian-eating monstrous races—and, in addition, leading the goblins, with their strikingly low intelligence, to common sensibilities—was an inconceivable judgment to make.

"That's…something I don't fully understand myself, actually."

Hiroto laughed a bit and looked at his own hands.

It wasn't clear where exactly Hiroto the Paradox's deviance as a visitor lay. Was it his silver tongue? His negotiation skills? A mentality that didn't possess any desire of his own?

"I thought that *would make them better*."

Or was it a different, far more fundamental ability?

"Make them better? You're saying that there was such room to improve among the goblins back then?"

"Yes. Undoubtedly… General Dant. Why were the goblins driven away from this continent?"

"Don't ask me questions you already know the answer to. Because they caused harm to minian races and ate them."

"In that case, what about goblins who don't eat humans?"

"…What do you mean?"

The monstrous races ate the minian races. As long as this fundamental principle existed, the sort of new society Zigita Zogi and Hiroto aimed for, where they would coexist together, could never arrive.

However, as long as Hiroto's committed pledge to Zigita Zogi didn't waver, it meant the means did exist.

"Indeed. They've *gotten better.*"

He smiled in the darkness.

"That problem has already been taken care of."

In Aureatia's seedy canal town, there was a tavern called the Cellar Steer.

A tavern without the hint of any glamorous performances that simply served cheap liquor. A year ago, the owner's daughter had played on a shoddy clavier, but she was wedded to someone in Toghie City, and the customers had dwindled from yesteryear.

Nevertheless, there still remained some number of strange birds that enjoyed this semibasement, gloomy, and dust-covered interior, and the scoundrels sitting in their seats, conversing together, were very much the type.

"It ain't no arrow! I know this. This thing's called a 'heart,' see... *Hee-hee*, you know. Like in your chest."

"No heart looks anything like this. You sure?"

"Wait, so this rounded area at the top's 'posed to be the atrium? Those visitors got some weird sensibilities, ain't they?"

"But thanks to me bein' here, now ya know, right? One of the trading partners with my little brother's shop? They got themselves one, a visitor. I'm positive. That's a heart."

"Fine, fine, I get it. We'll say it's a heart, then. The club's a tree mark. The diamond's a jewel. All right, so what the hell's a spade?"

"This looks even more like an arrow than the heart, yeah?"

"You dumbass, it's got to have some sorta object it's based off, like the other three, right? It ain't an arrow."

"Is it a tree or something?"

"That'd overlap with the club, right? Y'know, way I see it, there's gotta be a 'spade' thing shaped like this. Over there in their world, see."

There was a voice that cut into their worthless conversion.

"Looks like you're having fun."

The three stopped their conversation, looked over at the new customer, and realized it was a face they recognized.

A construct wrapped up in rags.

"...Hey there, Sound Slicer."

"Got some fun news or something, did ya, Sound Slicer?"

"Who's to say? Is that some game from the Beyond you got there?"

His white fingers picked up the card. The joints were exposed as well, and they were pure white in the truest definition of the word.

His name was Shalk the Sound Slicer. An empty frame that still lived on after losing his life and memories—a skeleton.

"We found it on the job this morning. We're using 'em for a new gambling game."

"Color cards would be way more fun for gambling, won't they? The quality of the Beyond's games is pretty hit-or-miss."

"Oh yeah, of course, but who doesn't want a bit of a change now and then?"

"What're you here for?"

Shalk pulled a chair from a neighboring table and sat down.

"My match is coming up and all. So now I'm looking for the rundown on the hero candidates. Any of you see some of the matches up until the fourth match?"

"That'd be me. Saw the first, second, and fourth."

"I only saw the third and fourth."

"I saw the second, the fourth…and maaan, I *bought* tickets for the fifth match, too. Even got my girl a seat."

"*Heh-heh*, that's awful!"

"Did you get your money back?"

"Nope. Elpcoza Peddler's are the worst, I swear. I ain't ever buying their stuff again; you can count on that."

There were some who laid out complex and mysterious conspiracies in order to investigate the strengths and weaknesses of the sixteen hero candidates.

However, Shalk the Sound Slicer took a simpler and more certain approach. In vast Aureatia, there were countless audience members who had seen the Sixways Exhibition for themselves. There were more than a few who had bought Aureatia citizenship just to watch the latest royal games. He just needed to hear their witness accounts straight from the horse's mouth.

There was also a reason he picked these sorts of taverns while he wandered about. These kinds of scoundrels worked jobs of a similar class as the construct mercenary, and few of them had any aversion toward other races. On top of that, they also hosted a clientele who could observe the match with the eyes of a warrior.

Ever since he had made contact with Tu the Magic at the Blue Beetle, Shalk had been putting a lot of work into this honest information gathering of his. Of course, Shalk's movements had probably already been leaked to the smarter candidates—but there wasn't any major issue with his own information getting out there.

He didn't have any relationships, like family or friends, that would be put in danger if targeted, and even if an enemy appeared right before his match to try assassinating him or injuring him, he thought he could just handle it when it happened. Shalk the Sound Slicer's strength was he could still *make it with time to spare*, even if he moved after his opponent.

"Did you buy seats, Sound Slicer? Even though you're a hero candidate yourself?"

"I watched all of them except the second match. And the fifth, too."

"What happened with the second match?"

"I was omitted from the caravan lottery. Probably didn't want to let a dead body on board and get mistaken for a funeral car. The date for the second match, I had a forced march anyway."

"For that one, I just gotta pat myself on the back."

A stocky ruffian smacked his chest proudly.

"I had a car booked before the first match and made arrangements to get on the next ride out there. I'm the biggest winner outta this gang, eh?"

"...It was the second match where everyone got evacuated

midfight, right? They tacked that onto the caravan booking fee, so you lost out."

"*Bah*, you're too stingy about what really counts—that's your problem! We're talking Lucnoca the Winter here! I ain't seen anything like that breath of hers…! I even got a look at Alus the Star Runner's treasures, too!"

Three glasses were brought over to them. Drinks Shalk had ordered.

Putting them in front of the three as a gift, he continued his questions.

"If those eyes of yours aren't hollow holes like mine here, then you're probably the best to ask about the second match. Before that, though, how'd the first match look to you?"

"Ahhh, that fight? Toroa the Awful's enchanted swords ended up being the real deal after all. He had a whole lineup of enchanted swords, and despite it all, he got trounced by a lowly ooze—"

"Oh yeah?"

"—least, that's what some bums are spouting. That's where I come in. I saw everything real clear. Those techniques ain't something you learn through regular sword training, I'll tell ya that. You think if he was in front of ya, you'd catch his movements when he was switching out swords? Honestly made my blood run cold."

"I agree there. During that match, Psianop's ability to read Toroa's movements was frighteningly precise. It felt like no matter what enchanted sword he swapped to, the ooze seemed able to handle every technique and characteristic they had. That might be that guy's strength."

Shalk improved his estimations of the large man in front of him, too. Given that he was able to verbalize the main strength of Toroa in the match, Shalk might be able get some helpful information about the second match from him as well.

Shalk turned the conversation to include the gloomy man sitting beside the larger one.

"You're the one who saw the third match."

"I'm not a big fan of these types of events, but...I have a personal debt to the Fourteenth General and used that connection for a chance to watch."

"Then let me ask you about that match..."

"............"

"...Can't help feeling like the story around that match's off. You're not the only one. The others I went and met with tonight were the same, and I'm the same. The match should've been an impressive spectacle, too. What was it?"

"...I don't really want to think about it."

"Ozonezma the Capricious."

At first, for the third match, Shalk had turned his attention toward Soujirou the Willow-Sword—a deviant visitor he had briefly crossed swords with during the Lithia War. Throughout his entire life, this man was the only one who had ever been able to *cross swords* with Shalk the Sound Slicer straight on.

He thought the match was going to be a good opportunity to see his skills one more time—right up until the actual start of the match.

Soujirou's opponent, Ozonezma the Capricious, was the strongest chimera in the land. That was clear.

An innumerable number of arms that seemed to blaspheme the minian form. Knife-throwing skills that launched the blades like beams of light. Detaching his physical body.

…Still, though, Shalk the Sound-Slicer thought:

Is all that really something to be scared of at this point? When I'm a dead body already.

Shalk had tried to search for the true identity of this fear, but he had yet to meet anyone who could accurately guess the reason behind it.

In any event, Ozonezma lost. Certainly not an unwelcome result for the remaining hero candidates.

Appearing unable to bear the silence that'd changed the atmosphere at the table, the shorter man chimed in.

"Let's talk about the fourth match."

"Aw, yeah, this is what I've been waiting for! Rosclay really is the greatest guy in the world, huh? Can't believe he stuck it out through all that."

"Yeaaaah, I don't know. I keep saying this, but he should've cut Kia down before he got his legs broken. I don't know what sorta ne'er-do-well was using the poor girl, but an accomplice's still an accomplice. Rosclay's dumb."

"'Scuse me? Did I just hear the dumbest thing I've ever heard? What's wrong with saving a kid's life? Go ahead, enlighten me."

"Liiiisten, the enemy factored that in and chose a girl like Kia on purpose to send out there! Him not killing Kia meant he ended up caught in their trap!"

"...Wait, wait. In the end, who was behind it all in the first place? That's what I'm curious about."

"I don't know, but the Iznock school comes to mind immediately, given the sorta deranged Word Arts she was capable of...but even they're not that good, right? The assembly hasn't made an official announcement, either."

"Who cares? The important thing is that Rosclay managed to hold out against that sick Word Arts attack. Without harming the kid at all the whole time, to boot. He knew the real enemy he was supposed to defeat. That's a true champion right there. Now, who was this big-shot asshole who had the gall to complain about that? Huh?"

"I get it... Fine, fine. I'll apologize. Esteemed General Rosclay is a true champion. I'll treat you to some pork sausage or something, so c'mon, cheer up."

"*Tch*...you just wanna eat some for yourself."

...*Absolute nonsense.*

Shalk didn't have anything regarding the fourth match that was worth bringing up. In regard to Rosclay's match, he merely thought that the man had desperately done the best he could to win out in the end.

It was a mystery what sort of mechanism the young girl Kia had utilized to accomplish those attacks of hers. Thus, between the two, Kia was no doubt the more troublesome one to have advance into the next round.

Rosclay had overturned what should have been a complete

and certain victory and advanced on instead while being heavily injured in the process. All things considered, Rosclay could probably say it was a fortunate result.

As for the one who lost, though...is it really okay not to think about that yet?

If Kia herself was capable of such tremendous Word Arts—not that Shalk himself believed she could be at all—the possibility she could still be out there somewhere in Aureatia might end up being incredibly dangerous.

The next was the fifth. Shalk had some questions about Tu the Magic as well. Their relationship started and ended with the brief conversation they had at the Blue Beetle, but Tu that day appeared to possess an invincible body and spirit.

That same Tu was supposed to have cowered at the true duel and refused to appear in the fifth match. Shalk had no way of knowing what had actually happened.

...I'm the seventh match.

It was likely simple luck. Shalk the Sound Slicer, his match coming later down the line, had been given the chance to look over the whole picture of the Sixways Exhibition.

This battle wasn't a simple clash of combat prowess. If his match had come sooner, he might have been defeated without even learning that much.

...I probably should've thought through my moves a bit more carefully, huh.

◆

There was a man lying in wait at the top of the stairs to the surface when Shalk exited the establishment. The man held an umbrella, and the skeleton realized it had begun drizzling while Shalk was in the tavern.

He was a plump man with a mysterious machine of some kind hanging from his neck.

"What?"

Shalk wasn't so reckless as to make an attack without saying a word. He'd merely called out to the man, sounding annoyed.

"Oh, okay if we chat, then? Do you have time?" asked Shalk.

"All I asked you was 'What?'"

"Hmm, well, let's start with introductions, then. My name is Yukiharu the Twilight Diver. As far as *what* I am, I suppose that would be a news reporter. How exactly would you like me to answer that?"

"......I'll rephrase. What do you want?"

Yukiharu the Twilight Diver. If this man was who he claimed to be, he was the land's apex information broker, known even in Okafu. There were also rumors that given his abnormal gifts of survival, treading through all sorts of certain death to grab his information, perhaps he was, in fact, a visitor from the Beyond.

"Mister Shalk the Sound Slicer. There is someone who wishes to employ you."

"Depends on who and for what. Go on."

"The commission comes from the Gray-Haired Child. The job would be searching for hidden vampires and corpses."

"...Vampires? In this day and age, and here, in Aureatia?"

"Ah, right, vampires are seen as a frontier epidemic, aren't they? Still, this commission is completely serious. There are suspicions that there's a source of vampiric contagion active here in Aureatia, and their corpses have infiltrated several organizations, including the Aureatia army."

"The pay?"

"Information regarding the True Hero."

"……"

"…How does that sound?"

Shalk stopped walking and turned around toward Yukiharu for the first time. A friendly smile. Save for the apparatus around his neck, he looked like any other rotund man he could find on any street corner.

"Sounds like…you've looked into me pretty well."

"The New Principality of Lithia, then the Free City of Okafu. You're roaming between the countries of self-proclaimed demon kings because you're searching to see if there are any traces of the Hero left in the Final Land, yes?"

Shalk the Sound Slicer didn't know who exactly he was himself.

It was said that the hero who killed the True Demon King had yet to be found. Even their body.

Ever since this skeleton life of his began, terror and irritation would stir in his empty chest whenever he heard the word *hero*.

"No thanks."

"…May I ask the reason why?"

"Because I'm participating in the Sixways Exhibition. I've accepted a job from my sponsor to advance through this tournament. See, I don't really want to take on two overlapping commissions."

"I understand. Well, that's fine. I didn't think you'd be immediately receptive to the idea."

Yukiharu waved his hand back and forth.

It was almost as if he had known Shalk was going to answer this way.

"...If you're really Yukiharu the Twilight Diver, this is a great chance. Let me ask you something."

Shalk looked up at the sky, covered in thick clouds.

The light from the gas lamps illuminating the road flickered and twinkled, perhaps a side effect from the rain.

"Have you ever...tried to search for who the Hero is?"

"...Outside the Final Land, yes. However, the timing of the True Demon King's death is a bit vague. I couldn't even collect eyewitness accounts about if someone was heading toward the Final Land or not. It's natural, really. There wasn't anyone still sane around there."

"In that case, just a guess is fine. If there was indeed a True Hero...then what does the world's premier information broker, Yukiharu the Twilight Diver, think he was like?"

"......Shalk. In both Lithia and in Okafu, you always postponed your reward, information on the Final Land, until the last minute. You could've even gone there on your own two feet, after all. In my eyes, you seem to be searching for the Hero *as though you're making sure you absolutely never find them.*"

"...That's how it looks to you?"

He was right. Shalk should have wanted to know the truth more than anyone else, but at the same time, he wished for the exact opposite.

Yukiharu laughed cynically.

"*Ha-ha.* It's not just you, Shalk. In truth, everyone has understood for a long while…and are just pretending they don't. I mean, am I wrong? The more you know about the terror of the True Demon King, the more *obvious it becomes*, doesn't it?"

It was said that the hero who killed the True Demon King had yet to be found. Even their body.

Perhaps this wasn't because no one had been able to find them, but instead…

"The True Hero is *terrifying.*"

It was over ten years ago.

At Sine Riverstead, there was an area called the Needle Forest that had been there for a long, long time. Thick metal pillars stuck out from the hill like a grove of trees, and when one gazed up at the hill from the village, it looked like a mountain of needles.

Mele the Horizon's Roar was always in the Needle Forest. He'd sleep like a log for however long he wanted to and stay sprawled out as he gazed up at the shapes of the clouds. If someone came to visit from the village, he would begrudgingly keep them company.

On that day, there was a child visiting Mele from the village.

"Why're you sleeping?"

The child was named Misna. The young boy's personality made it hard for him to fit in with the other children, and he always did everything alone.

Wearing glasses so thick that they seemed to be little more than shaved-down lumps of glass, he held a grammar book of the Order's script underneath his arm. Mele had heard he was the cleverest kid among the village children. Not that Mele seriously remembered that sort of small stuff.

"I can sleep or get up whenever I damn well feel like it. Ahhh...
Noon already?"

In truth, Mele had been awake for a little while at that point.
He just felt too bothered to get up and simply found himself want-
ing to watch the sky's color change for a little while.

Such days continued on for a spell after the Demon King Army
had passed by Sine Riverstead.

"...Why didn't you fight, Mele?"

"......"

Mele scratched his neck, not understanding the intentions
behind the remark.

Misna's words were often perplexing, in a different way from the
other young children, and he never knew how to approach them.

"Everyone is saying that you're a champion who saved our village. I don't think so at all."

"Oh yeah, that right? Well, doesn't make a difference to me
what a runt like you might think about me."

—One small month earlier, this village had been threatened
with annihilation.

The True Demon King and the Demon King Army, which
accompanied them, had surged up close to the village's border.
The beasts in the forest began to go mad, and bodies were found
of birds and rabbits tangled up together and eating one another.
A large number of deer had thrown themselves into the river, and
the villagers had locked up their doors and windows in several
layers to ensure none of the children accidentally laid eyes on the
Demon King Army.

It was only a matter of time before the madness spread to the residents of Sine Riverstead.

There was very little Mele could do. He had simply stood on top of the hill and glared at the Demon King Army.

The gigant, who had been lying on his back for two hundred and fifty years, kept his colossal black bow ready to fire at a moment's notice and remained standing there from before sunrise to long after sunset.

It continued like this for several days. The villagers were worried for Mele, who was no longer eating or cracking lighthearted jokes, but they, too, remained unable to do anything in the face of the surging terror.

The tension seemed close to rending the village itself apart.

…And then they passed on by.

The Demon King Army went around the small village and headed off toward some other place.

"Listen here, go home and take a nap yourself. Me, I can barely keep these eyes open," said Mele.

"…Is it true that you're the one who stops the flooding every year?"

"Hell if I know. I'm just practicing with my bow."

"They say that you're the one who shoots down all the wyverns that come to the village."

"It's my food. I ain't handing any of my grub over to you guys."

Misna looked up at Mele, tears filling his eyes.

In contrast to his matter-of-fact tone, his face seemed to be mixed with anger and frustration.

"…If you're so strong, why didn't you fire any arrows?"

"Hah?"

"The True Demon King was nearby. You could've killed them. If you had just shot them, everyone would've been saved… Everyone in the world."

Still lying down, Mele absentmindedly extended out his dominant right hand, opening and closing it.

The True Demon King had come right up next to the village. If he had shot his arrow, it would've reached them.

Mele's arrows brought unilateral destruction, impossible to defend against. Even without precise knowledge of the True Demon King's whereabouts, he could've laid complete and utter waste to the entire topography itself.

Anyone should've been able to arrive at such a simple conclusion.

So why hadn't he been able to shoot?

"*Hah*, shooting arrows tires me out… It's a big pain in the ass, so I didn't."

"That's not it. You avoided it."

"……"

"Y-you were scared of the True Demon King and couldn't shoot your bow. You could've saved us all, but you didn't have the courage to do it!"

The True Demon King had annihilated the True Northern Kingdom.

In order to fight the terror threatening the world, the remaining two kingdoms had been gathering soldiers from all over the land and strategizing about how to eradicate the True Demon King.

What about luring them to a city deep in the mountains and burning the whole mountain down with them?

What about building moats and walls too big for the True Demon King to scale and isolating them?

What about throwing poison in the wells along their invasion route and making them run out of food and starve?

What about using an artificial pathogen or a giant army of constructs to take them down?

Perhaps this time, they would finally be able to defeat the True Demon King. Maybe, just maybe, there was still hope left in the world.

—Such attempts ended without accomplishing anything.

There were stories of operation commanders going mad. Stories of the soldiers suddenly deserting right before they were meant to enact their plan. Stories of citizens opposing things from a humanitarian perspective. Or in some cases, it was none of these things...and it simply faded naturally.

For some reason, no one was able to pull the trigger to destroy the enemy of all.

Any and all will to fight against this enemy was stolen. Unable to do what was needed, they found themselves doing what they shouldn't instead.

Anyone in the world, no matter who it was, no matter how far away they were, whether they were openly opposing them or not, would be forced to confront that terror. Such was the True Demon King.

I should've been able to fire.

In truth, Mele had awakened long before Misna's visit.

With his body lying down, he had continued to ponder the same thing over and over again.

The entire time, long after the Demon King Army had passed by Sine Riverstead.

All I could do was stand at the ready.

"You saved the village. But the Demon King Army... They went past this village and destroyed Gilano Forestland. My friend Yuren lived there."

"...Like I'd know. Don't give a rat's ass either way. Long as I get to protect my napping spot, that's good enough for me. Anywhere else's got nothing to do with me."

"B-but...all the adults... I-it's cruel! They treat you like a champion, and you couldn't shoot at all! When you know the truth better than anyone! And you're really fine with that?! Doesn't it bother you?!"

The villagers said that Mele had won. That the Sine Riverstead's guardian had driven off the Demon King Army.

—They were wrong. Mele had lost to the terror. For the first time, he hadn't been able to shoot at an enemy he needed to defeat.

If he just had a bit more courage. If he was just a bit stronger.

The Mele of the past might have been able to shoot the True Demon King. He couldn't help thinking so.

"I told you, I don't care, okay?! Enough of your shouting already—go home. I wanna get back to sleep already."

"I...I thought...that our Mele could've become a real hero...!"

"............"

Misna didn't say anything further, and his tiny back descended down the hill.

From the next day, Mele no longer saw Misna anywhere.

He heard later that the following day after his visit to Mele's hill, Misna boarded a caravan and left the village. That the boy had decided to study outside the village and fight against the True Demon King on his own.

However, that was all.

Since that True Demon King was never defeated by any champion.

◆

Several years passed by.

Mele remembered the day a single lone wyvern flew down to the Needle Forest.

Although a wyvern appearing in the Sine Riverstead was a somewhat rare occurrence, to Mele, it wasn't a matter worth remembering, and he nocked an arrow to his black bow just like always.

He didn't use one of the iron pillars in moments like this, when he was driving wyverns away. It was an arrow made with Craft Arts out of soil.

....

However, at the time, Mele kept his arrow nocked and waited until this wyvern perched itself atop one of the iron pillars sticking out of the mountain. He could tell that with this opponent, if they engaged in a fight, neither of them would make it out of the scrap unscathed.

—This wyvern had three arms growing from his body.

"……So you're Mele the Horizon's Roar…?"

His name was Alus the Star Runner. The strongest wyvern in the land, arrogating all the legendary treasures remaining in the world and crushing champions beneath him. His arrival always meant the end for the legends at his destination.

"And what if I am? Ain't got nothing here. 'Cept for me." Mele dauntlessly smiled yet replied in a low tone.

The fact that Alus the Star Runner had appeared meant Mele's turn had come.

A great number of this world's legends hadn't been able to take down this wyvern, but Mele the Horizon's Roar could do it.

Sine Riverstead was home to a peaceful people—for over two hundred and fifty years, no enemy had appeared worthy of Mele's full power.

Finally come here to do me in, eh? I'm happy to hear it, Alus the Star Runner.

He drew power into the hand holding his black bow. If he was going to attack, the sooner the better. With one shot, carved out from the hill, he'd scatter dirt and sand into the air and take away Alus's ability to fly freely. If Alus avoided it by flying low, he'd use a trajectory that'd send him down over the village's pastures—

"…………"

Mele was unable to fire.

Even though he was well inside his bow range, Alus the Star Runner stood stock-still atop a pillar and quietly observed Mele.

"......That bow. Is it strong...?"

"*Ha*, curious, are ya? I don't know who the hell out there made it or whatever materials they used, but this fella doesn't break no matter what. Gonna try stealing this, then, ya scaly pigeon?"

"...No thanks... Looks like a pain to carry around."

For this rogue, it was enough of a reason to give up on an item for his collection. On the other hand, it meant that were the black bow a weapon Alus could use, he would've absolutely stolen it from him.

"Besides, your real treasure...isn't that."

Alus craned his head and looked in the direction of Sine Riverstead.

"...What does it feel like?"

"You don't know a damn thing about me... What the hell are you here for, Star Runner?"

Mere didn't take his fingers off his arrow.

Mele was an ancient gigant warrior. He hadn't only fought against floods and wyvern flocks, but krakens and dragons as well. His proudest accomplishment was battling and winning against all such opponents, and nothing should have made him happier than to face off against a powerful opponent.

And yet—what would happen if he did?

He'd be forced to fight here, at Sine Riverstead.

He wouldn't have it any other way.

If you're looking for a fight, then I'll give ya just that.

There was a voice whispering to him the same question he had heard when the Demon King Army surged close to the village.

"What are you afraid of?"

Past Mele hadn't needed to protect anything. He had been able to throw his own life away if it was all for the thrill of battle. He was strong and courageous.

Until he had *laid down roots* here in Sine Riverstead.

…What the hell's that crap? Doesn't matter. Ain't got nothing to do with it.

He had spent the impossibly long years of his gigant life polishing his skills with the ultimate bow. He always hit his mark, and he always destroyed his targets.

But should Mele the Horizon's Roar fight with everything he had, what would then come of Sine Riverstead?

This small village couldn't hope to withstand his full fighting power. This place was an all-too-miniature village of minia, the gap in scale so vast that he was unable to live together with them. If the arc of his arrow grazed the ground, the village would be unrooted entirely, and if his colossal body ran through it, he'd crush both their houses and their fields.

It had been the same on that day when the Demon King Army was right in front of his eyes.

He became unable to do the very thing he had always wished for.

This gigant, more powerful than any other, could do exactly that simply by letting go of his finger.

And yet Mele the Horizon's Roar was scared.

"…………"

Alus didn't move. Did he think that Mele wouldn't shoot?

Or perhaps, Alus the Star Runner, having witnessed all the treasures across the land...had managed to see through to what type of treasure Mele now found himself needing to protect.

"I'll say it one more time. What...do you want?" asked Mele.

"...Nothing, really."

Alus turned his head in a completely different direction, as if Mele's existence was of no concern to him.

He didn't seem interested in the slightest with anything that didn't capture his interest.

...From the very beginning, he hadn't appeared there looking for a fight.

"I just wanted to ask you, that's all... What it feels like..."

"What *what* feels like?"

"Having a homeland...a country."

"...This puny village? Like hell it's any of that stuff."

Mele's true treasure wasn't this black bow he had from the time of the Wordmaker, nor was it the iron needles stuck into the mountain, nor even his pride as the strongest in the land. It had all been supplanted somewhere along the line.

Had the ancient gigant, while living under the standards of the small and weak, accidentally grown smaller and weaker himself as well?

He felt scared to lose this village.

"It ain't bad," Mele said, trying to laugh it off.

Sine Riverstead had been a shackle to him. In the Needle Forest, Mele continued to protect this village from the flooding that came once a year. As long as he was here, he would never be able to truly battle.

"It ain't bad, having a place you belong."

Nevertheless, he didn't want to blame the villagers for him growing weaker.

Sine Riverstead wasn't at fault at all. Things like this happened when one lived for a long time.

It wasn't bad. It was much, much better than fighting to his heart's content and annihilating the tiny village instead.

That's what he believed.

"...Really."

Alus flapped his wings wide. His visit to the Needle Forest had been for a remarkably trivial reason, purely just to ask Mele his question.

"Hey, Alus!" Mele shouted as Alus was taking his leave.

He asked a question like a past child had asked him once before.

"Why don't you fight?! If you're all about bringing down the world's legends, there's one of them who's a helluva lot bigger than the rest, right?! The strongest one out there, the one who no one's able to bring down!"

".......? ......Ohhh, you mean the True Demon King..."

Having conquered legends far and wide, this wyvern could've defeated such a person and become a hero. There may have been a lot of people who selfishly placed their hopes in Alus the Star Runner.

However, Alus didn't fight for anyone. He was always fickle and lived free.

His way of life was the exact opposite of Mele, who had chosen bondage for the sake of the villagers he needed to protect.

"The Demon King doesn't have anything, right…? No treasure…or place they belong. Defeating them's meaningless…"

The wyvern was right. The True Demon King was sure to be alone, without anything to protect.

His wings disappeared far off into the chartreuse sky, waiting for dusk.

The legend and the legend-slayer parted ways without a fight.

It had been Mele's sole chance in the past two hundred and fifty years.

"…*Heh*, he leaves with a sorry excuse like that?"

The gigant, left behind without anyone to fight, stayed standing alone on the hill.

Mele the Horizon's Roar, holding his true-shot bow, for the second time in his life, let his target get away.

◆

"Excuuuuse me! Where do you get off, sleeping past noon?!"

Then present day—a shrill voice echoed through Aureatia's gigant town.

Aureatia's Twenty-Fifth General, Cayon the Skythunder. He was Mele the Horizon's Roar's sponsor.

"Why, evening will be here soon!"

"Ah, pipe down, will ya?"

Mele the Horizon's Roar opened his eyes underneath a roof.

House though it was, it was plainly built, little more than a giant box, with four walls and a ceiling constructed in a rush. Compared with the other gigant staying in Aureatia's gigant town, he easily required four times as much area for himself.

"*Heh-heh-heh.*"

"*Heh-heh-heh* my foot! Are you still half asleep—is that it...? Have a dream or something?"

That was it. He had a dream. Long happy days, peaceful, and starved for battle.

"Well, see...how can I put it? Just let myself get a bit happy is all."

This wasn't Sine Riverstead. None of the small, weak friends he needed to protect were here, either.

He could be his strong former self, without anything to fear. Everyone had wished for it.

Sine Riverstead's colossal hero would be appearing in the seventh match. A true legend, spoken of together with Lucnoca the Winter. Mele the Horizon's Roar.

He had waited two hundred and fifty years for this chance.

"It ain't bad, having a place you belong."

The strong and powerful were gathering together.

Aureatia's Nineteenth Minister, Hyakka the Heat Haze, was sometimes called a young prodigy.

Looking from one side of things, that was a possible interpretation.

Hyakka the Heat Haze wasn't quite as young as Mizial the Iron-Piercing Plumeshade or Elea the Red Tag, and he didn't have either the superb brains of Hidow the Clamp or Quewai the Moon Fragment, nor the excellent physical abilities of Qwell the Wax Flower.

Hyakka's reason for being in his present position was due to a single occasion of good fortune.

In the past, there was a visitor named Luisa the Morning Dew. A self-proclaimed demon king, by spreading a new variety of wheat that was extremely tenacious and resistant to bugs and diseases, she completely changed the ecology of the eastern farmlands. On top of that, she brought tenant farmers with her when she seceded from Aureatia, creating a massive food crisis.

Negotiations with Luisa, appealing for a radical reformation to the system of farmland ownership, had broken down a number of times, and while a military clash seemed nigh unavoidable, the man chosen to serve as the diplomat was Hyakka. Lacking experience and given the job even when, by that point, the Aureatia assembly's policy had already been decided, there were even dubious voices suggesting he may have just been appointed to allow the former Twenty-Ninth Minister to flee from his responsibility in starting the war.

However, with his seat at the peace negotiations, little more than a formality at that point, the situation completely changed.

Luisa the Morning Dew seemed to take a one-sided fancy to something in Hyakka's personality and what he said. Things went almost absurdly smoothly from that point until both sides reached peace... Hyakka was thought to have *exceptional executive abilities* that brought with them great successes—the reason behind such successes being a mystery to Hyakka himself until he was sworn in as the Nineteenth Minister, in charge of the agricultural division.

I was simply lucky.

It was Hyakka's custom to admonish himself with this mantra.

Aureatia's Twenty-Nine Officials were a realm where bureaucrats, far more capable than him, exerted influence over minian race politics. It was inconceivable to think something convenient specifically for Hyakka would occur a second time.

In which case—his next accomplishment absolutely needed to be through his own efforts. That was what he believed.

There was an opportunity to do just that, too. The Sixways Exhibition.

He had single-handedly found the nameless skeleton mercenary who'd slayed *the* Kazuki the Black Tone.

Luckily, the end of the war with the Free City of Okafu was a big part of it as well. It allowed him to sponsor Shalk the Sound Slicer, a former Okafu mercenary, as a hero candidate.

However.

"Shalk the Sound Slicer!"

He called out the name of his hero candidate right as he threw the door open.

The room was in a luxurious inn in Aureatia's central district. Shalk the Sound Slicer was leaning up against the back wall and gazing outside the window at the night cityscape.

Hyakka brought both legs together, adjusted his posture, and looked up Shalk, who was taller than the minian man.

"I heard! You were apparently present during the violent fracas at the Blue Beetle?! Why can't you immediately report that sort of stuff to me?! It's outrageous that I, your sponsor, am not being informed of what's happening with his own candidate without hearing about it from other officials!"

"...A fracas? That's the phrasing you all use for a minor scrape like that, eh?"

Shalk the Sound Slicer's skull face had no expression. This was just as true whenever he joked and spoke sarcastically.

"I'll be more careful next time, but should I 'immediately report' to you stuff like a rock in the road someone could trip over or if the booze I ordered is out of stock, too?"

"D-don't... Don't belittle me, thank you very much!"

Hyakka sat down at the table in the middle of the room, poured himself a drink, and held his cup in both hands, taking a big gulp.

This room was rented by Hyakka the Heat Haze as well. After investigating the crime and safety in the surrounding districts, as well as the level of service each inn showed their lodgers, he had picked one that was also equipped with perfect security protections. However, all that effort seemed totally useless to this guest himself, who would go out walking the city streets night in and night out.

"Don't get too rowdy with the alcohol now," said Shalk.

"I should be asking you to stop trouncing around to different taverns when you can't even drink yourself! Especially the haunts of the low-class scoundrels! Are you trying to degrade the hero candidates' integrity?!"

"I've got my own way of thinking about things. That and I don't have a lot of fond memories associated with inns like this."

Shalk had never shown any interest in the high-quality bottle of alcohol the inn provided every night.

Obviously, he wouldn't. Skeletons didn't need food or drink and may not have needed a safe place to stay at all. Hyakka was only able to able to provide him with lodgings based on minia standards of quality.

"I'm sure you can fend off the likes of a petty thief, but the ones seriously out to assassinate you aren't gonna hesitate. If you value your life, I wouldn't be dropping by this room too much."

Hyakka silently drained the next glass.

For him, he had wished for his hero candidate to be nothing more than a tool.

However, it was then he was faced with nothing but an all-too-reasonable reality... Someone possessing power that far eclipsed his own was never going to obediently serve under him as his tool in the first place.

Shalk the Sound Slicer didn't want anything.

Neither food, women, nor money could be used as a bargaining chip against the dead.

Hyakka couldn't even imagine it. How were the other sponsors controlling their own hero candidates?

"...Dammit, damn it all."

"You okay? You're not gonna tell me you can't hold your liquor after chugging it down like that, right?"

"Wh-what...does it matter to you?!"

◆

"What, Hyakka? Come to kvetch at me again, have you?"

A noontime café. The man sitting in a seat on the terrace was the Fifteenth General, Haizesta the Gathering Spot.

"That's not it!"

Hyakka got the sense he was constantly being tormented by misbehavers like the man in front of him. It had always been like this, before he even got involved with Shalk the Sound Slicer.

"General Haizesta! Just today, I had *multiple* women come up to talk with me! There've been six complaints as well! And for some reason, all of them came to me! Do you realize how much trouble this is causing for me?!"

"Oh, six complaints, eh... *Nyeh-heh-heh.* I tried seducing eight today, but if that's the case, that means two showed some interest. Ain't bad."

Haizesta's voice and laugh were always lower-pitched, even lower than a male opera singer.

He was uncouth, with a large frame. A military officer who gave the completely opposite first impression compared with small and fidgety Hyakka.

"It is bad! First of all, all six of the people who came to see me were *married*! Four among them even had grandchildren! I cannot fathom how such a frivolous and irresponsible man like you ended up in the Twenty-Nine Officials!"

"See, you're kvetching after all... *Nyeh-heh-heheheh.*"

As it was for almost all the military officers among the Twenty-Nine Officials, Haizesta the Gathering Spot, too, had been included in their ranks thanks to his past battlefield achievements. However, there was a fundamental problem with him as a government official: his terrible behavior.

Thus, there were not very many, even among the other Twenty-Nine Officials, who willingly involved themselves with Haizesta. Hyakka had never seen anyone besides himself lecture the man about his behavior straight to his face.

Despite being over a decade younger than the man, for some reason, this responsibility had landed on Hyakka's shoulders.

"First of all, General Haizesta, what are you even doing during the day? I'm always the one who's forced to figure out where in hell's name you are and whether you're goofing off or actually working!"

"C'mon, I'm doing a bunch of stuff on my end, too, okay... The Sixways Exhibition's bound to get interesting from here, lemme tell you."

"This isn't the time to kick back and enjoy yourself!"

At this point, it wasn't public knowledge that Haizesta the Gathering Spot was, in fact, part of Kaete's camp and actively working behind the scenes. In Hyakka's eyes, he simply came off as an even lazier man than he thought he was.

Hyakka placed both hands on the table.

"Even if you're not a sponsor, you should address the situation seriously! The Sixways Exhibition is an extremely important true duel event, with the future life of Aureatia on the line!"

"Your promotion's on the line, too, and all."

"That's right! Wait, no, that's not it! I—I simply believe that being royal games, we should be even more disciplined than usual! And yet Shalk will go outside without my permission, and there's delinquents like you lying around, too..."

"Ohhh. So you want your hero candidate to obey your orders, too, huh?"

"Yes! Wait, no, that's not the point here! Gaaah, I give up!"

"You're a goody-goody, but still a real worldly fella, aren't you?"

Normally, this wasn't the time to trouble himself with a man like Haizesta. His present problem was Shalk the Sound Slicer.

On top of it, once he got control of Shalk, he'd have to put him up against the legendary champion, Mele the Horizon's Roar, and he needed to win. It was his sponsor, Hyakka, who needed to think about how exactly to make that happen.

"...*Nyeh-heh-heheheh.*"

"What are you laughing at now...?"

Hyakka groaned, with his face flat on the table. This was a battle that no one else had ever experienced before. There wasn't anyone out there who could tell him how he was supposed to fight it.

"What...am I supposed to do?"

"Good question."

Haizesta let out a big yawn.

"I mean, you handled the arena situation pretty well, right? Should go fine if you just keep that up, yeah?"

"......?"

This might have been the first time he had felt something was off.

At this point in time, there hadn't been any negotiations at all regarding the arena for the seventh match.

◆

Hyakka learned about the fortunate change in the situation after a big month had gone by.

He was in the middle of a conversation with one of his subordinates in his office.

"By the way, Hyakka, sir. I heard that the Dogae Basin was decided on for the seventh match."

"What......?"

The Dogae Basin was a modest caldera in Aureatia's southern area.

The ground had collapsed into a circle, like a stadium; it was evenly leveled and surrounded by a high rock face.

Indeed, the Dogae Basin was far and away the venue that would give Shalk the best advantage when going up against Mele the Horizon's Roar. Hyakka himself had even planned on requesting it for the venue.

Talk about the arena's already going around?

Naturally, Hyakka had no recollection of making such an arrangement with Mele's sponsor, Cayon the Skythunder. There certainly hadn't been any official negotiations, but there hadn't been any talk of any personal verbal promises, either.

"Who exactly did you hear that from?"

"Umm, who? I mean everyone's talking about it. Is that not the case?"

"...I haven't entered into any talks about the venue yet."

"Really? Then someone must have jumped the gun, perhaps. I myself thought that Dogae Basin would be the absolute best possible terrain for Shalk, though."

Like the Mari Wastes, it was an arena removed from Aureatia city proper. Although the fighting field was spacious, due to the prominent topography that encircled the area, it didn't allow enough space for Mele's archery.

The most advantageous development for me is to get Cayon the Skythunder to agree to this venue...or it was. *With Shalk's speed, far faster than Mele could nock an arrow with his sluggish, giant body, he'd be able to close inside the gigant's bow range from the starting position in an instant. He could gain a decisive advantage right from the start of the match.*

The only arenas that could handle fights against irregularly large bodies like Lucnoca the Winter and Mele the Horizon's Roar were the Mari Wastes and Dogae Basin. With that in mind, Hyakka could understand this rumor itself. There was obviously someone making assumptions ahead of time about the venue for the seventh match.

…In which case, can I use this rumor to my advantage?

This fact might be a second visit of good fortune for Hyakka.

He proposed something to his subordinate who had brought the rumor to his attention.

"Could we spread that rumor around to more people?"

"I suppose…? But you haven't decided on the arena yet, right?"

"That's exactly why. We just have to pretend any advantageous terms for the match are an established fact. If there's a rumor going around that the venue's already been decided, next can come a rumor about the number of spectator seats. Once that's dispersed enough, next can be a rumor about the day and time for the match. If the shops and citizens take it as true and everything trends toward Dogae Basin as the venue—by that point, even Cayon wouldn't be able to go back on it. I'll be able to force through the exact conditions I want!"

There was more than enough time left until the date of their negotiations in the Coordinating Room.

Until then, he would remove every obstacle in his way and suppress Mele the Horizon's Roar abilities before the match even begun.

I might be able to do it.

An unexpected exaltation welled up from within Hyakka.

The strategy he just blurted out on the spot, to make use of these rumors for himself, didn't seem like too much of a long shot. If it succeeded, he'd gain a decisive advantage, and if it failed, it wouldn't cost him anything.

Above all, this scheme was one Hyakka had thought up on his own.

No, I can do it. I...I'll win the Sixways Exhibition with my own abilities!

◆

The rumors about the seventh match's arena had begun spreading even among the citizenry.

It was the match of Mele the Horizon's Roar, the living legend who had protected the Sine Riverstead from any threat against it. The people were highly interested in him, only dwarfed by their interest in Rosclay the Absolute, Alus the Star Runner, and Toroa the Awful, and when Hyakka went into the city, every day, he'd hear the topic come up around him more and more.

That day, Hyakka entered a general store to do some inconsequential shopping.

"Good day, Hyakka, sir! I've heard the rumors about the royal games!"

"Thanks! This, please…and three of those lampwicks."

"Yes, right away. Our supplier's changed from last month, but I've already confirmed their quality for myself. Rest easy… Incidentally, will the match arena really be Dogae Basin?"

"No, it hasn't exactly been decided on yet!"

Hyakka gave this sort of answer whenever he was directly asked about the subject. He was a man concerned with worldly pursuits, but he was still an upright civil official. He couldn't give false answers no matter what.

"However, it does seem like things will turn out like that soon."

Therefore, he tempered people's impressions with responses that weren't technically lies.

It could be said that this future was on the horizon, though, now that the rumor was spreading voluntarily among the people.

"*Ha-ha.* Is that right? So it's not set in stone?"

"I assume, then, people really are talking like it is, after all?"

"Both the blacksmith Yewty and the boss at the Sparkling Stag were saying as much! After all, I mean, it's Mele the Horizon's Roar's match we're talking about here. Anyone who says they're not interested is a liar."

"Are tickets already being sold? I need to take care on my end to know if there are any shops accepting reservations before everything's decided, after all!"

"For the seventh match… I haven't heard any myself. The second match apparently filled up with reservations a long time ago. Is it true that Lucnoca the Winter's gonna take part? *Eh-hee-hee-hee!*"

...Mrrrm. I guess things aren't going to turn out that perfectly for me.

If hasty shops were already getting to work, he would've been able to present the rumors of the arena as indisputable facts.

However, for that reason, tickets sales were being strictly regulated.

The results of any negotiations were submitted to Aureatia's Third Minister, who was in charge of trade and commerce—Jel the Swift Ink. As long as he didn't acknowledge the situation, it would mean it'd be impossible to have the shops clear the way for him ahead of time.

"Though, well, that's good," said the shopkeeper.

"What's good?"

"Oh, no, nothing, nothing, just talking to myself. We'll be eagerly awaiting your next visit to our shop, Hyakka, sir!"

The rumor was spreading among the people. Things were going smoothly—that's how it seemed to Hyakka.

◆

The decisive turning point arrived four days ahead of the negotiations over the match conditions.

Just past midday, a report suddenly came to Hyakka as he attended to his duties.

"Milord Hyakka. We've received a complaint from the people. They have a matter they wish to petition you about directly."

"Not again! More problems with General Haizesta?!"

Dealing with complaints involving Haizesta was almost becoming a routine part of Hyakka's daily workload.

Hyakka didn't know the reason why, but it seemed people considered him the one to bring any complaints against Haizesta, and it was an entirely meaningless bypass of proper procedure. Hyakka had firmly resolved to bring up this inefficiency at the next assembly meeting, no matter what.

"No, sir. It concerns you."

"What?"

"Their complaint is lodged toward you, sir."

Hyakka was at a loss on how to answer.

He listened to the opinions of those he governed in the agriculture division whenever necessary and had set things up that, outside a truly serious emergency, there wouldn't be any situation that would bring the concerned parties directly to him to lodge their complaint.

Then had such an emergency broken out now, of all times, with the Sixways Exhibition close on the horizon?

When he headed to the reception room, unable to hide his confusion, there were already several woman sitting inside.

"Thank you for waiting. I am the Nineteenth Minister, Hyakka the Heat Haze! How may I help you all today?"

"Thank you for making time for us. I'm Yubalk the Goblet Hall, mayor of the sixth northeastern ward."

The slender, middle-aged woman finished her slightly hasty self-introduction as soon as Hyakka sat down.

She was the type of person that Hyakka didn't really enjoy dealing with, with the fact that she was there to lodge a complaint not helping the matter. Her position as ward mayor represented the opinions of all the citizens in her ward, and if she was making a direct petition on top of that, it was difficult even for one of the Twenty-Nine Officials to ignore.

"I'll begin by saying I don't want to waste your precious time, so I'll get straight to the point—Master Hyakka, what sort of perception do you have of a true duel fight?"

"P-perception... By that, you mean...?"

"I am asking you if you believe combatants will be able to display their true skills in a battle on unequal terms."

"Ahhh, you don't happen to mean the seventh match's—"

"Why, whatever else could I mean, when it is you yourself who designated Dogae Basin as its venue, isn't that right? Everyone's heard the rumors saying such. You realize your opponent is Mele the Horizon's Roar, don't you? The champion who protects Sine Riverstead, who took down the Particle Storm, and who's known to everyone across the land. I can hardly believe I'm asking this, but you're not trying to defeat him before he can fire a single arrow, are you?!"

The middle-aged woman slammed the table. She was trying to browbeat Hyakka with the gesture.

...Dammit. Just because I'm young doesn't mean...

It was maddening. Supposing it was Haade or Jel sitting where he was, he knew she wouldn't have been acting the same way.

The same thing happened with Haizesta, too. In the end, Hyakka was simply an easier person to throw complaints at. That was why he always ended up suffering losses like this.

In any case, he had already thought up the wording he'd use in response to such complaints.

"Please calm yourself, Yubalk! If I may? We have yet to confirm the match terms. Thus, if you've come to complain about simply rumors, I—"

"That doesn't matter."

"Huh?"

"It doesn't matter! Everyone has reached a consensus on the matter."

The middle-aged woman ostentatiously threw down a bag stuffed full of bundles of paper strips.

There were several different patterns of seals lined across the page—voting seals. Each registered family in Aureatia possessed a unique seal, and pressing this in with a stamp signified agreement with the opinion in question.

"Th-this many... Um, is there really enough to fill the bag like that?"

"I still have two more! You're one of the Twenty-Nine Officials, right? Haven't you heard the talk on the street? Holding the match in Dogae Basin, why, it's obviously ludicrous!"

"Like I said...that hasn't been set in stone yet—"

"Listen here, Hyakka! We've come here to advise you—refrain from causing any suspicions of foul play during this very important event!"

Hyakka lightly rubbed his head. He wasn't getting through to them... No—

Even if her initial preconception was wrong, she was sticking to it.

Basically, she was forcibly demanding him to retract the match terms that she was personally unsatisfied with.

Y-you've got to be kidding me...! Did she really think that'd be enough?! A measly reason like that?!

Hyakka could admit that seeing *the* Mele the Horizon's Roar put his technique on display in a public event for the first time had been a large part of the Sixways Exhibition's publicity. His opponent, Shalk the Sound Slicer, was a no-name. The citizens one-sidedly focusing on Mele might have been the natural outcome.

However, the significance of a true duel absolutely did not lay in that time of showy performance.

Expending all of one's efforts under mutually agreed-upon conditions. As long as there was a consensus, each of the hero candidates took responsibility in following them. That was how it was to be.

"...I understand your feelings on the matter very well. I will be sure to think over your complaints," Hyakka replied with an artificial smile.

After continuing to voice her complaints for a time, the middle-aged woman left satisfied.

It wasn't his first time dealing with someone like her. Even when in a position like the Twenty-Nine Officials, as long as he governed over people, there would be times he'd have to endure such unreasonableness.

…However, something about her words stuck with him.

Is that how everyone's discussing the rumors?

He stopped on the way back to his office and thought.

I had instructed…my subordinate to spread the decision of the arena for the seventh match. But how was it being conveyed to the citizenry? How were they talking about it?

What had been a tiny thorn of anxiety suddenly began to swell.

This was everyone's consensus. Then did that mean everyone was talking about *how they didn't want it to happen?*

"Refrain from causing any suspicions of foul play"—that would then mean he was *under such suspicions,* wouldn't it?

Back then…what did the general store owner say?

"Though, well, that's good."

Perhaps, then, was his implication that he was glad it wouldn't be held in Dogae Basin?

Without realizing it, he was doubling back down the hallway.

He needed to get a clear grasp on the content of the rumors spreading on the streets.

◆

That night. In a rare move, Shalk had returned to his own inn.

"You're here, Hyakka. Perfect timing. Sorry, but for the first time, I got a bit of a request for you."

"…Shalk."

There were several empty liquor bottles rolling around on the floor.

Shalk gazed at them without seeming particularly interested, before shifting his gaze back to Hyakka.

"Been a problem or something?"

"What's it to you?"

As it had turned out, all his apprehensions had been right on the mark.

The number of voting seals he'd seen had certainly not been wrong. It was abundantly clear that in regard to Shalk's advantageous match terms, the citizens were, if anything, displeased. It was merely that no one openly mentioned it in front of him, and behind the topic of the seventh match, there had been all kinds of unfavorable criticism toward Hyakka the Heat Haze, groundlessly suspecting him of bargaining and secret maneuvering.

...Something this simple—if I just looked into it a little, I could've figured it all out immediately. I came up with countermeasures and everything... I... I was supposed to be thinking things through as I fought, but in the end, I didn't see through anything. I wasn't thorough. My failure. My...

He had pounced wholeheartedly on the unexpected good fortune presenting itself in the Dogae Basin rumors. Without at all thinking what sort of end result would follow.

As his sponsor, he already knew about the formidable strength of Shalk the Sound Slicer, but most of the people of Aureatia were looking forward to Mele the Horizon's Roar instead.

Perhaps, back in the moment, he shouldn't have spread such rumors and instead used any method to stamp them out entirely.

"Mind if I keep going with what I was saying?" asked Shalk.

"……"

"Make the Mari Wastes the arena for the seventh match. Quit overthinking things."

"……! Not you too! Shalk!"

Make Mari Wastes the arena. He had heard the words over and over all day. Hyakka smacked the table and shouted:

"You have to take this seriously! You're basically throwing away your chance to win!"

"Now, that's weird. I remember someone going on and on about the integrity of the hero candidate or something."

"…This is nonsense! Did those tavern scoundrels say something to you?! Is that why your stubborn, worthless pride's got you purposely trying to fight a losing battle, huh?! The sponsor's the one who gets to decide the match terms! Me! Y-you're my hero candidate…and you don't get to order your sponsor around!"

"Doesn't matter."

The head of his white spear was pressed up to Hyakka's neck.

An undead who found no value in anything else. A man who couldn't be bargained with.

"Whether it's some tavern scoundrel. The boss of some shop or another. No matter who it is, I can't stand to have anyone looking down on me. I'm dead—what else do you think I've got left?"

"Hic… Hngh…"

"Hell, even I don't know what I've got left for me besides this worthless pride."

The negotiations determining the match terms were a consensus between hero candidates.

In actuality, it was their sponsors in the Twenty-Nine Officials who did the negotiating as their representatives. That was where their talents were put to the test.

However…supposing circumstances had induced the hero candidate himself to wish for conditions that disadvantaged him, at that point, Hyakka's hands were tied.

"I…I just—! Listen to me, Shalk!! I want to win! I want to win, Shalk!"

"Yeah. I'll get you your win."

The hollow warrior seemed to be smiling with his expressionless skull.

"I'll fight my opponent at his full strength and win."

◆

The day of the negotiations. Cayon the Skythunder appeared in the Coordinating Room, where the one-on-one conversation would be held.

A one-armed man with decorous facial features. He looked at the emaciated and haggard Hyakka and announced:

"Well, how about we wrap this up quick?"

"……"

Sitting in the chair opposite Hyakka, he gave his conditions.

"Seems like the whole city's settled on Dogae Basin, hasn't it? I'd feel bad throwing them for a loop, so if you two are fine with that, then—"

"Nhg…hngg."

Hyakka was terrified by his enemy's lack of quarter.

Many, Rosclay first and foremost, had avoided a battle against Mele the Horizon's Roar, who assumedly had a distinct weakness in close-quarter combat. More than Mele, they were avoiding a battle against Cayon the Skythunder. Without either the power of a faction or a vast amount of wealth, he achieved his goals with the barest stratagems necessary, having full knowledge of his opponent's capability to deal with him.

Hyakka had been locked into a battle with the absolute worst opponent.

"Um…well, those terms are unacceptable!"

All he could do was force the words from his own mouth.

It wasn't enough to stamp out the rumors. He was supposed to have investigated where they had started.

Who was the person who'd first circulated the rumors involving the seventh match?

Chewing on the all-too-distant gap in their abilities, he had to say it.

"The Mari Wastes… For the seventh match, I r-request t-to have the…candidates…at bow range…!"

"Oh, really? Thanks."

Match seven. Shalk the Sound Slicer versus Mele the Horizon's Roar.

◆

An arctic wave, normally an inconceivable phenomenon in the region, brushed against the spectators, who were gathered together at a safe distance.

All of them were at a loss for words, gazing at the impossible landscape—even those who had already heard about the circumstances of the second match.

The Mari Wastes.

Yet the once-level topography was twisted like a billowing wave, and the lithologic nature of the earth, previously dried out and littered with fissures, was condensed. A chill that changed the very weather still lingered.

However, today, they weren't witnessing a fight from Lucnoca the Winter.

On top of the hills where, in the second match, two of history's ultimate dragonkin faced off, there were now two different people standing there and waiting for the match to begin.

One of them could be easily picked out even without a monocular looking glass: the gigant Mele the Horizon's Roar. His body was remarkably enormous, even among his own kin, with his height extending well over twenty meters tall. A colossal body piercing the sky.

The other one should've have been standing on a hill as well, but he couldn't be seen. Shalk the Sound Slicer's height was no different from any normal minia. The mercenary who'd slain Kazuki the Black Tone, a legendary champion known to all in Aureatia, was said to be this Shalk the Sound Slicer himself.

Their opening distance from each other was identical to the opening distance between Alus the Star Runner and Lucnoca the Winter. The space was set up with the flight speed of dragonkin in mind, but when compared with the maximum range of Mele's arrows, it was also an extremely short distance.

Moments before the start of the match, Cayon the Skythunder, standing beside Mele the Horizon's Roar, was peering through a monocular looking glass.

"The one over there, that's Shalk the Sound Slicer. Can you see him? I certainly can't."

"Ohhh, that guy who looks like a walking rag? He's so small, I can't see 'im too well."

"You better take this seriously now. Your opponent's faster than Kazuki the Black Tone's bullets. I haven't checked anything out, got it? Get a good look at him yourself and fight it out."

Aureatia's Twenty-Fifth General, Cayon the Skythunder. The man who'd engineered this match at the Mari Wastes.

However, for this match, he hadn't done anything beyond inducing the current terms of the duel with his information warfare. He could have secretly maneuvered to enact even more, but he hadn't.

Things really would get dicey otherwise.

Cayon wasn't a part of any of the major factions fighting the political war in Aureatia. Belonging neither to Rosclay's camp nor Haade's, he was battling in the Sixways Exhibition under his own personal motives.

The operation to intercept the Particle Storm, making use

of Mele the Horizon's Roar, had been another facet of his initial preparations. Utilizing his massive achievements from the successful operation, Cayon formed a secret pact of nonaggression with all the other camps. However, in exchange, Mele needed to be burdened with *properly established* matches in order to satisfy the bare minimum of what the Sixways Exhibition promised.

That was something that Cayon's side wanted as well.

Why, winning without showing Mele's fight to anyone—it's completely out of the question.

Mele the Horizon's Roar stood up and fixed his eyes on his enemy.

He had a gallant air and vigor that made him look like a completely different person from the Mele whom Cayon knew.

"Go out and win, Mele."

"Who the hell do you think you're talking to? I'll blow your mind."

"...*Hmph.* I'm cheering for you, okay?"

◆

On the hill opposite Mele, Shalk the Sound Slicer and Hyakka the Heat Haze prepared for the start of the battle.

His tiny frame shivering in the Mari Wastes' cold air, Hyakka moaned.

"H-he's...looking at us."

Mele the Horizon's Roar was clearly visible as he stood on the other side. Hyakka was looking squarely at the gigant, who was readying himself for a fight. That mean that he was within the range of death, with all chance of evasion impossible.

"You'll be able to avoid it, right?! We may be this far away, but I can tell he's focusing his sights on us! He'll fire an arrow right as the match begins! Mele's vision is special!"

"I get it. Move."

The enemy obviously had Shalk's figure, smaller than a speck, in his sights. Shalk had swallowed the disadvantageous terms to the match, but that definitely wasn't because he scorned Mele's strength. It was the opposite.

Since his opponent was the most gifted long-range fighter in the land, then if he, holding nothing but a single spear in his heads, was then able to get inside Mele's melee range...

...Who am I? This time, I might find out for sure.

Shalk the Sound Slicer was strong. He remained oblivious to the reason why.

The strength was there to fight against something. That much he was sure of. Given that he was a construct...someone out there in the world created Shalk the Sound Slicer in order to defeat an enemy that only someone with his strength could oppose.

It was possible that this enemy was the True Demon King. It could have been something different, but similarly strong. Perhaps it was even Mele the Horizon's Roar himself.

This was why he continued to fight as a mercenary.

Putting his entire being on the line, he kept fighting those who were close to this fundamental principle of his being. More than knowing the name of the True Hero, he felt that this was what would get him closer to the true identity he so desperately desired.

Beyond that, it was win or die.

"...You have to win," Hyakka quietly murmured at Shalk's back. "If you don't win, pride, stubbornness—it won't mean anything. Isn't that right, Shalk?!"

"...Get outta the way. You'll get hit by the arrow."

Hyakka was speaking the truth. Shalk thought so.

If he didn't fight with everything he had, he wouldn't be able to realize his wishes. Then should he end up losing, nothing would be left. His answer only lay beyond the true line between life and death.

He defied the norms. Even Shalk himself understood that.

"You're going to make me say it a third time?" asked Shalk.

"......"

He made the nuisance Hyakka evacuate. No matter where he was in the vast Mari Wastes, as long Mele could turn his eyes toward him, he risked death. Especially right here next to Shalk once the match started.

"...All right, then, come at me."

The only thing that would remain behind would be the frozen loneliness.

He readied his spear, stark white, parallel to the ground. Mele's bow, opposite him, was black darkness.

The stone pillar that had been used as a sundial to signal the match's start had been destroyed in the tremendous battle prior.

A brief silence passed between them.

Fireworks, instead of a starting gun, began the match.

—*It's coming.*

Far off, hazy in the pale-blue air, Shalk could see Mele pick up his bow. During Shalk's subjective view of the time frame, he had gotten in his stance to rush at full speed far before Mele had begun.

He had stripped off one of his two layers of rags and tossed it behind him. A decoy, little more than self-comfort. However, assuming the gigant's eyes were drawn to it even just once, at this long range, it would then be impossible for him to keep track of Shalk's real movements.

Together with his acceleration, Shalk the Sound Slicer transformed into a belt-like trail.

Godlike speed impossible of any living creature that the average person couldn't even visually recognize.

It's already coming. Fast.

With thoughts keeping up with his speed, Shalk had recognized it.

The arrow. The mass of Mele's first shot, like a tower closing in.

He didn't take the bait. It's following me. Twenty paces in range. Seven. Now—

The air screamed like a lightning strike.

The terrifyingly massive and boiling-hot earthen arrow passed through Shalk's position.

The speed as it pierced the atmosphere was so great, the soil burned from the high temperature of the adiabatic compression. The arrow passing through the surface was enough to melt the ground, which had been frozen over, bedrock and all, by a dragon's breath.

A carved-out ditch extended in a clean straight line to the horizon, and even after the arrow stuck into the ground, it signaled that the unobstructed destruction had been etched into the topography.

"...Hold up now."

Shalk, escaping to a point slightly removed from the arrow's flight path, became freshly cognizant of his enemy's might.

He had seen the trajectory. He had seen the moment of impact, too. Even evading it wasn't impossible.

However, it was monstrous. A voice, half-appalled and half marveling, slipped out of his mouth.

"Trying to cremate me here, are you?"

He knew from this attack that instantaneous destructive force wasn't what he truly needed to fear.

It was that, from a distance far enough away for the atmosphere to haze, Mele had accurately caught Shalk the Sound Slicer's movements, without being tricked by the decoy...and to go even further, he'd successfully calculated Shalk's supernatural agility and led his shot at where Shalk would end up.

I had been on guard to see if he would match up with my speed or not, but if I moved carelessly, it would've been all over with that first arrow.

His first act to try to close the distance between Mele and himself hadn't been made at Shalk's max speed. In the moment the arrow hit its target, he had been able to increase his speed one step further and avoid the ace shot.

Shalk's speed was neck and neck with the size of the arrows' moving inertia, and he was fully aware from the start that against the overwhelming area of attack of such a colossal arrow, dodging with a clever last-minute change in direction would be meaningless.

It meant he needed to constantly surmount a calamity more terrifying than lightning with just simple speed.

Three geographic reliefs I can see from here. Hide behind one of them, then I can cut off his line of sight, at the very least. Right now, he's nocking an arrow... He's creating them with Craft Arts. There's an interval between shots. If I use the reliefs and move at top speed— two shots. If I can stave off two shots, then I'll be at his throat.

Shalk's thoughts boasted the same abnormal speed as his movements. He could observe the process Mele took to nock an arrow, but to the average person, it all went by in the span of a single second.

Mele the Horizon's Roar. The minian-race champion who saved Sine Riverstead.

However, looking at him from Shalk's distance, he seemed like a mechanism of disaster given minian shape, wielding power easily capable of bringing ruin to everything within his bow range. A mountain moves, and life ends.

Even with his colossal frame, due to the long distance between the two, Shalk couldn't grasp the gigant's finer motions.

Conversely, Mele was watching Shalk's preliminary motions down to the littlest twitch.

Including his initial movement when he began to run. Just then, the next arrow flew—

In that moment, Shalk's trajectory reversed.

After visually confirming the arrow's release, he didn't continue forward and retreated farther away from Mele instead.

"What in the world?!"

Sitting far off in a carriage and watching over the course of events, Hyakka couldn't suppress his shout.

Even a child could understand it was a bad move to go *away* from someone skilled in long-range combat like Mele. It was a move that went horribly against standard strategy.

The line of destruction once again licked the ground.

It threw up clouds of frozen soil as it carved its destruction, but it didn't, of course, hit Shalk, having hidden which direction he would advance with his monstrously explosive speed.

"...Can you see me real well?"

For now, he had made his move. Shalk called out to his enemy, who could not hear him.

"The better sights you got on someone, the more you're supposed to get tripped up by feints."

While he dampened his movement by stabbing his white spear into the ground, Shalk hadn't taken his sights off Mele.

He watched his enemy's initial motions, moved after he saw them, and reacted according to said movements.

This was the fighting style that Shalk the Sound Slicer had always utilized. If he made his enemy act first and could observe it properly with his ultra-high-speed thinking, he could then come up with the perfect countermeasures against any opponent.

It was at that moment.

At three points simultaneously, streaks of lightning rained down from beyond the sky.

At least, that was the only thing Shalk's perception registered it as.

The earth burst and split open together with terrifyingly resonant earthquakes, and heated soil and gravel erupted like a volcano up to the clouds. The blast wave didn't stop.

"......"

Three points. He had never even thought about it.

The arrows hit the three areas Shalk had, mere moments prior, considered as possible places where he could hide himself.

Did that mean Mele had shot them to the heavens, to make them land with a slight delay?

If Shalk hadn't reversed course, instead electing to dodge the first arrow and close in on Mele...then the very moment he hid behind cover after evading the first shot...

No. Him seeing through my ideas isn't that big of a problem. What the hell was that? It's impossible.

The essence behind it wasn't Mele's eyes, which could fully grasp the flow of the terrain; nor his combat judgment, which could accurately track Shalk's thoughts; nor was it even the precision of his archery, freely manipulating his arrow's descent through the sky.

Three spots at once? All this power...

There was a lot of distance between them. Even though he watched out for the moment Mele fired, Shalk's vision couldn't get any handle on what sort of movements the gigant's hands were making.

It meant that, just as Shalk had done himself, Mele, too, had techniques to beguile what his movements were when firing. Even then, that wasn't the essence of it, either.

And he shot four times?

Many people knew about Mele the Horizon's Roar. He was the most tremendous archer in the land.

His fierce arrow fire of unparalleled accuracy had always shot down whatever target he aimed at with a single arrow.

Thus, no one had ever even imagined it.

That Mele the Horizon's Roar could shoot his bow rapid-fire.

◆

Shalk the Sound Slicer was faster than any other being in the world.

Even if the distance was far-off in the horizon, he could quickly cross it as if he was cutting across a garden. Even in this current battle, that fact hadn't changed.

It had simply lost all meaning.

He's far.

Shalk was calculating his distance from Mele. How much he would have to dodge certain death until he reached the gigant's feet, hazy on the very edge of the horizon.

Neither distance nor speed were concerned when it came to the concept of "farness" on this battle.

There was a single standard to measure: how many times Shalk would need to avoid Mele's attacks before he reached his destination.

The boundless space separating Shalk and Mele, completely and without exception, was a death zone.

He could make *at least* four rapid shots in a single breath. At this point, Shalk should have quintupled his estimations about the number of arrows Mele would fire until Shalk reached him.

Nah. He can probably get off more than four shots, and I don't even have any cover to break his line of sight. My means of escape are dwindling one after another.

When he arrived at that thought, he had already begun to run. There was a chance he was too late.

He couldn't use the areas of cover that had been drilled by the sky-falling arrows. There was likely nothing left behind but a black pit, without any footing to speak of.

The soil and sand were soaring like volcanic smoke from the three points, and not all of it had fallen back down to the ground yet.

Shalk had an urge to hide himself in the shadow of the dust cloud.

I know. It's a trap, isn't it?

The scenery on the left and right melted like a light sugar syrup in Shalk's vision as he ran at godlike speeds. He could make out Mele readying his next arrow from afar. He accelerated both his legs and his thoughts.

Though the cloud of dust would block Mele's view, it wasn't actual cover. Mele had an attack radius that was capable of instantly killing a target just by aiming broadly in its vicinity. If Mele shot at him through the smoke screen, Shalk would be erased in a single attack.

He ran. He continued running right on through. Was there any possible plan for Shalk?

He didn't hide in the dirt smoke screen and close in; the instant he hid inside, he cut back and dodged.

Shalk gambled on leaving a decoy behind, hiding his own body and leading Mele to lose sight of him.

Predictable.

Mele the Horizon's Roar was strong even without aiming. That one point was unmistakable.

Combining transcendental precision with his unreal attack radius and speed was, as a combat technique, excessive to begin with.

In a place like Sine Riverstead, lacking any enemy that required using such technique, Shalk couldn't possibly imagine exactly what sort of enemy had warranted such devoted training of his craft.

He had no choice but to close the distance in a straight line. He had to move faster than his maximum speed.

He continued to run.

Even as he went through all these thoughts one after another, to everything outside Shalk, it all happened in an instant.

He's not firing in my direction.

Mele had stopped Shalk in his tracks by demolishing anywhere safe, kicking up clouds of dirt, and showing off for the first time to anyone his trump card: his rapid-fire archery. There was a single second until Shalk rushed off and began thinking again.

It wasn't that Mele hadn't fired.

In that time that he stopped Shalk's ultra-high-speed running, Mele *had already fired.*

Mid acceleration, Shalk gazed up at the deep-blue sky.

He saw a straight, sideways line of twinkling and terrifying midday stars.

The same as before. Rapid-fire shots to drill vertically into the ground. This guy's...

The row of arrows rained down on the ground up ahead of him. Seven uninterrupted shots.

Shalk perceived their trajectory with a slowed-down sense of time, like the moments before death. For someone long dead like him, perhaps that was the only world he'd ever be able to see.

Turning to face the raining meteor swarm, Shalk plunged into it himself.

He was destined to be unable to obtain what he sought unless on the brink of death.

He tilted deeply forward. Smoothly and sharply, to the absolute limit.

...trying to split apart the damn terrain.

Mele changed the first rapid-fire volley, destroying three places he foresaw as potential points of shelter into groundwork for his next move.

His real aim was, through destructively drilling into the earth and connecting the three previous holes together, to create a completely unassailable cliff in the Mari Wastes.

Creating geography itself that would seal off his enemy's approach and allow him alone to continue his one-sided offensive. Once that happened, Shalk wouldn't have any hope left to win. They were frighteningly levelheaded tactics that left no chance to be undone.

Not only that, but these tactics also hadn't been planned from the start, either. It would have meant that he had derived a means of certain victory, enacted only after seeing Shalk's move to instead put more distance between them, with a decision-making speed on par with Shalk's mobility.

A damn monster. Mele the Horizon's Roar. What a bastard.

If he didn't make it before the division, he would die.

If he was directly hit by the destructive rain, he would die.

Even if he climbed over the precipice of death, if he then couldn't escape the destruction's radius, he would die.

He raced. He tilted forward. Ever deeper. Ever faster.

Shalk was a skeleton who could transform himself in ways that were impossible for any normal bone structure. He was capable of various tricks, like combining his right and left arms instantly to extend the throwing range of his spear. In his skeletal structure, he had movement joints in his ribs, his hip bone, and even his skull. His movement was fluid. Exact.

Though the shape was impossible for anyone to understand due to his speed transcending all perception, it was similar to the aircraft of the Beyond. At the very least, it wasn't the shape of any minian at all.

Tilting forward to the limit. Rushing on all fours like a beast, Shalk housed his skull and his white spear inside his own rib cage. The gaps in his bones were closed and blocking airflow, and with his whole body changing into a sharp, streamlined shape, he cut through the sound barrier.

Shalk the Sound Slicer was a spear himself.

Light rained from the sky, piercing the crust and exploding. There was a blast directly ahead of him and off to the right.

The falling stars continued one after another, trying to fragment the ground as they landed.

The second impact. The third. The fourth.

They were close. Closing in. He himself continued to get closer.

The fifth. The sixth.

Shalk perpendicularly intersected the destruction that had now drawn up directly beside him.

Now. He had crossed over the fragmenting line dividing life and death.

Not yet.

The seventh shot landed at his back. The destruction was catching up with him.

Though not hit directly, he had entered the arrow's attack radius.

Through the rocks and pebbles flying about wildly, he got a glimpse of Mele the Horizon's Roar. His stance following a shot. Already, a fresh arrow.

Shalk had slipped through the final brief opening in the raining row of destruction.

Surely Mele had assumed there was such a possibility. From in front came the *eighth shot*.

"I get it."

Mele had, from the very beginning of the fight, continued to fire shots that gouged out the earth.

That was because, as long as one stood in their path, the line of destruction they drew would be lethal.

Against Shalk the Sound Slicer and his transcendental mobility in a land battle, Mele understood that shots aimed precisely at a single point were impossible.

As it annihilated the path forward before him, the eighth arrow was closing in right before Shalk's eyes.

It was a direct line of destruction that completely blocked off Shalk's route of evacuation, which had been led into the position from the fragmenting arrows before it.

Mele the Horizon's Roar was an archer.

Even if his enemy wasn't going to be finished off in one shot, he knew the tricks to chase his prey into a corner with his attacks.

Shalk grabbed a large rock fragment flying toward him from behind.

Kicking off the ground and jumping high, he evaded the eighth arrow just in time.

He needed to.

"From the beginning, this was…your…!"

Mele had repeatedly caused lines of destruction and hadn't aimed at a single point.

—In order to instill the impression in Shalk that the air was his last route of escape.

Shalk had jumped off the ground. The ultrafast spearman couldn't evade in midair without footing.

And there came the ninth arrow, aimed at a single point in midair.

◆

Going back moments in time. Right after Shalk had reversed course and the three arrows reached the ground.

Mele had released seven arrows straight up into the air, without waiting for Shalk's next movements.

One shot matching up with the beginning of Shalk's high-speed maneuvering. One shot he had dodged by reversing course. Three shots to destroy the terrain.

And now seven arrows, one right after another.

Unfaltering movements, free of any hesitation, as if decided on from the very start.

"*Merre io mali. Akovst. Renterte. Nakkotay. Torfarmict.*" (From Mele to Mali soil. Conduit. Sunlight and claw. Undulation. Extend.)

Mele incanted his Craft Arts and made another pillar-like earthen arrow. As long as there was soil he could use for Word Arts, his quiver was endless.

"Say, Mele. You're not using your iron arrows at all?"

Surprisingly, Cayon hadn't fled and remained at Mele's side. Sitting down on a boulder, he wore a faint smile as he gazed at Mele's ongoing fight.

"These were a real pain to bring here, you know," said Cayon.

The *iron arrows* that Cayon mentioned were colossal iron pillars stuck vertically into the ground. The ultra-heavyweight mass of iron, able to stop a flood in a single shot, had been carried from the Needle Forest at Sine Riverstead as Mele's trump card in the Sixways Exhibition.

"I'm concentrating here."

Mele's reply was short.

From Cayon's vantage point, he couldn't see Shalk the Sound Slicer's figure. He was practically nonexistent, smaller than a piece of dust—and on top of that, he was running at a speed beyond all minian comprehension.

Mele hadn't lost sight of his target once and even managed to read all his opponent's movements.

Mele. I was right. You really are unbelievably strong.

Cayon gazed up at the sky to see seven streaks of fire raining down to the ground.

Then like a meteoric curtain, the lines pierced into the ground and split it into two.

Amid the earth rumbling, as if the end of days had arrived, Cayon thought the burning light was beautiful.

◆

He had shot down dragons.

He had crossed blades with gigant.

The sort of fights that had become myth were everyday struggles in the age Mele had lived in.

He was always optimistically smiling. He enjoyed the moments of struggle, expending all his energy to make sure that whenever he died, he didn't leave any regrets behind. If he lost, he could smile at being defeated by someone strong enough to surpass him and die without any lingering feelings.

The weak tearfully feared death, but for the strong, even death was something to be proud of.

Mele the Horizon's Roar had been in the middle of the conflict spiral. The strong who slew many enemies with their superb power were defeated by those even stronger. Or the clever, able to take hold of advantageous positions and golden opportunities for themselves, were defeated by the even cleverer.

The first races of the world—the dragons and gigant—were said not to die from old age. To them, dying in battle was the true and rightful way to die.

Mele the Horizon's Roar was a warrior who had fought through and survived this spiraling age.

He hadn't hesitated to put his life on the line, but the fact that he had still managed through it made him proud. It wasn't the life of a coward, seized while fleeing in constant terror. The life at the terminus of conflict became proof in and of itself that he was stronger than all.

...Which was why some settlement of minian wholly ignorant of battle should've been completely insignificant.

Mari Wastes. Shalk the Sound Slicer had accelerated even faster to dodge the first arrow launched right after the start of the match.

He was fast. Even Mele's eyes, able to distinguish everything down to the smallest tree nut on the edge of the horizon and determine the complex floodwater currents, could only continue to chase his movements. The only option was to anticipate his movements and guess.

"He's strong, all right. Real wild bastard."

Mele smirked, turning up one side of his mouth. It was a ferocious smile that he had never worn in Sine Riverstead.

He had reclaimed his life from that bygone time. The vivid brilliance of a life of honor, filled with euphoria. That fire that he thought he had lost from living peacefully in Sine Riverstead had now, at long last, been kindled again inside his soul.

Aaah. Those hills over there...

Mele was already shooting four arrows.

...are all in the way.

Three of them were aimed at the terrain his enemy was likely to utilize in his approach.

The three arrows, launched up into the heavens, came slightly after the one he had fired at Shalk himself, *erasing* the three hills from the topography. Pierced vertically, they swelled up and exploded.

By Mele the Horizon's Roar's standards, even colossal geographic features were the same as any other obstruction.

He chased Shalk the Sound Slicer's movements with his eyes. The skeleton had backed off. He'd deceived him with his movements and evaded.

From this distance...he had done that by using the fact that Mele could see all the moves he'd made.

"Real damn strong."

Mele smiled.

He was always optimistically smiling. Not because he was confident in his victory.

It was a smile of bliss about being once again in the spiral of conflict.

"Perfect. All right, Shalk. I'll tear you apart and take the whole world down with ya."

Smiling the whole while, he released seven arrows up into the air.

Like a child tearing up clay work with their fingers, Mele could divide up the world itself with his arrows.

Craft Arts. He created several fresh arrows all at once.

"*Merre io mali. Akovst. Renterte. Nakkotay. Torfarmict.*" (From Mele to Mali soil. Conduit. Sunlight and claw. Undulation. Extend.)

"Say, Mele. You're not using your iron arrows at all? These were a real pain to bring here, you know."

"I'm concentrating here."

Cayon was still standing there? The thought flashed in the corner of his mind.

He could leave him for later. His experience from ancient times, surviving through life-and-death struggles, was largely moving Mele's body automatically.

Mele had already let twelve arrows fly.

No matter how far back in his history he went, he had never gone through so many arrows on a single target before.

Shalk wasn't a dragon. Not even another gigant. He was a nameless construct and a dead man, his identity unknown to everyone.

Nevertheless, Shalk the Sound Slicer was the same type of enemy as *back then*.

An opponent that Mele the Horizon's Roar had always longed for, one he could battle with his full strength without needing to protect anything.

"You're a real strong one, Shalk the Sound Slicer!"

Mele loosed his eighth arrow. At this point, without even looking, he was able to aim at the spot he assumed Shalk would end up, likely having the arrow pass through terrain itself. He nocked the next arrow.

There wasn't a single hesitation in Mele's movements. This still wasn't enough to finish off his enemy.

Because Shalk was strong. Without fail, his enemy found the optimal solution.

The eighth arrow left him a path to escape into the air. Mele fired the ninth arrow to hit that exact point. The ninth arrow continued after the eighth, chasing its shadow. They succeeded like flowing water. Two releases, made in what seemed nearly one single motion.

More.

He nocked the next arrow.

You're strong, ain't ya? I know you can do it!

It was physically impossible to evade the ninth arrow, aimed at a specific point in midair.

However. If on the off chance there was some sort of method left to survive Mele's arrow—if Shalk the Sound Slicer was indeed that sort of enemy—nothing would have made him happier.

The tenth arrow was aimed at where Shalk would land. He steadied his sights.

Shalk pierced through a dust cloud from the fragmenting terrain and appeared.

The eighth arrow was already close to arriving at the spot where the skeleton reappeared.

The white spearman jumped and dodged it.

Exactly as Mele predicted, the most optimal and fastest option for evasion.

"—"

As if intersecting with his trajectory, the ninth arrow arrived in midair. An arrow with force that made defense impossible.

Even if Shalk managed to successfully hold out, the tenth

arrow was heading for the skeleton's landing point. Mele assembled his next arrow.

"*Merre io mali. Sai fartari. Nemkau*— (From Mele to Mali soil. Unstuck bramble. Frozen sea—)"

At that moment, there was a strange phenomenon.

"—*jin a tol* (bug and moon)— What?"

Shalk appeared to dodge the ninth arrow *in midair*.

The trajectory of his jump made an inconceivable zigzag, and he landed diagonally forward.

As a result, the tenth arrow, aimed at his original touchdown point, didn't hit its mark.

I ain't ever seen that.

The movements went against reason. The sudden acceleration, far too unnatural to be explained by some sort of flight ability, much less by kicking off a piece of debris, had been done in midair, without any footing.

"*Kanderkor.*" (Extend.)

Mele finished his Word Arts incantation.

With his stunningly abnormal landing just now, Shalk was closing the distance to Mele more and more. His midair acceleration even made sure to propel him in a forward direction.

"—*Ha!* I haven't...ever seen a guy like this before!"

Shalk's ultra-high-speed rush began again. How many more arrows could he fire in the remaining distance?

"Mele. What is that...?"

Watching over the fight, Cayon gasped at the shape of the arrow Mele created.

It wasn't a straight line. Like a gnarled tree branch, it was twisted and warped along the shaft, an impossibly deformed arrow.

A technique called Mystic Arrow. Naturally, it wasn't meant for firing far off into the distance.

It was meant to kill an approaching enemy.

"Get crushed."

In order to block Shalk's advance, he fired it into the earth.

With a dreadful rotation, the arrow ricocheted off the ground and bent.

Its trajectory resembling a snake's death throes, it thrashed, gouging the earth, whirling up, and pounding it.

An arrow of annihilation, bringing destruction not in a line but across an entire surface, returning every inch of the terrain to vacant, raw soil.

However.

"......!"

Mele pulled out one of the iron pillars nearby. He immediately nocked it and fired. Not a single thought had time to slip in.

The iron arrow landed right in front of him and largely destroyed the very hill he was standing on.

He had to.

In order to stop his enemy's advance.

"...An iron arrow, eh?"

He could hear a voice from the shadow of the iron pillar after its impact.

A voice—this skeleton had now already gotten in close enough for Mele to hear his voice.

"This arrow's a whole lot better behaved than that last one."

He'd broken through the ruinous rapid fire that had sealed off all methods of survival.

He'd evaded the Mystic Arrow, which had irregularly raged amok, on first sight.

He had, at that very moment, turned the distance, an archer's lifeline, into naught.

This man was inside his arrow's firing range. Nevertheless.

The position where Shalk now stood was the line between life and death.

—Shalk the Sound Slicer was strong.

Stronger than anyone else Mele had encountered. More than any calamity he had seen.

More than any of mighty foes who lived in that age of spiraling conflict.

"Been waiting for ya."

The gigant sneered.

◆

The ninth arrow, aimed at Shalk in midair, had passed right over his head.

There was a change in Shalk's trajectory after his jump. This emergency evasion was an ace up his sleeve he had carried with him secretly until he had reached this distance.

If Mele had suspected that Shalk had the means to do so, then he definitely would have countered it in kind.

This guy's a damn monster. Way too strong.

Behind him. The tenth arrow touched down in his original landing spot.

If Shalk had made the slightest incorrect movement, he would've died, every part of him smashed into dust.

Too bad.

Just a bit farther to reach him—taking stock of this as he re-accelerated, a gloomy shadow loomed over Shalk's heart.

Mele the Horizon's Roar was a far more tremendous enemy than the legends, or Shalk's own expectations, had made him out to be.

The truth to these gloomy emotions was the delight in standing before Mele the Horizon's Roar and being able to battle with him.

As well as resignation.

I have to kill him.

This enemy couldn't be beat without killing him.

Mele the Horizon's Roar was too strong. Even if Shalk fully closed the distance between them, this enemy could surely bring out any number of sublime techniques to blast Shalk away.

If there was some method to outdo Mele in this match, it was to definitively end his life with a single strike exceeding the gigant's reaction speed.

Amid these thoughts, the landscape around him changed into light passing him by.

Mele had launched the next arrow.

It wasn't a rapid-fire volley. The interval between shots had been strangely long.

Facing the arrow, which was closing in with destructive relative velocity, Shalk tried to consider what the pause could mean.

He attempted to evade.

"!"

The arrow, piercing into the earth, was the one to thrash about and evade Shalk instead.

Twisting. Scattering. Snaking. Destruction.

Uh-oh.

He was surrounded.

This bizarre arrow had broken down the surrounding earth and lifted it up with its violent roiling. Shalk's way forward was blocked by a large mass of rock, and he had no footing for himself on the continuously splitting and breaking ground. It wasn't only in front of him, either. Right. Behind him to the left. He needed to decide in a split second on his alternative route.

Already accelerating close to his absolute limit, Shalk pulled out the white spear from his deformed bones and pierced the rock in front of him. Using the point of his thrust as a fulcrum, he made a sharp turn. A storm of rock, like buckshot, swept through the position he had just been standing in, scraping away everything with it.

The arrow. The arrow thrashing around. Where is its actual body?

Even in the midst of his high-speed turn, he could perceive the entire scene before him like a still-life painting transmitted piece by piece.

He confirmed the arrow diving into the ground about sixty meters up ahead of him. However, his high-speed senses alone couldn't estimate how its irregular trajectory would jump about.

Right? Left? Would it leap back?

He never took his sights off the arrow's movements. He sensed the initial motion as it began to reverse backward at super-high speed.

Don't get taken in. I just need to cope with what I can see.

In any case, sight was the only sense that would be any help. The explosive sound of the ground being struck, rupturing, and scattering about encircled Shalk's area. He needed to break through this hell, or he'd die.

The arrow reversed course. If anything, to chase after it...I need to go forward.

Both the arrow's trajectory and the onrushing rocks were merely being perceived as elongated phenomena via his high-speed thought process. From the perspective of any other living creature, everything had occurred in just a second. If he could just ascertain the optimal path forward, Shalk would immediately be able to get out of range of this destructive surface attack.

He wouldn't use any *emergency methods* like before. The boulders, their relative velocity slower when compared with Shalk himself, seemed to be frozen in the air. He kicked off them in midair and accelerated.

He landed on the flat ground in front of him. Even this piece of bedrock was waning away, and he was able to recognize anew that the previous arrow was an attack meant to destroy the very geography itself.

However, even if his footing crumbled away in an instant, in a world of blinding speeds, it was enough. He evaded a colossal boulder flying and closing in on him with a lower stance.

He raced through the middle of the crumbling maze on the flat rock bed, as fast as electric signals through nerve synapses.

The arrow that Shalk chased after also bounded in every direction. There were no surprises from the arrow itself.

Geographic division. Rapid-fire sniper attacks. The Mystic Arrow.

He had completely dealt with all the ranged attacks. Now he wouldn't give Mele any time to nock the next arrow.

Shalk could very quickly get on top of the hill where Mele the Horizon's Roar stood. Closing the distance at max speed, with one decisive attack—

A crackling shock ran through him.

"......!"

The bizarre arrow was flying right past Shalk.

Impossible.

He had only passed five paces behind it. He hadn't been directly hit at all.

Nevertheless, against the raw power behind the arrows Mele shot, *at this distance*, evasion wasn't an option. The wind pressure from the arrow's passage alone tore off his right arm from the shoulder of his now half-length body and sent it flying.

Where the hell did that come from?

Up until that exact moment, he was supposed to have been tracking the actual body of the bounding arrow. It couldn't possibly have gotten around behind him in an instant.

What was going on? He tried to comprehend things with his high-speed thinking.

"Ohhh."

He understood immediately. The arrow that suddenly jumped out, digging up and smashing the surface behind him, had just been a fragmented piece of the tip.

The warped shape. Thrashing around and breaking apart. So it was a scatter shot *from the very beginning.*

No time was left for him to rejoin his arm.

He only had one arm left. Shalk ran.

"My body's gotten...lighter now!"

Shalk went up the hill like a reverse lightning bolt. He readied his white spear and held it straight.

Just beforehand, he extended out all the bones in his body wide.

He pierced his spear into the flat ground. He forcibly slowed himself with the air turbulence.

Impact.

Right in front of his eyes, an iron pillar stuck out of the ground.

Abominable precision, right up to the very end.

Perhaps due to the instantaneous rapid release, there wasn't much power to it. Even then, Shalk could tell the shock wave from the impact alone had made all the joints in his body creak.

"...An iron arrow, eh?"

With just a single arrow, a fissure ran through the hill, and the side of the level ground Shalk stood on dropped a little.

A quick shot to stop his advance and prevent him from getting close.

Cayon the Skythunder, his sponsor, had been at Mele's side up until a few moments ago—he must have stopped Shalk from going farther like this to buy time for the man to escape.

"This arrow's a whole lot better behaved than that last one."

Which was why, for just long enough to make a sarcastic quip, Shalk decided to accommodate his adversary's intentions.

"Been waiting for ya."

Mele didn't exploit the opening, either.

This was the first and the only conversation exchanged between the equally peerless skeleton and gigant.

"Merre io article. Wikognen." (From Mele to Sartile needle. Move earth.)

At the same time as Mele's incantation, Shalk stepped forward.

Fiercely flying out from the iron pillar's shadow, he had arrived inside Mele's bow range.

Mele the Horizon's Roar was an archer skilled at long-range sniper fire.

A battlefield where he couldn't keep space between himself and his opponent curbed this specialty.

However.

That didn't mean that he *wasn't skilled* at close-range combat, either.

"Amzst, fotima." (Heaven's clasp, raindrop.)

While still continuing his incantation, Mele held his black bow and dropped his waist low.

The colossal weight of a twenty-meter-tall gigant. He had the gargantuan strength to change the terrain itself. His movements, in proportion to his massive frame, were fast.

While his indestructible bow was like a supermassive hammer.

"—Slow."

A huge mass of flesh flew off—it was Mele's right thumb.

Cleaving his leg in a spiral, the white gust ascended.

Before the vast amount of blood could even wet the ground, the swift death god had reached Mele's backbone.

It was faster than Mele could register the pain.

Shalk's target was his spine.

"Far too slow."

Naturally ruinous power. Overwhelming speed. A transcendental weapon. None of them held any meaning whatsoever.

It was impossible to perceive.

As long Shalk the Sound Slicer's spear was within range, there was no longer any time to counter it.

Therefore, the only thing left…

"*Lettemiks.*" (Bloom.)

…was the speed of the mind.

The iron pillar that had just impaled the earth. It was a vessel that Mele the Horizon's Roar trusted more than any other and felt the most familiar with, resonating with him. His Word Arts could immediately communicate with it.

The mass of the tremendous pillar instantly transformed.

Wire—

The iron pillar split apart into countless pieces and came undone.

An enormous and fine wave of wire closed in.

Right before Shalk could deliver the coup de grâce—Shalk, holding fast on to Mele's back, was forced to give up on his attack and dodge. This wasn't like any bullet or arrow. He wouldn't be able to evade the wire through the gaps in his bones.

If the wires passed through the openings and tangled in his bones, Shalk the Sound Slicer would be incapacitated.

This guy…

He dodged. Jumping off Mele's massive body, he escaped the space as it began to be blanketed over.

Mele had begun incanting Word Arts from the very start. His real goal hadn't been a close-range brawl with his black bow, but these iron wires.

…used his own body to slow me down!

Below his eyes was an eternally extending sea of iron wire. Shalk dangled down from his spear, stabbed into Mele's thigh, and was just barely holding out in midair.

If he fell, he'd stop. Coming to a stop before Mele the Horizon's Roar meant death.

He had to dig hard into Mele's body once more and stab deeply into his spinal cord. Either that or sever his main artery.

Even from this position, grabbing on solely with his arms, if Shalk transformed his body, then one more time…

Just a little…

Even that chance collapsed with what happened next.

An intense impact and acceleration assaulted Shalk's body, and he was thrown into the air.

The tip of his spear, which he'd thought had sunken deep into Mele's body, cast a futile arc in midair.

Shalk kicked his high-speed thoughts into gear. He had to think through what exactly just happened.

Mele jumped.

The action, nigh unbelievable when considering the gigant's appearance, had sent Shalk's body flying off its vise grip.

Mele's initial move to lower his body hadn't been to attack, but to prepare for this leap.

He went high. From high up in the air, Mele looked down over Shalk.

From the moment Shalk had stepped in to melee range, Shalk was instead backed into danger—

No.

The sea of iron wire was descending. The iron wire, pulsating as it expanded, tangled in Shalk's left arm. He had now been blocked from throwing the spear in his hand, too.

If he had his right arm. If he had just the slightest bit of time to stab with his spear.

...That's not it.

He didn't have the time to brandish his spear to throw.

He didn't have the time to sever the iron wire and escape.

He didn't have the time to detach his bones and then reconstruct them.

"...No... There's no way I'm slow...!"

The massive shadow blocking the sky got ready. To Mele, who was looking down from the heavens, the airspace Shalk descended through and the entire scenery laid out below—was in range of his cataclysmal bow.

The line of death—his line of sight. In the backlight of the sun behind him, only the light of his two eyes glared.

Which was why Shalk could fix his aim on them.

Shalk launched his white spear.

"You're far—"

The white flash streaked and pierced the gigant's left eye.

It was a perfectly motionless release, faster than Mele's bow.

Immediately after. The arrow, launched together with a low groan, grazed Shalk and blasted his left leg off.

Before then annihilating the ground below.

"That's all!"

The colossus fell. Shalk, too, having lost all his weapons, was sinking down into the sea of iron wire.

◆

...If those eyes of yours aren't hollow holes like mine here.

How was Shalk the Sound Slicer, supposedly with all the methods at his disposal cut off, able to drill into Mele the Horizon's Roar's left eye? The inexplicable phenomenon had occurred at an earlier stage of the fight than that.

Shalk had dodged the ninth arrow, shot with full foresight into his evasion route, with abnormal midair mobility. With neither recoil from kicking debris nor some flight ability, he had been able to instantaneously and acutely change his trajectory angle.

The principle Shalk used for midair control was the recoil stemming from a powerful action.

Shalk the Sound Slicer *launched* the heavy stone debris secured right before his jump directly behind him and, like the rocket engines of the Beyond, gained reaction-based propulsion midjump without any footing.

Launching debris at high speed for emergency evasion. Launching his white spear to decide the fight.

The truth behind it all was the ultimate trump card Shalk had secretly brought to the match.

Right after the start of the match, why had Shalk mysteriously reversed course away from Mele?

Was the move not just to catch his enemy off guard, or was there some aim behind the movement itself?

What if he had known from the very start that there was something there at the spot he had shifted toward?

I even got a look at Alus the Star Runner's treasures, too!

"Heshed Elis the Fire Pipe..."

Shalk the Sound Slicer's entire body was tangled in the iron wire. At this point, he could no longer move. He had let go of his white spear, too.

"...is what it's called, apparently. Alus the Star Runner's

treasure. Just wanted to make sure I told you that it wasn't that my skills bested yours."

One of the magic items that Alus had used right before Hidow the Clamp led everyone to evacuate.

Merely an iron pipe, not even loaded with gunpowder, it could shoot any object that touched the tip of its barrel with bullet-like speeds. It was a magical gun that had launched Alus out of range of Lucnoca's breath with power to spare.

Shalk had thought of two possibilities after gaining info on the second match from the tavern scoundrels—the first was that Lucnoca the Winter had made a direct hit, and Heshed Elis the Fire Pipe had been disintegrated as well.

Then there was the other. The possibility that after firing off Alus's body, Heshed Elis the Fire Pipe itself had also been launched outside the breath attack from the recoil.

Mari Wastes had been decided on for the seventh match.

If Alus the Star Runner's magical items were still stuck in the ground, then would Shalk be able to use them? Keeping his eyes on the area he estimated it'd landed and observing the bottom of the hill from before the match started was what made it possible for Shalk to come across the item.

It may have been the briefest moment possible. But in it had been a nigh-endless back-and-forth.

Just how closely had Shalk the Sound Slicer escaped his demise?

If he hadn't reversed back for the Fire Pipe, Mele would have seen through his potential areas of shelter, then Shalk would've taken his rapid-fire volley and died.

If the distance separating them had been just a bit farther apart, the terrain would have been divided apart, and he would have died.

If the arrow that had thrashed across the ground had moved differently, he would've died from a coincidental collision.

In the end, if the throw he'd aimed at Mele's eyeball had missed the mark, the arrow fired in return would've killed him.

"Can't stand up, Mele?"

He looked at Sine Riverstead's champion, collapsed on the ground and unmoving.

The conversation they'd exchanged had been a brief, single back-and-forth.

"...Well then. You were one hell of an opponent."

Nevertheless, Shalk felt like he understood Mele.

What the man was proud of, why he had fought.

Shalk turned around. He had to retrieve the other arm he had lost along the way.

"I'll let you have that spear. Mele the Horizon's Roar."

◆

The seventh match was over. Shalk the Sound Slicer walked alone, blending in with the nighttime hustle and bustle.

He would go on living as if he was a low-class scoundrel.

Even as he won against champions, standing colossal above all others, he didn't need a single one of the glamorous luxuries of a champion.

...There's some who purposely wish to become a monster. Like a totally different creature... Merciless, without pain or fear, solely dedicated to battle...

Mele the Horizon's Roar had surely been that way.

He had fought like an incarnation of calamity and turned into carnage itself, his face looking completely different from the one he wore as the guardian of Sine Riverstead.

That couldn't have been out of hatred or loathing toward Shalk himself. Mele had been happy to have that sort of battle.

I'm the same type of monster. Unchanging, from the moment I was born.

—Who exactly was Shalk the Sound Slicer?

"But I get it now," he quietly murmured. The answer was certainly out there. Somewhere out there in the world, in the middle of battle.

"I... I really do need this fight."

Fighting. It may have been the only thing Shalk the Sound Slicer was capable of, but he certainly wasn't a lonely creature. There were indeed others like him in this land, and by continuing to fight, he had to eventually be able to learn the truth behind his identity, the identity he'd lost in death.

He would continue battling in this Sixways Exhibition. The skeleton, unknown to anyone and who didn't find anything necessary at all, had at last obtained a desire of his own.

Shalk had the next match to fight. Was he supposed to get a new spear for himself?

Perhaps he could have Hyakka buy him a present.

Mixed in the city crowds, Shalk felt his hand settling on something.

The sensation made it clear what it was.

A white spear.

The one that he had lost in the middle of his fight.

Something surprised him even more than this fact.

Although he was mixed in with the crowd—was there someone who pushed through a gap in Shalk's consciousness *to hand something over to him*?

Someone, only as tall as Shalk's thigh, seemed to pass right by his side.

They spoke.

"...Alena?"

The ooze-like silhouette slipped into the flow of the crowd and disappeared.

Shalk probably could have followed after him.

With Shalk the Sound Slicer's speed, surely both catching up and searching around to locate him would have been easier than spotting the moon in the night sky.

He didn't pursue.

With the white spear still in his hand, he couldn't even turn back around.

It was an name he didn't know.

Nor was there any name like it in his memory as a skeleton.

"......................"

◆

The seventh match was decided.

"...Why're you sleeping? Get up."

Cayon sat down beside Mele, who remained collapsed on the ground, motionless.

All the onlookers who had watched the match were already nowhere to be seen.

The caravan that Shalk and Hyakka had boarded was likely back in Aureatia by now.

The magnificent battle to the death was settled, and there was nothing but silence over the frozen land.

"You are really such an idiot."

Aureatia's Twenty-Fifth General. Cayon the Skythunder.

Though a famed general, superbly resourceful and valiant, living through battles fierce enough to lose an arm, there were not many who knew his true origins.

The evening sun illuminating the chilled wastes also shone light on Cayon's cheeks.

"Why— Why didn't you fight...? You're this strong, so why? You wanted to fight, didn't you?"

There were a number of scars, bored by Mele's bow, carved into the Mari Wastes. Was there any other champion in this planet's history, besides Mele the Horizon's Roar, who was capable of performing such a feat with a bow and arrow?

He was a warrior. He'd left Sine Riverstead, and indeed, he had fought.

The champion's power, which had beaten back the True

Demon King themselves, had been put on display for all the people to witness.

"You're such an idiot."

Even if he wasn't the hero who'd defeated the True Demon King.

Cayon wanted to boast that Sine Riverstead's true champion really did exist.

Cayon wanted to show him fighting at full strength. The mightiest archer in the land.

No matter what sort of other schemes he could have pulled over, that alone would have been enough.

He buried his head in his arm.

He had his back turned to Mele, just like he had on that day.

"...Give it a rest already."

Cayon heard a voice.

"You got it all wrong. I don't want a runt like you giving me crap," Mele said...sounding displeased and still lying down on his back.

Cayon was at a loss for words, and he looked at Mele, who still had his eyes closed.

His tearful face twisted into a smile.

"*Ha... Ah-ha-ha...!* What the hell are you sleeping for...?"

"'Cause getting up's a pain, why else?"

"You could've kept fighting after all."

"Damn right. May as well've been stabbed with a toothpick. That bastard Shalk the Sound Slicer's got a lotta nerve acting like a tough guy... Who the hell'd want a puny spear like this?"

His right leg had been pierced deep enough that he couldn't stand, and his left eye was pulverized. Even with such terrible wounds, Mele the warrior could've continued to fight.

He was supposed to have been wishing for just such a fight for so long. Cayon could tell.

Closer to him than anyone else, he had seen Mele's face and the exhilaration in his heart.

No matter how close danger loomed, Cayon had an obligation to watch such a fight unfurl.

"What the hell, then? It was just stuff some kids said; you should've just forgotten all about it... E-everyone...called you a champion..."

"*Gwa-ha-ha-ha-ha...* Then don't cry about it, runt. You ain't gonna grow taller like that."

Still lying on his back, the gigant reached out his hand and rubbed Cayon with his pointer finger.

—Even then, Mele had stopped fighting.

Even as he hungered for the spiral of conflict, he hadn't truly thrown his everything into the genuine duel to the death.

"Mele... You were... You were a true champion, but... I'm sorry, Mele..."

Had the peaceful days with the villagers weakened Mele?

If he had spent all his time fighting, would he have been able to live the past two hundred and fifty years without knowing the hunger in his soul?

Even if he had never made his promise with Ilieh long ago,

could he have continued to fire his arrows up at the shining stars every night without fail?

No. Surely that wasn't true.

Everything had made Mele the champion stronger. None of it was pointless.

"Hell if I care. Whatever you chirped at me... I forgot all about it a long time ago. So smile."

The gigant almost never called the children, even tinier than the already small minia, by their names.

It was perhaps because he feared growing too attached to the lives of such weak creatures.

...However, he remembered them. Forever. Without a single exception.

"Go on, Misna. Smile."

He was always optimistically smiling.

Match seven. Winner, Shalk the Sound Slicer.

CHAPTER 13 ◄□► New Continent

—Just how far in the past was it? Long ago, before Hiroto the Paradox visited this continent anew, before the True Demon King appeared.

The memory of the first time someone set off from this continent. Hiroto was gazing out at the sea with his companions.

A red hull, expanding out wider than a castle's walls. Brand new sails lined up in white. The colossal sailing vessel that was going to navigate them to the new world was right in front of his eyes—a ship named "Knowledge's Gate."

Hiroto the Paradox's companions were not minia, but a group of goblins. Hunted as base vermin in this era, they studied science, gained the power of intelligence and group harmony for themselves, and at last, built the Knowledge's Gate.

These goblins had achieved an undertaking that everyone else asserted as impossible.

Pioneering a new world beyond this continent—it was the end of a dream.

"…It zook a while. We're halfway zhere, Hiroto."

Zegegu Zogi the Stone Dam had arrived at the beach much earlier than Hiroto and appeared to have been gazing at the boat.

Nothing but a mere chief warrior ten years prior, Zegegu had grown older, too, and had now become the leader of his clan.

"Indeed. But still halfway to go," Hiroto replied similarly. He thought about Zegegu Zogi's long journey.

Zegegu Zogi had a talent that other goblins didn't: the capability to logically ascertain disadvantages and advantages and iterate on plans aimed toward the future. Hiroto had assisted with Zegegu Zogi's fight, and conversely, Zegegu Zogi had protected Hiroto's life from harm, slowly raising Hiroto's position up among his people.

"With zis, I'll have no regrez left behind..."

To a goblin, with their short lifespans, a mere ten years was a considerably long among of time.

To Zegegu Zogi, it seemed like far back in his past.

"World... The new world. It has a nice ring to it. For us goblins, a world of vast pozential."

"No, not yet. Venerable Zegegu. Looking at the world isn't enough. In your case... You have a duty to see the people you lead prosper and thrive. It's a future that will absolutely become a reality."

"*Hah, hah, hah...* I don't zhink I'll be living zhat long. Been alive zhirty years. If I arrive zhere, and see it wiz zhese eyes... zhat alone is already zoo good for me."

"You can't go dying now, okay?"

A woman's voice cut in between the two's conversation.

Her back was facing the pair, and her pale feet kissed the water's edge. She had long golden hair and a slender frame.

She was a vampire woman named Ephelina the Snow Sunlight.

"You die, and there might be more goblins looking to chow down on Hiroto again. I need you to be strict with them, or I'll end up with more work."

Hiroto the Paradox, a mysterious and odd visitor, had lived a long time amid the people-eating monstrous races. If he hadn't met his bodyguard, Ephelina, early on, he likely wouldn't have survived this long.

"I'm grateful to Miszer Hiroto. He was zhe only one to lend a hand to us as we were fated for extinczion... Zhere aren't any ozhers among our clan who have inzeracted with a single minian for so long."

"I am simply fulfilling my promise, and nothing more. Transforming this goblin clan into a society that properly recognizes intelligence and cooperation. The next, to protect the goblins themselves from the threat of the minia. It wasn't me who saved you from being destroyed, but your dream, venerable Zegegu."

"Why did you choose us?"

"Because you all chose me."

"You...picked a difficult path."

"Not at all. I believe this will make things better."

A foreign sky where visitors who deviated wildly from the worldly principles and natural laws of the Beyond found themselves. That was this world.

The information that Hiroto had first sought after crossing

worlds was if there were any other visitors like him who had appeared across this world's history—and records of the fates they met.

The first conclusion he received from this information was that it was impossible to achieve immediate reform of minia society centralized around the three kingdoms.

The deviant presences that brought instability to the world—visitors who brandished their outstanding technology and knowledge—had been largely deemed demon kings throughout history and exterminated through the collective efforts of the minian races.

This world knew that rapid development reliant on a single individual would have harmful effects on their civilization. They didn't integrate the demon kings themselves, but just the vestiges of the technology and power they left behind, and continued on developing their world with stability.

It was almost like this world's antibody mechanism, raised over a long history, against these foreign threats called visitors. A refined and excellent tradition. Therefore, it would be hard to undermine it.

"I simply chose the path where I saw possibility. Not the already-stabilized minia kingdoms...but the other community that energetically reproduced, had a social nature, and was filled with desire and zeal. That was how you appeared to me."

"*Ha-ha-ha.* An inexperienced and foolish group. My mind here would be bested by a minian child's, surely. Dizappointed by minian groups, witnessing our goblin foolishness firsthand...you must have walked a difficult pazh to reach zoday, Mizter Hiroto."

"...*Pfft*. Not at all."

Hiroto fearlessly laughed. It wasn't a strong front, but his true, heartfelt enjoyment for this grand endeavor. He had loved the path he had traveled to get here.

"Venerable Zegegu. I believe this world is a wonderful place. I haven't abandoned my expectations for the minia, while at the same time, I truly believe your people are clever, absorbing every experience you face. This world has possibilities that far exceed those in the Beyond! Much like you and I are able to talk right now, venerable Zegegu!"

"You mean...Word Arts? Zhat is what pozzibility is to a polizician like yourself?"

"That's right. In the world of the Beyond, minia can't affect societies outside their own. That is different in this world. The goblin clan I joined forces with has developed technology just as you and I wished, learned language, and are now trying to discover a new world! As a politician, could there be anything so delightful?! There's a chance to bring everyone happiness and riches! This world needs us!"

There was no language barrier in this world. Visitors, without any natural life span, could enact any long-term plan they could ever want. There wasn't any more ideal of a world for a politician.

The many long moons spent fostering goblin culture together with Zegegu Zogi were sure to save more than just the goblins. It was bound to help out a great many people as long as the day came where minian races and goblins could join hands together.

"Yooo! Hiroto!"

Someone called Hiroto's name from up in the sky. A blue wyvern.

Raheek the Wet Scale.

"Don't head out now! Real dangerous out there! Kraken'll swallow ya whole!"

"I know. That's why we're waiting like this until it's time to depart."

Normally, wyverns were the natural enemies of goblins.

Amid all the contributions Hiroto had made to this plan, the ones he prided himself above all else were enlisting the help of the prodigy Raheek, who had discovered a sea course unknown to even the minian races, and making him agree not to eat the goblins.

"We're counting on you, Raheek."

"That so, huuuh? Well, you guys are all idiots, see! Don't know anything about the sea! I figured you already forgot and got worried for ya! I'm hungry!"

"Your meal's piled up in that carriage over there. Go ahead and do whatever you'd like until sunset."

"*Heh-heh-heh!* Yer a great guy, Hiroto! May be stupid, but still a great guy! Ahhh, I can't wait! Settin' sail! Looking forward to it!"

The boisterous, shrill voice passed on by. Ephelina shielded her eyes with her hand and watched him depart. Shrugging her shoulders slightly, she turned around to Zegegu Zogi.

"Idiots are nice and easy to manipulate, aren't they? Sure are loud, though."

"Nonzheless...he has discovered a route from zhe skies for us to cross the sea wizhout kraken azzacks. Raheek deserves commendazion zhe mozt here."

"Yeah, sure, it might be that way for you, but still."

Ephelina was coming back up the beach, seemingly grown bored of playing in the water.

Of all of Hiroto's companions, she was the only one who didn't seem to have been deeply affected by their expedition at all.

Ephelina placed both hands behind her back and turned around to Hiroto.

"Hey, Hiroto. So in the legends of the Beyond, vampires can't cross the ocean, right?"

"Ah, yes, there were some stories that said as much."

"So then what'll you do? If I melt or something the instant I cross the sea?"

"It'll make me very sad. But that's just superstition. You vampires, for a long while, didn't know the truth behind your own identity. That's why the superstitions from the Beyond managed to spread like that."

"Huh, that so...? You're not gonna give up on this, are you? Going out to sea, I mean."

"I'm not."

Hiroto had been together with Ephelina even longer than he had known Zegegu Zogi. She was Hiroto's sole bodyguard and close friend.

When the end of his experiment in the new continent was finished, he was sure to return back to these shores. A day may come when not only goblins, but Ephelina could also live as she wished among the minian world.

In Hiroto the Paradox's future, it was indeed them…the companions who held dreams in his stead who would be necessary going forward. Not a single one of them could be lost.

"Miszer Hiroto…someday, one smarzer zhan myself will be born."

"……"

Whether he had gazed at the future far across the ocean or read the thoughts in Hiroto's mind, Zegegu Zogi brought up this promise.

"Our lives are short. However, we will be born anew. Zhough each individual one is short…zhat brief life span will pass on into zhe new age, stronger. Zhat is what we goblins do. Not our name or our second name…but zhe third name you beszowed us with, Mizter Hiroto. I guarantee you zhe clan bearing zhis name will be raised to be clever. I alone am not zhe last. One will be born smarter zhan any ozher. Zhat is my…way of repaying you after my death."

"*Heh-heh-heh.* Me, well… I'll also go along with you, Hiroto. It'd be a waste to hand over something this fun to a bunch of kids or someone else. I'm definitely not going to die, either. Got it?"

"……"

Hiroto faced off into the sun to ensure the other two couldn't see his face.

He thought he was an innately inhuman person. He had been so back in the Beyond and still was now.

Hiroto hadn't been emotionally pained to see goblins attack his fellow minia, and he was able to live on without any desires or dreams of his own.

"Thank you very much."

Nevertheless, he felt happy.

Drawing in others' trust made him able to experience these warm feelings.

He could feel the desire to see a world together with them that no one else had ever witnessed before.

The position of the sun was low. The time to set sail would come eventually.

With this, he made a promise that wouldn't be kept.

"Let us step foot on this land once more again. All of us, together."

Many days and months passed. Crossing the sea, Hiroto the Paradox realized one of his big goals.

Among the companions he was with on that day, he alone returned to their original continent.

—For their dream. To create a society where minian and monstrous races coexisted together.

◆

Aureatia. Third floor of an apartment complex, the third match finished.

Dant the Heath Furrow heard, earlier than anyone else on this continent, about the vision Hiroto indicated for the world's future and its feasibility.

Could goblins who didn't eat people exist?

That problem has already been taken care of.

"On the new continent, we continued to research. Monstrous races eat the minian races. Naturally, this could be willfully suppressed on an individual basis, but as long as the race exhibited this tendency on a whole, it would be difficult to quell such desires. However, if that was the biggest obstacle to reconciliation between races, we researched if we could selectively breed livestock to serve as a substitute."

"...This isn't a problem that can be solved with a substitute food source, though. The logical perspectives of the minian and monstrous races are completely different. Lycans, for example, are said to not actively eat people, but they're still a race that kills them for fun."

"And if that was nothing more than prejudice? Milord Dant. The difference between us is much smaller than I thought... I have, in actuality, lived for a long time in goblin society. If they were truly a race incapable of mutual understanding, then I certainly could've never done such a thing."

"Isn't that just an issue of individual wills like you mentioned before? Making them comply with a prohibition on eating any and all members of the minian races is much harder than forbidding them from eating a single, designated individual."

"Of course, I cannot deny that may also be a factor."

Hiroto forced a smile. The truth was he had been in danger of being preyed upon many times.

"However, in that case, why is it that goblins do not eat their fellow goblins? It's simply that they adhere to a clear prohibition not to eat their own comrades and consume hostile races instead. The example that you put forth, about forbidding them from eating any member of the minian races—to them, it's a simple and easily understood rule of thumb. As long as the minian races accept them and they are given plenty of provisions to curb any need to eat people, then it will be possible to include us minian races into their definition of *comrade*."

"Even then, logical perspective's an issue. There are none among the minian races who believe it's okay to attack others capable of mutual Word Arts understanding in order to eat them. That's the disparity that defines them as the monstrous races in our society."

"...Is that true, though? As I am a visitor, I can't help but find that questionable. The ability or inability to understand Word Arts. In truth, there isn't as major of a difference as the people of this world think there is. Yes, I'll cede that only gigant eat wyverns, given their flavor, but in actuality, wyverns are an exception here, being preyed upon despite communicating with Word Arts. If you're talking about killing adversaries who understand Word Arts, well then, all the minian races do that as well. Is it really that big of a difference on whether or not the body is eaten afterward?"

"...A visitor's thought process there, Hiroto the Paradox. That's completely alien to our world."

"I know. That's precisely why an outsider like myself needs to act in order to bring harmony between the monstrous and minian races."

"You're going so far to introduce goblins into our society, but what do you gain—?"

In the middle of his sentence, Dant fell silent.

That was, in fact, precisely what Hiroto was doing. Hiroto and Zigita Zogi were participating in the Sixways Exhibition in order to prove the benefits of letting goblins enter minian society.

They had suppressed the Old Kingdoms' loyalists, who opposed Aureatia, and even influenced the continent's civilization with the technological innovation of his muskets. If anyone wanted proof of the benefits, he had been achieving exactly that for a while.

"That's precisely why the Sixways Exhibition was necessary. If the hero's the one who *defeated the enemy to all...* then whoever it ultimately is, they can unconditionally *become an ally to all.* It's a once-in-a-lifetime opportunity. Through the title of *hero,* we'll control the people's emotional backlash and, over a long period of time, systematically permeate society.

"By specifically doing what?"

"First, it'll begin with a slave class. Goblins and other monstrous races will be allowed to integrate as part of a labor force, and with their living areas isolated from minia, we'll give them our substitute food source. Without either starvation or hostility, little by little, we'll see some among them interact with minia and begin a cultural exchange."

After an outcry for equal rights among minian races, it had become difficult to make slaves of elves and dwarves on the continent as in eras prior. In recent years, the value of slaves had been drastically rising day by day. Thus, there was open space in the market for cheap labor whose rights were differentiated from the minian races.

There was no need to seek equal rights from the start. Slowly, gradually. Until eventually, it became too difficult to cut them off from society. That was Hiroto the Paradox's strategy.

"That must mean you've completed it...this substitute food source or whatever."

"Of course."

Hiroto carried a wood box, big enough to need both his hands, from a corner in the room. It was Zigita Zogi's personal property.

Since his arrival in Aureatia, Zigita Zogi hadn't eaten anybody. The same for the goblin army he commanded. Even just Dant's surveillance alone was enough to make the fact undeniable.

"This is our substitute meal."

"......What in the...?"

Dant looked inside the box and was rendered speechless. He also needed to endure the nausea.

The box was stuffed with tumors. The tightly packed and chaotically engorged masses of meat seemed to still be alive and pulsating.

A single...clouded eyeball peeked through a gap in the sarcoma pile, and its sight seemed dozy, wandering through the air. It had no will of its own. Or at least, it shouldn't have had one.

"What exactly is this?"

"I already mentioned this before...that we *rewarded* Ozonezma with one of the spots in the Sixways Exhibition, yes?"

Hiroto's camp had made Ozonezma enter the tournament not because they had anything to gain from his participation.

Giving him the spot in and of itself, allowing him to achieve his own aims, had been the goal.

"That was compensation for this contribution. By calling him to the new continent, we were able to overcome the final hurdle and mass-produce this construct. Ozonezma's skills as a doctor are likely the most cutting-edge medical care this world has. Ozonezma can genetically transfer and incubate cells using a virus. Even testing the faculty to maintain a bare-minimum homeostasis without brain cells is within the scope of their ability."

"Th-that's not... That's not it... You know...what I'm trying to say here. This thing here—if you're telling the truth, then—is a minian?"

"No, absolutely not. Even though its flavor and texture may be the same, and the raw materials came from a minia, it's absolutely nothing like them. HeLa cells— Oh well, that sort of example isn't going to get things across, will it? These cells, repeatedly modified, are now something completely different entirely, even in a genetic sense."

"But the original minia then—"

"Would be me."

Hiroto closed the lid of the box without peering into the flesh mass's single pupil.

The people who had continuously protected Hiroto, Zegegu Zogi and Ephelina, had both left this world a long time ago. However, the goblins never attacked Hiroto. He gave them a substitute.

"Visitors don't have a natural life span. This primary supernatural factor brings eternal youth. In which case, say their cells are ageless cytologically as well—what would happen if they grew cancerous and multiplied endlessly? I've named them Taisai. While they exist as living creatures, they don't die, continuously regenerating as long as they receive nutrients, and serve as a minian replacement for the monstrous races...a new artificial life-form, a construct crafted with the hands of science, so to speak."

"Hiroto the Paradox... This is a truly foolish endeavor. What will the people think when they see that—that thing...? Why... Why would you reveal something like this to me?"

"For your trust. You're able to put much more trust in this than in eating minia, correct? While it is easy to proclaim that these goblins are ones who don't eat people, that won't be enough to instill trust. It's the same as a politician without any personal ambitions. The existence of the Taisai...is the minimum and necessary truth for us to reach a compromise."

"Trust? You expect me to look at that and trust you?"

"That's what I hope."

Dant glanced over the closed wooden box with an acrid look.

"...Maybe it might be right. Introducing the monstrous races into society may actually help to restore the world. Just how many citizens in this country would be freed from their toil with the ogres' strength or the goblins' sheer numbers? But...you're telling us to do so, even if it means relying on something that horrifying?"

"Yes. It was necessary to inform you of everything, Milord Dant, as our collaborator."

"...Give me some time to think."

"Absolutely. I'll be waiting."

Save the goblins, who were expelled by the minian races and previously driven off the continent.

Save the royal family, now changed into an untenable authority, with the young queen being the sole living survivor.

Save the Order, now persecuted with the loss of faith in the Wordmaker.

"You are one of my constituents as well, after all."

Hiroto the Paradox had decided to ally himself with them. He intended to make every one of his promises become reality.

The sixth match ended in defeat for Mestelexil the Box of Desperate Knowledge.

Kaete the Round Table, considered to be the third faction involved in the Aureatia political conflict, had fallen from power, cited as the perpetrator behind the castle garden theater bombing. Mestelexil's whereabouts were unknown directly following the match, and with a warrant out for Kaete's arrest, Kaete the Round Table was believed to be on the run within Aureatia, together with Kiyazuna the Axle.

However, there was one more unknown collaborator within Kaete's camp.

Aureatia's Fifteenth General, Haizesta the Gathering Spot.

Losing the faction he had stealthily been a part of, Haizesta made an appearance at the Aureatia Central Assembly Hall for the first time in a long while.

As he walked through the corridor on the way to his destination, he spotted a familiar face. Since they tried to pass by without a word, he smacked them on the back.

"Hiya."

"Ow! Wh-what in the world is your problem, Haizesta?! I'd ask you to keep the meaningless violence to a minimum!"

Nineteenth Minister, Hyakka the Heat Haze. A petite and seemingly high-strung civil officer, the complete opposite of the boorish and large-built Haizesta.

"Got a real annoyed look, don't we?"

"It's got nothing to do with you."

"C'mon, you won your match, didn't you? You could stand to be happy about it."

"What do you know about how I feel?! Anyway, why are you here in the Central Assembly Hall and not the Military Ministry?! I've told you over and over again that there are several important matters piling up while you've neglected to visit your office in the Military Ministry!"

"Sorry, but I've got some other minor business to handle today... This sermon sounds like it'll be a long one. Give the Sixways Exhibition stuff all you got, Hyakka."

"Ow!"

Haizesta smacked Hyakka on the back two more times and went to take his leave.

"...General Haizesta! Um!" Hyakka called out to the departing man. He appeared to have blurted it out without thinking. "I...I'm taking my work seriously. Not just the Sixways Exhibition—always. But... well...I always bemoan that...there must have been some other way to do things..."

"Hmm."

Hyakka the Heat Haze was a man unable to honestly revel in good fortune.

The fact that he had confronted the Sixways Exhibition with all his effort and might, only to claim victory in spite of his own personal blunder, had further exacerbated his sense of inferiority.

"*Nyeh-heh-heh...* Being able to do things seriously is quite a feat already, isn't it? I don't have the talent for that whatsoever... Downright jealous, really."

"B-but that alone... It's meaningless if you're not strong, isn't it?"

"I wonder. Being strong ain't always a good thing, see."

At the very least, the strong weren't always guaranteed to survive.

Kaete the Round Table, Kiyazuna the Axle, and Mestelexil the Box of Desperate Knowledge were all powerful beyond imagination. Losing shouldn't have ever been a possibility for them, and they still ended up defeated.

In the Sixways Exhibition, Hyakka had won, and Haizesta had lost. That said everything.

"Way I see it... Those guys who can win while they're weak are a helluva lot more advantaged than the ones who've gotta be strong to have any hope of winning..."

"...That doesn't sound like a compliment at all."

"Well, that's 'cause I wasn't complimenting you... *Nyeh-heh-heh...*"

With that simple response, Haizesta began to walk off once more.

It was something that didn't concern him at all. He thought it had been out of character for him.

If I had been able to take things seriously, heck, maybe Kaete would've won out, too...

Most likely, that wasn't the case. Kaete's group must have exhausted every possibility the best they could.

Even if Haizesta had made his own moves, the enemy may have just gone one or two moves above him.

However, he did want to try carrying through his duty to the other three in his own frivolous way. Nothing more than a flight of whimsy.

He arrived at the documents room at the end of the hallway. He put his hand on the door, but it was locked.

"I'm coming in."

He grabbed the steel doorknob. He twisted it.

There was a dull, groaning sensation. Haizesta the Gathering Spot didn't actually possess any lockpicking skills.

"...I don't remember giving you permission to enter."

There was only one person lingering in the records room—Aureatia's Thirteenth Minister, Enu the Distant Mirror.

In the backlight peeking in from the window behind him, it was only his two eyes, wide like an owl, that stood out.

"Really? Well, I mean, I'm already in here and all... Say something first next time," Haizesta said.

Haizesta remained in his spot in front of the door and fixed his eyes on Enu.

An eccentric man who didn't belong to any faction despite how extremely capable he was and who sponsored, in the Sixways Exhibition, a survivor from the same Obsidian Eyes he himself destroyed. Haizesta's responsibility within Kaete's camp was to investigate the personal background of the man in front of him.

Even after Mestelexil's defeat in turn made Kaete's entire camp vanish, Haizesta continued to investigate Enu with his uncouth intuition and tenacity...and he had arrived at a single conclusion.

"You weren't a corpse to begin with, huh."

"Hmph."

"The person leading an antivampire mission's obviously gonna be forced to undergo a thorough quarantine, but...even if someone hasn't been turned into a corpse, that doesn't necessarily mean they can't be manipulated... *Nyeh-heh-heheh*. Like someone's been taken hostage to make you fall in line, for example, or there's something set up to kill you at a moment's notice..."

"...The Obsidian Eyes matter, is it? I am indeed cooperating with them during the Sixways Exhibition. I'll admit that. Now then, Haizesta, do you plan on indicting me?"

"Well, I don't know, see... Just bringing this information over to Rosclay or Haade doesn't guarantee they'll believe me, for one... It's lonely not having a faction for your own."

"Whether you're being honest or not, with the first round over, it's too late anyway. Zeljirga's already returned to Obsidian Eyes' main force. Supposing you did kill me right here, it likely wouldn't put a stop to their activities," Enu matter-of-factly replied. He had eyes that seldom blinked. It was said that one could tell if a person had been turned into a corpse or not by their pupils' reactions, but he clearly seemed to still be minian.

"Basically, your plan from the very beginning was to capture Mestelexil in the first round—but it doesn't seem that way to me, really... *Nyeh-heh-heheh.*"

In the cramped records room, Haizesta's low laughter reverberated with an eerie clarity.

Conspiring with Obsidian Eyes to seize Mestelexil the Box of Desperate Knowledge—if that was Enu the Distant Mirror's goal as well, his own actions didn't line up.

Enu was put in charge of vampire subjugation from before the Sixways Exhibition was ever decided on. It would have been impossible for him to be cognizant of Mestelexil's existence prior to the Particle Storm interception campaign.

"Enu. You've interacted with that National Defense Research Institute a number of times now, haven't you? Despite that *national defense* name, the organization hasn't been officially sanctioned by the Aureatia government, has it...? What did you do?"

"......"

"Before the Sixways Exhibition...*you had your own plan* you were pushing forward. Isn't that right?"

Enu closed the document he was holding in his hand.

A long silence passed between them, but his eyes remained fixed straight on Haizesta's own.

There was nowhere to run in the tiny records room. Should Enu try to fly out from the window behind him, Haizesta could likely grab hold of him far before he could pull it off.

"Haizesta. What do you think about Taren the Punished?"

"She was a real fine woman... I mean, I bet that's not what you're asking, but that's how I saw her."

"In this age...there remain numerous powerful figures that could potentially destroy the world. I believe Taren was trying to control these figures and bring about ruin through an absolute fear in place of the True Demon King. Ultimately, it merely shaped a war that forced even more death and destruction on the people."

"*Nhehehheh...* That cruel streak of hers really drove me wild, too."

"On the point of forcing sacrifices to maintain control, the Sixways Exhibition underway right now is the same as Taren's war. There needs to be some way beyond fear to control the people. Kaete was trying to accomplish that through the technology of the Beyond... My way of doing things is different. A means to unify their minds and *not under their control.*"

Enu's objective was unknown. What was he trying to do?

Nevertheless, as he made progress through his string of investigations, there was one thing Haizesta came to understand.

The man sponsoring Obsidian Eyes was not just being used by a vampire.

It was that he was *trying to use a vampire* for himself.

"...Hmph. If you're done saying your piece, then I may as well ask... Any plans on giving Mestelexil back?" asked Haizesta.

"Impossible. Now that he has been handed over to Obsidian Eyes, I'm unable to intervene."

"What about lifting the manhunt for the bombing culprit?"

"If you're able to fabricate a more likely suspect and the evidence to back him, that can be done. Of course, it's a matter of whether you can manage that or not."

"Sheesh. Not much fun threatening you, huh?"

"......"

For a brief moment, a silence fell between the two men.

For one moment.

"Sheeh!"

It was not a laugh that slipped from Haizesta's lips.

It was a sharp exhale, bestial and almost abrasive.

A crack rent the floorboards where he stepped, while at the same time, he grabbed Enu's throat with his right arm.

"Whatever your...pet theory or goals are...doesn't make a damn difference to me. Enu the Distant Mirror."

"......Ngh! Glngh......"

Haizesta was using as little strength as possible. The power of his grip, enough to twist the lock off a door, could've crushed a person's neck down to the bone.

Haizesta the Gathering Spot was himself one of the monsters born from the era of the Demon King. A powerful individual, equipped with aberrant brute force, as if birthed as a reversion from minia to beast.

"If you don't understand something, then you just gotta kill it instead. Y'know...that faction matched my character to a T. Nyeh-heh-heheh..."

The only way in and out of the room lay at Haizesta's back. However, if he jumped down from the window, he could exit out from the building through a blind spot. He would twist off the iron fence surrounding the grounds and make off with Enu.

A savage plan with no regard to the consequences. If Kaete was still around, he would've never allowed him to act so arbitrarily.

"You're coming with me. Enu the Distant Mirror."

"General Haizesta!"

A completely different voice interrupted the scene.

It was a familiar face. Opening the door, Hyakka the Heat Haze entered the records room.

Haizesta hadn't seen anyone besides Enu and himself have any business with the records room, and of all people, Hyakka was the most problematic person to deal with.

"Wh-what in the…? What're are you doing?!"

There was a *thump*.

"Whoa now, Hyakka. Sorry, but now's not the—"

Haizesta's words were cut off.

His breathing itself was interrupted with a sudden intense pain.

"……"

Hyakka was in a bizarre stance, the palm of his right hand held upward and stretched out in front of him.

By flipping his right wrist down, he threw the second and third pebble. Two thumps.

They stabbed into Haizesta's chest in succession. His fingertips went numb, no longer able to keep his grip on Enu, and Haizesta's massive body collapsed to the ground.

"…Don't cause us any unneeded trouble. Enu the Distant Mirror."

Hyakka the Heat Haze spoke in a cold voice, as if an entirely different person.

Had Hyakka's voice even from a moment prior actually been the man's voice?

"Your death could be brushed off with a laugh, but we need to dispose of every person who gets information out of you."

"...*Koff, gahak...* I'm aware. If he hadn't tried to, you wouldn't be saving me at all."

Haizesta, collapsed on the ground, could only see the shadow Hyakka cast from the hallway. That alone was already unlike the man. Its height, and even its sex, was entirely different.

The thing that transformed into *what appeared* to be an elf woman's form had both eyes covered with bandages.

"Don't think we'll be saving you like this the next time. Especially in my case...as I can only move these eyes of mine unprotected for a limited amount of time."

A mimic...

Constructs created by altering the cells of undifferentiated races. A species that could mutate into any form at will, with an extremely low confirmed population.

—Not only that, but she was simultaneously a corpse of Obsidian Eyes.

First-formation vanguard, Lena the Obscured.

"...Middle of the damn day in the Central Assembly Hall and you're telling me...someone this abhorrent...slipped right on in..."

The strong weren't guaranteed to survive. That was absolutely right. Haizesta knew that.

With a tiny pebble. Just a few drops of poison.

Within a single second of his attention going astray.

"Nyeh-heh-heheh..."

Haizesta the Gathering Spot's consciousness ended right at that moment.

Aureatia's Industrial Ministry. Its departments and agencies had been under former Fourth Minister Kaete's jurisdiction, but now a different bureaucrat was commanding the withdrawal of weapons from their storerooms.

"All right, all right, careful how you handle these things!"

A woman with her grizzled hair tied behind her head. Aureatia's Twenty-First General, Tuturi the Blue Violet Foam.

"There's a chance that any movable part could be a trigger, so no touching! With weapons from the Beyond, their power isn't proportional to their size, okay? Even for the small items, carry them one at a time and leave yourselves lotsa space! Sloooow and steady now."

The castle garden theater bombing wasn't the only reason why Kaete the Round Table had gone from part of Aureatia's government to wanted criminal.

For the forces taking advantage of Kaete and Kiyazuna's disappearance after the end of the sixth match, the suspicions around the garden theater bombing were a windfall excuse to forcibly execute a search for the weapons belonging to his camp.

On top of the many suspicions surrounding the events of the sixth match, there were a large number of golems and weapons from the Beyond that Aureatia wasn't aware of. Kaete the Round Table's scheming to revolt against the kingdom had already become indisputable fact.

As for which power would eventually impound these weapons, which were set to become evidence, there had, of course, been a dispute among Aureatia's main factions, but...

"Hey there, Tuturi. How's the extraction going?"

"Smoothly. I've already picked out for myself a few of the more interesting-looking ones, mind you."

Calling out to Tuturi was an elderly general with dry white hair and a long scar on his right cheek.

Twenty-Seventh General, Haade the Flashpoint.

"Not only that, but that crone Kiyazuna must've made up a whole fleet of those Chariot Golems... Ha! Makes me really glad I joined up with you, General Haade, that's for sure. If I had gone along with Rosclay and friends, I definitely wouldn't've gotten to experience anything this interesting."

"Ah, well, I could've gone ahead and let Rosclay have the win here, but..."

The secret struggle surrounding Kaete's left-behind property had ended in victory for Haade's camp with almost-disappointing ease.

A savage smile came to Haade's face as he watched the unknown weapons carried off right before his eyes.

"No matter how old I get, I still love to get my hands on new toys, see."

"*Hee-hee!* When I was a young lass, I was also scolded that a young girl *shouldn't play war.* This would've been a golden chance for Rosclay's reformation faction to prepare for what lies ahead, so why didn't they make any serious attempt to jump on this?"

"Even if they obtained these new and functionally complex weapons, it's still up in the air if they'll have enough leeway to get use out of them until a war actually breaks out. The reformation faction's winning out against us in the numbers game. Either they determined that the Beyond's weapons don't have the power to overturn that superiority…or it might mean they've gotten stuff that powerful elsewhere."

"…What do you mean?"

"Aureatia's already secured some enchanted swords and magic items, right? Of course, those items've all been divided up among the Twenty-Nine Officials to keep a watch on, but the reformation faction's got a lot of the Twenty-Nine on their side to begin with. Basically, when the time comes, their group's got plenty of trump cards already up their sleeve."

"Yikes… So then we might have to battle against the Cold Star and stuff at some point? That'll be trouble…"

"Of course. Too late to gripe about it now… Though, even without that, there's the biggest reason those guys couldn't do anything about it—the head of their faction was seriously wounded in the fourth match. On top of that, with the whole almshouse raid and the chaos around the sixth match, their other leader Jelky's probably dealing with more work than he can keep up with, too, see. The bickering over seizing Kaete's weapons was probably a bit too much of a burden for those guys right now."

Rosclay's camp was the largest faction within Aureatia's political struggle, but it had a very big weakness.

The first was that Rosclay, inevitably due to becoming a symbol as a hero candidate, needed to participate in the matches himself, and their camp could never avoid the effects from his match results.

Additionally, since they were the largest faction of all, there was a wide range of matters that they needed to control. In particular, Jel the Swift Ink essentially bore full responsibility for all of Aureatia's economic activity, and the other facet of wielding enormous power and authority was the need for him to deal with problems whenever they came about.

"The reformation party lost old man Nophtok, too, didn't they? Did you see him, General Haade? That poor guy—he must've gone completely nutty. Rumors say he slipped outta the hospital and rubbed his head hard enough in prayer to draw blood in some church ruins. Isn't that terrifying? It sounds like something ripped from a ghost story."

"Once someone's gotten that bad, it actually gets more annoying to keep 'em alive. It'd be best to just kill the poor guy and erase Kuze's slot in the tournament, but… If Kuze's side is taking precautions against it, that'll make it real hard to do."

Immediately after the end of the fifth match, there was an

incident involving an Order almshouse. It was obvious that Noph-tok the Crepuscle Bell was dealt some sort of reprisal, whether by Kuze or a collaborator.

According to the physician's diagnoses, he wasn't said to have any physical wounds at all.

"Old man Iriolde disappeared, Taren left—then there's Elea, Kaete, probably Nofelt, too, and Harghent is pretty much finished already, so guess that'd make seven."

Tuturi smiled as she used her fingers to count the Twenty-Nine Officials who had vanished.

She was always cheerful and heartless.

"All that's left is Rosclay, depending on the condition he's in, but the Twenty-Nine Officials may just keep dropping left and right at this rate! I better be careful myself, huh."

"*Bweh-heh-heh-heh-heh,* you and I aren't going be dying any-time soon."

"*Pfft.* We better not. Else, there was no point in even hitching my wagon to your side."

Even now, with Kaete's camp wiped out, the fire of the inter-factional political struggle remained burning.

More than that, they were incorporating leftover embers and beginning to strengthen their flames even further.

Aureatia's second faction, Haade's camp.

Aureatia outskirts. There, a mansion sat on the shores of a lake, the forest casting a dark shadow over it.

Yuno the Distant Talon had already spent nearly a big month living within this mansion, which almost didn't see any sunlight even in the middle of the day.

During her life here, the only people she had to converse with were the housekeeping matron, Frey; and the young lady Linaris.

"…Are you bored, Miss Yuno?"

"Nope. I'm fine."

She shook her head.

Linaris's visits to her room would often come in the middle of the night like this.

She was radiantly beautiful, yet the quiet light of the moon suited the girl more than the rays of the sun.

"When I think about it, honestly…just because I was in Aureatia, I didn't really head outside to enjoy myself or go converse with a lot of different people or anything… Actually, that sort of stuff made me feel awful."

Whether she was conscious of it or not, that sensation had always been within Yuno.

Since surviving Nagan's ruination, acting freely or enjoying things for herself had come to feel like blasphemy to her.

This building repression inside her might have been what occasionally drove Yuno to madness.

She was unable to believe in her own sanity. Nor that right now, she was living here in the home base of Aureatia's enemy.

"…Linaris, are you okay? Um, it seems like…you have a harder time being outside for long."

"My apologies. It wasn't my wish to make you worry as well, Miss Yuno."

Linaris put her hand to her breast and smiled.

Back then, when she had first met her, Linaris had staggered under the rays of the sun.

However, from what Yuno saw of her lifestyle, it wasn't that she was especially weak to sunlight—she had a fundamentally frail constitution. For Linaris, even the smallest outing would have been equivalent to extreme hard labor.

"However, I have been perfectly fine as of late. Because I am also able to chat with you, Miss Yuno. Um. If possible, would you continue teaching me the rest of set theory? I always enjoy listening to your stories of the college at Nagan."

Linaris leaned forward, and Yuno couldn't help but pull her body back in turn.

Had she forgotten that Yuno had once inflicted harm on her?

Linaris was always meek and wise, unguarded in surprising

ways, and had something within her that unconsciously stirred the hearts of those she spoke with.

"U-um...maybe tomorrow. You're so smart, Linaris, that I end up losing confidence in myself."

"That is because you teach me so well, Miss Yuno."

"*Ah-ha-ha*, that's not..."

She suddenly covered her mouth.

Yuno had let a laugh slip again. Despite how much she wanted never to act like that again.

I...ran away from General Haade's side and came to Linaris's mansion. From here...what am I supposed to do? Just because we've gotten friendlier, that doesn't mean there's any way Linaris will let someone who knows internal information about Obsidian Eyes go.

Yuno had pondered the same thing over and over again since arriving at this manor.

It always ended without her reaching any answers. Even after breaking through a situation that blocked her from achieving her vengeance, she had been surrounded by yet another obstacle.

It's really nothing short of a miracle I haven't been killed yet. I'm living in comfort, but my present situation is really no different from when I was captured in the New Principality...except this time, there's no way Soujirou is coming all this way to fight for me.

After Yuno had left—had Soujirou been able to beat Ozonezma in his match? Even this remained unknown to her.

She might have been able to find out immediately if she asked.

However, for some reason, she didn't want to bring up Soujirou when she was sitting before the girl in front of her.

Am I even supposed to escape *from here in the first place? No question that Obsidian Eyes is dangerous. But…they could be beneficial for my revenge. I still haven't settled on that answer…*

"Miss Yuno?"

"Wah!"

Linaris was peering close into her face again. Yuno's bashfulness and nerves had sent her heartbeat into high gear. It was agony.

"L-Linaris…are you the type of girl to do that stuff?"

"What stuff exactly?"

Linaris blinked her golden eyes, perplexed. When she gazed at Yuno's face and her breasts up close, she felt very glad that, at the very least, she was a woman, too.

"…If you get so close to everyone like that, well…it's really dangerous, isn't it?"

"Why, it's not dangerous. You're my friend, after all."

"That's not what I mean; you're so pretty that—"

"Oh, please…"

"…It's true."

She stared back into Linaris's eyes. Her behavior may have stemmed not from Yuno being another girl or that they were close in age…but because she didn't know how much distance to keep between them from not having much experience interacting with friends. Yuno was sure that during Linaris's lifetime, there had been far fewer people whom she could interact with so intimately like this.

"…Um," said Linaris.

Her golden eyes averted from Yuno's, embarrassed.

"No, never mind... It's okay. I don't mind."

She was lying.

"Thank you for always coming by and talking to me."

"Not at all. I'm the one...who brought you here, Miss Yuno. Perhaps I simply wish to free myself from the guilt."

Linaris gave a strained smile. She, too, had secrets that she couldn't tell to Yuno.

"...Still, though, thanks."

Nevertheless, she had shown trust in Yuno, even though she might have originally been her enemy, and treated her like a friend.

If it was possible...I'd like to show as much trust in her as she had in me.

The thoughts came to Yuno, unrelated to her revenge.

It didn't go just for Linaris. Soujirou and Haade, too.

Though they may have been a loathed archenemy or someone she betrayed...if Yuno could, she wished she could return their trust.

Though that's probably far too egotistical for someone like me.

Yuno still remained a powerless young girl, making it impossible to even imagine when such a day would come.

◆

In a spot slightly removed from the black mansion, there existed a cave just deep enough for shelter from the wind and rain.

Starting from the day prior, there was a colossal and inhuman mass of metal enshrined within.

"Mestelexil."

Lingering at his feet was an elderly leprechaun woman with a cane. A member of Obsidian Eyes and Linaris's devoted household matron. Frey the Waking.

"If you're able to speak properly, then answer me. Mestelexil."

"Un-nnh."

The golem answered with an inarticulate groan.

Mestelexil, meant to be Obsidian Eyes' final trump card, was now under particularly elaborate mental dominion. The load had been tantamount to completely reconstructing his sense of self.

"Wh-where is, nice lady?"

"My lady isn't here. However, I have come with a message from her. You will listen to what she says, of course, won't you? Mestelexil."

"Y-yeah. I-I'll listen…to what nice lady, says."

Therefore, it was only at this stage that it became possible to disrupt his directive system.

Even among all the agents throughout history, Frey the Waking was the only one who knew the weakness of Obsidian's technique. If Rehart the Obsidian had learned of this fact, Frey would have been disposed of without question.

However, Frey hadn't the slightest intention whatsoever of using this secret in revolt. If anything, she believed that it was meant to be used explicitly to protect the young mistress she loved and respected.

"At this position here in Central Aureatia, there is a small clinic."

Frey took out a detailed map of Aureatia's streets. There was a cross etched at a single point on the map. Beside it was an accurately reproduced portrait of their target.

"There is a clinic where this mark is. Aim just for this building and burn it completely to the ground without a trace. If the person with this face flees from the building...pursue them as long as it takes and kill them. Understand?"

The next operation would be, for Obsidian Eyes, the most critical one of all. They couldn't allow the slightest chance for this natural enemy of theirs to intervene. Frey needed to be the one to make this move, which had become a blind spot for Linaris.

"I-if the nice lady...orders it, I will, do my best! *Ha-ha-ha-ha.*"

"That's right. I myself and my lady will be watching you work."

"*Ha-ha-ha-ha-ha-ha-ha. Exil io mestel. Waskert bafewar. Fain myuewm. Hangmot netlicon. Uladzmot.*" (From Exil to Mestel. Star reversion. Howling rain and wind. Earthmoving darkness. Release.)

Incanting Word Arts together with loud, staccato laughter, Mestelexil generated a new armament on his back. In the Beyond, it was a mechanism known as a rocket engine.

"XR-4A3."

The demonic weapon flew off into the sky, like a death-bringing shooting star.

◆

Central Aureatia. Inside a hospital, a creature resembling a songbird flapped about in glee.

"Wow, Toroa, that's amazing! You can hop up and down like that?! I didn't think you'd get better so fast! Wowee!"

It wasn't a bird, but a tiny girl with blue wings. A homunculus named Cuneigh the Wanderer.

In the middle of the girl's whirling flight stood a hulking dwarf with a somewhat troubled look on his face.

A minian child sat with his legs crossed in a chair within the same hospital room, while a leprechaun wrapped in a dark-brown coat leaned against the wall in front of the door.

Toroa the Awful, and his sponsor, Mizial the Iron-Piercing Plumeshade. Along with Kuuro the Careful.

"You gotta calm down for me, Cuneigh. I don't mind you flying and hopping left and right, but I'm scared I'll smack you if you fly in too close."

"Really? You're worried, Toroa? Sorry. I'll still be watching from where Kuuro is, okay?!"

Cuneigh returned to her usual position inside Kuuro's coat pocket.

Kuuro let out a sigh, a mixture of relief and astonishment.

"...Seriously, I don't even believe my own eyes. Psianop the Inexhaustible Stagnation risked his life to injure those knees of yours, didn't he?"

"I heard it from Dad too many times to count, but...apparently, my body's special. I gotta thank my parents...my real parents. Though—"

Toroa the Awful looked at Kuuro and smiled faintly.

"I bet I'll be bragging for a while about pulling off something even those clairvoyant eyes of yours couldn't believe."

"Yeah. Go right ahead and brag about that even more than those enchanted swords of yours."

Mizial, sitting in a corner of the room, kicked his feet up and down.

"Hey, Toroa. You're still going to be in Aureatia, right?"

"...Probably. I've got the citizenship you gave me and all. Guess I could crash here for a little while longer."

"...! Right?! I thought you'd say that! I mean, you got super banged up in the first round, so you haven't gotten any chance to go around the city at all, right?! I'm, well...coming along."

Mizial's four limbs were still thickly wrapped up in bandages, and his right arm remained in a splint.

"My injuries have healed a fair amount, so let's go explore the ruins of the old kingdom's fortress or something! It's really, really dark and goes super deep! I promise, it'll be scary, and a lot of fun! I can show you around!"

"Sure. That'd be nice..."

As he gazed at the two conversing with each other, Cuuro pondered the true identity of this enchanted swordsman.

When he first laid eyes on him that fateful day, he thought the dead had come back to life. That the Toroa the Awful who was supposed to have been killed by Alus the Star Runner had revived and wouldn't stop until he had slaughtered any others who wielded enchanted swords.

However, after Kuuro had his life saved by Toroa, talked with him face-to-face, and watched him deepen his bonds with Mizial and Cuneigh, it had become wholly impossible to believe this man was some mysterious and unknown monster.

True, his skills with enchanted swords were not inferior to the legendary Toroa, or maybe his nightmarish killing blades might've even surprised the legends. However, the Toroa the Awful standing before him, at least, was an artless and good-natured, if slightly inarticulate, young dwarven man from the countryside.

...Toroa. Just who exactly are you?

Kuuro found himself wishing that the man was an impostor.

That it would be best if the horror-story monster drenched by blood and slaughter wasn't the man smiling with Mizial in front of him.

"Right! What about you, Kuuro? If there's anything you wanna eat, I'll treat you! My family's loaded, so no need to hold back, okay?"

"You shouldn't be the one to say it like that..."

Toroa sighed with exasperation.

Mizial the Iron-Piercing Plumeshade was an honest young boy who acted his age, standing out from the Twenty-Nine Officials, which were rampant with devils and wickedness. He was a well-suited sponsor for Toroa, to the point where it made Kuuro think so just from looking at the two of them from the sidelines.

There wasn't any need to be on guard against traps, like Kuuro had throughout his life up until now. He found himself wishing he could fully indulge in their friendly dispositions.

And that he could talk with them, just a little bit longer.

"…No thanks. I'm planning on leaving Aureatia now."

"But, Kuuro."

Cuneigh raised an anxious voice from within his breast pocket. He gently patted her through his coat to try calming her down.

"I decided from the very start I'd take off once Toroa's legs were healthy again. Looks like I'm fated to never stay in one town for too long."

Toroa the Awful's wounds had fully healed far faster than he had imagined.

For Kuuro, he couldn't have asked for anything better. Leaving Aureatia and spending his days ensuring he didn't get involved with Obsidian Eyes. The optimal path for survival. That was what he'd follow.

From inside his chest, Cuneigh's worried tone came again.

"But, Kuuro. Listen. Won't you be lonely?"

"…Me? I wonder. I'm more worried about whether you'll get lonely or not, Cuneigh."

"I… I'd like to get to know Toroa and Mizial a bit better, I think…"

"Yeah. I know—"

It was at that moment.

You're too slow.

Anger was the very first emotion that welled up inside him.

He was looking not toward Toroa or toward Mizial, but outside the window of the clinic.

What the hell are you doing with your clairvoyance, Kuuro? You noticed it too late. *Shouldn't you be able to sense life-threatening danger* before *it's moments away?*

His clairvoyance could foresee everything. Not only limited to perceiving everything in the present across an ultra-wide area, he could even sense a destined future, deduced by bringing all the information of his senses together.

"Toroa!"

Kuuro was the only one inside the hospital losing his composure. No one else in the area had the same reaction.

"I'm leaving Cuneigh with you! You and Mizial need to run!"

"…What happened, Kuuro…? No—"

Toroa the Awful pulled his jet-black hood deep over his face.

"—*what's going to happen?*"

"Don't try to fight! Keep Mizial alive!"

"W-wait a second, Kuuro, so you're saying that clairvoyance of yours…can see something, right?"

"Mestelexil's coming!" Kuuro declared. He could sense the cold sweat that began to pour out all at once. "You all will die! I'll be the only one left!"

They were out of time. His Clairvoyance's perception wasn't too slow. His enemy *was too fast.*

The rocket engine, delivering continuous flight at supersonic speeds, was a machine of the Beyond that greatly eclipsed the wisdom of this world.

This won't work. If they ask me to repeat myself again, it'll be too late. I need them to believe me right now.

Kuuro aimed the crossbow hidden up his sleeve at Mizial.

Cuneigh shouted:

"Kuuro!"

"If you don't want this boy shot, then you need to take these two with you and get out of here! Right now!"

"Got it," Toroa briefly replied.

Then his large hand scooped up Mizial. His other hand was then stretched out in front of Kuuro—

Though he knew he hadn't a single second to waste, to the leprechaun, the movement felt like an eternity.

Cuneigh. He had to part ways with the partner he cherished more than anyone.

Just as Cuneigh had entrusted his life to Toroa on that fateful day.

"Kuuro!"

"...Take her!"

"Kuuro! Nooo!" Cuneigh tearfully screamed. Kuuro wished he could tell her something, anything, to help reassure her, but there wasn't any time. Toroa believed Kuuro's words, then immediately kicked through the clinic window and ran off down the road.

...*Right now. It's coming.*

What Kuuro sensed was nothing but a premonition right before his enemy had starting moving. Mestelexil had *flown off at that moment*. Clairvoyance, in extreme situations, prognosticated even the future itself with unparalleled accuracy.

Nevertheless, if Toroa had carried Kuuro off and withdrawn from this location, he knew for certain that they would be tracked and attacked all together. Since the enemy's target was Kuuro the Careful. He understood that, too.

It's not the young mistress... Either Frey or Wieze. If they had just trusted me for a bit longer. Then I would've...without killing anyone...

Going by Mestelexil's flight speed, he had barely a few seconds left.

He could see the method of attack coming after those few seconds. A bomb containing a large quantity of incendiaries would reduce the whole area around the clinic to ash. The weapon was referred to as a cluster bomb in the Beyond, but Kuuro's Clairvoyance wasn't comprehensive enough to give him this name.

The coordinates where Mestelexil would generate the bomb, and the bombing angle. Air resistance. Terrain cover. Estimation of the fuel properties. Where the closest water source was from this position. Whether or not there was a route that would allow him to endure the several seconds following the impact, when chemicals were scattered into the air. Breathing. Posture. Body maneuvering. Allowable injuries. Limitless information, everything and anything in the world around him, was being processed in the span of a microsecond.

Cuneigh and Mizial had gotten away. However, that wasn't because Kuuro had given up on his own life.

This is the best way. If I'm by myself...I can survive. As long as I have my Clairvoyance!

The sky let out a roar. It likely appeared as nothing more than a single streak of light through the air. It was too fast to visually grasp its presence.

Explosion. Descent.

Kuuro was the only one who saw, through the ceiling cover, the malefic comet, navy blue, passing overhead.

It was Mestelexil who had, on the day of the Particle Storm, saved him together with Toroa.

The clinic dissolved.

The raging blaze, flowing like a river, instantly swallowed up the entire building, burning thirty-six townspeople, including the hospital's patients, in the blink of an eye.

From that day, all news of Kuuro the Careful's whereabouts ceased.

Half a day after the end of the sixth match.

There were quiet whispers being exchanged in an abandoned house on an overpass in the old town.

"Hey, Kaete. Don't go nodding off, you idiot."

"I'm not…! Don't put it like that! Something happen?"

"We've got trouble."

Aureatia's former Fourth Minister, Kaete the Round Table. With him, self-proclaimed demon king Kiyazuna the Axle.

They were charged with serious foul play in the sixth match, and both had become wanted fugitives—with the even more pressing problem being the presence of their pursuers, who were aiming to kill them.

The spy organization that had framed the pair and spun conspiracy like ghosts behind the scenes of the Sixways Exhibition, Obsidian Eyes. A squad of unknown scale, with each individual member possessing fighting skills that could rival any champion.

Not only this, but Kaete's and Kiyazuna's once trump card, Mestelexil the Box of Desperate Knowledge, had his controlling authority seized by the same Obsidian Eyes.

"We've been spotted. They're calling their little friends."

"Radzio wiretapping?! That's a clever move, all right!"

"*Heh!* That's 'cause the people here don't know anything about cell splitting or spread spectrum. The radzio ore's too damn convenient, so there's no way for tech to keep up... More importantly, though, these bastards are gonna surround us here soon. That happens, and we're done for."

"Launching ourselves out there's all we got. I had planned to do that eventually anyway!"

"That's what I like to hear. Let's kill 'em, Kaete..."

When the old woman raised a fist in the air, wooden golems resembling praying mantises thronged out of every nook and cranny in the abandoned house. They were merely a makeshift fighting force, constructed while lacking both materials and time, and their only capability was to cut down anything deemed an enemy. On top of that, they were thoroughly silent, making less noise than a single ant's footsteps.

Though they were isolated and holding out on their own, it was possible to produce a fighting force from the lumber taken from the floorboards and walls. Kiyazuna the Axle was the ultimate golem user, whom no one else across the land could best.

Kaete, too, having just lost his sword, had created a new one with his own Word Arts. Kaete's duty was that of a civilian official, but he was a prodigy with distinguished abilities even when it came to swordplay or Word Arts.

"Only one enemy. Uses a straight sword."

"Got it."

The praying mantis–like Wood Golem army first surged like an avalanche and attacked—

"Hwah!"

The straight-sword wielder—Hyakrai the Tower—opened up plenty of space for himself.

As he leaped back and drew his sword, he swept aside the blades of the jumping golems and slipped through the surrounding horde.

Meanwhile, Kaete and Kiyazuna rushed off in the direction of the alleyway's blind spot, which they'd driven their enemy into.

As he ran, Kaete grabbed the torso of golem that was following along at his feet.

"Sniper fire!"

"*Geh!*"

The golem Kaete raised up high squeaked. A chakram flew in from somewhere, biting into its composite armor and charring the wood layer until it was finally severed in two.

Three golems automatically jumped up and stopped the next long-range attack with their body. All of them were destroyed.

There was a tall building that could look down over this overpass bridge.

"...There were two of them after all!"

"Hey, Kaete! Those're *my* golems, dammit!"

The several dozen wood golems were about as big as a minia's balled fist. Nevertheless, each one possessed armor and combat capabilities on par with Aureatia soldiers. Four of them had been destroyed all at once.

Then from behind them.

"…Ahhh… What do we do?"

Hyakrai the Tower was closing in. The wood golems that were supposed to be swarming him, in the span of an instant, were culled in significant numbers.

One after another, the golems' blades closed in from three directions. Hyakrai casually dropped his body and evaded them.

Finishing them off from below with a minimum number of thrusts, he held back the opening moves from a golem's scythes using the hand not holding his sword and destroyed the golem with a kick.

Then moving as if he weighed nothing at all, he rose back up once again.

His sword vanished for an instant in the kickback from getting up, then it slashed a golem in two, blades and all.

"Y-you should've waited…just a bit longer for me… If they got away, it'd b-be my responsibility…"

"Set your mind at ease."

While hiding in a blind spot away from the long-range chakram attacks, Kaete turned back to this enemy.

How many of these golems had gone down? Five… Ten. They could still definitely fight with these numbers. There was always a chance of victory. That's what he tried to believe.

Kaete had his back up against the abandoned house's wall. Close enough to be slashed if he stepped forward.

The enemy was a swordsman like him. For their range, his was slightly wider, given the length of his arms. Kaete tried to lure in his enemy's attention with his words.

"You can take care of that responsibility of yours in the next life."

"*Hoo...*"

Hyakrai suddenly stumbled a step forward and fell to the side. The same abnormal opening move as before.

However, this time, it wasn't a sword attack, but a throwing move aimed at a different target beside Kaete. Kiyazuna immediately pulled in her arm and evaded the dagger swooping toward her. The blade stuck itself nearly halfway into the stone wall behind her.

Hyakrai stuck one leg straight up into the air right as he collapsed, and the tip of this foot touched one of the two golems that'd flown toward him at that same moment. That single touch seemed to have slightly deviated its direction, as the golem's scythes destroyed the other golem.

Kaete thought to stab during the opening caused by Hyakrai's collapsing posture, but he listened to his gut telling him to hold his ground.

"Too bad."

The series of movements had been a rotational motion. As if foreseeing that Kaete would catch him off guard, Hyakrai swept with his sword using the height of his shin. As he slashed through the air, he smoothly stood back up.

If he had lost his balance the slightest bit, he would then have fallen straight down from atop the bridge.

It was a completely unnatural recovery, as if he was raising up his entire upper body with just his ankle.

...What exactly...is with this guy's joints? Going off balance doesn't leave any opening at all. He can fight with this much force from that stance? Damn abomination.

Hyakrai the Tower held out against the incessant slicing from the golems assailing him and kept Kiyazuna in check, all while shortening the distance between them little by little. As if he was the god of death himself.

"Ohhh... D-do you think if you hide like that, those ranged attacks won't reach you? Surely not."

"......!"

A chakram was stuck in the wall. It was the wall surface that Kaete was hiding behind, creating a dead angle for the long-range attacks. The throwing weapon could rotate to change its trajectory. Even long-range attacks that curved around corners were possible for him, too?

"...Calm down, Kaete! As long as he's launching those from that distance, there'll be a limit to the curvature radius! Don't move, and it won't hit you!" yelled Kiyazuna.

"*Heh-heh.* That's true. But it's too late," said Hyakrai.

Hyakrai turned his sights up above him.

"Rehem!"

"*Tch!*"

Kaete followed his sights and braced himself.

Supposing the chakram thrown just now, knowing it would miss, was launched to keep him and Kiyazuna in their place.

Their enemy squad wasn't necessarily a group of two—

An elbow was stabbing into his ribs. Kaete dropped his sword.

"……!"

Accelerating in an instant, Hyakrai pinned Kaete up against the wall.

It was simple good luck that stopped Kaete from being skewered on the spot. Hyakrai had used the momentum of his rotation to stab his elbow into Kaete while he curbed the encroaching golem swarm from the rear by swinging his sword behind him.

There was no advance warning to his stance change. The enemy's range was, from the very start, longer than Kaete's.

This guy... No, both of them...!

They had tried to convince him there was a third among them. That was why the sharpshooter had purposely thrown his projectile.

In addition to these sword skills, which outmatched the Twenty-Nine Officials, they possessed enough proficiency to work with such precise coordination, even when separated by such a distance. They were mysterious. There were only two enemies. Each one of them was abnormally strong.

"...Grams!" Kaete shouted. Over Hyakrai's shoulder, he saw Kiyazuna collapsed on the ground, lying on her back. A short sword was stabbed into her stomach, and she wasn't moving. This swordsman had, in the brief second he had created with his words, incapacitated two people simultaneously.

The right half of his body neutralized, Kaete tried to fight back with his free left arm. Even then, the enemy was faster and would split Kaete's head open with the pommel of his sword.

"Ah."

However, said sword was guarding against a slash from behind.

A hatchet, resembling a meaty kitchen knife, was turned away by the straight sword and smacked the ground.

A hatchet. Someone freshly arriving to the fight had assaulted Hyakrai.

"......!"

She was a burly and muscular woman, taller than Kaete. Her deeply taut smirk and narrowed eyes, combined with the scars on her face, had a monsterlike ferocity.

Who is this?

"Not good enough..." said Hyakrai.

Hyakrai the Tower was a master who hadn't missed a beat while taking several dozen golems on all at once.

Even if a single fighter came in to help, with his flexible body posture, he could instantly slash back with his straight sword and—

Then he turned in Kiyazuna's direction.

There was a bursting sound— *Pop, pop, pop, pop, pop.*

"Hngh...! Augh! Gah!"

The straight sword he guarded with shattered into pieces.

Blood burst from Hyakrai's hands and feet, and he collapsed in a knot where he stood.

"The HK MP5. You got sloppy, brat."

The weapon Kiyazuna the Axle had whipped out was called a submachine gun. A remainder of the Mestelexil-produced weapons from the Beyond.

"I-impossible..."

Much like his reaction to the incoming projectile moments prior, Hyakrai hadn't neglected to remain constantly vigilant against any movements from Kiyazuna. However...in that brief second, his attention was diverted to the sudden arrival of the giant woman.

The old crone smirked amid the smoke of gunpowder.

"You think a golem master...didn't prep any golem armor for herself, did ya?"

The composite armor hidden within her clothes fell, and there was a metallic echo on the stone pavement.

Of course, Hyakrai's dagger had pierced through that armor and lightly tore into her abdominal muscle, so her performance had also been a bluff that required her to muster all the strength she had.

"*Gahak...ngh.*"

Severely wounded, Hyakrai began to sink lower, teetering.

Kaete didn't hesitate to step right in front of him and go to cut off his head.

"Back, Kaete!" shouted Kiyazuna.

With a light, tumbling motion, Hyakrai's sword flashed smoothly. Kaete's forehead was lightly grazed, and Hyakrai fell down, face looking upward. Down below the overpass bridge.

"...Dammit! I should've won...!"

"Hey, what about the sniper?"

Kiyazuna looked at the building across from the bridge.

He had vanished without a trace. They'd immediately retreated the moment Hyakrai was knocked out of the fight.

On top of the bridge stood Kiyazuna and Kaete. As well as the mysterious hatchet-wielding woman.

"...Who're you?"

"I'm not your enemy, former Fourth Minister Kaete the Round Table. You two are going to come together with us."

She was undeniably a skilled fighter. She didn't appear to have lost any composure during the series of offensive and defensive back-and-forths just now.

However, Kaete the Round Table had no recollection of seeing a warrior such as her among Aureatia's soldiers.

In which case, which power did she belong with?

"Don't piss me off. Who are you? Can't reveal who you're with—is that it?"

"Caneeya the Fruit Trimming."

The woman spun her meaty hatchet with one hand.

Kaete had heard the name before. The abnormal and valiant woman who had battled against Twenty-Fourth General Dant on the Toghie City lines. It was said she brandished an enormous hatchet and always wore a smile on the battlefield.

More than anything, however...she wasn't an Aureatia soldier.

"I'm an Old Kingdoms' loyalist. You two don't have any options... Of course..."

Kaete the Round Table, believing that this day of the sixth match marked the doomed fate of it all, ended up having his doomed life saved through a wholly unforeseen encounter.

Nevertheless, it absolutely didn't mean that the situation had changed for the better.

"...that's only if you want to survive."

The stable owned by Aureatia's Fourteenth General, Yuca the Halation Gaol, housed a bizarre and colossal beast. From a distance, it seemed similar to a wolf, but it didn't resemble any other creature the world knew.

That was because he was a chimera. The hero candidate defeated in the third match, Ozonezma the Capricious.

"…I NO LONGER HAVE ANYTHING TO DO WITH YOUR FIGHT."

The person he was conversing with was a goblin. A messenger from Zigita Zogi the Thousandth.

"I ASSISTED HIROTO AS LONG AS I ADVANCED THROUGH THE SIXWAYS EXHIBITION. THEREFORE, HIROTO HELPED TO ENSURE MY VICTORY. THAT WAS THE AGREEMENT. THERE IS NOTHING MORE BEYOND THAT."

"This matter isn't about assisting with Zigita Zogi's operation."

"IT IS NO DIFFERENT, GIVEN THE END RESULT WILL HELP HIM WIN."

Ozonezma's objective was finished. He no longer had any reason to be involved with the Sixways Exhibition, and he didn't desire to continue his contact with Hiroto's camp after losing his match, given it would bring with it danger and risk.

His contractual relationship with Zigita Zogi was finished. Even considering that fact, the situation might have required Ozonezma's help; however—

"Then what about as a doctor?"

"...WHAT?"

"There is a possibility that behind the scenes of the Sixways Exhibition, a new species of corpse is running rampant. We believe that with your medical skills, perhaps healing patients who have been turned into corpses could be possible."

"...I WON'T SAY IT IS IMPOSSIBLE. HOWEVER, THE TREATMENT CAN ONLY BE DONE DIRECTLY AFTER INFECTION. A LARGE QUANTITY OF BLOOD FOR TRANSFUSION WILL ALSO BE CRITICAL. IF THAT DOES NOT DISSUADE YOU, THEN...I WILL SAVE EMERGING PATIENTS AS BEST I CAN."

Ozonezma the Capricious was a medic along with being a chimera.

Killing many champions in the past, he had left this continent behind in despair following the death of the True Demon King.

With the techniques he'd used to continue his murders as well as improve his own body, he tried to dispel the curse over his own body by saving innocent people to make up for all those whose lives he had taken.

All while carrying something like the Demon King's arm inside me. Truly foolish.

Ultimately, though, in reality, the gnawing at his heart wasn't a sense of guilt over his continued killing at all.

It was because the most loathsome origin of said curse had been quite literally inside him all along.

"...I DO NOT MEAN TO DIRECTLY ASSIST WITH ZIGITA ZOGI'S BATTLE. TO AVOID INVITING ANY UNWANTED SUSPICIONS, IDEALLY, I WILL DEPART RIGHT AFTER THE EIGHTH MATCH. I ASK YOU TO TAKE THAT INTO ACCOUNT."

"Understood. In that case, we'll be waiting for you at the castle garden theater."

The messenger slipped through the window he had left open and disappeared. Not a single trace was left behind.

DURING THE EIGHTH MATCH, THERE WILL BE A LARGE-SCALE OUTBREAK OF CORPSES. THAT WOULD THEN MEAN...SOMEONE IS TARGETING ZIGITA ZOGI'S MATCH TO BRING ABOUT SUCH AN EVENT.

After the messenger departed, Ozonezma went to sleep for a spell.

He woke when this stable's master, Yuca the Halation Gaol, appeared.

"How are you feeling?"

"...NOT BAD."

"*Ha-ha-hah.* That's some impressive resilience, I'll say that. Chimeras are something. You can already fight freely now, right?"

"I HAVE NOT TESTED THAT EXACTLY. IS THE SEARCH GOING WELL?

"You mean Kaete and Kiyazuna? Not at all. The day of the sixth match, we found a large number of bloodstains in a back alley inside the old town. But there's been no bodies yet—there's talk that even that could've been a diversionary tactic, too. It's Kaete and all. He's definitely thinks things through a lot more than me; it's annoying."

BLOODSTAINS? IF THERE IS A VAMPIRE MIXED IN WITHIN THE HERO CANDIDATES...I SHOULD HAVE AT LEAST TRIED TO GET THAT MUCH INFORMATION OUT OF THAT MESSENGER.

For the Sixways Exhibition, Ozonezma's chosen strategy had been to cut off information about himself and others from Gimeena City, then focus everything he had on his own match. He didn't possess any information on the other hero candidates that didn't directly involve himself.

It was a purposeful strategy. Since Zigita Zogi was such a brilliant tactician, any information shared from him couldn't possibly be gotten for free. He had determined that knowing too much information about the other hero candidates would risk other camps targeting him as well.

However, now he would be going on his own to the castle garden theater. Due to a forecasted corpse infection, at that. He would also need information on Zigita Zogi's opponent.

Ozonezma looked at the clock.

THE EIGHTH MATCH SHOULD BE STARTING SOON.

—Uhak the Silent. He only knew the name and had no idea what sort of person they were.

"YUCA. HOW DO YOU SEE THE EIGHTH MATCH PLAY-ING OUT?"

"Hmm? You mean who'll win? Normally, a fight between an ogre and a goblin, it'd be obvious who'd win there, but...Zigita Zogi's real strong and all."

"...OGRE."

With that single word, he felt as if all the hair on his body had stood up on end.

He tossed his head. Why hadn't the thought come to him?

The entire time, up until his loss in the third match, Ozonezma had been lost in madness.

Even though what he saw, or *what he didn't try to see*, didn't serve him at all in his judgments.

"DID YOU SAY 'OGRE'?"

"Yeah. A gray-colored ogre, doesn't speak a word. That said, though, I haven't heard anything about him myself. No idea where he came from or— Ozonezma?"

Ozonezma kicked off the ground before Yuca could stop him.

By the time the hay thrown up by the gust had fallen to the ground, he was already gone.

◆

The day of the eighth match. The waiting room at the castle garden theater.

Hiroto the Paradox wasn't present in Zigita Zogi's waiting room.

No matter how close their collaborative relationship may have been, during the Sixways Exhibition, the only ones allowed in the waiting room areas were his sponsor or people directly involved with them.

As the match drew close at hand, the door opened, and someone entered the room.

"Zigita Zogi. Got a minute?"

Twenty-Fourth General, Dant the Heath Furrow. Zigita Zogi's sponsor.

"Certainly. There's still some time left."

"...I know this is right before your match, but it seems Nofelt still hasn't returned to Aureatia."

Sixteenth General, Nofelt the Somber Wind. Uhak the Silent's sponsor.

"I see. Any investigation on Aureatia's end?"

"It hasn't turned into an incident yet. Nofelt's schedule has him returning to the city today. But...wouldn't he have come back in the morning? As of right now, no one has been able to get a handle on his movements."

"Supposing Nofelt never returns, what would then happen to me?"

"......I can assume that you've done something, then, haven't you?"

"Well now. For the time being, it would seem our luck isn't all that bad."

Although he was a part of Hiroto's camp as well, Dant, one of the Twenty-Nine Officials, was unaware of the full circumstances regarding Nofelt. The man hadn't responded to Kuze the Passing Disaster's persuasions and was cut down by the blade of death on the spot.

As long as his sponsor's death hadn't been verified, Uhak the Silent, strictly speaking, wasn't disqualified. Much like the hero candidate swap in the fourth match, even if a candidate's sponsor met a sudden untimely end, a hero candidate could continue on in the Sixways Exhibition by naming a replacement sponsor.

However, Nofelt couldn't arrive at the garden theater. Zigita Zogi believed that the chances of Uhak showing up were also extremely low.

...Uhak the Silent has no initiative of his own.

From the start, Uhak wasn't a shura who had become a hero candidate of his own volition. He was brought all the way to Aureatia by Nofelt, registered as a hero candidate, and merely fought to go along with some orders or obligations.

The Alimo Row massacre was the one and only case where it appeared he had taken action of his own will.

What was his objective, and why is he appearing in the Sixways Exhibition...? Ideally, I would've liked to gather information about his motives as well. No matter how deeply we probed into his personal background, that alone seemed practically nonexistent.

"Just what is Uhak the Silent's goal in participating anyway?"

Dant vocalized the same question in Zigita Zogi's thoughts.

"...I have investigated Uhak the Silent's past. Nothing at all is known about before he appeared in Alimo Row, but...right now, the only thing Uhak has is his connection to the Order. First, he was saved by Cunodey the Ring Seat, then he followed Nofelt, a child raised by the Order, to become a hero candidate...and I've been told by Master Kuze the Passing Disaster himself that during the raid on the almshouse, the ogre saved him. Although we still don't know the 'why'...at present, it's clear to see who he serves."

"......"

Zigita Zogi had collected information on all the Order children across the entire continent and used that to bring Kuze the Passing Disaster into Hiroto's camp. His reasoning didn't just stop at the man's usefulness as an assassin, but was also used as a part of his long-term plan to use the Order connection to manage Uhak the Silent.

Securing Uhak the Silent was an essential requirement for Zigita Zogi, the individually weakest candidate in the tournament, to advance through the Sixways Exhibition.

"What about you?" asked Dant.

"...By me, you mean what, exactly?"

"Are you following the orders of Hiroto the Paradox the individual? Or do you seek to manipulate Hiroto's power, too, if it helps your goal of seeping into Aureatia? In your case, you've never deliberately talked through it all."

"I see. Master Hiroto is more the one who would enjoy these sorts of topics. I myself... Well, it's not in my nature to bring up my own goals, or what have you, on my own."

Zigita Zogi the Thousandth was a Zogi blood descendant, continuing down from Zegegu Zogi the Stone Dam. His forefather, Zegegu Zogi, was the wisest goblin of his age, one of the first companions Hiroto the Paradox gained for himself, and Zigita Zogi was told he had perished soon after fulfilling his grand undertaking of searching for the new continent.

Zigita Zogi was fighting in part to fulfill Zegegu Zogi's ardent wish.

Even when he, a commander, was confronted with the condition to participate in the Sixways Exhibition, as a hostage from capitulated Okafu, the agreement had come without a moment's hesitation.

However, that was purely because he had thought, of his own will, that was best.

"It's not about whether I serve Master Hiroto or if I'm using him. Let's see. While this may not sound like something a tactician such as myself would say—"

The minia who had, since the age of a faceless ancestor, striven harder toward the goblins' growth than anyone else.

The minia who hadn't hesitated to declare that the single dose of vampire antiserum that they received from Haade the Flashpoint as compensation for their cooperation would be given to Zigita Zogi and not himself.

Who had said that as long as Zigita Zogi remained, there was a future for goblins.

"I like him. Master Hiroto."

"...I can believe it," Dant quietly replied. "The man's a truly terrifying politician, after all. Jovialness, friendliness, a striking gift for attracting others—I can't help but see the man as the complete opposite of what makes a suitable politician. He's argumentative, weird, and even a bit suspicious, yet for some reason, I can't help wishing *that I would become a friend of his.*"

"Master Dant... So you do *not* seek to become a friend of Master Hiroto's, then, I take it?"

"...That's right."

Dant had said that all the tactical decisions were made by Zigita Zogi, but that wasn't true.

When it came time for them to come to Aureatia as a hero candidate, it was Hiroto the Paradox who'd chosen Dant. At the time, it didn't only have an element of currying favor...but there was something else. Something that Dant the Heath Furrow possessed that Hiroto needed to smoothly move things toward the future.

...Eventually turning him into an ally. Whoever it may be, as long as they could become an ally, there wasn't anything more to ask for.

The door opened.

"Zigita Zogi the Thousandth. The match will begin shortly."

It was a soldier with the castle garden theater, charged with leading the hero candidates to the arena.

"Get your equipment in order until then and wait until someone comes to summon you."

"...The match?"

"Yes, General Dant. Is something the matter?"

"No, well...nothing that major. This means that Uhak the Silent's arrived, then...? Is Nofelt with him?"

"......? Yes, that's right, they both turned up a short while ago. Now then, if you'll excuse me."

"……"

The soldier left the room. Zigita Zogi and Dant both remained silent for a time.

Uhak the Silent had appeared. The principle governing his conduct still remained a mystery.

"…Well then, with that, I'll have no choice left but to fight. Reluctant though I am."

"Zigita Zogi. You said that this invisible army behind the scenes of the Sixways Exhibition had a vampire, right? That Obsidian Eyes, connected with Zeljirga, was moving as an independent faction of its own."

"…Yes. With all likelihood."

"What if Uhak the Silent is being controlled to appear in this match?"

"That would be impossible. The vampire's virus should fall under the effects of Uhak's Word Arts nullification. Like dragons and oozes, their very activity would be erased."

"In that case, what of the possibility that Uhak's appearance at this match is the outcome Obsidian Eyes planned for?"

"That is very plausible, yes… The point about Nofelt's arrival is worrisome… There's a chance, for example, that the perceptions of everyone in the area are being manipulated and misled."

Zigita Zogi raised one finger.

"I made a single error in this battle—having Okafu's mercenaries withdraw from Aureatia in response to the invisible army's infiltration. In other words, Obsidian realized that at least one person in Hiroto's camp, that person highly likely to be myself, *had immediately caught on* to their existence. We have been spreading the information that this enemy is a vampire to various other camps, but there are still very few who are earnestly responding to the news. If there was one person to target first, it would be me."

"In that case...Zigita Zogi. This match is dangerous. Assuming Uhak's defeated, there's the chance some other intruder could appear in the arena and try to dispose of you. If the enemy's a vampire, that's a possible option for them."

"Oh my, I am surprised to hear you, Master Dant, showing any concern my way... Please, no need to worry. If they do barge into the arena, then surely there won't be any problem with throwing in an intruder of our own."

"...Ozonezma?"

"I know he won't be one to sit on the side quietly. In addition, I have laid some number of our own army in the audience as well. If there is any suspicious movement in the stands or near the arena entrance, our force of numbers will be able to keep them back."

"...*Hmph*. You plan on using that proud military force of yours? The Sixways Exhibition is one-on-one, you know."

"Yes. So long as the other side follows the same rules, of course."

Zigita Zogi muffled his voice and smiled, and even serious and stern Dant couldn't help following it with a half-arced smirk of his own.

"...Master Dant. If possible, can I ask you to make contact with Nofelt? Seventh Minister Flinsuda's medical team will arrive in short order. Please meet up with them. I'm certain that there will be someone involved with this invisible army waiting to ambush you. Please make the proper provisions, assuming there will be hostilities."

"...You even arranged for a medical team?"

"Yes. Flinsuda the Portent is someone *who will act for the right price*, you see. In terms of economic clout, Hiroto does not fall behind the other camps at all, mind you. Besides, that isn't the only strategy being put into action today."

"Geez, you people..."

Spitting statements that sounded irritated yet resembled words of confidence, Dant took his sword.

"Go out there and win, Zigita Zogi the Thousandth."

"The same to you, Dant the Heath Furrow. Give everything you have for the Queen."

Dant disappeared from the waiting room.

What remained was Zigita Zogi's own preparations for his match.

He donned a thick iron helm that completely enveloped his face.

Along with protecting his head, it was meant to hide his features from the large unknown masses witnessing the match—additionally, this helmet had a third function in this fight.

He planned on bringing a crossbow into the arena with him, but to Zigita Zogi, that was little more than a backup weapon. The weapon he utilized was a large and long alloy ax strapped to his back.

In a one-on-one true duel, Zigita Zogi was unable to bring

his true weapon, his army of goblin soldiers, into the arena. Even then, the unparalleled tactician was still able to ready surefire tactics for his victory.

"Zigita Zogi the Thousandth. It's match time. I shall reaffirm your will to battle in this match here."

Zigita Zogi replied to the soldier guide who had appeared again.

"That won't be necessary. Let's head out now."

"As you wish."

The soldier guide had one arm slung in a bandage. From the conversation he'd heard during the negotiations with Haade, there had been a disturbance behind the scenes of the third match, and one person had been injured.

The invisible army is everywhere.

There was always the possibility of being ambushed, even during the short walk to the arena.

Vampires and corpses infected others either through direct mucous contact or by pouring a large amount of blood through an open wound. Was there any possibility that this soldier had been turned into a corpse when he was cut by the invisible army?

Zigita Zogi's equipment was also a means to immediately suppress such an enemy.

"...I smell blood. I believe you should have a doctor look at that wound of yours."

"It's already undergone Life Arts treatment."

"Quite... However, I merely thought I could introduce you to a more skilled physician, perhaps."

Before long, Zigita Zogi arrived at the arena.

At the same time, a colossal ogre appeared from the opposite corridor—Uhak the Silent.

He did come after all.

In between the pair, the adjudicator, Twenty-Sixth Minister Meeka the Whispered, shouted:

"Combatants, take your appointed positions and face each other!"

As he checked the direction of the wind, Zigita Zogi faced toward Uhak.

Even among other ogres, Uhak was remarkably large. Compared with Zigita Zogi, he was more than three times his size.

Both of his eyes, staring back at Zigita Zogi, were fathomless and white, like a mirror.

"…Well then. I didn't wish to fight at all, if possible."

Zigita Zogi entwined the fingers of his hands together.

Confronting an ogre one-on-one was, for a majority of the creatures in the land, synonymous with death.

Goblins were a species that relied on numbers from their fecundity, and their individual strength was inferior to even a minia's. Nor did they excel with Word Arts when compared with other races, either.

However, when it came to Zigita Zogi the Thousandth, even overturning this racial disparity was possible.

The weapons Zigita Zogi was utilizing in the Sixways Exhibition were not superb racial physical strength or supernatural ability. It wasn't any lethal technical prowess he had honed to perfection. It wasn't even some irreproducible magic item, either.

Electrolyzing table salt produces sodium hydroxide. If this was heated and melted down together with naturally occurring quartz, it generated sodium silicate. From that sodium silicate, one could obtain sodium metasilicate.

There was a third mechanism to the iron helmet that completely covered the goblin's head. It consisted of goggles to protect his eyes and a sodium-metasilicate respirator that filtered outside air—in essence, to give it an internal gasproof filter.

Uhak the Silent. Just what sort of moves do you have, then? Strategies? Tricks? Techniques?

Additionally, on Zigita Zogi's back, he bore an alloy metal ax.

Even in a world without large-scale processing plants or stringent laboratory environments, it wasn't impossible to create such a substance. By combusting coke under a constant temperature, it was possible to produce carbon monoxide. Through the process of electrolyzing table salt, one was able to obtain chlorine.

There was a substance that could be produced by reacting carbon monoxide and chlorine under sunlight.

If it came into contact with the membrane of the ocular mucosa, it would immediately produce hydrochloric acid and induce intense inflammation, rendering one unable to fight.

From there, it would invade the respiratory organs, inducing aftereffects leading to pulmonary edema.

In the Beyond, it was a key substance in chemical manufacturing as well as a deadly poison that terrorized soldiers in a great war... Its name meant "synthesized from the sun" in the Greek language.

Carbonyl dichloride—phosgene.

This will be my first move.

Even Uhak, negating any and all Word Arts, was unable to deny its power.

The power Zigita Zogi wielded was the power of civilization itself.

◆

The spectator seats.

As Hiroto the Paradox watched intently, the eighth match was about to get underway.

...Kuze didn't kill Nofelt?

Uhak the Silent had appeared. It was clear he had a sponsor. Hiroto, not witnessing the moment in person, hadn't confirmed Nofelt's death with his own eyes, but it was impossible to think Zigita Zogi, the one who'd commanded the operation, hadn't verified the body for himself.

Supposing that there was possibility that this "angel" who haunted Kuze could induce not instant death but a temporary state of suspended animation.

Or instead, the possibility that there was some deal between Kuze and Zigita Zogi, and they had left Nofelt alive for a future stratagem. When considering Kuze's personality, this seemed like the far more likely possibility.

...Even then, there isn't much I can do. When it comes to matters martial and tactical, I can't lend any help to Zigita Zogi from here.

"......"

He realized that the audience around him was withdrawing like a receding tide. Hiroto muttered, still facing toward the arena. "...I would avoid interacting with me."

A massive beast, his single body seemingly filling up all the space the retreating audience left behind, was present at his side.

Everyone besides Hiroto feared the grotesque creature and looked at it from afar.

A streamlined beast, resembling a massive and bizarre wolf, with bluish-silver fur. Ozonezma the Capricious.

"*HAAAH, HAAAH...*"

His breathing was terribly ragged. It was hard to believe a creature like Ozonezma would get like this just from running at full speed. This breathing was psychogenic. He was scared.

"Or maybe...Ozonezma. Do you have some personal business with me?"

"DID—DID YOU KNOW?"

The fiendish and wicked tone in his voice was unlike anything Hiroto had ever heard from the chimera before.

"DID YOU REALLY KNOW WHO EXACTLY ZIGITA ZOGI'S OPPONENT WAS?"

"Of course I knew. We've done plenty of preliminary research into Uhak the Silent's origins and his abilities. However—"

Hiroto sensed it with his mercurial wit. That wasn't it.

This was decidedly not the answer to Ozonezma's question.

He wasn't even looking at Hiroto. With bloodshot eyes, he was staring at Uhak in the arena.

"Ozonezma. You...know something. Something about Uhak the Silent."

"HIROTO! QUICK... YOU HAVE TO CALL OFF ZIGITA ZOGI'S MATCH IMMEDIATELY! IT CANNOT BE ALLOWED TO PASS! THAT IS ONE THING...HE CANNOT BE ALLOWED TO LOSE!"

"What...? Just what exactly do you know...?"

A cold sweat flowed down the back of Hiroto's neck. Was it fear of the truth?

Zigita Zogi hadn't passed any information regarding Uhak the Silent over to Ozonezma the Capricious whatsoever. Ozonezma was supposed to be the trump card of Hiroto's camp's, and it had been to prevent Uhak's abilities from being handed over to another camp.

In which case, what could he, without having a single change to interact with Uhak at all, possibly know about him?

"I KNOW!"

Uhak possessed the power of true and pure dispelling. Before him, any and all Word Arts were meaningless.

Why was he battling in the Sixways Exhibition? Why had he come here?

No one knew the answers.

Perhaps, that wasn't because one had never been able to find them...

"I KNOW EVERYTHING FROM THE BEGINNING. UHAK THE SILENT... THAT NAME IS WRONG, TOO!"

The starting gun ringing out from the band felt horribly far away. The match began.

At any moment, Zigita Zogi would deal with the ogre. Hiroto couldn't stop him.

The only thing that resounded was the cry:

"SETERA! HIS NAME IS SETERA! THE ONE WHO KILLED THE DEMON KING... HE'S THE TRUE HERO!"

Match eight. Zigita Zogi the Thousandth versus Uhak the Silent.

At the end of the age of the True Demon King, a man and a beast continued a yearlong journey. An aimless journey with no destination, and no guarantee they would be able find what they sought.

Even then, it was by no means a trying journey. Ozonezma the Capricious had the power to fend off any threats that approached them, and Olukt the Drifting Compass Needle had his soothing songs.

"Thus, blessed rains washed over the land / The soldiers' swords at last fell / Ahhhh, none at all doubted / the sincerity of the princess who gave her life / the realm now tranquil / that beautiful wish."

Ozonezma closed his eyes and listened to Olukt's song until the last reverberations of his instruments died down.

The beast, born for battle, had lived for nothing but slaughter, and felt like that sole drive was enough to save him.

As if by magic, the song could heal terror.

"......There's a boar."

"INDEED."

There were in the middle of a forest. Apparently, Olukt and his dulled sense of danger had noticed the presence of the beasts resting in the shade of the roadside trees. Ozonezma could tell their numbers as well. Four. Or perhaps, it was a mother with her farrow.

"THEY DON'T INTEND TO FIGHT. WE CAN LET THEM BE."

"*Ha-ha!* Look, I'm not bragging, all right? But even beasts will listen to my songs. So if that's the case, don't you think I might have a shot at defeating the Demon King, too?"

"IMPOSSIBLE."

Ozonezma agreed that there was indeed a power within Olukt the Drifting Compass Needle's song.

Soulless beasts were enthralled by the beauty of the melody and stopped their legs and wings. Even those with explicit hostile intentions were unable to help themselves from listening along.

Though Ozonezma recognized the wonder of his music, which could touch those in the realm of madness, he still believed the man's experiment was reckless.

That didn't change the fact that Ozonezma, accompanying Olukt on his experiment, was just as reckless himself.

"DO YOU REALLY THINK YOU'LL FIND THIS THING YOU ARE AFTER WITH THIS METHOD OF YOURS?"

"In all honesty, there's no real way to know without asking the Wordmaker themselves. I'm doing it *because* I don't know, see? We're getting to the next town before the day's out, okay?"

"...WE'LL ARRIVE IN THE EVENING. WE SHOULD QUICKEN OUR PACE A SLIGHT BIT."

From one town and then onto the next. Olukt would earn coin with his songs and travel onto the next place.

Towns didn't always welcome the company of a drifter bard. Without Ozonezma at his side to protect him, Olukt was in more danger inside town limits than on the open road.

As if he had exchanged everything for his lyrical talents to resonate with the very world itself, Olukt was astonishingly inept as a fighter. While he was blessed with the physique for it, both his technique and his decision-making were hopelessly slow.

It probably seemed like a cruel joke to anyone who looked at him that the man remained on his journey to defeat the True Demon King.

"OLUKT. WHAT IF... WHAT IF YOU DO NOT FIND THE SORT OF INDIVIDUAL YOU SEEK? WHAT WOULD HAPPEN THEN?"

"When that time comes, it'll probably be the end of it for us. Everything would turn into a big, wasted effort... But that'd be all. Or perhaps, someone else will defeat the True Demon King for us—how about that? There's probably others out there like us, attempting this stupid endeavor...trying out a loony method of their own."

"...A LOONY METHOD..."

"You know the story? There was some smart guy out there who tried to poison the Demon King to defeat them. If I remember, inside the champion's bag was some mechanism to discharge a deadly poisonous gas when opened up. The idea being that if this fella closed in on the Demon King without realizing it, then just by taking out his weapon, the Demon King would die."

"...WHAT HAPPENED?"

"In the middle of the night, he *opened up his bag himself*. The champion who tried to set up the trap died and took everyone else in the same building along with him. The end."

The Demon King's terror eroded the very intent to resist them. The people themselves feared their decision-making. Even should one attempt to kill them via soulless constructs, automatic machinery, or explosives, as long as the person setting up the trap had a soul of their own, they would be terrorized by their own actions and driven mad. Regardless of the distance and timing, they would avoid *putting their plans into action*.

Would attacking indiscriminately do the trick? Did they need to keep the True Demon King out of their perception? Did they need to make sure their own self-destruction was incorporated somehow?

Anyone with a bit of a head on their shoulders could come up with any number of different methods to defeat a tremendous fear that they couldn't approach or think about.

An innumerable number had done exactly that.

During this twenty-five-year span, there was no doubt the world had exhausted every possible means its people could come up with.

Even the First Party had been defeated. Including the most wicked demon king of all and Ozonezma's creator, Izick the Chromatic. If victory was impossible for those seven, then no matter how powerful one may have been, it must have been impossible to lay a single finger on the True Demon King.

Which was why, in actuality, their quest was nothing like a

tactical operation—unable to discover a method to defeat their enemy, it was like they were clinging hopefully to some baseless and enigmatic magic charm.

What they were doing was something the weak did when forced up against oblivion.

IT'S STRANGE, Ozonezma thought as he walked behind Olukt down the road.

This journey, the first he had done with a companion since creation, was by no means a trying one.

DESPITE BEING SO UTTERLY RECKLESS, IT DOESN'T SEEM LIKE A HOPELESS QUEST—OR PERHAPS, HE REALLY CAN...

—Sure enough, at the end of that year, they would meet him.

Olukt found the ogre that, most likely, no one else would have ever been able to find.

Had it been a revelation, bestowed by his talents for song, that led Olukt to discover him?

Or perhaps, it was but a piece of cruel destiny.

At the time, no one knew the answer.

◆

The traveling company of just two had increased to three.

The ogre, lacking the power of Word Arts, was given the name Setera the External.

He was *terribly small* for an ogre, being only half a head taller than Olukt.

Just what sort of name had Setera been given originally?

Or perhaps, had he never felt such a thing was necessary from the beginning?

Setera didn't insist on anything at all himself, but nevertheless, he silently accompanied Olukt on his journey.

When danger arrived, he fought with just as much bravery as Ozonezma, never eating people despite being an ogre, living disciplined as though he was an oracle, and solemnly joined their journey.

While they were unable to exchange conversation, Ozonezma started to put a bizarre trust in the ogre, occasionally leaving his own life in his hands during a battle.

The ogre, unable to understand Word Arts, still listened to Olukt's music together with Ozonezma.

In those moments, Setera seemed calm, as if his mind was at peace.

The three continued their journey.

Until they reached their final destination.

"…Kuta Silver City. This place is Kuta. No doubt about it."

Olukt looked at the charred remains of the sign bearing the town insignia, and he broke into a twitching, taut smile.

The shape-shifting city, a new building popping up each time one visited, had teemed with people and activity.

Indeed, that was how it had once been. Now it had changed shape entirely. All of it.

"WITH THE LOSS OF SHINJI THE PIECE COLUMN, THIS DOWNFALL WAS AN INEVITABILITY. BEFORE THE

THREAT OF THE TRUE DEMON KING, A CITY'S SIZE IS INSIGNIFICANT."

"I know. I know, but...now that I'm seeing it for myself, the reality really hits you hard."

Olukt's unrest didn't only come from the drastically changed cityscape before him.

Dyed in gruesome blood, with the vestiges of agony and death left behind everywhere they looked, the town was completely finished.

In this day and age, such ruins could be found all across the land.

But Kuta Silver City was different.

The Demon King *was here*. The source that was painting over the land with a dark, black terror.

"...Ozonezma. Do you know where the Demon King is?"

"......"

Ozonezma was levelheaded. He had stopped and didn't move.

Just like the brilliant warriors who had come before him, he could sense the terrible menace.

He knew where it was coming from. Amid the silence of death, there was a single life lingering.

He didn't want to face it. He didn't want to get close.

Ozonezma was an artificial life-form, created by the self-proclaimed demon king Izick to collect biomaterial and equipped with all the functions needed for combat.

Even still, there was one function, courage, that he hadn't been given. He had been made this way to act as an assistant to Izick and never disobey him.

Beside him was Olukt, while Setera vigilantly protected their rear.

Still, it was frightening.

"Setera..."

"............"

The ogre didn't let out a single groan, even in the thick of such soul-crushing terror.

Setera was a chosen being. He had the power to erase any and all mysteries of the world with just a thought.

It wasn't only Word Arts. All supernatural phenomena—including the paranormal effects of magic items, clearly not the product of Word Arts—were meaningless to Setera the External.

He negated anything that lay outside the natural laws of the physical—a supremely powerful supernatural skill, even capable of killing a dragon without a fight.

That was truly what Olukt had continued to pursue: a being inconceivable to this world.

A power to negate everything. A power that didn't cause anything.

With him at their side, Ozonezma believed that they could manage to fight against the Demon King.

However.

Now that the time had come, now that they were standing here, this conviction disappeared without a trace.

Would *that really be enough* to make killing the Demon King possible?

"...OLUKT. I WAS RIGHT; THIS EXPERIMENT IS RECKLESS."

"*Ha-ha-ha... What's the matter, Ozonezma? Getting cold feet now that we're here?*"

"THAT IS EXACTLY RIGHT. IS IT NOT SO FOR YOU?"

Ozonezma couldn't advance another step farther. No matter how much bravery he tried to drum up within himself, he couldn't do it. He rued his lack of such a function.

Perspiration. Pulse. Breathing. He could tell that Olukt was terrified beside him.

For someone who wasn't a warrior like him, the fear alone was enough to endanger his life.

"O-OLUKT. PLEASE. WE CAN'T GO ANY FARTHER."

He just needed to pretend he hadn't seen anything.

Pretend that their journey had been a waste of time.

If they turned back now, they would simply go back to the lives they had lived beforehand with nothing changed, and no one would criticize them. From the start, Ozonezma hadn't held any belief that their method would actually be able to defeat the Demon King.

Eventually, this world might be annihilated, but that wasn't a burden that a single person was meant to bear.

"......*U-uuunh...*"

They had come this far.

He had listened to Olukt's songs on the main roads, the sun peeking through the trees.

Ozonezma had even felt proud watching the city people applauding the bard from afar, as if they were cheering for himself, too.

Their nigh-impossible quest, which they themselves hadn't truly believed in, had finally been completed.

Freed from his duty of blood and slaughter, Ozonezma had been able to witness it, witness the beautiful world for the first time. He may not have been the hero. Even then, he had adventured with his companions.

Ozonezma didn't want to believe that those days of adventuring had all been leading to this kind of ending.

Beyond them lay only despair.

"Setera!"

Ozonezma looked at Setera. Was he really going to defeat the True Demon King for them?

Setera remained silent. He quietly lingered where he stood, showing no signs of moving forward.

In which case, their quest had been a mistake.

The fact that Setera was unable to move forward with such terror in front of him was the proof, wasn't it?

"Ha-ha-ha-ha... I told you, Ozonezma... Someday...someday."

Ozonezma would die. Ozonezma could clearly understand that if he continued from there, he would die.

Olukt must have understood it just as much himself.

"Even if we don't move forward now, someday, the fight will come. If that bravado I showed you... If that can't protect me right now, then what else is there?!"

"NO...! WAIT... STOP! THERE IS NO HOPE OF WINNING AGAINST SOMETHING LIKE THIS. EVERYTHING WAS A FAILURE FROM THE START."

Ozonezma could tell that by stepping out in front of them all, Olukt was trying to give them the courage to move forward. Despite being nothing more than a bard, with no warrior strength to speak of.

"I CANNOT GO! FORGIVE ME... FORGIVE ME, OLUKT..."

"Really? Well, makes sense, doesn't it? Of course, huh... Well, that's fine. I get it, I know... Ozonezma. Sorry for making you go along with my selfishness."

Placing a hand on the downturned head of the beast many times bigger than himself, the bard smiled.

Then he walked off.

"Take care of Setera for me."

No matter how much Ozonezma wished that he would stop, Olukt continued to walk.

It was a scene Ozonezma had seen countless times in the past.

Many... So very many champions doing the same thing and walking to their deaths.

Alas. Why did people decide to attempt bravery?

"You've got courage. I know that for sure, after all our time together."

"......!"

Ozonezma tried to advance. Warily, he took two steps forward.

His legs trembled, and his strength gave way. If he didn't follow after Olukt, the man would die.

"I said this to you right at the beginning, too, didn't I?! I'm doing things whether you're coming with me or not!"

He spread his arms out wide, right in the middle of the deathly scenery.

His departing figure grew smaller and smaller.

So far.

So far was the difference between himself and this mere minia.

Courage was the one function the invincible chimera hadn't been equipped with.

"I'm gonna move the heart of this True Demon Lord with my music!"

The man laughed at the all-too-preposterous words himself.

◆

Among the Final Party, there was only a single person who, in the truest sense, challenged the True Demon King.

He was Olukt the Drifting Compass Needle. This man didn't carry a weapon.

Following the obvious presence of terror, he had arrived at a singular abode.

A completely ordinary residence. Red roof. White walls, and a green garden.

Any signs of the residents had long disappeared, and amid the dilapidated residential street, this house was the only one that maintained a rather trim and neat look to it.

There appeared to be a thin, dried-up corpse collapsed in the garden, but that was the extent of it all.

It was the Demon King's final stronghold.

"…Sheesh, what the hell are they eating to survive around here?"

Olukt tried to sarcastically crack a smile, but nothing beyond a muffled hoarse whisper escaped his lips, and his facial muscles couldn't possibly keep up.

I haven't gone mad. Not yet. I've still got time.

He desperately tried to convince himself of his sanity.

In that case, maybe even I've got the qualities of champion, too. Right? I mean, I've gotten this far, haven't I? That's not something anybody could do.

Now there wasn't a single companion to whom he could display such false bravado.

Nevertheless, he needed to put on this brave front for none other than himself.

He placed his trembling hand on the door leading into the room.

If it had been locked, that would have been enough of a reason for him to turn right back around.

However, it wasn't the case. The door easily swayed open.

"Gwah, bleeerg!"

Olukt vomited. He couldn't stay standing in the face of such terror.

The True Demon King hadn't even showed themselves yet. Their heart, not of a champion, had been completely hobbled.

His body tried to flee, faster than his thoughts could keep up. He felt like he had to get away from this room as quickly as he could.

"*Bleh, hngh... Ha! Ha-ha-ha... Ha-ha...*"

It was a laugh of resignation. He had realized that it was already impossible for him to turn around now.

There was no other path for anyone who had reached this destination.

Faced with this danger he was meant to immediately flee, his body went stiff. Circumstances that he couldn't let himself ponder instead filled up his thoughts completely. There wasn't a single shred of rationality within the phenomenon at all.

He had accepted something he was meant to avoid. He was being forced to do something he shouldn't be.

Olukt couldn't defeat them, either. Nor could he flee.

Because it was frightening.

There was a common anomaly that was more familiar, and more inescapable, than any other in the world.

Even though there wasn't anyone out there who wished to fear, the faculty dwelled in everyone's hearts.

The emotion of "terror."

"...Is it—? *Ha-ha*, is it really...this h-hopeless...? You're kidding... *Ha-ha-ha-ha... Bwa-ha-ha-ha!*"

Laughing out of despair and misery, Olukt continued unabated, crawling along the house's corridor.

Completely understanding the fate, gruesome above all, that would come for him, it was the only thing he could do.

"Gah...my voice... Dammit, my voice's...gettin' hoarse..."

The hallway connected into an average, everyday living room.

The furniture had all been left as is. The chairs surrounding the table, along with a wooden chair two sizes smaller than the rest.

It must have been a happy family living here. Olukt could tell.

In one of the chairs, she sat.

Black, long, and glossy hair.

Not making any movements, she was looking at the blue sky beyond the window.

"It's nice out, isn't it?"

The black hair smoothly traced along her cheek as she slowly turned around.

Amid the ghastly hell, she alone remained herself.

Long black hair, still maintaining its luster. Skin without the slightest blemish.

There wasn't a single fray to be seen on her black sailor outfit.

That was how she was.

An existence that should not be.

Her eyes, seemingly absorbing all the light around her, looked at Olukt, and she smiled.

"What's your name?"

Olukt repl—

He had to remember how to breathe.

"*Glrng—*"

A gurgling sound was the only thing out of his lips.

Bubbles of blood.

He realized that the terrible tension in his muscles had caused one of the blood vessels in the back of his throat to burst open.

"...Y-you're— *Glahak!*"

The True Demon King was a powerless, normal young girl.

Olukt had known that from the beginning.

To those maddened with terror, his songs were able to provide a brief...and ephemeral moment of soothing.

He could encourage them to speak the truth, impossible to broach, while gripped with terror.

Olukt had heard the truth of the True Demon King from one of the extremely few cases of someone witnessing them and managing to return home—Romzo the Star Map from the First Party— and it was from that moment, he set off on his journey.

Olukt had begun it from the hopeless knowledge that the all-consuming fear bringing ruin to the world was, without reason, from nobody special.

A journey unthinkable to anyone else: to defeat the True Demon King.

"...Have you... Have you heard songs before...?"

"......"

He remembered—

With the power of his songs, able to move the hearts of all living things, he tried searching for the hero meant to defeat the True Demon King.

His travels with Ozonezma, the only one who had never laughed at his preposterous and romantic plan.

The countless moments of danger, the times he was saved by the chimera's strength.

Then...encountering the possibility he had long sought, like a miracle.

He remembered having Ozonezma listen to more songs than anyone else.

The bard was never going to be saved by weaving songs all by himself.

In which case, Olukt's journey, always with someone to listen to them at his side—

"...Or...maybe it's just...? Y-you forgot...all about songs, huh...?"

With trembling fingers, he grabbed the dinner knife lying on the floor.

Olukt understood what he planned to do.

Tears bubbled up from the awful terror. He wanted to make her listen to his song.

If Olukt could just sing, he may have been able to move this young girl's heart, too.

"What a pitiful man."

Then he lacerated his own windpipe.

The throat that had woven the most brilliant songs in the land, the voice capable of resonating with soulless beasts, was rent by the dull blade and transformed into nothing more than a hideous tangle of muscle fiber.

Breath leaked out from his respiratory tract like a cruel, miserable flute, and it was no song.

"Songs? ...Oh, right, songs..."

The True Demon King simply looked down at the man, robbed of his greatest pride and dying in agonized despair.

With an ironically pretty voice, she absentmindedly murmured:

"...I'd like to hear one again."

Olukt's journey was over.

Without leaving anything behind. Without any reward to speak of.

All except for one.

A silhouette appeared in the residential window.

Destroying the whole wall along with it, an enormous creature leaped into the room to protect Olukt.

It resembled a colossal wolf, but its fur, shining bluish silver, was unlike any wolf in the wild.

"OLUKT!"

Ozonezma looked at Olukt's pitiful corpse.

His bravery had come too late.

Just moments before Ozonezma appeared, he had slit his own throat.

His songs were gone forever.

"DEMON KING. CURSE YOU. AAAH!"

Ozonezma went to slice up his enemy.

"AAAH..."

He realized there wasn't a single thing he could do.

The True Demon King. A powerless, delicate young girl was right before him.

He was close enough to kill her, if he just reached out his leg slightly.

Ozonezma didn't need limitless courage. He only needed enough to do this.

This chimera didn't possess any innate courageous faculties.

Nevertheless, he had managed to get this far.

"HNG, AHHHH! AHHHHHH!"

He remembered—

—that this bard had sung more songs than anyone else.

Grand stories of legendary champions defeating powerful beasts and fiends.

The nobility in the powerless being able to stand up to the powerful.

He remembered songs of courage.

"DEMON KING...! HOW DARE... HOW DARE YOU! *HNG, GWAAAH!"*

Thus, Ozonezma felt it was fair, just this once, for a miracle to happen.

Courage.

With his mind long since given in to the terror, nevertheless, Ozonezma tried continuing forward.

His feet didn't advance a single step.

The True Demon King wasn't even facing him.

She continued to look down at the dead bard on the ground, as if curiously examining an oddity.

"MRNGH... MRRRRNGH...!"

He was close enough to kill her, with just a small extension of his hand.

However, that slight distance was the infinitely unreachable yonder.

Thus was the True Demon King.

The ultimate terror couldn't be overcome with the power of one's heart.

If the very idea of courage was to overcome such fears, then—

—*it meant that those with courage felt fear.*

Such strength of will was needed to fight against her, and yet the essence of that will, the heart and soul, gradually descended into ruin.

The efforts of everyone in their world had all been meaningless.

Unparalleled techniques that slew enemies far and wide, minute and limitless planning, an enormous amount of gunpowder, a small dagger, strength, weakness, the mind, the body. All the means in the Beyond, and all the means in their world.

Everything. All of it. In totality.

"AAAAHHH! KILL...DEMON KING...! K-KILL... KILL HER...!

—However.

Faced with this terror, was there really nothing he could do?

No, that wasn't it. There was one sole thing that everyone had been able to do.

Everything and anyone was clearly able to wish for it.

"*KILL HER FOR US! SETERA!*"

Ozonezma was no exception.

He was able to *entrust the task to someone else.*

Simply believe that it wouldn't be himself...but that the Hero would defeat the Demon King for them.

"Ahhh, songs..."

The True Demon King...went to say something, as if she had suddenly remembered something.

The chimera's enormous back gapped open.

From within a gray ogre, small enough to fit inside Ozonezma's body, emerged.

The True Demon King turned around at them for the first time.

An unbelievably beautiful yet lonesome face.

A visitor, her existence impermissible to both this world and her own.

The young girl's lips opened.

"___"

The boorish club split the girl's head in two.

Setera's single swing pierced through flesh and bone, even leaving a crack in the floorboards below.

A terrible and wet crunching sound covered the area.

There had been an enemy to all, who terrorized the entire land.

A singular enemy whom no one could oppose, who brought nothing but terror and slaughter to their world.

The True Demon King had now, from the top of her head to her waist, changed into a nondescript mass of flesh and bone.

Her porcelain legs, still standing on the floor, finally collapsed in a heap.

"HAAAAH, HAAAH! AH... AHHH..."

Ozonezma was frightened, his breath ragged. He continued to be frightened.

Setera had killed the True Demon King.

He had achieved the truly remarkable triumph that all others had feared, had been unable to achieve.

"IMPOSSIBLE, IT CAN'T BE...! SETERA..."

Nevertheless, he was *still* in fear.

Since now he understood.

Who exactly Setera was. What exactly Olukt had accidentally accomplished.

The Demon King's final words were in a language that Ozonezma didn't understand.

A power that didn't allow Word Arts communication had activated.

In which case, that moment that he jumped out from Ozonezma's back, Setera should have negated any and all supernatural phenomena. The single glance he made should have negated all the terror.

Yet the terror of the True Demon King carried on. Even now.

＊　　＊　　＊

A terror without any cause or origin couldn't possibly be negated.

"SETERA... Y-YOU'VE..."

Setera the External...was simply looking down at the Demon King, now transformed into fragments of red flesh.

Quiet, he looked to be deep in thought, as if in mourning.

The experiment was a success.

What had Olukt long been putting to the test?

His songs were music capable of reaching the souls of living creatures far and wide.

Those driven mad by the Demon King's fear. Supposedly, even soulless beasts.

If, perhaps...the heart that feared the Demon King and the heart susceptible to soul-stirring song both shared the same identical origin.

If he, simply wandering from town to town and playing his songs for the people, had something he truly sought after. It hadn't been this invincible ogre who negated any supernatural powers and defeated his enemies with his tremendous physical abilities.

He had observed the whole time. It wasn't a reaction to his songs. The opposite.

He realized there was one who, even while able to hear his songs, deep down in their heart, *didn't react to them whatsoever.*

"OLUKT... A-AHHH...! I AM SORRY... FORGIVE ME...!"

Facing the long-dead Olukt, Ozonezma apologized over and over again.

He hadn't made it in time.

Ozonezma didn't have any courage whatsoever. Nor did Setera the External, either. In their world, there wasn't a single person who possessed the true courage to oppose the Demon King.

Otherwise…such a terrifying idea wouldn't have ever flickered in the back of Ozonezma's thoughts.

He himself was doing something terrifying.

"NGH… NO! AHHH, AHHHH!"

Something terrifying enough to drive him mad.

"NO…! NO…!"

Where Ozonezma looked, there was a white arm torn off and sent flying alongside the wall.

Unlike the hideously crushed body…

…it was an incredibly well-preserved and beautiful arm.

Even if it was conjoined with someone else's body…

…it was surely in good-enough condition to make movement possible.

"AHHHHH…! NOT THIS— THIS IS…SUCH BLASPHEMY… FORGIVE ME, OLUKT…!"

Setera was greedily devouring the True Demon King's corpse.

He was eating the thing he'd killed by his own hand.

An absolutely impossible feat for anyone who felt the slightest hint of fear.

He, beyond a shadow of a doubt, possessed a singular, personal will. Not a construct or machine with his intentions controlled by others. He could freely decide for himself what he would do.

That was why Ozonezma and Olukt had entrusted their wish to slay the Demon King to this ogre.

However…he was a presence that normally should have been wholly inconceivable in their world.

Setera the External. Philosophically speaking, he was no different from the dead. From the very start.

"…………"

"SETERA! SETERA! *AH, AHHH, AUUUUUGH!*"

The chimera tearfully wailed.

He understood the words would never ever reach the heart of another.

"TELL ME, WHY…?! WHY?! WHY…DID YOU COME THIS FAR?!"

…Three years ago. There had been a man named Olukt the Drifting Compass Needle.

It was a black age. He was one of the innumerable champions who had been slaughtered by the True Demon King.

Unable to make his singing voice ring, he ended up dying without leaving his name behind.

However. He had, at least, found a hero.

One who should have never existed, unable to comprehend the Word Arts that all minds communicated with.

—*Truth is, that guy… He hates all of it. The whole world and everything in it.*

—*"When you killed people, was it painful?"*

—"*Uhak. You have a soul inside you. A soul just the same as anyone else's.*"

He perceived the world without understanding the concept of innate Word Arts.

He possessed the true power to dispel, thrusting the same reality he saw onto others.

He was a simple ogre, equipped with the grim reality of strength and size.

And he was, from the very beginning...

...Hero. Ogre.

Setera the External.

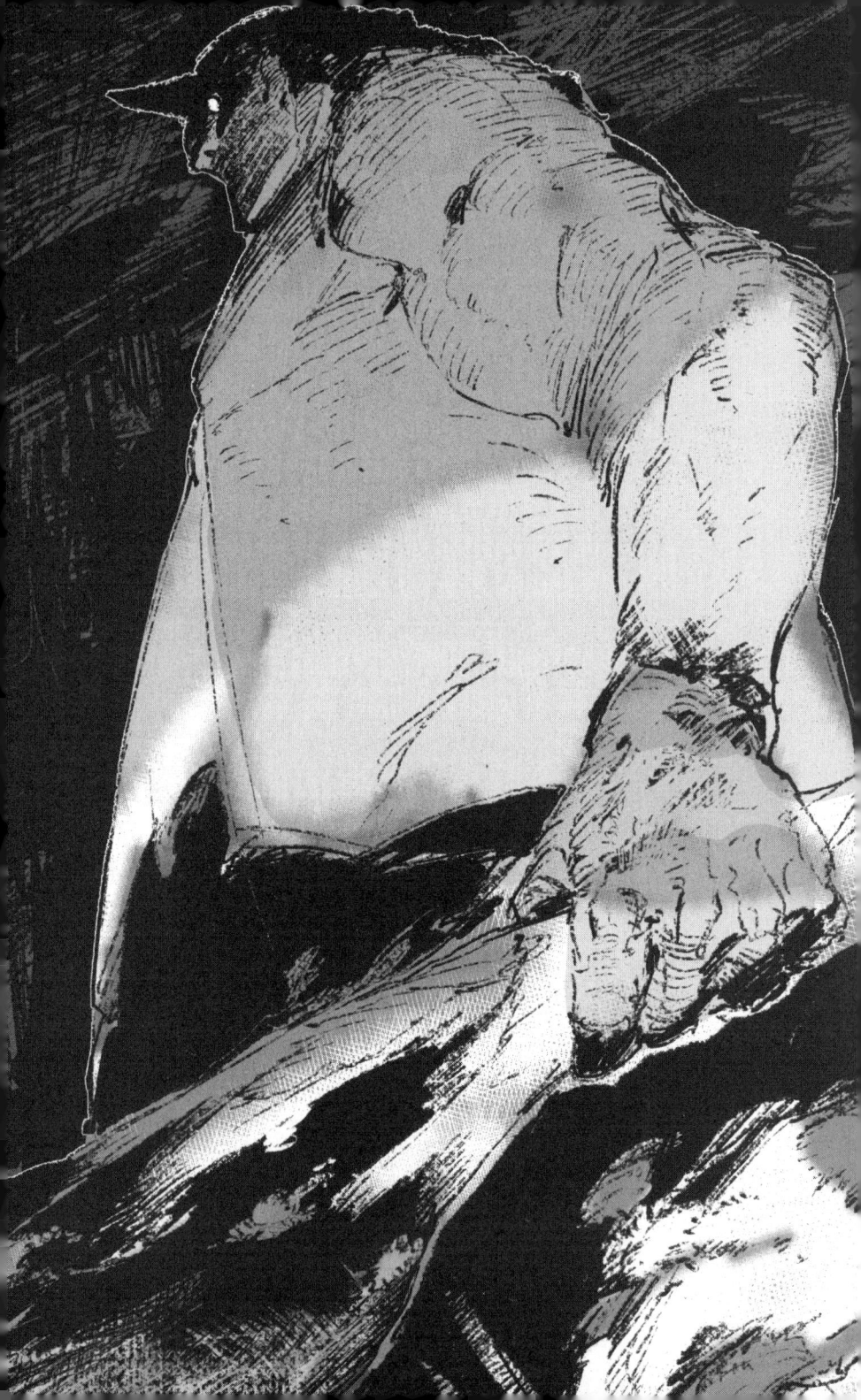

Uhak the Silent was massive.

Just *what did he have to eat* to grow so huge?

There was little Zigita Zogi the Thousandth could speculate.

One could rephrase the ability of tactical strategy as the ability to create options.

Cut down the enemy from the front? Scheme behind the scenes and cut off an enemy's path to victory?

None of the methods were superior or inferior to one another. Here in the Sixways Exhibition, all the candidates had prepared their own strategies for victory as well.

However, there were those who only held a single option to advance through the tournament, and those who confronted the tournament with countless different options prepared ahead of time. Zigita Zogi the Thousandth was the latter.

He had utilized a great number of troops to probe into the state of affairs in Aureatia; he was at a stage where he could manipulate the citizens through forecasting the weather with an impromptu meteorologic station far off in Imag City or through his complete command of the flow of goods.

If victory was all he was after, then there were other methods to make it possible.

There were many reasons he had planned to use chemical weapons in his match.

Phosgene was a weapon that incapacitated the opponent and induced a number of side effects; however, as long as the victim was immediately given medical treatment, the chances of death were low.

If the attack came with any serious aftereffects, then it would serve as a reason to have Ozonezma treat him long-term. He would usurp Uhak the Silent's physical fighting abilities while simultaneously increasing the chances for them to interact. It would become easier to control him. It was not his physical ogre strength but his unique power that Zigita Zogi saw as necessary.

There was an additional point as well.

Phosgene's relative density was heavier than air and, once used, would linger behind in an area.

...In short, he could use it against anyone who immediately approached them following the end of the match as well.

That way, it would create a chance to investigate said individuals' bodies under the pretext of treating their exposure to the gas.

The target of his tactics was not only Uhak the Silent.

It was a trap to capture the corpse intruders, using Zigita Zogi in the arena as bait.

◆

Underneath the garden theater. Dant the Heath Furrow was walking down the corridor, accompanied by several soldiers and a doctor.

Uhak the Silent's sponsor, whom Zigita Zogi was supposed to have disposed of—Sixteenth General Nofelt the Somber Wind—had suspiciously made his return to the city. Dant needed to ascertain the truth of the situation.

"There's something I'd like to ask. Had Nofelt been inoculated with the vampire antiserum?"

"No. Since cases of vampire infection themselves have died down, even among the Twenty-Nine Officials, less than half have purchased the antiserum," the doctor replied. Using the word *purchase* was the characteristic turn of phrase for all of Flinsuda's subordinates.

"I figured. I haven't, either."

Select personnel from Flinsuda's medical team had arrived ahead of them.

The emergency vehicle, flying white and blue flags to signal they were with the medical division, would also be arriving eventually.

Must be a way to make the enemy mistime our arrival. Always calculating, isn't he?

The soldiers accompanying Dant were elite troops, picked out to prepare against an ambush by the invisible army. Three minia, one goblin. The goblin was under Zigita Zogi's command. With them were the three doctors from the medical team they'd met up with. In the event they encountered a corpse or vampire, there were many circumstances that only doctors could handle.

...Should I bring one more with me?

Dant called out to a senior soldier on patrol.

"... I'm Twenty-Fourth General Dant. You there, a moment."

"Yessir...! What may I help you with, General Dant?"

"Ashamed to say it, but it seems all my men were solely focused on the perimeter. No one seems to know the layout of the garden theater. Can you be our guide?"

"*Ha-ha*, that is indeed a problem! After all, it's been rebuild after rebuild, so the underground's gotten quite complex. Where, then, are you heading?"

"Uhak the Silent's waiting room."

"Of course, right away!"

As though proud to be relied on by one of the Twenty-Nine Officials, the elderly soldier seemed a bit giddy, standing out in front of them all as he walked. Unfortunately, Dant didn't consider this man to be part of his fighting force.

His aim was to have the man act as their forward shield through the corridors leading to Nofelt's waiting room. If their enemy truly was Obsidian Eyes, then it was impossible to be too well-prepared against an ambush.

"However, sir, if you're heading there, I assume you have some business with General Nofelt?"

"Yeah, I do. Since Uhak the Silent's showed up, he's here, too, right?"

"Indeed. However, General Nofelt just walked down this corridor and left a few moments ago..."

"...What?"

"You didn't pass each other?"

Dant had no recollection of such a thing. Before he found the old soldier, he had passed by several other lightly armored soldiers, but he should've been able to immediately pick out an abnormally tall man like Nofelt.

Up until just a few moments ago Nofelt was here. Or at least someone who looked like Nofelt.

What sort of method had they used? Even assuming Obsidian Eyes possessed some degree of unknown infiltration techniques, were there any methods of disguise capable of reproducing the man's physique, too?

That can't be...

The soldiers who were supposed to be on guard outside Nofelt's room weren't there.

"......"

—They had been set up after all.

The eighth Match had been unusual right from the start.

"......! This is a compulsory investigation! We're entering this waiting room!"

Everyone except the elderly soldier shared a glance and came together in a battle formation.

Dant swung open the door.

If there were some other people besides Nofelt inside the room, then—

"Who's there?!"

Together with Dant's shout, a shadow lurking inside the room moved.

The shadow bared their teeth, a bestial sneer—

An explosive *boom*. The stone floor cracked.

It was the sound of an opening rush.

"General Dant— *Gnh!*"

One of the elite soldiers stepped in the way and protected Dant.

His throat was gouged with the single attack, slicing all the way down to the cervical vertebrae deeper within.

—All done with a single, bare finger.

Dant only knew of one person who was capable of such a deed.

"Haizesta the Gathering Spot...!"

"...*Nyeh-heh-heheh.*"

The Fifteenth General, unmistakably minian yet using his unbelievable and downright monstrous physical strength as his weapon.

Why is he here? One blow will do it.

Dant drew his sword. He thrust it forward, going through the armpit of the soldier in front of him.

Haizesta dodged, advanced, and rotated.

Abnormal agility.

Using the momentum of his turn, he drilled his fingers into the goblin soldier's skull.

The goblin's drawn pistol hadn't even been allowed to fire.

"*Hrnk...*"

He slowly extracted his spear hand. The goblin's brains stretched from his fingers.

Haizesta was on the right. Dant was unable to swing his sword, the soldier with his throat gouged out still standing in front of him.

Can I do it from this position?

He forcibly pushed the dying soldier forward with his left shoulder. The soldier's body collapsed, spinning to the right—blocking Haizesta's line of sight.

Dant sharply exhaled.

He would cleave through the armored soldier and take Haizesta behind him with it.

"Too slow."

Haizesta pinched down on the blade with two fingers and brought it to a stop. Inconceivably fast reaction speeds.

Dant murmured:

"Sorry."

He had already taken his hand off the sword in Haizesta's grip.

It was being pushed downward, still under the momentum of his vertical slash.

I'm going to have to lethally injure him in one attack.

Dant had pushed the soldier in front of him in a way that made the soldier spin to the right in order to turn the piece of equipment, strapped to his right hip, toward Dant. He grabbed the sheath. He immediately counterattacked. A diagonal slash, upward to the shoulder.

Cutting through several ribs, he knew he had severed the man's lungs.

"......!"

Spurting blood gushed forth.

Still with a bestial smile on his face, Haizesta the Gathering Spot's life came to an end.

"What...?"

Dant gnashed his teeth. One of his elite subordinates and a goblin, both slain in an instant.

Haizesta lay in the pool of blood as well. Aureatia's Fifteenth General.

"...What is going on?!"

Someone who looked like Nofelt the Somber Wind.

Haizesta the Gathering Spot waiting in ambush for Dant's arrival.

A preposterously abnormal set of circumstances had come about.

Dant shot a look to the elderly soldier quivering in the back of the formation.

"You! Did you see that?!"

"I mean, honestly...it was so fast, the details of it all were a blur... That and...th-the man just now was General Haizesta, wasn't it?!"

"That's plenty. You're our witness! The Fifteenth General suddenly went berserk and fatally wounded my soldiers, which left me no choice but to counterattack myself! There are suspicions of a corpse infection, so I, Dant the Heath Furrow, under my authority, will have this medical team perform an autopsy!"

"*Eep*, y-yes…sir!"

The insurance Dant had prepared was a success. He had thought that should the enemy be plotting to set up an attack between two internal Aureatia forces somehow, he needed to bring along a third party who wasn't a part of anyone's private forces to serve as a witness.

With a killing blow from a single attack, it served as definite proof that Haizesta had attacked them first.

Haizesta had lain in wait alone. A terrifying enemy. The plan enacted by the invisible army, architects of this situation…clearly didn't just include Dant the Heath Furrow's demise.

It was to lay the crime of the Fifteenth General's death on him.

"Dammit… I don't like it…! What happened?! Who is this, and what are they doing?!"

He didn't have any time to spare. If he brought this truth to light, would he make it in time before the match was decided?

"Let them know immediately! Right now, the eighth match is being held without Sixteenth General Nofelt's presence!"

What if the ogre who had never shown the slightest hint of ego…from the very start, hadn't paid any care to whether his own sponsor was there or not?

"Uhak the Silent is *participating illegally!*"

◆

At the same moment. In an alley that adjoined the castle garden theater's main avenue, a single carriage was rolled over.

Appearing to have toppled at full speed, the sturdy iron-carriage body was warped, and the driver was dead, pierced through by wood splinters.

The horse had died as well. Both of its forelegs had been ripped off and scattered from the knees down.

This was no traffic accident. Someone had attacked the carriage as it was traveling along.

"Enough."

The man who stepped out from the passenger car raised both of his hands up into the air and demonstrated no intent to resist.

"I surrender. Seriously, I'm sick and tired of this sorta stuff."

A man with a stubbly beard, dressed in black and with a slightly ominous air about him.

"This isn't an assassination, Kuze the Passing Disaster. It's a parley."

The voice came from above the shop. Sitting in a low stance and looking down at Kuze was a bipedal wolf.

Obsidian Eyes' ninth-formation vanguard, Harutoru the Light Grip.

"You're heading for the castle garden theater under the orders of Zigita Zogi the Thousandth, then?"

"Ah, well... Yeah, pretty much. Don't really plan on hiding it at this point. You ambushed me because you already know everything anyway, right? Feels like everyone I meet's real dangerous, I tell you..."

Kuze the Passing Disaster was one of the hero candidates, as well as an assassin cooperating with Hiroto's camp.

It was absolutely necessary to stop him if he was going to make an appearance at the eighth match.

"What's your reason for working with them? We're prepared to offer suitable conditions as well."

"Well...I can't answer that. Since it's a wish that you guys aren't gonna be able to make come true."

"..."

"*Bweh-ha-ha.* You're not attacking me, are you...? So even if you don't know my reason, you at least know that much."

Harutoru had the high ground over Kuze. The great shield Kuze used to fight was still left behind inside the carriage, and the lycan was in a position to make a one-sided surprise attack on the defenseless man.

"So then you weren't the one who attacked the carriage, were you?" said Kuze out of nowhere. "Sorry, but I'm going to have to head on to the garden theater. You should go check to see if your buddy's all right. Making the carriage roll over means that you were trying to kill me in the accident...and anyone who tries that sort of stuff will die. No matter how far away they may be, no matter how well they try to hide. Guaranteed."

"...Guaranteed?"

In that moment, a colossal mass descended down and crushed the iron carriage to pieces.

Navy-blue armor. A singular, purple eye.

There had been two lurking in the alley. Harutoru the Light Grip, and...

As his Gatling gun begun to spin, Mestelexil laughed hysterically.

"Ha-ha! Ha-ha-ha-ha-ha-ha, ha-ha-ha-ha-ha-ha-ha-ha-ha-ha-ha-ha-ha-ha!"

"Whoa, whoa now...! You gotta be kidding me!"

What did one need to do to finish off a man with the supernatural ability to bring instant death to anyone who tried to kill him?

"Let me tell you something, Kuze the Passing Disaster."

—Throw *someone who kept going even when dead* at him.

As the loud guffaw echoed across the alley, Harutoru similarly bared his fangs with a smile.

"The side holding the most information's the only one with the right to use a word like *guaranteed*."

◆

Linaris the Obsidian had spent almost all her childhood years confined to the bed in her home.

From birth, her body was so weak that she couldn't adequately stand up and walk by herself, and Rehart the Obsidian had to throw all his personal funds into ensuring his daughter would live on.

That had been her way of life for close to half of her seventeen years.

Though vampires may have looked no different at all, the mere fact that she was one made her the enemy of all minian races, and to ensure no one would try to take her life, she hadn't been able to freely leave the house even after she had become able to walk.

She had no one she could call a friend.

In the end, there were only a handful of those remaining she could even call comrades.

Frey the Waking. Harutoru the Light Grip. Lena the Obscured. Wieze the Variation. Hyakrai the Tower. Lendelt the Immaculate. Finally, Zeljirga the Abyss Web. Each one was indomitable with unrivaled strength, but once the existence of Obsidian Eyes became clear, there were no longer the numbers to ensure everyone survived.

There were also some who had left the organization. Kuuro the Clairvoyant. Hyne the Swaying Indigolite. Zizma the Miasma. Lana the Moon Tempest. Rook the Shredding Trineedle—all of them possessed the superb skills that allowed them to survive in the outside world, yet despite this, all of them, without exception, chose livelihoods embracing conflict.

This was because the entirety of Obsidian Eyes had, in the end, become totally separate creatures from the people of the outside world. It wasn't just because they were corpses. They were creatures who had adapted themselves to the spiral of endless conflict, staining their hands with blood simply by living their lives.

She needed to keep them all alive.

Creating a warring chaos that would preserve Obsidian Eyes' existence was the method to ensure they did.

If creating war was the extent of it, she could make an armed force of corpses under her control fight with a force that was not.

Linaris the Obsidian was able to bring annihilation to Aureatia.

The Queen and certain members of the Twenty-Nine Officials

had been inoculated with antiserum, but most of the citizens in the country didn't have any resistance to the vampire virus. Even without setting her sights directly on the central figures, if she controlled every single one of the high-ranking bureaucrats tasked with the day-to-day business, she could easily bring about the collapse of Aureatia's societal structure.

However, that wasn't a victory for Obsidian Eyes. That was Linaris's thinking.

Even if she successfully guided the world toward war, should Obsidian Eyes' secret activities and Linaris's existence as the source of a vampire-infection epidemic be brought to the light of day, they would end up fighting on with the whole world as their enemy.

Even if they destroyed Aureatia, the sort of shura who appeared in the Sixways Exhibition would kill them off. Lucnoca the Winter, able to lay waste to a nation with a single breath. Or perhaps Shalk the Sound Slicer, who was physically impossible to infect. There were countless threats still remaining in the world that couldn't be bested either through exhausting individual strength or through manipulating an entire army.

The Sixways Exhibition, meant to control said threats all at once, was necessary for Obsidian Eyes as well.

They would push through this battle until the end and purge all the exceptionally powerful players that could threaten their existence.

In the process, they had forcefully stolen the ultimate strategic weapon in Mestelexil the Box of Desperate Knowledge, using the exhibition arena where his combat abilities were limited as much as possible.

What Linaris was trying to create was the spark to ignite war following the conclusion of the Sixways Exhibition.

The conflict needed to be born *from the intent of those involved*, without any getting wise to the secret maneuvering behind the scenes.

The key to it all lay with Hiroto the Paradox's camp.

With the combined power of the Free City of Okafu and the nation on the new continent Hiroto had behind him, they would become a force able to stand shoulder to shoulder with Aureatia both in scale and national strength. They could create a long entrenched period of war.

Obsidian Eyes had repeatedly used their control over Okafu mercenaries to provoke Aureatia and the hero candidates, trying to sow discord between Okafu and Aureatia. Ambushing hero candidates. The sniper attack on Haade's envoy. A large number of suspicious deaths.

However, there was someone who had seen through all their sabotage both material and immaterial and immediately taken actions to block their objectives—Zigita Zogi the Thousandth.

A goblin genius. The tactician who avoided any and all conflict with strategies that surpassed Linaris's own thoughts.

He had defined her organization as the invisible army and dealt with Linaris's schemes with terrifying speed. If he secured one of Linaris's corpses as evidence, Obsidian Eyes would be clearly identified. She needed to dispose of Zigita Zogi for good before they reached such a conclusion.

What was the most suitable situation to try finishing off the most brilliant tactician in the land?

A situation where their enemy was assured to be by himself, when it was impossible to set up any traps ahead of time, and when he was surrounded by people other than his allies. The only choice was in the middle of the eighth match.

During the third match, Linaris had infiltrated the castle garden theater in order to look into Haade the Flashpoint's movements. On that occasion, she had turned many of the garden theater's soldiers into corpses under her control.

She had sent Uhak the Silent, originally supposed to be unable to participate, into the arena with the help of Lena the Obscured's mimicry.

Intervention from Hiroto's most powerful pawn, Kuze the Passing Disaster, had been blocked off by Mestelexil.

They would bring about Dant the Heath Furrow's fall from power by making him kill Haizesta the Gathering Spot.

Then Obsidian Eyes' powerful members would infect Hiroto the Paradox in the spectator seats.

The biggest difference between Hiroto's camp and Aureatia was the existence of a leader who could influence the camp all by themselves. Though it appeared that he hadn't contributed one bit to the tactical decisions, Hiroto was truly the cornerstone of the camp, controlling all the political relationships himself. Linaris was cognizant of this fact herself.

By killing Zigita Zogi and controlling Hiroto, they would then be able to manipulate two nations, the Free City of Okafu and the goblin nation, with minimal active participation. She would then use Hiroto to manipulate Okafu and the goblins into choosing war with Aureatia of their own volition.

The seeds of war had been scattered in untold numbers.

After the conclusion of the Sixways Exhibition, a war would begin between Aureatia and the Free City of Okafu.

With both sides now lacking any shura of their own, the conflict…was sure to become a long and drawn-out war, completely different in nature from the Lithia War and the suppression of the Old Kingdoms' loyalists.

The eighth match, the keystone to all of Hiroto's camp's plans.

To Linaris the Obsidian as well, it held even more importance to her than the outcome of the sixth.

She would kill Zigita Zogi in a way that no one would suspect Obsidian Eyes of being involved at all.

Linaris didn't need to gain anything else. She didn't need to kill anyone else.

With it, Obsidian Eyes' battle would end in victory.

◆

Mestelexil the Box of Desperate Knowledge was no longer a hero candidate in the Sixways Exhibition.

He was a weapon within Obsidian Eyes' arsenal.

"Ha-ha-ha-ha-ha-ha-ha! Ha-ha-ha-ha-ha-ha-ha-ha-ha-ha-ha-ha!"

Laughter. Destruction. A line of fire ran through the alley.

The largest sweep of the Gatling gun from the Beyond, even in a narrow alleyway preventing it from being wielded perfectly, was capable of biting down into the terrain itself and destroying it.

Kuze the Passing Calamity tried to hide behind the carriage debris, but even if he had his shield in his hands, the gun had enough firepower to pierce right through it and the cover in front of him.

"Stop! If you do that, then—"

"Ha...ha."

The raking gunfire that had mowed down everything in front of him stopped right before it could reach Kuze.

The light in the single eye faded, and Mestelexil fell to his knees.

Kuze flashed a pained smile.

"See. You'll just...die immediately."

The white angel whom only Kuze could perceive was floating in the air above Mestelexil's head.

Nastique, right next to Kuze a mere moment ago, had moved instantaneously. She'd killed—faster than any attack could reach Kuze, as if forestalling his fated death.

"That supernatural power's just as the rumors say, Kuze the Passing Disaster," Harutoru the Light Grip stated, observing the fight from a rooftop.

The massive lycan didn't make a single creak on the wooden rooftop, as if he weighed absolutely nothing at all.

"No special technique can do this. No signs of poison, electric currents, or heat. So you can do it in a way that's completely divorced from your own strength and abilities. Go on, show me more of just exactly how you fight."

...Dammit. This guy...doesn't intend on killing me at all, does he?

Nastique's absolute and instant death was an unmatched power.

However, it certainly couldn't stop the person she killed from *reviving*.

"Weresm otampea nete haires tesnainmestorte rwem gwis kelber quomexos—" (Permeating sheet laminate handwriting excite the soul torchlight, separate, flow, wrap celestial sphere in notochordal phase, create planet—)

Kuze only knew the information Hiroto the Paradox had given him from Toroa and Mestelexil's clash: that he could infinitely produce weapons from the Beyond that far eclipsed all knowledge this world had to offer, that he possessed an immortality that allowed him to revive no matter how many times he died, and that he could even create golem replicas of himself.

However, Hiroto's camp hadn't acquired the knowledge behind the absolute mechanism that formed this core of his.

When the golem's life was taken, the homunculus core would reconstruct the golem.

When the homunculus died, the golem body would reproduce the homunculus.

This was what comprised Mestelexil the Box of Desperate Knowledge.

"Ah, ahhhhh... Ah. R-re—stored."

Nastique's previous attack had stopped Mestelexil right before his bullets could rip through Kuze.

However, if their enemy continued to attack *without death even stopping them*, then the chance of survival was extremely low.

Not only that, but as for the enemy's objective.

These two...are trying to keep me here. Keep me right here until the eighth match is finished!

"*Exil io mestel. Ueetes jodo. Lin hey tede. Wa notketm—sinkart.*" (From Exil to Mestel. Congealed raindrops. Swaying red. Revolving marrow—join together.)

A box-shaped weapon formed from Mestelexil's back. Faster than Kuze could breathe.

"LRAD 2000X."

"......!"

The directional acoustic weapon activated.

Faster than the electrical current flowing through it, Nastique's blade had taken the golem's life.

This guy's way too dangerous. Seriously.

Just now, Nastique had prevented some sort of attack from Mestelexil. It meant that this box the golem created was a weapon that went beyond the realm of Kuze's comprehension.

How aware, exactly, was the angel of a threat against Kuze's life, and how big was the scope of her automatic counterattacks? Once the counterattack's interpretation had repeatedly expanded into a range of understanding that was unfathomable by his own standards, was it possible Nastique would then no longer be something Kuze could individually control?

"I-if I attack, I d-die."

Yet that didn't apply to Mestelexil, completing his revival once again.

"...Then I just shouldn't."

An invincible weapon that learned according to any and all methods of attack it faced, then responded accordingly.

I'll forcibly break through. Before this thing can pull out his next trick—

"Mestelexil, block him off," Harutoru coldly muttered from the rooftop.

"Exil io kouto. Diel ab. Meosi yuwet. Pierzi fortea 6. Chardketia." (From Exil to Kouto soil. True indigo jaw. Sequence of buds. Axle is horizon six. Spread.)

Mestelexil immediately finished his Craft Arts incantation. The terrain itself transformed and rearranged on its own, producing a large iron wall that blocked off the route to the main avenue. Breaking through had now become physically impossible.

"Hey now... Whoa, whoa, whoa, c'mon! This is crazy!"

"Topographical transformation. As long as the attack's not directed at you yourself, you can't use that instant-death ability of yours. My hypothesis was right on the mark."

Kuze turned around behind him. The surrounding terrain had been completely transformed, with even its mineral properties transfigured, but there was an escape path behind him. However, that was likely to be sealed off with Mestelexil's next move.

Then on top of it all...

"Exil io kouto. Zavortes. Ottportel. Shyake bibot. Chorte."

(From Exil to Kouto soil. Cord of light. Sextuple star. Thousand rotation stone. Arise.)

...at Mestelexil's side, a machine formed that resembled a gun battery sprouting up from an emplacement.

Sweat ran down his brow. Even Kuze could understand what the machine meant without any knowledge of the weaponry from the Beyond.

As long as I survive.

An unmanned turret. Mestelexil sought to kill Kuze with neither a piece of equipment nor a golem but instead a simple, automatic machine.

Angels couldn't kill machines that never possessed a Word Arts life force. Unlike the terror of the True Demon King, she couldn't find fault with the intentions behind the one who set it up, either.

Could he stop Mestelexil's next attack? What about the one after that? Did this golem enemy before him ever tire?

His opening was...

"Make him stop! Please!"

Kuze shouted to Harutoru up above him.

One of the invisible army, meant to keep their identities hidden, had purposely revealed himself before Kuze, even knowing he personally couldn't participate in the fight at all. Most likely, it was required by his mission, whatever that was.

Kuze theorized: They were trying to make Kuze do something, using the threat of Mestelexil as a deterrent.

"You said it at the start, right?! You came here to parley, didn't you?!"

The gun barrel Mestelexil had set up moved.

He could tell that its sights were aimed directly at Kuze's undefended gut and head.

Amid the powder keg situation, Kuze gulped.

"...Fine. I'll continue with our parley, then. Enough, Mestelexil. If he makes any suspicious moves, kill him."

"O-oh...okay. I will do, as you say!"

"W-well now, he's...a real obedient fella, isn't he? Mind if I ask how exactly you tamed him?"

"We only have one demand."

Harutoru completely ignored Kuze's question.

"You don't need to promise us anything or switch sides to some other faction. Once you've accepted my demand, you can even continue on to the garden theater if you want, and we definitely won't cause you any harm. That goes for you...and those orphans who Okafu is protecting, too."

"................"

Kuze went silent. Even though he smiled, it felt like his torso's temperature was gradually going cold.

Harutoru took out a cloth-wrapped vial and tossed it to the ground.

"Drink that."

"*Bweh-ha-ha.* Excuse me?"

"It's mostly water. Not poison. If I planned on killing you with chemicals, I could have let Mestelexil finish you off just now."

"......Y'know... Zigita Zogi? He mentioned something. That the invisible army could possibly have a vampire in their ranks."

Vampires made additional corpses by transfusing blood through an open wound—or by contact through the mucuous membrane.

To look at it another way, it required intimate contact, and even ingesting a drop or two of blood wouldn't immediately turn someone into a corpse.

Normally, the pathogen shouldn't be able to infect someone through a single small vial like this.

"It's *mostly* water, huh? *Bweh-ha-ha.* So basically, inside this thing is the smallest amount of your parents' blood in here...and if I drink this thing, I'll end up as one of your myrmidons, is that it?"

"No. It's my blood in there."

Harutoru snarled with a smile.

"That way, if that automatic counterattack of yours considers the infection as an attack against you, too...I'll be the only one who ends up dead."

"*Bweh-ha-ha...* That so, eh..."

Kuze bent down where he stood and picked up the vial.

Still in that position, he opened it up and brought it up to his mouth.

"Hey, listen. All right if I ask you...one more thing?"

The iron wall, blocking out the surroundings, cast thick shadows down around him.

"When you said you wouldn't harm the kids, is that true? See, I...I want to protect them. Whatever happens to me doesn't matter, as long as I can help all of them..."

"Yeah. I promise."

"Say."

With a whirl—

—blank eyes looked up at Harutoru.

The moment he felt the cold shiver run down his spine, Harutoru used his sheer force of will to stop the instinct engrained in him telling him to counterattack.

"Try all you want…to make me attack; it's me—"

A red line ran across Harutoru's throat.

A brief holy pause.

Harutoru hadn't harmed Kuze in the slightest. He was confident he had shut out any intent to kill Kuze from his mind.

His massive frame slipped down from the roof, spasming, and landed right at Kuze's feet.

"…So in other words, I can't protect those kids unless I kill every last one of you, right?"

The man stared, looking down like a death god over Harutoru, who was no longer able to move.

The vial was in Kuze's hands. He hadn't drunk from it.

"*Gahak, hgnk!*"

Nastique's power over instant death would kill all those who tried to kill Kuze.

However—there was another condition that could induce it, one that even Obsidian Eyes didn't know about.

Kuze himself *wishing to kill someone* who was in his line of sight.

"Mestel…"

"*Ha-ha-ha*, what's wrong?"

Gazing at Mestelexil, standing by exactly as Harutoru ordered, Kuze muttered:

"...*I* haven't made any suspicious movements. Right? You're an honest fella. Like a kid."

"*Hrngh, glrnk, augh.*"

Harutoru's tenacious body, even with his death fated, continued to wriggle in agony.

His claws scrapped the ground as he tried to breathe.

"Don't get in my way."

Kuze's dense pupils, like a mire, looked down into Harutoru's own.

"Don't interfere with what I'm doing. I'm not going to extend salvation to you all, too."

There was no longer any voice to answer him.

"...*Bweh-ha-ha.* Hey, Mestelexil."

"...?"

"See, I'm thinking about running away, actually..."

"*Ha-ha-ha-ha-ha*, really now—"

Mestelexil visibly reacted to Kuze's words. Movement with intent to kill.

At the same time, the unmanned turret on the perimeter moved.

"To the right."

One second before Mestelexil and the turret could, Kuze sent Nastique into action of his own will.

Just as Kuze had told her, Mestelexil died instantly, collapsing to the right. The precision rapid fire from the unmanned turret was blocked by Mestelexil's massive frame and armor, which were now collapsed on the ground.

After the dust had settled, Kuze had disappeared from the alley.

...Dammit!

It had taken up too much time. The road was blocked off.

He wouldn't make it in time for the eighth match anymore.

If Mestelexil was going to faithfully stand by just as ordered, then killing the person giving him orders in the moment, Harutoru, had been the surest method of survival.

There was also still room for his enemy to interpret Harutoru's cause of death as the virus itself being perceived as a *hostile attack* against him. That was why he'd opened up the vial and brought it up to his mouth without showing Harutoru or Mestelexil.

It was a situation that required his trump card. He was certain.

...That's just an excuse.

When Sun's Conifer attacked the almshouse, Kuze had to be able to get through without killing anyone.

However, if Uhak hadn't been there that day, what would he have done?

When the lycan brought up the kids, he couldn't avoid thinking it.

I wanted to kill him. The truth is, I...

He clenched the vial in his hands.

Why was the angel who killed everything haunting him and him alone?

Was it perhaps that her existence itself revealed Kuze the Passing Disaster's true character?

The white angel made sure to fly right at Kuze's side while he walked, and she smiled at him.

...I'm so full of loathing, I want to kill absolutely everything in the world.

He had a hunch. The day would come when he could no longer keep Nastique under control.

◆

"To all gathered! Uhak the Silent has been shackled with the burden of deafness from birth! We in the assembly guarantee the blame for this lies not with Uhak himself and that he is not a minian-eating ogre! As such, Uhak has a special right to know the true duel accords through the written word!" Meeka the Whispered declared before establishing the rules of the match.

This declaration was likely how Uhak's sponsor, Nofelt, had explained it—that it wasn't that he didn't comprehend Word Arts, but that he was simply a mute ogre with a hearing impairment.

He inherently perceived the sounds that people's voices made without any difficulty. He was merely missing the blessing of Word Arts to interpret and comprehend them.

A creature who shared the same nature as Words Arts–ignorant beasts.

"A combatant is knocked down and doesn't get up. A combatant willingly admits their defeat with their own words. These two things shall decide the match, and on these grounds, any and all weapons, and any and all techniques, are permitted. Any outcome that does not adhere to these two conditions shall be relegated to my, Meeka the Whispered's, adjudication. Do we have an agreement?!"

Meeka informed the two combatants about the rules behind the true duel.

Uhak was handed a piece of paper with the Order's script written on it, and he gave his assent with a nod.

...Meeka the Whispered. I truly respect you for putting yourself on the line here.

The heavy responsibility and danger she purposely shouldered as the adjudicator for the Sixways Exhibition, enshrouded in schemes, were extraordinary. She was definitely involved in unfair play, however—she was trying to ensure victory for Rosclay the Absolute.

Nevertheless, there was certainly a plethora of different powers that were targeting her and the huge authority she had over each victory. It was possible for her to earn the resentment and ire of defeated hero candidates as well.

Meeka the Whispered was putting herself right on the front lines of danger, far more than any other of the Twenty-Nine Officials.

However, I know very well why you have gone so far to expose yourself to danger.

She wasn't able to entrust it to anyone else.

If it was someone else standing in her place, the slightest slip of their tongue could cause Aureatia to lose public prestige. If they were swayed by the honeyed words of one of the other factions, they might betray everyone's belief in them. It was precisely because she held such confidence in her ability to make truly correct judgments that she couldn't stand to have someone else here in her stead.

Zigita Zogi understood that. It was a risk, and a heavy responsibility, she carried because of her excellence.

He was the hero burdened with the future of the goblin race.

Their race had grown shockingly more intelligent in the past ten years. Even then, they couldn't compare with the cunning of the minia. That was all the more reason why, right now, no one else could be sent out into this arena.

To ensure that on this continent, they didn't play a subordinate role to the minian races once again.

Zigita Zogi knew that the Sixways Exhibition was a scheme to eliminate the hero candidates.

The one who, despite this, stood forward as a hero was someone who wouldn't be daunted by whatever bargaining was at play, nor make any mistakes in their judgment—in other words, it had to be him himself.

"Uhak the Silent has given his consent! Zigita Zogi the Thousandth! Do you agree to the accords of this true duel?!"

"Yes. I'll fight under those conditions."

"The match will begin with the sound of the band's starting gun! Prepare yourselves!"

Meeka's large frame disappeared into the underground corridor.

Zigita Zogi gripped a metal stopper inside his right fist.

He utilized military strategy, but he couldn't employ any breaches in the rules during the match. It could potentially become an exploitable chance for another hostile force. However, this was a true duel battle. An ultimate fight where any and all methods of attack were permitted. After the signal to start the match, even chemical weapons would be beyond any scorn.

The band's cannon fire echoed. He could see Uhak begin to advance.

Yet it would only take a blink of an eye for him to twist the stopper and release the gas valve—

"......"

He couldn't move.

Me, of all people—I can't believe it.

Zigita Zogi's muscles had completely stiffened up. He couldn't even move a single fingertip.

There hadn't been any interference from someone else.

Zigita Zogi had been turned into a corpse.

The gray ogre raised his club up in the air.

Zigita Zogi knew exactly how fatal this single instant was.

Using the increased mental agility that came moments before one's death and using brain cells more outstanding than any others', he thought:

Food. Lesions. Or a bug, perhaps. None of those seem to fit, really. Ahhh... I see. The blood smell. In which case, my initial premise was wrong. If only there had been a bit more material to predict this development... A mutation to airborne transmission. Unbelievable. So this is our enemy's true form. Finally... With this, there's a chance of victory...

He was the thousandth, genius, most eminent of all.

Up until the end of his life, he thought through tactics and plans, and finally...

Ah, but still. I'm glad it was Hiroto...and not me who was given the antiserum.

The boorish wooden club was closing in before his eyes.

Uhak didn't erase any supernatural abilities—because he could win without having to do so.

Zigita Zogi wasn't allowed a single movement.

While he had arrived at the correct solution, far closer than any other, how was he to pass it along?

I've reached an impasse.

The barbaric mass crushed the thick metal helmet along with the cranium underneath.

The dream that Hiroto the Paradox had awaited.

A true genius, the likes of which would never appear among the goblins again.

His brains were turned into a light-pink mass of blood and flesh and scattered across the graveled earth.

◆

A café terrace in front of castle garden theater—it was the same seat where she had once shared a meal with Yuno.

Listening to the clamor from within its walls, Linaris stared silently in the direction of the garden theater.

She almost came across as the innocent child of a respectable, well-to-do family, taking an early afternoon breather.

"...Farewell, Master Zigita Zogi," the young lady murmured, not with a smile at the loss of her greatest enemy, but instead with a tinge of sorrow.

One could rephrase the ability of tactical strategy as the ability to create options.

Obsidian Eyes had a massive amount of information they'd accumulated from their investigations.

What sort of shape did the duties of the castle garden soldiers take? If there was someone among the other sponsors who would try to use Zigita Zogi's camp for themselves, who would it be? Was there an opportunity to assassinate Zigita Zogi with certainty and without any suspicions being sent their way?

If they were going to make a move on a strategist of Zigita Zogi's caliber, he was sure to outwit their attack, then trace it back to the source. If he did, he would likely arrive at the true form of Obsidian Eyes, which she needed to keep secret... In which case, they weren't the ones who were supposed to deal with him.

There was only one person who could assassinate him with certainty and without casting any suspicions toward Obsidian Eyes' possible involvement.

His opponent in the eighth match. Uhak the Silent was the only one who could do it.

All the preparations had finished in the middle of the third match.

Secretly switching out the keys, the corpse-transformed soldiers inside the garden theater were able to come and go freely.

Identifying the soldiers who belonged to the garden theater using the information gleaned from her infiltration, she had turned those involved with the eighth match into corpses.

Therefore, Linaris didn't even need to enter the garden theater at all during the eighth match.

The surveying of the garden theater that Enu had pushed forward had, from the very beginning, laid the groundwork to determine whether the range of her vampire pheromones could reach the arena from the outside or not.

The means didn't need to be complicated.

If anything, it needed to be something so simple that Zigita Zogi couldn't outsmart it.

At that same moment.

Inside the garden theater, a soldier threw something into a furnace.

Hidden inside the bandages that covered his wounds...was a handkerchief soaked in fresh blood that was not his own.

Linaris the Obsidian was a vampire who could spread the vampiric infection through the air. Even just a single part of her body, a smattering of blood, was no exception.

Evading all his precautions, she'd infected Zigita Zogi *just by having him stand in the same space as her blood.*

The simplest method, and impossible to avoid.

Our biggest obstacle has disappeared. With this, at last...I can finish my mission.

Zigita Zogi was sure to have stationed his goblin forces within the garden theater to be ready against their powerful enemy, the invisible army. Dant the Heath Furrow and Hiroto the Paradox were also there as well.

It was possible she had led them to summon their previous collaborator, Ozonezma the Capricious. Even then, it would be no problem for Linaris.

She had made part of the Obsidian Eyes forces slip into the castle garden spectator seats. Lena the Obscured. Frey the Waking.

Once the results of the eighth match were confirmed, these two would immediately begin to act. With their level of skill, it was possible to infect Hiroto the Paradox without even making him aware of the fact. Furthermore, by using blood for an airborne infection, his bodyguard—the terrifying chimera Ozonezma—wouldn't have any hopes of resisting them, either.

Airborne infection, requiring Linaris's blood and unable to be spread from corpses, was a final resort. The potency of this tactic came at the cost of a greater chance of its truth being exposed. Now, with Zigita Zogi dead, they could put said method into action without any apprehension.

Now there was no one who possessed the brains to arrive at Obsidian Eyes' existence in the shadows.

"My lady."

There was a voice at her feet from underneath the tablecloth. A bizarre minia who walked on all fours.

Wieze the Variation. A sniper who snuffed out his enemies with chakrams.

Promptly noticing the new presences that came into his firing range, he cautioned her.

"Six carriages. They bear the Seventh Minister's flag."

"...Thank you very much. Continue to stay on guard for me."

Linaris was able to discern the same a fair bit of time after the sniper's eyes had picked them up.

The carriage designs were garnished extravagantly with silver. The white and blue flag signaled the presence of physicians. It was a cohort under the command of Flinsuda the Portent, leader of the medical division. They were, in essence, the bane of any vampire; however, that itself wasn't any reason to fear them.

Nevertheless.

An anxious shadow passed through Linaris's mind.

There's far too many here just to treat injuries or confirm the death of the losing candidate... Even assuming there were injured inside the garden theater...

The medical-division carriages came to a stop as she watched from her position.

Looking at the people who alighted from the carriage, her anxieties changed to conviction.

A woman wielding a massive war ax. Thick bangs that almost seem to block out her whole line of sight.

She was the Tenth General, Qwell the Wax Flower.

"A dhampir...! Why is the Tenth General with the Medical Division...?!"

A bodyguard who was resistant to the vampire's virus. There was only one thing that could possibly point to...

It was a team that'd been sent, *convinced* of a vampire's involvement, *to specifically deal with it.*

The Seventh Minister doesn't belong to any specific faction and is swayed by coin. Master Hiroto, the Gray-Haired Child, must have a large amount of Aureatian currency through his musket dealings. If he already had Miss Flinsuda working on his behalf before the start of the match...then we've already...

It meant they had been identified.

They knew that the "invisible army" was a vampire group, or perhaps even the fact that it was Obsidian Eyes itself.

Linaris had planned to erase Zigita Zogi with the fastest method possible, but the enemy's thinking had been far faster and meticulous enough to arrange for a medical team.

In that case...will infecting Master Hiroto while he's in the castle garden right now...actually be possible? If he had a chance to make a bargain with Aureatia in this short period of time, it isn't completely impossible that he's obtained the antiserum. If Master Ozonezma has been inoculated with the antiserum, then everyone will end up killed by the target... There's a chance they've gone one step further...and positioned some ally we are unaware of...and seen through this ambush.

"My lady. Shall I wipe out the medical team here?" Wieze said, below Linaris as she worked through her endlessly labyrinthine thoughts. "Even I alone could kill them all without leaving any survivors. Kill this dhampir here, and they're little different from any other minia."

"...No... The fact that this medical team has come here...

means that Master Zigita Zogi has already seen through our plans to mobilize a large number of corpses during the eighth match. They've already come to realize the 'invisible army' is a vampire... that Obsidian Eyes is in the shadows of the Sixways Exhibition..."

Obsidian Eyes had made a large number of moves related to the match.

The preliminary subterfuge using castle garden soldiers made into corpses. Airborne infection using Linaris's blood. Impersonating a sponsor with the mimic, Lena the Obscured. Suppressing Kuze the Passing Disaster's movements with Mestelexil.

To ensure they put an end to Zigita Zogi that day, they had no choice but to play many of their cards. Had the ultimate tactician managed to anticipate that a vampire parent unit would make a move during this match as well?

Nevertheless. I need to take control of Master Hiroto here, or we shall lose our golden opportunity to do so. All these misgivings are based on my own assumptions, and I haven't seen any definitive evidence, either.

This operation needed to continue. Even if Obsidian Eyes' covert plans had already been exposed, now that they had given their enemy so much information, backing down was the worst possible move they could make. She simply needed to control Hiroto the Paradox and take command of his country. That was what Linaris's brain told her to do.

Her father had done so. Sparing no thought to the sacrifices. Calmly and coldly choosing the optimal path forward.

I will create an era of war. That's all I need... If I can just finish Father's wishes, then I can be free...

◆

The castle-garden-theater spectator seats—

Lena the Obscured continued her surveillance as the venue erupted with the conclusion to the eighth match.

A mimic—a construct race capable of changing their form at will. After fulfilling her mission to disguise herself as Nofelt the Somber Wind, she had moved to the spectator seats to complete her next mission.

She had pinned down where Hiroto the Paradox was sitting. As well as confirming that Ozonezma the Capricious was right beside him.

Zigita Zogi had Ozonezma come to act as Hiroto's bodyguard after all. Exactly as anticipated.

Lena carried a small vial with her as well.

However, it wasn't a corpse's blood dissolved in the vial's water, but Linaris's blood, capable of airborne infection.

Regardless of the fighting capabilities Ozonezma the Capricious might possess, if she opened it up as she passed by at point-blank range and made them breathe it in, she could put them under her mistress's control. It didn't even require her to act suspiciously, let alone attack them.

If there's one problem...

Lena looked down at the arena. The garden-theater seating was constructed in a basin shape to ensure the arena was visible from any seat. In the spot slightly removed from the center of the basin was a red blood splotch.

What resembled a squashed bug was, in fact, the miserable end of Zigita Zogi.

...*That helm.*

She lifted up the bandage covering her eyes.

The light in her eyeballs, to an unstable construct like Lena, put a heavy strain on her and was a major limitation whenever she changed into someone else. Even then, she needed to visually confirm Zigita Zogi's death once more.

She verified that his corpse was still wearing his helm.

The metallic helm had been cracked open, together with the rest of the cranium, like shelling a tree nut, and stuck into his flesh, likely making it impossible to tear off.

The appearance of all the sixteen challengers in the Six-ways Exhibition had been verified beforehand by several of the Twenty-Nine Officials, then registered accordingly. If there was any equipment that completely covered one's face, then naturally, the organizers would verify the face of the person beneath it before and after the match.

Therefore, any impersonation of one of the candidates by another could never happen—the situation was completely different from the fourth match, where the hero candidate had been swapped out with another. At the very least, it had been verified that Zigita Zogi himself was beneath the helm.

For this match, they were no longer able to do the postmatch verification. *The head they were meant to double-check had been completely smashed.*

If, in the unlikely scenario...that getting his head caved by Uhak had been incorporated into his plan, then it's possible the goblin appearing in this arena had been expendable from the start. Can we pick out Zigita Zogi from other goblins without the head still intact...?

If she approached even closer, Lena might have been able to determine for herself. However, the castle garden theater was vast, and her only option was to judge from a distance. With all eyes fixed on the arena, sneaking in was impossible.

...I have to be cautious.

Caution. Nothing more. Lena's mission hadn't changed.

She would approach Hiroto and Ozonezma and infect them. Then she would depart from the scene.

As long as her mistress had ordered her to do so, she would carry out her duty, even if it cost her life. Simple as that.

However, Lena's feet stopped soon after she started walking toward Hiroto's seat. Her gaze drifted—on the exact opposite side of the spectator seats, there was another hero candidate, beside Ozonezma.

Shalk the Sound Slicer.

He was far away. A seat too far away to be guarding Hiroto.

Nevertheless, he was positioned with a good look at the area around the politician's seat.

Lena took out her radzio, fully aware of the danger of making any contact. It connected to Linaris, outside the garden theater, in case of emergency.

"My lady. It's Lena. Uhak the Silent has won without issue. However, there are a few points that bother me."

<...What would those be?>

"Shalk the Sound Slicer is spectating the match. Southwest side, twenty-fifth row, second from the right. Hiroto the Paradox's seat is on the eastern side, fourth row and tenth seat from the right."

<......>

"They are separate from each other, but if he seriously did go into action, no distance would be too far for him."

Shalk the Sound Slicer was one other of Obsidian Eyes' feared enemies, on par with Kuuro the Careful. His body, composed of white bone, wouldn't be infected by any blood-borne virus.

Furthermore, once his spear fixed on a target, no amount of sleight of hand would make it possible to escape.

<That...is not anything unusual. Master Shalk has spectated almost all the matches up until now.>

"I believe the same thing. However, there is a chance that he has made contact with Yukiharu the Twilight Diver. Right?"

<...Yes.>

It was impossible for anyone in Obsidian Eyes, no matter their agility, to surveil Shalk himself.

However, Obsidian Eyes was still the largest spy guild in the land. If someone was impossible to trail, they just needed to collect secondhand information instead—even by Lena's recollection, she clearly remembered hearing a witness account of Yukiharu the Twilight Diver conversing with Shalk the Sound Slicer.

"Also."

Lena looked at the arena. At the body lying on the gravel.

"Zigita Zogi the Thousandth wore a helm. Uhak's attack defeated him by crushing his entire head with the helm. I ask for your judgment regarding this situation, my lady."

<............>

◆

The café terrace, outside the castle garden theater—

That isn't a problem.

Linaris closed her golden eyes, as if in prayer.

Even if the helm was to feign his death, Master Zigita Zogi wouldn't use any strategy that involved in the Sixways Exhibition... since his goal is to make Aureatia accept his people. He wouldn't do anything that would entail abandoning his original goal simply to deal with us.

Linaris was endowed with that power. The gift to penetrate a person's heart and deeply consider their emotions.

Sparing no thought to the sacrifices. Calmly and coldly taking the optimal action—if there was a possibility she would stray from the correct path, it would stem from Linaris herself and the weakness in her heart.

Master Zigita Zogi made sure to appear with an iron helmet on. Clearly a move to confound his enemies should he lose, making it impossible to confirm his death. *Master Shalk's seat positioning isn't a coincidence, either. It wasn't Master Shalk himself but* Master Hiroto *who chose his seat to curb any movements from those who were aware of the details behind Master Shalk and Master Yukiharu's contact—in other words, to curb us.*

Lena's voice came through to her from the radzio.

<*If I am to act on this information, I wish for your orders. Now that a medical team is here, there's no time to delay. What should I do?*>

"Carr—"

She attempted to tell her to "carry out her mission."

Linaris forcefully pressed down on her chest. Was this really the best move?

<*My lady. It's Lendelt.*>

A voice cut into the radzio call.

It belonged to Lendelt the Immaculate, charged with guerilla-style attacks. However, the line he utilized should have been in Harutoru's hands...

<*Harutoru was killed.*>

"......Ngh!"

She tried to hold her lamenting cry back but failed.

Harutoru the Light Grip had died.

"That can't be..."

<*Mestelexil was recovered safely, but Kuze the Passing Disaster appears to have fled. The particulars of Harutoru's time of death are unknown. I will follow up with Mestelexil.*>

"No...it can't be..."

Even with Mestelexil the Box of Desperate Knowledge with him, Harutoru had fallen in battle.

She could imagine the reason why. Harutoru may have tried to make some attack on his own. Perhaps an unexpected amount of reinforcements came to Kuze's aid.

If they were able to win today, everything was supposed to be over. It was why they had laid out multiple layers of intrigue and deceit.

Even then, the power of subterfuge was unreliable. Linaris knew that.

"Miss Lena. Quickly—"

She could no longer believe in it.

Linaris handed down her orders to Lena inside the garden theater.

"—please leave the garden theater immediately and bring everyone along with you. You are free to abandon your infection mission. Please move quickly and ensure no one else takes notice."

If Linaris commanded her to execute her orders, Lena would have gone forward without hesitation.

<Operation suspended. Understood, my lady.>

"...*Koff, koff.*"

Right as she ended the transmission, Linaris coughed harshly.

"*Koff, hrk...ngh!*"

The stress of traveling outside the manor a number of times in a short period, and the extreme psychological tension, gnawed at her thin, frail body.

Suspension had been the only option. If, by any chance, Linaris had misread the situation, then she would lose everything.

She had needed to bestow on Obsidian Eyes a path for their future survival, without sacrificing a single one of them in the process.

Despite that, Hyakrai the Tower had been heavily wounded by a slight, accidental deviation.

Now she had let Harutoru the Light Grip die.

"Koff, augh... Why...? Why...?"

She covered her face with both hands and dropped her head down flat on the table.

Despite knowing such unladylike behavior was sure to earn her a terrible reprimanding.

She was supposed to be here in her father's stead.

I wasn't able to claim victory. I threw all our plans into this, and even then... Master Zigita Zogi was a true genius. If Father was here... If it had been Father here right now, I'm sure then that...

Linaris had thought if she could fulfill every part of the mission entrusted to her, she could begin her own life.

If she could do that, then surely there wouldn't be any further need to keep abandoning her friends.

At her feet, Wieze spoke up.

"...My lady. I will stay behind here. Please escape with Lena or Frey once you've confirmed they've made it out. I will keep watch on the medical team."

"Yes... Very well. I will leave it in your hands."

Linaris returned Wieze's smile as he departed. She was crying.

She smiled and let the tears simply fall down her cheeks, as her etiquette had trained her.

I'm sorry.

Zigita Zogi the Thousandth may have truly been dead.

The iron helm he had worn might have been a way to implant a nonexistent shadow of doubt in his enemies' minds.

Similarly, Shalk the Sound Slicer sitting in a position where he could guard Hiroto the Paradox may have simply been because Hiroto had chosen that seat to instill such a thought in his enemy's mind, and nothing more.

The fear might have all been in Linaris's mind, and if she fought now, she might be able to win.

Even then, I can't do it. I just can't... Sacrificing everyone else is the one thing I cannot do.

Being born and raised within Obsidian Eyes, she had no means to live a life outside it.

Among the comrades she had spent her life with, only a few remained. If she lost them, then there wouldn't be a single thing left in Linaris's life.

More than all that...

"I...I can't possibly put everything on the line like that... I mean...I-I'm merely borrowing it...from Father, after all."

Neither Obsidian Eyes nor any of the agents in its ranks belonged to Linaris.

She wasn't Obsidian. She hadn't been able to inherit that from her father.

—She remembered that day.

Her beloved father stained with blood, with Linaris looking on at him in shock.

Who had killed him?

No. He hadn't been killed at all.

Thus, Rehart the Obsidian wasn't dead.

If he wasn't dead, then she should have still been able to accomplish his goal.

That was why she still needed to keep thinking. Calmly and coldly, just like her father, regardless of any potential sacrifices, just like her father. Even the slightest chance of defeat was unforgivable. She didn't wish to blemish her father's name with her own failure.

She wished to be a daughter who wasn't ashamed to act in Rehart the Obsidian's stead.

"...Please forgive me..."

She begged for forgiveness.

There was no one else out there who could keep Linaris in check.

◆

Even after the fierce battle in the underground waiting room was over, Dant stayed behind and worked to preserve the scene.

Dant alone wasn't able to read to what extent the enemy had infiltrated inside the castle garden. He also feared that evidence, including Haizesta's corpse, would end up being destroyed.

One minia soldier, and one goblin soldier. Along with Haizesta. There had been three casualties right as the match was going on.

This would be enough of a reason to suspend the match and lobby for Uhak's disqualification, but—

"...General Dant!"

Several soldiers appeared, faces pale.

There was definitely some emergency situation, but first, Dant was wary of the soldiers. There was a chance a corpse was mixed in among them.

"You have to flee this place immediately! We'll secure the scene," said a soldier.

"Can't do that. This is a serious example of unlawful behavior. The match should immediately be suspended, and the scoundrels who sullied the Sixways Exhibition need to be identified. Besides, I need to provide my own testimony for the investigation."

"U-um, well...th-that's not it, General. This isn't about this incident."

"What else could it possibly be about, then?"

Dant was suspicious.

Was there any other matter that could be more pressing than a member of the Twenty-Nine Officials being manipulated and killed during the royal games?

If there was, it would have to be on a national scale...

"My apologies, General! It most likely happened right around the time you arrived here, sir. The eighth match is over! Zigita Zogi the Thousandth is dead! Without a moment's delay following the results, an alarm was sounded, which—"

"Wait. An alarm?! What's going on?!"

"Ministers Jel and Grasse have already departed the garden theater! Furthermore...you've been *ordered to sortie*, General!"

"...It can't be."

Dant quickly silenced everyone gathered before him, and he perked his ears up amid the silence.

He could faintly catch the bell ringing up on the surface. Two strikes. Three strikes. Two strikes. Three strikes.

Every single member of the Twenty-Nine Officials was well acquainted with what exactly this signal meant.

"Dammit! Things are in enough of mess already...!"

"We were just now dispatched here as reinforcements. With the suspicion of corpse infiltration, Minister Flinsuda's medical team is accompanying us. From here, we will restrain the castle garden soldiers, examine them, and identify who is behind this incident. We'll also ask you to appear for an examination at a later date, General Dant...!"

"Somewhere around here... You—you look like an official medical team. Take a look at my pupils here, then. Examination's a bit simple, but it'll be enough, right?"

Showing his pupils to one of the physicians running through the area, Dant proved that he wasn't a corpse himself.

Vampires. A plague that was thought to already have been largely eradicated. The enemy of Zigita Zogi, who needed to be brought down first and foremost. Naturally, Dant had been informed of it all as well, and it was something he had been on guard against.

However, Haizesta's appearance moments prior had been something else.

The enemy possessed skills of manipulation on a far deeper level than simply controlling a corpse's actions through pheromones.

Most likely, that was the truth of Obsidian Eyes. Something capable of multiplying their scouts, without any of the many other organizations taking notice, had already infiltrated Aureatia.

"I'll head out immediately."

"Good luck in your campaign, General Dant. Are there any other matters to check on?"

Dant stopped his feet.

"...Right. One thing I'd like to ask."

While he had clearly heard the truth himself, he couldn't help but confirm it again.

The cunning tactician, more intelligent than any minia, who had been able to see through every development...

"Zigita Zogi died?"

"Yes. His head was split open in a single strike, and he died instantly."

"......"

With a small nod, Dant rushed off.

He bitterly mumbled to himself.

"To hell with this..."

The goblin who had suddenly appeared on Dant's battlefield, stealing all his military achievements out from under him.

Everything about the tactician had rubbed him the wrong way.

Even the feeling of loss the goblin left with his death vexed him.

"Zigita Zogi!"

Zigita Zogi was dead. He didn't want to believe it.

Dant's face was twisted with rage.

It was what he was supposed to do.

"Damn you for pushing all this trouble onto me!"

◆

Ozonezma looked down at the scene.

In the center of the garden theater, Zigita Zogi had become a widening blotch of blood, and the spectators, witnessing such a gruesome demise, were left speechless, while others whispered and murmured among one another.

Amid the stir, Hiroto alone simply remained quiet.

"The true duel has been decided! The winner, Uhak the Silent!" the adjudicator, Meeka, shouted.

The woman's firm voice clearly reached Hiroto, sitting frozen, and Ozonezma at his side.

"...HIROTO..."

"..."

Ozonezma didn't have the words for how Ozonezma was meant to face the scene of finality before him.

Was he meant to mourn the man's death—a comrade in arms, albeit for a brief time?

Or perhaps, should he have felt relieved that the True Hero had advanced to the second round?

What had happened to his memories around the end of the Final Party's journey?

By the time he had finished agonizing and writhing from the surgery to incorporate the True Demon King's arm and regained his sanity—or at least, what he had believed was his sanity—Setera had vanished.

Only he alone could be rightfully labeled the True Hero.

Ozonezma had thought he needed to search for the ogre, but his fear toward Setera's true identity prevented him from doing so.

…He had believed him to be dead.

If there was any being in this world who could calmly live on after consuming the corpse of the True Demon King, then they were a true and unequivocal monster.

He hadn't wanted to think that the last remaining companion from his travels was such a thing.

Thus, he had kept silent on the ogre's achievement while being simultaneously unable to overlook anyone who falsely claimed they were a hero.

It was something no one else had been able to do…that no one should have done.

The deed was far too great, and frightening.

The True Hero was *terrifying*.

Nevertheless, Setera had returned.

To the Sixways Exhibition, to tell without any words to speak, that the Hero did truly exist in their world.

" … "

Ozonezma went to say something to Hiroto, but an alarm bell began to ring from afar.

It propagated through the spires in each of the districts quickly, turning into a piercingly loud din.

"…WHAT IS THIS?"

The tall black smoke rising up in the distance could be seen even from the spectator seats.

Ozonezma realized what exactly the implications of it all were.

"Everyone, please calm down and move as commanded!"

A soldier came running up the seats, shouting with all the volume his voice could muster.

"This is a life-threatening disaster! Line up in order and evacuate as instructed! Match pace with children, the elderly, and the injured and don't disturb the line! We are fully prepared to get everyone out of the arena!"

"Those closest to the east exit, come this way! We are arranging carriages for you outside!"

Ozonezma—and all the hero candidates—knew. This alarm bell didn't signal any ordinary disaster.

"…HIROTO! YOU NEED TO FLEE IMMEDIATELY, TOO. THIS LOCATION IS ALREADY IN DANGER, JUST AS THEY SAID."

"…Yes. I suppose so."

Hiroto was perfectly calm, his hands folded together on his lap as he stared at the arena.

The supernatural politician wasn't at all rattled by Zigita Zogi's death.

"I'll follow after you. Go ahead without me."

"…I…"

Setera had vanished. Among all the chaos, had he already headed off to do the job he was meant to do?

Ozonezma was scared of him. He overlooked him.

He was unable to forget the ogre. He rued him.

Ozonezma wanted to convey something, even a single word, to the ogre, but he didn't know what exactly he was supposed to say.

Zigita Zogi's body hadn't been devoured but left exposed in the arena.

If there was even one person who believed in the horrible truth behind the Hero, then would this Sixways Exhibition have ever happened in the first place? If Ozonezma hadn't completed the tai-sai, would Hiroto have returned from across that sea? Or perhaps, if Zigita Zogi hadn't isolated Ozonezma outside Aureatia? If the information on Uhak had been made clear to him. If Ozonezma hadn't ended up losing to Soujirou the Willow-Sword.

Izick the Chromatic. Olukt the Drifting Compass Needle. Setera the External. The True Demon King. Hiroto the Paradox. Zigita Zogi the Thousandth. Soujirou the Willow-Sword. Ozonezma the Capricious.

No one had planned for it to happen at all.

In some place beyond the reach of anybody, all their fates had grown intertwined.

Was what lay ahead in the future of the Sixways Exhibition the answer to this fate?

"...HIROTO. I WAS NOT ABLE TO DO ANYTHING IN THIS BATTLE. CALL FOR ME IF THERE COMES A TIME I AM NEEDED."

"That's much appreciated. I'll do exactly that."

The colossal beast scaled the castle garden walls with a single jump and then disappeared.

Hiroto continued to stay seated in the now-blank, snow-white spectator seats.

Just as Hiroto the Paradox had been a perfect politician, Zigita Zogi had been a perfect tactician.

Foreseeing even his own future, dying without accomplishing his objective, he had used every method at his disposal to protect the politician's life.

Even in death, the tactician had beaten the land's most wicked spy colony.

The politician left behind merely had to achieve the tactician's goal.

A perfect politician didn't have any personal feelings. Without a single desire of his own, he moved solely to realize the promises to his constituents. The goblins' renaissance. That was possible even without Zigita Zogi the individual.

As long as Hiroto could accomplish that, their wishes would come true. There was no problem. As long as someone wished for it, there wasn't anything that Hiroto the Paradox couldn't accomplish. It had been so up until now, and it would be true going forward.

He smiled slightly, then pressed his fist up against his brow.

"*Ahhh*...goddamn it..."

Zigita Zogi had been a goblin the likes of which would never be seen again.

It had been a dream, passed down by Zegegu Zogi, by Ephelina, by Raheek.

From afar, the alarm bells continued to clang.

Thus, there wasn't anyone to hear his wail.

"Goddamn it aaaaall...!"

Match eight. Winner, Uhak the Silent.

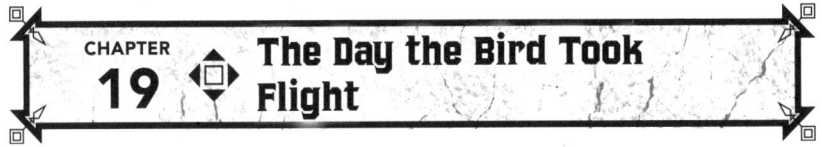

Slipping back in time—the day of the eighth match. A faint twilight before the sunrise.

Toroa the Awful quietly sat up in his appointed bed inside Mizial the Iron-Piercing Plumeshade's residence.

He needed to leave in the early morning while everyone else was still fast asleep.

Sitting in a wood chair, he bent his right leg and then extended it. He repeated the same with the left.

...Fully healed.

Attending to him until both of the knees Psianop had pierced through were healed—and in the end, even risking his own life to protect Toroa—Kuuro the Careful had allowed Toroa to recover his true strength.

In that brief second, there hadn't been any time to hear the details from Kuuro.

He was able to interpret from the few fragmented words that Kuuro was being targeted.

However, Kaete's camp was the power that had previously raided the clinic, aiming to acquire Toroa's enchanted swords. Was it possible that Mestelexil—Kaete's hero candidate—had fixed his aim on Toroa and caught the uninvolved Kuuro up in the disaster?

"...Enchanted swords invite conflict..."

He couldn't say for certain that another attack like it wasn't coming.

His presence in Mizial's home might bring death to those he cared about.

After Kuuro the Careful, he didn't want to lose Mizial the Iron-Piercing Plumeshade or Cuneigh the Wanderer as well.

...*That's right. Ultimately, I'm meant to stay inside people's ghost stories.*

He took all his possessions and left his room.

Pulling his hood down low, he hid his own face.

He carried countless enchanted swords with him.

"......"

The room of his sponsor, Twenty-Second General Mizial, was located right by the stairs.

The young boy had innocently admired the enchanted swordsman, who was feared by all others, and extended him a helping hand.

Toroa had long felt envious of the boy's honest way of being, deciding everything based on his own artless curiosity, unrelated to any political power plays or sense of duty.

"...You're leaving, Toroa?"

Toroa heard a voice come from over his shoulder as he went to descend the staircase.

So he had been awake.

Toroa answered back over his shoulder.

"Yeah. Going back to Wyte. Thanks for everything."

"Hmm... Back home, huh. I guess after what happened, it makes sense."

"Sorry for the trouble. Cuneigh still asleep?"

"...She was still crying when I went to bed, but...... Yup. Fast asleep. Must've been exhausted. I put her down in some old clothing scraps—hope it's comfortable."

"Can I leave her with you?"

"......"

If Kuuro was going to return someday, he would definitely track Cuneigh down.

"Hey, Toroa, listen! You're going to back to gather enchanted swords again, right?"

"...Nah. Not going to kill those who wield enchanted swords anymore. I'm going home to Wyte Mountains...to live a quiet life tending to my vegetable garden. I always knew from the beginning what I wanted to do. This sort of stuff'll end with me."

"......"

"Disappointed? Listen, Mizial... I'll tell you the truth."

A silence stretched out briefly behind him in the dark corridor.

It would have been much better if he had disappeared without saying anything. Perhaps, as part of his duty from inheriting the name *Toroa the Awful*, he was meant to preserve the enchanted-swordsman illusion, like the children-scaring ghost story he was supposed to be.

However, Toroa didn't want to treat Mizial like a child.

"I'm not Toroa the Awful."

"……"

"Take care of yourself. You always leave vegetables behind on your plate. Gotta eat right. It's good to be enthusiastic about your studies, but you shouldn't stay up late reading books all the time. You're a real self-indulgent kid, and it might end up giving someone a real headache. Even then... Ahhh..."

Toroa finally understood.

—What his father had wished for had really been something this obvious.

"...Stay true to yourself. Don't end up becoming someone else and take care of yourself the most of all."

"…………Thanks."

Mizial the Iron-Piercing Plumeshade. The Twenty-Second General had known no fear of anyone nor shown deference to anyone.

With Toroa's form still concealed in the dark, the boy said his good-bye.

"You really were just like the real Toroa the Awful, you know... Sorry for being so unreasonable all the time."

"There's not anything you gotta apologize for."

"We'll still be friends even after you're back in Wyte, right?"

"Of course."

This was the end of Toroa the Awful's journey.

He departed from Aureatia on the morning's first long-distance carriage.

◆

Toroa was familiar with the one sitting diagonally opposite him in the carriage bound for the Mari Wastes.

They didn't possess a fixed shape, but they had a tiny book open up in the pseudopods sprouting out of them.

"Quite the coincidence, now isn't this, Toroa the Awful?"

"Inexhaustible Stagnation. That talkative mouth of yours is the same outside the arena, then."

"My mouth's just the same as my muscles. If I don't keep it going, it'll grow weaker, and I won't be able to get the necessary words out when the time comes. There's no reason for an intellectual creature not to temper such a weapon. When I was in the sand labyrinth, I used to speak the words in the books out loud and strove hard to keep my mouth working."

"Our match together…taught me a lot. I'd even like a rematch if possible, honestly."

"In that case, I wouldn't mind going right here, right now. Shall we?"

"Definitely don't have the strength for that."

"Me neither."

Psianop's expression was unfathomable. Even then, Toroa believed that the slime was making yet another joke.

The scenery outside the carriage, little by little, began to be tinged silvery white.

Toroa's thoughts went to Psianop's opponent in the second round.

If he had won his match, they were the enemy he would have gone up against.

Lucnoca the Winter. Among the land's strongest race of creatures, the dragons, she stood on top as their strongest.

He had heard she was a calamity that exceeded all possible limits of the imagination.

Alus the Star Runner, thought to be a lock to advance on—and Toroa's ultimate enemy, having killed Toroa the Awful once before—hadn't been able to get close to taking the legendary dragon's life, even throwing everything he had at her.

"…Inexhaustible Stagnation. You going to battle Lucnoca the Winter?"

"If you're going to speak of her strength, I've heard more than enough already. I'm going to see it with my own eyes."

"I would've dropped out of the tournament, probably. What're you fighting for?"

"……"

Barehanded strikes and all manner of enchanted swords. If the technical apexes they had each honed and tempered on their own shared the same qualities…and if the reason Psianop the Inexhaustible Stagnation had surpassed Toroa the Awful lay within Psianop's heart and mind, Toroa wished to know what it was.

The loquacious ooze went silent for a brief moment.

"…Willpower and pride, I'd say."

"That's the same for everyone, though."

"And that's precisely why."

Toroa didn't know about the ooze's past.

Nor did he know the reason why the ooze aimed to be the strongest of all or why he didn't hesitate to use Life Arts that chipped away at his own vitality.

"It's a reason that everyone shares, and that's precisely why I don't want to lose."

What about the other fourteen hero candidates?

There were bound to be some who fought carrying reasons unknown to him or ways of life unknown to him.

It was the ones who had reached their strongest peaks who continued to search for the logical conclusion of their life.

Even in this land, where the True Demon King lay dead and all reason to fight had gone away.

"...Well. It appears, during our idle chitchat, we've arrived."

"Looks like it."

Outside the window, the surface was blanketed completely white.

The cold air seeped through the carriage's walls. A terrible and abrupt change in temperature.

It was neither a natural phenomenon nor the end result of a long history.

A scenery had been changed in the brief moment of a single breath by a singular creature.

A landscape of ruin.

"Mari Wastes... So this is it."

In this land rested the final job that Toroa the Awful had inherited.

◆

Toroa the Awful continued to descend down the sheer rock face of the abyssal fissures running through the frozen soil.

The vertical cliff didn't have the slightest protrusion to get his fingers on. He was using an enchanted sword like a walking stick.

It was called Wicked Sword Selfesk. The arrangement of its blade, composed from countless, floating rivets, could be manipulated with an almost magnetic force. He stuck the rivets into the rock face to create footing for himself. The rivets above him would collect in his sheath again then spread out below into a new piece of footing.

Though it wasn't the sword's original purpose, he thought it was much a better way of using it than for killing others.

"...That's right. This is better than killing," he mumbled. Despite the fact that he was searching deep down in the unfathomable bottom of the earth and that he was the only one here on this frozen soil.

It was all so much better than killing someone and plundering from them.

The second match—Alus the Star Runner lost to Lucnoca the Winter and dropped down to the bottom of the earth.

Together with the hoard of treasure he had collected from his travels across the land.

Among all the many magical items that were in the wyvern's possession, Toroa's objective, from the very beginning, had been one thing and one thing only.

The world's ultimate enchanted sword, able to sever any and all matter, including dragon scale. Hillensingen the enchanted light sword.

"Real cold out here…"

If anything, he grew more talkative when alone.

His quip at Psianop just might have applied to none other than Toroa himself as well.

…At long last, the end of the tall, perpetual cliff came into view.

Previously in the Mari Wastes, a river had run through the deep crevices in the ground, with a holdover of those times being the road chipped level into the bottom of the fissure.

It was earth, like the frontiers of hell, that no one had ever trodden before.

"……"

The walls rising up on each side of him were so high that he couldn't see the sky.

The thin, winding path stretched out before him.

Toroa was unaccustomed to carrying a watch with him, but noon should have been approaching soon. He needed to recover the enchanted sword of light and make it back up to the surface before the sun set.

Lighting a lantern, he walked the depths, which the sun's light couldn't reach.

Only the sounds of his shoe soles crunching on the frozen soil echoed for a short while.

Although he had generally pinpointed where Alus the Star Runner had fallen, there was no guarantee that he would truly reach the end of his search. He could find the wyvern himself, but there was the possibility that the enchanted sword of light had been scattered into a different fissure.

He continued walking.

Born with a degree of stamina far exceeding the average person's, Toroa didn't require any breaks.

Dark frozen soil without end.

Lonely earth, completely isolated.

He continued walking.

And walked some more.

Then finally—

"...Found you."

A narrow-bladed sword, with a brown, dingy sheath and an equally dirtied wooden hilt.

Although the cross guard was gone, it had been flung to the ground and remained there.

Hillensingen the enchanted light sword.

The be-all and end-all enchanted sword that had been stolen from his father.

The thing Toroa the Awful had sought... The very last fragment to a life of his own.

Toroa approached. Then up ahead along the serpentine path— there was one other presence crouching down in the shadow of the cliff wall.

"............"

It was silent.

Just like a true dragon would do itself, he did nothing but greedily continue to protect his treasure.

There lay the final enemy the immortal, death-bringing enchanted swordsman was meant to kill.

"..........."

"We meet again. I'm Toroa the Awful."

He was alive. In exchange, half of his body had been swapped out for metallic machinery with a brass luster, losing even the organs that all living creatures were meant to have...and abandoned by everything here in the depths of this now-frozen land.

Proliferating inside him, imitating living tissue, and forcibly driving his body.

It continued to maintain his bodily function, without any need of biogenic activity and regardless of the will of its wielder.

The name of the magic tool this rogue had used at the very end of his battle was Chiklorakk the Eternity Machine.

"I came to collect the enchanted light sword."

".........Keep your hands..."

The wyvern champion who had visited countless of the land's legends.

Alus the Star Runner spread his wings—one living, and one metal.

"...off my treasure."

Afterword

Thank you for reading. I am Keiso. *Ishura* has been continuing for a fairly long while now, and because of the support from everyone reading this story, I've been able to publish five full volumes now. With this volume, all eight matches of the first round have finished. If I was to label all the shura introductory episodes— up until the beginning of the Sixways Exhibition in Volume 3— as part one, then with the last episode of the next volume in the series, I believe that the second part of the story will have come to a close.

The fact that I was able to continue the *Ishura* series up until this point is thanks to Kureta, for all the wonderful illustrations they have provided the story; to Nagahori, who I am constantly giving deadline-related nightmares; to all the many people involved in publishing and marketing *Ishura*, as well as to all of you, the readers. I am truly grateful. I will continue to work hard until I'm able to bring the story of *Ishura* to a close.

In honor of the fifth volume, I will write out how to make a five-meal serving of Napolitan spaghetti.

First, spread oil in a deep saucepot and cook half an onion, diced, until translucent. Once the onions have cooled slightly, add three hundred grams of ground beef and pork mixture directly to the pot. After adding in five grams of salt, one egg, and ground pepper and nutmeg to taste, you should take whatever you used to stir the onions around—either a spatula or a ladle—and mix the meat with the onions, pressing it all up against the sides of the pot as you work it. By doing this, it's possible to create the main base of hamburger steak inside the pot without ever having to get your hands dirty. If your style is to use bread crumbs or some other ingredient to keep it all together, add that in as well. Apparently, you can use leftover rice to do the same thing. I don't really feel like it does much to add to the flavor at all, so I generally don't throw anything else in.

Use your spatula or ladle to divide the hamburger-steak base into three sections, and if you use the walls of the pot to adjust how it looks, you should be able to bring them together into the shape of a rugby ball. From there, heat them up, and after heating them on high to get a nice char, flip them over, following relatively the same motions as when you shaped them, and then finally place the lid on the pot. Heat them all the way through on low to medium heat, and your hamburger steak is finished. You'll make three at once, so you'll be able to have three meals' worth of hamburger steak all set to go.

Wait, I just remembered, but I actually mentioned how to make Napolitan spaghetti at the beginning. As long as you aren't cooking your hamburger steaks only after they've been completely packed together, there should be leftover pieces of ground meat